for
GEOFF *and* PETE

Jade Tiger

Also by Craig Thomas

RAT TRAP
FIREFOX
WOLFSBANE
SNOW FALCON
SEA LEOPARD

Jade Tiger

Craig Thomas

BOOK CLUB ASSOCIATES LONDON

This edition published 1982 by
Book Club Associates
by arrangement with Michael Joseph Ltd

© 1982 by Craig Thomas

All Rights Reserved. No part of this publication may be reproduced,
stored in a retrieval system, or transmitted in any form or by any
means, electronic, mechanical, photocopying, recording or
otherwise, without the prior permission of the Copyright holder.

Printed in Great Britain by
Richard Clay (The Chaucer Press) Ltd
Bungay, Suffolk

ACKNOWLEDGEMENTS

I wish to acknowledge at the beginning of this book, and most importantly, the companions of my travels, especially my wife, Jill, for being secretary, assistant, prompter, ally and editor.

I would especially like to thank Ms. Dorothy Goss, of Melbourne, for her generous and valuable assistance in tracing maps, reference works and the like, while also acting as hostess and guide.

Lastly, I wish to pay tribute belatedly to the late Anthea Joseph, whose untimely death occurred last year. She was responsible for accepting my first novel, *Rat Trap*, for publication, and it was her encouragement and enthusiasm that launched me upon my present course. She is gone, and I miss her, as do countless others.

The poetry of Meng Chiao which is reproduced in chapter 8 is taken from Penguin's *Poems of the Late T'ang*, translated by A. C. Graham; the quotation which prefaces the novel is taken from the Penguin collection of poems by Li Po and Tu Fu, China's two greatest poets, in Arthur Cooper's translation. Both are reprinted by permission of Penguin Books Ltd.

Hard is the Journey,
Hard is the Journey,
So many turnings,
And now where am I?

—Li Po (AD 701—62)

The senior foreign operations officer from the Ministry of Public Tranquility reached his slim, long-fingered hand into the pool of light cast by the anglepoise lamp at the edge of his desk. The fingers stroked the back and flanks of a jade ornament carved in the shape of a tiger. Its green was too light, artificial and almost plastic to the American's eyes. It did not look valuable, though he supposed it was. The tiger had been remounted on a cheap, varnished wooden plinth which bore a small brass plaque with an inscription in Chinese which commended the socialist revolutionary zeal of the occupant of that desk and that office. The inscription faced outwards into the darkened room, presumably to impress visitors. To the American, also, the tiger appeared tubby, ill-formed, Buddha-like. Smug, too.

The occupant of the office then spoke, in an American-accented English without slurs or hesitation; and with great politeness.

'Yes, with your permission, of course, we shall call this operation *Jade Tiger*. Do you agree?'

The American nodded. 'Sure. Good name. I agree.'

'Excellent.'

The overweight, fat-sleeked tiger continued to smile smugly from its little plinth in the white lamplight.

PRELUDES

He had been swimming now for a long time—for a little under three hours, he corrected himself sharply, feeling the edges of his consciousness curl and become fuzzy even as he attempted clarity of thought. Ahead of him, no longer retreating with every stroke but rendered a haze of light that had neither form nor movement, Kowloon and Victoria blazed. There was a patch of darkness between those two bunches of light hanging from the night sky, which was Victoria Harbour. The Star Ferries—there was one of them now, a bell clanging almost lost in the weariness-sounds in his ears—moved across that ten-minute gap between the lights. Then, at once, he was no longer certain of what he had registered, what he had thought . . .

The ferry, yes, that was it. Fingers of lights reached up into the darkness; the hotels on Kowloon. Then the roar of an airliner, lights pricking beneath its belly, coming in to land at Kai Tak.

Colonel Wei knew that if he was not picked up by one of the police patrols soon he would stop swimming, tread water wearily for a while, then slip beneath the dark, placid, oil-tasting water. And it would all have been for nothing. He splashed forward feebly, arms wrenching in their sockets. He had trained to swim much farther than he had come; from the Chinese mainland, a deserted though patrolled spot on the coast where swimmers launched themselves off from the People's Republic, making for the slums and the junk ghettoes of Aberdeen harbour. Yet he was wearied already, after less than ten miles, to the point of surrender. His body was warm rather than cold, warm and numb, and he could not make himself afraid and wary of that. The adrenalin had flowed too quickly, too crudely in his veins, dissipating itself. Now, nothing remained, nothing spurred him on.

Where were the nightly harbour patrols? He knew their routine well, their assiduous sweeps of the bays and harbours and roads around the islands. He should have encountered a patrol boat, been pinned gratefully in its searchlight beam, long before this, while he was still swimming across Deep Bay, or Urmston Road. A map flickered like an old piece of celluloid in his mind, and was gone. The names cost him an effort of thought. Hundreds of other swimmers would have been picked up by now, why not him? They would be sent back, he would not. Did they not realize that, out here in the dark water, he was beginning to drown? He, Colonel Wei Fu-Chun of the Ministry of Public Tranquility, Foreign Department, was drowning, and all the uniqueness that was him and the more valuable uniqueness of what he knew and could tell was drowning with him. Rage filled him for a moment, a back-of-the-throat rage like the last vomit of an emptied stomach, a thin bile of anger.

His body stopped. He worked his legs, so far away from him and so numbly warm, but he felt the weight of his torso pressing down into the water. His mouth closed as it went below the water, then he thrust up, arms waving and back arched, his breath roaring as if he had been submerged for minutes. He bobbed more successfully on the water, his head swinging slowly, like that of a tired and wounded bull, searching for the prick or wash of light across the harbour. He should have made straight for the shore, he should not have tried this over-elaboration, he should have . . .

He blew the water from his mouth, but he had already swallowed some and it made him cough and retch. No lights, no darkness, the rush and press of the water, the frantic, copulatory arch of the body, as he thrust back to the surface. Leaden arms, legs no longer there at all, slim body so heavy. Lights again, the hazy sunrise of lights and the gap of darkness between them now growing, seeming closer. His past life invaded him as a vague, hopeless, infinite longing to which images—pale and shadowy and unimportant—clung like burrs. His mission, his importance, his game-plan, all were rendered meaningless by the imminence of his death, a death he perceived with a dimmed kind of certainty. He felt abandoned by his past, by his self.

He shook his head with great effort. The water and his panic roared in his ears. The noise would prevent his hearing the puttering of the launch when it came. Light was flowing over him like pale lava. The noise of his blood, calling now. Something in him was trying to attract his attention.

Water as solid as earth in his nose and throat. He was being buried alive. He could not breathe. Darkness.

4

Then a thrust of futility, and a sound chuckled through the water, its laughter surrounded him. Puttering. Then only the arms, his body being moved, the dragging sensation, the pressure on his back, his legs being worked, something clamping over his mouth while something else held his nostrils tight. Again and again, spasms injected into his lungs. He kept his eyes closed, retched water in a dribble from the slack corner of his mouth, dragged in air without assistance, retched again, coughed in a spasm.

A white face was staring down at him, out of focus. An indifferent face, a face already expressive of decision, and dismissal. One more to be sent back.

'No——' he said, and began coughing again. He grabbed the man's arm, detaining him. 'No! My—my name is Wei, I am a senior official of the Ministry—Ministry of Public Tranquility. I wish—wish to talk to someone from the British int-intelligence service. Do you understand? Colonel Wei Fu-Chun——'

The face went on looking down at him. He could do no more to make his situation clear. It was a crucial moment, perhaps the most crucial. Everything—*everything*, he reminded himself—depended upon that moment. Yet he could not repeat his words. The face slipped out of focus, lost form, went. Wei slept.

'My languages aren't what they might be, Peter, but I definitely heard German—as you'd expect—and I *know* I heard Russian, too.'

Peter Shelley stood at the drawing-room windows, watching the garden slip into shadow. The tree that was the focal point of the part of the garden on which his attention was fixed was a blaze of crab-apples. Some of the earliest to fall lay like bright beads on the grass. A large Victorian house in a village to the north of Birmingham, and after dinner, with the sound of a last, distant lawnmower from a neighbouring property, Michael Davies had made his announcement, almost without preamble. It was as if he were continuing the telephone call that had invited Shelley from London in the brief interval while his wife, Marian, stacked the dinner service in the dishwasher. Shelley stared down at the brandy balloon in his hand, and swilled the pale liquor slowly.

'But—Zimmermann? Russian?' he said, without turning from the window, as if consciously posed against its last golden light

5

like an actor positioned upstage of Davies, at ease in an arm-chair.

'Yes.'

'Tell me again. You fell ill in Wu Han—business trip.'

'Yes. Food poisoning or something.' Davies chuckled. 'Over-doing the food and drink, no doubt. In hospital for a couple of days, business colleagues solicitous and out to steal the contracts I wanted to negotiate with the Chinese at the same time.' He chuckled again. 'The second day I was in, Zimmermann is rushed in. He's got food poisoning or something, as well. You'd have seen it all in the papers.'

'Yes, I did. Very embarrassing for the People's Republic. Deng makes a brief appearance in Wu Han to commiserate. The German Chancellor's top adviser, his strong right hand, struck down by sweet and sour pork. Too bad.'

Michael Davies laughed loudly. 'Didn't do the Krauts any harm, mind. Their trade mission scooped up orders left, right and centre—sort of apology, I suppose. By the time Zimmermann was transferred to Shanghai Hospital, there must have been a dozen deals on the cards—ball-bearings to TV sets. My illness didn't produce such spectacular results.'

Shelley turned from the window. Davies's florid features, good-humoured, shrewd, amused, were caught by the setting sun, which made him squint-eyed and golden. A successful Mid-lands' businessman, owning his light engineering company, and an occasional—in times past—courier for SIS. Uncaught and unsuspected, unlike poor old Greville Wynne and others like him. Someone Shelley had operated, instructed, liked. Trusted.

'Michael,' Shelley said, almost proffering his glass, 'thank you for dinner, which was excellent—Marian's cooking continues towards perfection—and thank you for the pleasure of your home.' Shelley's eyes wandered over the drawing-room. 'But this tale of yours, the purpose of my visit?' Davies nodded, his face ex-pectant. 'What is it you're really trying to tell me?'

'I want you to do something about it—can you tell Aubrey?'

'Is there anything to tell?'

'Look, Peter, you're Aubrey's closest confidant. What's he now, by the way—deputy director?' Shelley nodded. 'In that case, he ought to know. He ought to be interested.'

'In what, precisely, Michael?'

'I heard Zimmermann talking in Russian, bawling out, crying,

6

weeping, screaming, stuttering. You couldn't avoid it. I was in the room across the corridor. He was like a bad five-act tragedy in there, and you know as well as me what that means.'

'Do I?'

'Dammit, Peter, don't be so cagey! He was drugged, and not to make him sleep. There were little, official-looking Chinamen in and out of his room like a railway station. Staying for hours. *Not* locals—the kow-towed-to brigade was there in force. Then they whisked him off to Shanghai. A week later he was back in Bonn, at Chancellor Vogel's right or left hand. The second most power- ful man in the West German political firmament, the architect of *Ostpolitik*, was in a provincial Chinese hospital, yelling for his mother in Russian and attracting a lot of *professional* attention! Don't you think it all rather strange, Peter?'

Shelley sat on the chaise in front of the french windows, smooth- ing the creases in his trousers with his free hand. Again, he studied the brandy in his glass, his face exhibiting the concen- tration of a drunk at his car wheel attempting to count his alcohol intake. Finally, he looked up.

'Probably nothing in it—merely curious.' He raised his hand. 'Very well. Aubrey's on holiday, but I'll ring him about it, since you're worried——'

'I'm not. I just think Aubrey should be. Zimmermann was being interrogated in that hospital room—it was like one of my old courier's nightmares half the time—and he was being inter- rogated in Russian.'

The house was perched above Hong Kong Central, looking down from Peak Road over Victoria Harbour and Causeway Bay to the Manhattan-like skyline of Kowloon across the blue water. Colonel Wei, however, was not given the privilege of the view. His room overlooked a dusty, bright courtyard, and the hills rose directly behind the house, cramping the perspective from the locked window. There was ineffectual-looking wire netting across the window. The room was hot, the dusty fan turning slowly, as if continually losing power. Colonel Wei lay on the narrow bed, dressed in borrowed shirt and slacks, a belt pulling the waistband into his flat stomach. Unfortunately, too, he had to turn up the trouser legs a matter of three inches. He considered that the clothes represented a planned humiliation.

For most of the morning, after the doctor had left him, Colonel

7

Wei gave himself up to the task of filling the metal ashtray, blazoned with a brand of local beer, with cigarette stubs, and clouding the room with blue smoke which the fan moved like an element as viscous as treacle. Godwin, when he came in, unlocking the door noisily, wafted a disparaging hand at the smoke. He re-locked the door, and drew a chair to the side of the bed. Colonel Wei pushed his body into a more upright position against the bedhead.

Godwin was young, ruddy complexioned, his forehead showing a white, sunhatted line between his fair hair and the folds of his brow. He perspired freely in the humid atmosphere of Hong Kong. His pale suit was creased and rumpled. His pale blue eyes appeared ill at ease, almost furtive. He seemed to exude the kind of nervousness he might have displayed before his own superiors.

'You——' he began, then cleared his throat. 'You claim to be Colonel Wei Fu-Chun of the Foreign Department of the Ministry of Public Tranquility, the intelligence service of the People's Republic.'

Wei shrugged. 'I am he—I do not claim it.' He touched the small, waterproof packet suspended from his neck by a thin gold chain. They had inspected it, then evidently replaced it while he slept.

'We know about that,' Godwin said dismissively.

'You have had the photographic negatives developed and enlarged?'

Godwin nodded. 'Yes. If you're not Wei, you obviously seem just as important as he is. Unless the pictures are faked.'

'They are not.'

'Why does an intelligence colonel take the peasants' route into Hong Kong? You almost drowned.'

'It seemed safer.'

'You could have provided yourself with false papers, with travel warrants, with anything you needed to arrive anywhere in the West officially. If you are who you say you are.'

'I realise that. I am sorry, I can only ask you to believe that I was watched, that I was under suspicion, that I could not do the things you have suggested without being unmasked.'

'Why was that? Had you fallen into disgrace?'

'I was falling, shall we say?' Wei lit another cigarette from the butt of the one he had finished. He drew in the smoke like an

8

opiate, exhaling reluctantly and after a lengthy pause. The blue smoke enfolded the fan that moved sluggishly through its soup. 'I was in the Ministry of Public Tranquility in Shanghai. Does that give you a clue?'

'How long had you been there?'

'I am from Shanghai—I grew up there.'

'You learned your English in America.'

Wei shook his head. 'No, my teachers did, not I. As I was saying, I entered and progressed in the MPT in Shanghai. I am now forty years of age. During the Cultural Revolution——'

'Ah,' Godwin said, his eyes widening, growing bright with perception and self-congratulation, 'you're tainted by the Gang of Four, then?'

Wei nodded. 'Yes. The present leadership is suffering a renewed bout of Party purification. Now it is associates of associates of associates who are suspect, who will be disgraced. Myself among them.' Wei shrugged. 'It was becoming difficult, almost too late. I arranged a provincial journey, to Guangzhou—Canton, as you call it—to retrieve an individual arrested for bourgeois revisionism and crimes of counter-revolutionary publication. Instead of going there, I came here, swimming just like, as you say, a peasant.'

'I see.' Godwin's voice became official-sounding. 'What, precisely, do you want, Colonel Wei?'

'A great deal of money. And I wish to go to the United States of America—to the arms of the Great Enemy.' Wei smiled humourlessly. Even for an Oriental, he seemed to lack expressive facial muscles. He might have been lightly drugged, so bland and unchanging had been his expression throughout the interview.

'I see. America. Money. What have you to offer?'

'A great deal. But not to you. I will talk only to a senior officer of the CIA, *and* to your deputy-director.'

'There isn't a deputy-director here. You're misinformed. My senior is the station head, Mr McIntosh. He's in Macau at the moment.'

'I mean the deputy-director in London. Mr Aubrey. I will talk to him, perhaps only to him.'

'What?' Godwin's mouth had fallen open. 'Impossible, I'm afraid——'

It was as if Wei had moved in to finish off a boxing match. Another body blow winded Godwin. 'You must signal London.

9

Tell them I have information—a great deal of information—concerning a plot by the Soviet revisionists to discredit the whole government of West Germany. A man named Zimmermann is the keystone of this plot. Please tell Mr Aubrey in London that I will talk of this only to him. And please inform the senior CIA officer in Hong Kong of my arrival.' Now Wei smiled broadly, but his eyes were directed at his hands, at the smoke that curled from between his fingers. 'The name is Zimmermann, remember.'

'So, Shelley has rung Aubrey?'

'At least, yes. There was no way to hurry matters. The man Davies could not be prompted. A free agent.'

'I accept that. Shelley also has received signals from Hong Kong concerning Wei. That was confirmed this morning.'

'Good. A pleasing and effective conjunction, then?'

'It is to be hoped so. Aubrey's curiosity is famed. Sometimes, it clouds his judgment.'

'I agree. Is Wei good enough, do you think?'

'Aubrey is clever—so is Wei. He has been trained in Aubrey's methods of interrogation. He understands Aubrey. Yes, Wei will perform his task.'

'There'll be quite a convergence on Hong Kong, then. Everyone will be running for the train.'

'Indeed. The Germans, of course, will miss their train.'

'Let's hope so.'

'Do you really believe in the fortuitous, Peter?'

Kenneth Aubrey removed his straw hat and wiped his damp forehead. The noon sun glared above the garden in an almost colourless sky. Shelley's tall, angular figure remained beneath the shade of the low-boughed apple tree. In his dark suit, he had brought the atmosphere of conspiracy to the small, walled garden of Aubrey's Oxfordshire cottage, which seemed foreboding to Aubrey. As for himself, he felt diminished by the garden shears in his hand, his rolled-up sleeves, his momentary breathlessness.

'I—don't know what to think, sir.'

'I took your call here yesterday. Now, today, you arrive out of the blue to tell me that a very important Chinese intelligence defector has arrived in Hong Kong and regaled the station there with similar dark mutterings about the German Chancellor's principal political adviser. Do you really *believe* in it, Peter?'

While he spoke, Aubrey advanced on Shelley, shears extended as if to do him some physical injury. Aubrey entered the shade of the apple tree. Shelley wiped aside a lock of fair hair that had fallen over his brow.

'It's—curious, sir.'

'Perhaps. A Soviet scheme to discredit the German government, a German-speaking Russian in a provincial Chinese hospital. Curious is putting it rather mildly.' Aubrey replaced his straw hat, jamming it on his head as if a sudden wind might spring up. He studied the shears as if considering their purpose, then he let them fall, point first, into the grass. 'Mm.'

'Wei can be brought here, sir,' Shelley suggested.

Aubrey shook his head. He turned his back to Shelley and contemplated the whitewashed walls of the cottage, then its thatch. His study might have been valedictory. He sighed.

'I can't see that working. Godwin and McIntosh would have to come, too, denuding Hong Kong station. Time would elapse, Wei would be on guard. The CIA might have him *under wraps*, as they would put it, by that time. The man wants to go to America?' Shelley nodded. 'No. I shall have to go there.'

'Hong Kong, sir?'

'You don't think the trip worthwhile?'

'We're not even sure Wei is who he says he is.'

'Agreed.' Aubrey rubbed his mouth. 'I haven't offered you a beer, Peter.' He made no move towards the cottage. Birds quarrelled above their heads, amid leaves. 'Perhaps I would not take such a precipitate step except for the fact that the Berlin Treaty is to be formally ratified between the two Germanys and the Soviet Union in a fortnight's time. *There* is the real fortuitousness of these two pieces of information. There, perhaps, is their significance and their danger. I think I had better talk to this Colonel Wei.' Aubrey nodded vigorously. 'Yes, I had better.'

'You think this has something to do with the treaty, sir?'

'Zimmermann has *everything* to do with that treaty. Berlin to become an open city, virtually all travel restrictions between the DDR and the Federal Republic suspended for a trial period of a year. A referendum on reunification early next year. And the great symbolic act: the pulling down of the Berlin Wall. It is all Zimmermann's achievement, you know. He and Chancellor Vogel. They've gambled everything, including the imminent federal elections, on that treaty. It is a vastly important piece of legislation. *Ostpolitik* rules, OK?' Aubrey smiled. 'Talk of plots and schemes and the Russian language from a hospital room makes me a little jumpy.'

'You need me there, sir.'

'I'll take Hyde.'

'The swagman?' Shelley sounded disappointed rather than contemptuous.

'I'm old, Peter. I need legs. I need a Jason to carry me across the river, bundle of bones that I am. Hyde is a runner. Besides, I need you here.' He patted Shelley's arm. 'Come into the house. I have some rather gassy lager in the refrigerator.' He looked round the garden again, and sighed. 'I must arrange for the lawns to be cut, at the least,' he said, steering Shelley towards the cottage with his hand on the younger man's arm.

'You'll want the files pulled?'

'Of course. Did I tell you that I know Zimmermann—*knew* him rather? During the war. Beginning of the war, really, just before Dunkirk.' He looked up at Shelley. He was smiling broadly. His pale blue eyes sparkled with a kind of boyish mischief. 'Wolfgang Zimmermann was once my prisoner in France.'

12 May 1940

It was evident even to himself that he appeared more of an ornithologist than a man of action; thornproof tweed jacket and plus-fours, heavy walking shoes, a knurled stick, a deer-stalker. A costume that was an affectation in the Hague or Brussels or even yesterday in Arras, was here a piece of self-mockery, of self-deprecation that Kenneth Aubrey resented, lying at the crest of a hillock overlooking the Meuse and Sedan and Guderian's XIX Panzer Corps moving up to the river. The binoculars which brought him closer to the Germans also completed the inappropriateness of his appearance. The problem was, there was no prescribed uniform for spies, and there had been no time for a convincing gesture in the direction of French or Belgian peasant dress. There had only been enough time to contact his two local men, be led through narrow lanes and past tiny villages filling up with uniformed French, arrive at this hillock sheltered by heavy-boughed trees, and begin watching.

The French had abandoned Sedan on the other side of the river during the day, and the Germans had flooded into it and up to the eastern bank of the Meuse like a slow, inexorable tide of grey mud. Only an hour before, at seven, while the smoke was clearing from the demolition of the bridges and debris still bobbed and idled in the river, the assault infantry and the tanks had reached the far bank of the Meuse. With evening darkening the scene, Aubrey's certainty increased. Guderian would order his infantry, probably with artillery and aircraft cover, to cross the river the following morning. The battle for France was about to begin— was already lost?

Aubrey put away the thought. The Germans had been assumed incapable of negotiating the Ardennes, then assumed capable of being held for nine or ten days. That had been two days ago. Now they were across the French frontier, into Sedan, at the river. Tomorrow, they would cross. Now, Aubrey knew, French senior commanders would be assuming, possessed as they were by the spirits of the last war, that it would take the Germans five or six days to force a crossing. Aubrey, suddenly and utterly Francophobe, like the army commanders and intelligence seniors who had dispatched him from his SIS mobile unit with GHQ of the British Expeditionary Force, believed that Guderian's corps would cross the Meuse the following day.

Aubrey disliked the Francophobia, just as he disliked the defeatism that so easily and readily pervaded SIS during 1940. After the capture of two SIS senior officers in November 1939, morale in the intelligence service in the Low Countries had been dealt a blow from which it had never recovered. Raw and inexperienced young men, some of them with the correct languages, some of them with completed practical training, had been drafted in to replace blown agents and networks. Aubrey had been one of these barely-down-from-university young men. By May 1940, there was, for all effective practical purposes, no British intelligence service operating in Europe. Even here, above the river and the town of Sedan, Aubrey could conceive of himself in no other terms than that of the boy with his finger in the dyke.

'M'sieur?' Henri murmured behind him to attract his attention. Aubrey swept his glasses once more along the darkening river bank. Shattered bridges, a broad, moving stretch of water, the smoke of deliberate or inadvertent fires lowering above the town.

13

And field grey and artillery and tanks everywhere, a heavy margin drawn along the right bank. Aubrey rolled on to his back and sat up.

'Oui, Henri?'

'Food, M'sieur.' Henri offered him a hunk of bread he had cut from a long loaf with a clasp knife. There appeared to be no butter, but there was a strong-smelling cheese and some young red wine. Henri had obviously decided not to wait for the return of his brother, Philippe, before supper. Aubrey chewed on the bread, feeling it stick to his palate.

'Good,' he said. He had recruited the two brothers, who farmed near Verdun. Their intelligence responsibility had been the Franco-Belgian border from Verdun north along the Meuse to Charleville. They were enthusiastic, anti-German since their father had been killed in the last war and their farm destroyed around their childish heads during the battle of Verdun in 1916, and they were conscientious in the performance of their surveillance duties. They represented, in embryo, the kind of network that Aubrey believed, with the arrogance of inexperience, he could develop and maintain, given time. Guderian, as much as anyone, had robbed him of that time.

'Merci,' Henri murmured. Philippe, the younger brother, was more communicative than the darkly complexioned Henri. 'What do you intend M'sieur?' Henri continued, as if to contradict Aubrey's reflection on his taciturnity. 'Tomorrow, the Boche'— here, an obligatory spit—'will be across the river, uh?'

Aubrey nodded reluctantly. 'I think so, Henri.'

Henri pointed westward, where the clouds were dyed a violent pink against dark blue. He spat again. 'The French cavalry— ordered to hold Sedan! The retreat has begun.'

'What we need to know is . . . as much about their plan of campaign as possible.'

Wine dribbled from the corner of Henri's mouth. It made him look retarded. And his brother Philippe was in the nearest village, using an ordinary telephone to communicate with Aubrey's unit and pass on his report and conclusions. None of it seemed sufficiently serious, or sufficiently professional, to place in the path of Guderian's army like a buried mine. Henri wiped the wine from his chin.

'They'll be sending over patrols tonight,' Aubrey said. Henri nodded, and indicated his throat with a cutting motion. 'No. But

14

if they were like us, *spies*, they might know a great deal, don't you think? We might learn a great deal.'

'True, M'sieur.' Henri appeared disappointed. 'But only from an officer, uh? We need an officer.'

'Perhaps we can find one.'

Aubrey rolled onto his stomach again, and raised his binoculars to take advantage of the remaining daylight. He scanned the near bank of the Meuse, the concrete pill-boxes and the trenches of the French appearing stout, and yet shadowy and insubstantial in the gloom, behind the belt of barbed wire. Behind Aubrey, on the Marfée Heights overlooking Sedan and the river, the French had massed artillery. If the Germans sent out intelligence gathering patrols across the river, then it would be the heights that would interest them. Later in the night, perhaps, the small inflatable rafts might be putting out from the far bank.

He heard a click behind him, and rolled onto his back again. Henri was checking the big pistol he held in his hands, squinting down the barrel, pretending to fire. Aubrey found the gesture, and the concentration in the play-acting, strangely poignant. The gun belonged to the last war, a bulky, long-barrelled Mauser. It was effective, and out-dated. The tanks and artillery and P38s and new Mausers and machine pistols and Kar 98 rifles of a modern war lay on the other side of the Meuse. And he was a short man with thinning hair, dressed like a country squire. Ridiculous.

Yes, he would have a German, catch himself a Wehrmacht officer, when Philippe returned and before the night was through.

13 May 1940

Noises now, quiet mouse-pattering noises, the disturbances of old leaf-mould, new grass, the night air itself. Aubrey glanced at the luminous dial of his watch. Three-fifteen. Henri and Philippe were away to his left, towards where the copse straggled out on the Marfée Heights. The noises indicated a small party, perhaps three. The path through the copse lay like a parting in dark hair in the moonlight. It seemed impossibly arrogant that the German patrol would use the path, as if out for a stroll, for exercise. Perhaps they were that confident . . .

15

The noises ceased. The path slipped away from Aubrey, into the trees that marched down the slope towards the river. Distantly, the night was filled with the muted orchestration of German movements. Heavy artillery, the rumble of tanks, the occasional noise of aeroplanes overhead. A war gathering in the background, making itself real. Aubrey felt damp, stretched on the grass and leaf-mould; damp, ineffectual, reluctant, excited.

Noises again, and the bobbing of a helmet climbing the path, moonlight glancing on it above a bulky shadow. Then the glimpse of a slim rifle, caught in the pale light. Then a second German soldier toiling up the slope. No disguises, no real caution. The slope was already part of a greater Germany. The third man was an officer. Aubrey watched him pause and remove his cap, wiping his forehead. So confident . . .

The first soldier passed Aubrey's hiding-place, moving cautiously but steadily down the path towards Henri and Philippe. Aubrey experienced a sudden and fierce delight at the prospect of the man's death. The second soldier turned to look back at his officer, and was motioned forward. The officer replaced his cap, and hastened up the path. The second soldier moved on, his back now to Aubrey.

A long pause, each footstep the officer took punctuated by an intense silence where the noises from across the river seemed to have reduced to a static-like hum. The ether of war. Then sudden noise, muffled, struggling, hand-over-mouth noises that Aubrey could envisage vividly. Knife—the clasp knife that Henri had used to cut off chunks of the loaf—across throat, into side, up through ribs . . .

The German officer stiffened. There was an instant recognition that seemed without puzzlement or guesswork. This man *knew* the noise of assassination in the dark, and Aubrey was suddenly afraid of him. Aubrey pushed himself to his knees. The officer had drawn his pistol, and cocked it—cocked his head too, listening ahead of him. Aubrey moved the gun—it was clumsy, heavy now—out in front of his body in a two-handed grip, realising he had never killed, never even wounded, must not do so now . . .

'Halt!' he snapped in German. The German officer spun towards the sound of his voice. A crashing of something into a bush, then silence from further up the path.

The German's gun came up. Aubrey was still on his knees, as if praying, his Webley aimed at the middle of the German's form,

16

his hands white around the gun butt. The German saw the gun, didn't see the gun, *must* see the gun in this light . . .

The German officer lowered his pistol to his side. Aubrey was afraid to get up or to lower his own gun. He felt weak and help-less, anxious for the two Frenchmen and their arrival.

The German officer laughed softly, incongruously, then shrugged his shoulders. Then he spoke.

'You're not even a soldier,' he remarked, disappointment evident in his tone. He was no more than six or seven yards away, but his face was in shadow. He sounded young, looked tall and slim. Aubrey hated being still on his knees, damp from the ground soaking through the plus-fours. 'What are you? French? Not French?'

'Englander,' Aubrey felt obliged to explain.

'Where is your uniform?' Footsteps coming down the path. The German flinched, almost precipitated himself into activity, then shrugged again. He had Guderian's army at his back. It was bad luck, but only temporary. 'Wait—you're an agent—a spy, then.' The German laughed softly. Henri and Philippe appeared on the path. Aubrey could see their white teeth, grinning. They'd killed . . .

'Perhaps so. Like yourself, then.'

Aubrey felt excitement—a febrile, arcane, secret excitement he had rarely before felt—rise in his stomach like a tickling, mild indigestion. He had captured his first German of the war.

Henri tugged the pistol from the German officer's hand, and Philippe frisked him for other weapons. The German seemed indifferent, even bored. Aubrey stood up.

'Name, rank and serial number,' Aubrey snapped.

Yes, the German was taller, perhaps a few years younger; slim and handsome in uniform, unafraid.

'Hauptmann Zimmermann,' he said, nodding, 'at your service.'

PART ONE

TOWARDS THE UNKNOWN REGION

As cold waters to a thirsty soul,
So is good news from a far country.

Proverbs 25 : 25

ONE:

Orient Express

The rush of houses slipped beneath the belly of the aircraft—Hyde glimpsed washing thrust from windows on bamboo poles—and there was the sense of being amid the tall fingers of the hotel blocks, before the seeming lurch settled the 747 above the runway stretching out into the blue water. It was unnerving, as if the pilot had somehow shrugged the aircraft into alignment with the finger of concrete in the bay. Then the wheels skidded and bit, and the 747 was moving like a fast powerboat level with the water, and Kai-Tak's airport buildings were scurrying towards the windows.

Hyde shrugged himself upright in his seat as the aircraft slowed and taxied. The businessman who had kept him company all the way from London to Hong Kong looked rumpled, tired, but smelt of the applied wakefulness of after-shave. Hyde's knowledge of the clothing import business had become compendious during the flight, to his increasing boredom. His own biography as a freelance journalist had been used to fend off further assaults of information and anecdote. Aubrey, naturally, had travelled first class.

Hyde squeezed out from the window seat into the aisle before the rush to anticipate the disappearance of the seatbelt light, collected his bag from the locker over his head, and pushed down the aisle towards the nose of the aircraft. One stewardess watched him, but Aubrey had arranged matters satisfactorily, and his progress was not impeded nor was he instructed to return to his seat. He pushed aside the curtain into first class as the aircraft finally slowed to a halt. Aubrey's eyes instantly met his, and the old man smiled. He looked tired, and eager; an almost-hunger about his features, even in the pale eyes. In a room somewhere in the teeming city, a man waited to be interrogated. It was as if Aubrey could taste the man's presence, scent it in the dry air of the fuselage.

Immigration officials entered in crisp khaki shirts and shorts and sprayed the aircraft, which had stopped at Bombay, from

21

oversized aerosol cans. Five minutes later, Aubrey and Hyde stepped into the passenger gangway, Hyde carrying his own bag and Aubrey's, the old man's being emblazoned with the British Airways legend. It was virtually unused. Hyde wondered whether some of Aubrey's evident excitement was connected with the mere fact of travelling—a grandad journey, but not quite to relatives in Aussie.

The tunnel of the gangway was hot, insinuating a stifling, humid day outside. Then they stepped into the air-conditioning of the main airport building and its reasserted, artificial cool.

McIntosh and Godwin were waiting for them at passport control. Hyde observed a florid young man who emanated a subtle, and possibly crucial weakness, and an older, lined, sunburnt man who stooped, appeared clever, and was close to retirement. Aubrey shook hands with them, introduced Hyde, and was then ushered by the two men towards the terminal building doors. Godwin glanced at Hyde, following behind.

Hyde understood the way in which the two men from Hong Kong station had ignored him. They recognised him; recognised his type, his function, to be perfectly accurate. Aubrey's minder, his runner. The thug. Hyde grinned at McIntosh's stooping back in its creased linen jacket. Disrespect was something he offered freely, and received back by a process of compound interest. The uncomfortable, sidelong way in which the Third Secretaries and Trade Attachés of the intelligence service regarded him was in itself a marking-off, a distinction. He was one of the night-soil men, and there would always be a job with SIS.

He leant against the car, squinting in the hard sun. McIntosh was already in the car, inspecting his briefcase for something Aubrey had demanded. Aubrey, perspiring freely, visibly wilting in the temperature, which Hyde guessed was perhaps just nudging eighty degrees, and unable to cope with the high humidity, was fussing with his straw hat, then his club tie, then the creased jacket he wore.

'McIntosh,' he said suddenly, and the station head plucked himself from the hot interior of the small, battered Ford and looked at Hyde, startled; a sense of insult spread across his lined face immediately it emerged.

'Yes, Hyde?'

'Who's the little man watching us from the observation gallery?'

McIntosh's mocking smile revealed new and different folds and erosion gullies in his face. 'Local colour, Hyde—just local colour. One of the KGB irregulars. Taken photographs, as usual, has he?'

'Not yet. Get in the car, Mr Aubrey.'

'He goes everywhere with us,' McIntosh protested. 'You can't expect to come here without arousing professional interest, Mr Aubrey.'

'Agreed,' Aubrey said as he obediently got into the car.

'You could save on expenses by sharing the same transport,' Hyde remarked.

McIntosh shrugged dismissively at Hyde's back as the Australian climbed into the Ford. Godwin grinned.

As Godwin turned the car out of the airport and onto the road leading through Kowloon to the cross-harbour tunnel to Hong Kong central, McIntosh turned in the passenger seat and handed Aubrey a sheaf of papers.

'These are the full transcripts, Mr Aubrey.'

Aubrey glanced at them. Hyde slumped back in his seat, watching another 747 coming in to land. He had glanced to ensure that the car that had turned out behind them was still following, and then he relaxed. His talents and intervention were not, at that moment, required. A cooling breeze blew on his face from the open window of the car. On the opposite side of the road, the hotels crowded like white trees down towards the blue water.

'Your impressions, McIntosh,' Aubrey requested, looking up from the papers. 'What are they?'

'Of Wei?'

'I've talked to him most, sir,' Godwin remarked.

'Very well,' Aubrey replied in a heat-exasperated tone, 'what is your impression of Wei?'

'Very clever, sir.'

'What are his reasons for defecting to us?'

'Money and fear, I think.'

Ma Tau Wai Road was crowded with cars, rickshaws, bicycles. It poured humanity and vehicles along itself like a gully accepting new flood water. Hyde sensed the unimportance of one Chinese defector amid the seething, appalling collision of humanity that was Kowloon. He realised that Hong Kong was in the process of seducing him to its vision of itself.

'Fear? Does that fear of reprisal, of arrest and disgrace, ring true to you?'

'Yes, sir. As far as we can check back. He's a Shanghai MPT

23

man. We know there have been shake-ups there, a weeding out process. Deng's very thorough, sir, and he controls China now.'

'After smashing the Gang of Four . . .' Hyde recited in a mocking imitation accent that belonged to the music-hall.

'Precisely,' Godwin replied primly, his China-watcher's credentials mocked by the Australian thug. 'Deng's very thorough, and his people are prepared to sift and sift and sift, find anyone and *everyone* who might be suspect. He does not intend to find himself or his Great Leap Forward imperilled—*ever*. Chairman Hua has gone—Colonel Wei is just a minor case of purification.'

'Accepted, provisionally,' Aubrey remarked in a smoothing-over tone. 'He's given you sufficient background for you to believe he may have had superficial connections with the Gang of Four and the Shanghai People's Commune period?'

'Yes, sir, he has.'

'This money business—going to America. You find that equally convincing?'

'It . . . seems to fit the man——'

'Like a glove,' McIntosh interrupted. 'He's a greedy bugger. Clever, smart as paint, man-of-a-thousand-masks type. Oriental to the bone. No bloody Communist or Maoist or Dengist—just the usual selfist. An operator.'

'I see.'

The crowds pouring into the railway terminus on Hong Chong Road appeared to Hyde like a mass of the faithful pouring into some modernist temple. The search for faith was unceasing, desperate, hurried.

'The local CIA are very interested, sir.'

'I imagined they would be, Godwin. I've had signals from Langley expressing great concern. In fact, I expect no less a personage than the Deputy Director here to supervise.'

'Buckholz? He's coming?'

'He's as intrigued by the matter of Colonel Wei's proposed revelations as myself. I take it you have been unable to elicit anything further?'

McIntosh shook his head reluctantly. Hyde glimpsed the glittering, wild blue of Victoria Harbour from which Colonel Wei had been fished, then the tail-lights of cars glowed and bobbed ahead of them as they entered the cross-harbour tunnel.

'Tight-lipped bugger,' McIntosh muttered. 'Just Zimmermann, and a Soviet plot—dark hints, with that bland, cheesy, self-satisfied grin on his face and a fag in his mouth morning, noon, and night.'

Aubrey suppressed a smile.

'Does it add up to something important, sir?' Godwin asked in a voice that failed to conceal his excitement.

'I don't know, Godwin—I really don't.'

'But the Berlin Treaty, sir?'

'Yes, Godwin. Two weeks away from ratification. And you have a Chinaman you fished out of the harbour above us who suggests it is all a Russian plot. I take your point. But I wonder how a Chinaman knows, and why he should want to tell us, don't you?'

The car emerged into blinding sunlight at the end of the tunnel. Dark green hills climbed above Hong Kong into a haze of humidity that clung like mist. To Aubrey, the hills above the white concrete town resisted him. It was as if they concealed and sheltered Wei and what he knew. At the other end of the world from Zimmermann and his Chancellor and the Berlin Treaty, he had entered a world of secrets; a darkened room which contained a formidable, forewarned opponent.

'Kenneth.'

'My dear Charles, welcome!'

Aubrey shook hands with Charles Buckholz, Deputy Director of the CIA. The ice rattled in his tall glass of lime juice as he got up and crossed the room to the American. The last sunlight before the quick tropical night splashed against one wall of the fan-cooled, open-windowed room like a decorator's anger. Buckholz looked about him as if he expected Wei to join them, or to be concealed behind a piece of furniture. Then he looked at Aubrey intently, weighing him, his glance distinguishing the elderly Englishman as a relic of empire.

'I never realized how well you'd fit in surroundings like these,' he commented. Aubrey glanced down self-deprecatingly at his cream linen suit and recently whitened shoes.

'Ah,' was all he said in reply.

'You've talked to Wei?'

Aubrey motioned Godwin from the room, then indicated the drinks arranged on a sideboard. Buckholz inspected them without expectation, then found a bourbon and poured himself a large measure, adding a handful of ice to the tumbler. He raised his glass to Aubrey.

'Yes, I've talked to Wei.'

'What do you make of him, Kenneth?'

'He will be, as they say, a hard nut to crack. Something particularly hard and shrivelled and dry.' Aubrey remembered pickled horse chestnuts on knotted string. Conkers. A school quadrangle. The next day had been Armistice Day.

Buckholz looked puzzled. 'I thought he was eager to talk to you?'

'Oh, I have little doubt of that. I haven't allowed him to discuss the material he says he has brought—not yet. What I meant was—to establish the truth of what he says will be difficult. His genuineness.'

'Oh, yeah.' Buckholz walked to the open french windows to the first-floor balcony. He was outlined in orange sunlight, hard to look at without squinting. Aubrey sipped the chilled lime juice. What hadn't he asked Buckholz? The man seemed in such a hurry.

'Did you have a good flight?' Yes, that was it. Pleasantries.

'What . . . ?'

'Flight. A good flight?'

'Sure.' Buckholz turned to him. 'You have doubts about this guy Wei?'

'I would have doubts about anyone who claimed to know that the German Chancellor's closest adviser is a Russian agent-in-place.'

'He said that?'

'As near as dammit. Wolfgang Zimmermann was interrogated—so the claim runs—in Wu Han, then Shanghai, and officers of the intelligence service elicited that he was a long-term KGB agent.'

'Like Guillaume, who brought down Willy Brandt.'

'Precisely. Lightning striking twice.'

Buckholz moved away from the window towards Aubrey's chair. He appeared purposeful, quick, youthful. Aubrey glanced towards the sofa, where the small briefcase with which Buckholz had entered the room now lay. Buckholz swallowed at his tumbler of bourbon.

'We have to know the truth about this, Kenneth.'

'I realize that, Charles. I realize that.'

'Jesus, if it's true, then the whole of *Ostpolitik* is no more than playing into the Russians' hands—it could even be a Russian game that the German Chancellor is playing. Jesus.' He swallowed the last of his bourbon, refilled his glass, clinked in the handful of

26

ice, then turned once more to Aubrey. Orange light, darker now like a dying fire, lay like a birthmark on one cheek and fringed his cropped grey hair. 'I never liked that guy, Kenneth, and I never liked his games of footsie with the Kremlin. But this . . .' He shook his head, drank again. Then he moved like some caged and dangerous animal towards Aubrey's chair. The Englishman sipped like a nervous bird at his lime juice. 'You realise we've already withdrawn more than a hundred thousand troops from the Federal Republic, in agreement with this Berlin Treaty nonsense?' Aubrey nodded.

'We have done the same, in proportion. In two or three years there will be no more than token NATO forces in West Germany. It will be the probable case that West Germany will leave NATO. Will have to if any referendum on reunification proves—*successful*?' Aubrey smiled apologetically. 'These are world events, Charles. Not quite my responsibility. It is happening, it will happen.'

'And it could all be the motivation of a Russian agent? Listen, Kenneth, if Wei is telling the truth, that changes everything.'

'I suppose it does. Certainly, if it were proven against Zimmermann, there would be no Berlin Treaty.'

'We have to find out.'

'I agree.'

It was Buckholz's turn to appear apologetic.

'It's going to be difficult, Kenneth.' He sat down in a chair opposite Aubrey. 'Since this guy Wei went over the wall, all our people in Shanghai are under the closest surveillance.'

'Your Chinese nationals?'

'No. But my channels to them are stopped up. I can't get any-one near them.'

'It would be the same with my people. I realise that.'

'But we need to check this out. Wei has to be checked out. Zimmermann has to be checked out.'

'Quite. What do you propose?'

'Send in a man—a Chinese. One of my people.'

'And?'

'I have people he can talk to in Shanghai. He goes to this Wu Han place if necessary. He's got to learn if Zimmermann was in those hospitals, who visited him, when and how often—the whole ball of wax.'

'One man?'

'It has to be done. Everything you get from Wei—*we* get from

Wei—has to be checked out. Every detail he feeds us. You agree?'

Aubrey was thoughtful for only a moment. He disliked the haste being thrust upon him. It was more than simply Buckholz's characteristic thirst for action, the American's effective impatience. Yet the deadline was unavoidable. Aubrey felt himself pushed reluctantly into what he could only regard as an arena, an amphitheatre. Wei's story might be true. If it were not, then Aubrey could not comprehend the man's motive; if it were true, then its implications were appalling. If Zimmermann was a KGB agent . . .

Aubrey did not complete the speculation, but said: 'It goes back as far as 1938, you know.'

'What?'

'Zimmermann's relationship with Moscow. Not quite as long as Philby, but longer than most of your doubles.' He smiled.

'In my briefcase——' Buckholz began, indicating it with his tumbler. 'I debriefed Zimmermann, a long time ago.' Buckholz's eyes were gleaming with recollection and speculation. 'At the end of the war. I was with G-2 then, army intelligence. He was captured near Frankfurt. He was an Abwehr *Oberst*, but they all had to fire guns in the front line by that time.' He leaned towards Aubrey. 'Read the file, Kenneth. Zimmermann was no Nazi, not to me. He surprised me then. With what Wei has on offer, I wonder just what he was. I read the files on the airplane.'

Aubrey nodded, almost dismissively. 'This man of yours. Can he do any good?'

'He has to. My people are hamstrung by surveillance. We'll get nothing out of China on Wei without a new face. A Chinese face.'

'Where is this man?'

Buckholz looked at his watch. 'No more than two, three hours away. He's on the next flight from the States. Just in case you agreed we needed him.'

'Quick,' Aubrey murmured.

'He's one man, Kenneth. If we send him in and then come up with another idea, so what? We have nothing to lose, except by doing nothing.'

'I suppose not.' Aubrey paused, then added: 'Strange, isn't it? I once had Zimmermann as my prisoner.'

'You're kidding.'

'No. Early on in the war, before Dunkirk. In France. I interrogated him, too.'

'And?'

'Not a Nazi, as you say. No, not a Nazi. But that means nothing, of itself.'

'No? You read my file. Five years—*those* five years—are a long time. He may have changed—hardened.'

'I wonder. You say you can do nothing in Shanghai with your establishment there?'

Buckholz shook his head vigorously. 'No way. They're all pinned down in the foxhole. We need a wild card—my tame Chinaman.'

'Hospitals, you think?'

'Who was there, how often, the records, even the MPT. There are one or two low-graders in the ministry he can tap.' Buckholz shrugged. 'It's not just an offer of help, Kenneth. Everything looks like it could be coming down to the wire. We have to crack this one, and we've got two weeks. Just two weeks.'

Soft morning rain from a grey sky. Except for the temperature and the mugginess of the atmosphere, it might have been early winter in the Marienplatz in Munich. The rostrum had been set up on the steps of the Neues Rathaus, the town hall, and Wolfgang Zimmermann stood below it, looking up at the figure of Chancellor Dietrich Vogel as the West German leader addressed a large crowd in the main square of the Bavarian capital. Vogel was on his opponent's territory, in the heartland of right-wing, conservative Germany, and he was displaying the wares of the Berlin Treaty with all his customary style and simplicity and effectiveness. He held the microphone close to his mouth so that his tone and style remained conversational, and he was wearing his familiar check cap, borrowing an image of ordinariness for his purpose of self-portrayal as a man of the people. Elegant of mind, easy of manner, quietly passionate, Vogel demanded admiration, even affection, and Zimmermann rendered it.

It was a good crowd, and a receptive one. Whatever his opponents' suspicion of Moscow or East Berlin, and whatever right-wing fears he was able to mobilise, Vogel possessed the dream. It had been handed down from Adenauer and Erhard and Brandt, and it had lost none of its potency during the transmission. The German dream: the reunification of Germany. In the shadow of the Neues Rathaus and beneath the twin towers of the Frauenkirche away behind Zimmermann, Vogel paraded the dream-becoming-reality once more, and its magic was potent enough to win elections.

'Look,' Vogel said, without histrionics or rhetoric, 'I know you don't trust the Russians—I find it hard myself sometimes——' Laughter, a few cheers, very little adverse comment from the crowd. 'But if we don't trust, we get nowhere. And the people we really have to trust are in East Berlin, the people on the other side of that obscenity of a wall and a border fence. And they're Germans like you and me.' Cheering now, a swell of sound. To Zimmermann, it appeared that the crowd had raised its collective voice precisely because Vogel had not raised his. Vogel waved for silence, and continued. 'I know that's easy to say, and I could be accused of making cheap political capital out of it. But it's also true. They're Germans, just like us. They live in German cities like Dresden and Leipzig and Halle and Magdeburg and Berlin——' Vogel was interrupted by another cheer. He waved again for silence. 'They don't live in Russia or Poland, that's all I'm saying. And we have time to see whether it will work— whether East and West alike will let we Germans make it work. The referendum on reunification will not take place until next year, and then *you*—all of you—will have the chance to vote on it. We won't do anything without you. There are nearly sixty million of us, and less than twenty million of them. How can they impose on us? If *you* want a reunited Germany, then it's in *your* hands.'

More cheering. Zimmermann studied the nearest faces. Yes, he concluded. Vogel and the Social Democrats would win the election, and the Berlin Treaty would be signed. The Wall would come down.

Zimmermann suppressed a smile, knowing it would be smug, knowing there might be a film camera on him at that moment as he looked up towards Vogel. It would work, though, he repeated to himself. They would win. NATO would leave German soil. It would be, again and after so long, just Germany; not East and West. Germany. Nothing could go wrong now, nothing could stop them.

'Don't be afraid,' Vogel was saying, still in his conversational style. 'As a great American President once said, we have nothing to fear but fear itself. Don't be afraid.'

*

30

The french windows were still open, despite the moths and insects that flew into the room periodically, attracted by the soft light of the table lamps. In the darkness outside, Hong Kong glowed with light. Its noise ascended the hill to the house as a hum; urgent, vibrant, enervating. It was a noise that seemed to tauten the atmosphere of the room, to bring the walls closer to the soft lights. It emphasized shadows and rubbed against nerves. It was, Aubrey considered, the noise of a dentist's drill, heard from the waiting-room.

McIntosh and Godwin, present out of courtesy rather than necessity, hovered at the edge of the lamplight, as did Hyde, who leaned on the frame of the open windows, arms folded on his chest, an observer who might have been carved or inanimate in some other way. Aubrey and Buckholz sat on chairs drawn closer to the room's large sofa. On that piece of furniture sat an Oriental; small, slim, brown, he appeared diminished and made child-like by the size of the sofa. He looked very young and, to Aubrey at least, vulnerable. David Liu. Correctly, Liu Kuan-Fu. His American persona possessed the name David.

He should be wearing spectacles, and have neatly cut hair and be dressed in a narrow-lapelled suit and be white, Anglo-Saxon and Protestant, Aubrey reflected. In that skin, he would appear more clearly what he was, a recent college recruit to the CIA. There had been many such young men, during the sixties and seventies, who had melded into a single image of the young CIA officer in Aubrey's mind, so that he could not help but see this Liu's Oriental guise as no more than a veneer. It only partly disguised his experience, his youth, merely delayed the reluctance Aubrey felt at having to trust the verification of Colonel Wei to him. Hurry, hurry, he reminded himself. They were moving at Buckholz's pace, with his energy. Yet there seemed no virtue in deliberation, nothing to be gained from procrastination. It was best to let Buckholz continue to handle the penetration operation, while he concentrated upon the enigmatic Colonel Wei.

A small heap of papers and documents lay on the coffee-table before the sofa. Liu's new identity—identities, rather. Liu had brought them with him from CIA headquarters, Langley. They were safe and current. Liu had been thoroughly briefed by Buckholz, and the penetration operation had been planned and organized before either of them had left America. There was no reason—except an old man's reluctance—to delay Liu's departure any longer.

'From the border to Kwangchow, then you take the train to Shanghai,' Buckholz was saying. 'An army officer, returning from home leave in the south, to 20 Corps headquarters outside Shanghai.' Buckholz turned to Aubrey. 'He's Political Department, so he should be safe from any army personnel he meets.' Aubrey nodded. The repetition of Liu's route and cover were for the benefit of those in the room.

'We require medical certainties—if you can obtain them,' Aubrey said, addressing Liu. Liu's attention turned to the old man with a kind of robotic deference. Ancestor worship. 'Who came to see Zimmermann, yes, what they talked about—but why Zimmermann was there, what treatment he received, that kind of thing. If we know his illness and his treatment, that may tell us whether or not he was interrogated.' Aubrey turned to Buckholz. 'This man Davies's story indicates the administration of highly specialized drugs. One hint of that, one shred of proof, might be all we need.'

'Agreed.'

'What access to the hospital does your cell in Shanghai have?' Aubrey asked.

'Some. Probably enough. Shanghai station has built up a good range of contacts—industrial, political, domestic, even medical. They should be able to put Liu in touch with someone from the hospital. He has the freedom to frame his actions to the kind of person he reaches, and how much they can tell him.'

'You understand the gravity of your undertaking?' Aubrey persisted, addressing Liu.

Hyde, from his vantage at the open windows, a moth touching his neck at that moment and startling him to wakefulness, saw the movement of the old man as one of doubt, disquietude. Aubrey looked pale in the light, drawn. For his own part, Hyde sensed the inevitability of Liu's mission. He had weighed the Chinese-American for himself, and suspected reserves Aubrey evidently doubted.

'I do, sir,' Liu replied with archaic courtesy. 'I realise, also, that I am expendable as clearly as I understand the importance of my mission.' He smiled swiftly and briefly. 'I consider your task with Colonel Wei just as difficult as my own.'

Buckholz laughed. 'Get off the boy's back, Kenneth. He'll do a good job for you.' He turned back to Liu. Hyde studied the slim brown hands crossed almost primly on Liu's lap. They did not move, did not appear tense. 'OK, David, you know what we want, and how soon we want it. Mr Aubrey's added what he wanted to your Stateside briefing. You ready?'

Liu nodded, as if dismissing them from an audience he had held. 'I am, sir.'

Buckholz looked at Aubrey, who nodded, then up at McIntosh, who came forward into the light. 'OK, let's get this show on the road.'

Liu stood up abruptly, mechanically.

'Patrick, you accompany Mr Buckholz,' Aubrey instructed. Then he reached out his hand, and shook Liu's slim fingers. 'Good luck, young man,' he said. 'Very good luck.'

Wei was sitting up on the bed, almost in the same position he had adopted during Aubrey's first encounter with him that afternoon. The ashtray was again full of stubs, and Wei was smoking. He seemed to treat American tobacco—he had insisted on that—as a source of infinite satisfaction. Aubrey wondered whether the man was allaying, even sidetracking, an opium habit, and then dismissed the idea. There was too much control there for a smoker of the stuff.

Aubrey closed the door of the room behind him. A bright moth fluttered at the heavy mesh across the window, desperate to escape into the room. Wei seemed to possess no such urgency to leave it.

'Ah,' he said. 'Mr Aubrey. I heard a car leaving. I take it the young American-Chinese I glimpsed earlier is beginning his journey?'

The perspicacity Wei displayed surprised Aubrey. 'I beg your pardon?' he bluffed.

'Come, Mr Aubrey. You must check on me. Obviously, I am not to be trusted. I would imagine some new face would be required. Your people and those of the Americans would be under the heaviest surveillance since my disappearance.'

'I see.'

Wei lit another cigarette from the stub of the one he had been smoking. The nicotine of his habit was revealed even on his brown fingers. He stared upwards, watching his exhaled smoke roll like dragon's breath along the low ceiling. A long-legged insect that

33

had climbed through the mesh hovered around the bulb over-head.

'Well, Mr Aubrey?' he asked, still regarding the ceiling with an intent, satisfied gaze. His manner angered Aubrey, as it was meant to do. 'Are the arrangements proceeding for my reaching the United States of America?'

'At present, you're going nowhere,' Aubrey snapped impatiently. Wei shrugged. His face remained impassive. 'How did you come into possession of the information concerning Herr Zimmermann? Were you present at any of the interrogations you claim took place, either in Wu Han or later in Shanghai?'

'Ah,' Wei observed. Surprisingly, he stubbed out the unfinished cigarette, and did not light another. Aubrey stood by the bedside, and saw Zimmermann's face against the creased and soiled pillows, and wondered about the drug-truths the German was purported to have uttered. There was Davies's evidence, dammit, otherwise he could have freely chosen to disbelieve this Chinaman. 'No, I was not present.'

'Then it is all hearsay. It is a great pity, Colonel Wei Fu-Chun, that you could not have smuggled out some verification of your story, along with your photographs which may or may not prove you are who you say you are.'

'It was much too difficult,' Wei replied in a slightly apologetic tone.

'Then all of this could be nonsense, Wei!' Aubrey snapped, steeling himself to accelerate the interrogation and establish a new relationship between them. He moved closer to Wei, drawing a chair to the side of the bed. His movements were studiedly brusque and confident. 'Every piece of information you have supplied, or have hinted at, could be nothing more than fabrication on your part.'

'Perhaps.'

'Your motive is obvious.'

'Yes?'

'Certainly. What are you worth to us, in the present climate of growing cooperation between China and the West? We would be far more interested in a KGB officer from one of their foreign departments, perhaps even in a Cuban. So, you invent a grandiose lie concerning a senior German political figure, to make yourself more interesting. It is the shy and lonely child's effort to make himself interesting to others.' Aubrey spread his hands like a

34

benediction. 'In what other light, pray, am I to regard this story of yours?'

'As the truth?'

'Ah, what is truth? What are facts? I accept, for the moment, that you are who you say you are, but I can accept nothing else. We know that Wolfgang Zimmermann fell ill in Wu Han, and was transferred to Shanghai. Within a week, he was back in Bonn, none the worse for his experiences. Yet in that time, you tell me, he confessed to being a long-term Russian agent? Why haven't your superiors used and exposed this vital piece of information? Why does it need your escape to bring it to light?'

Wei shrugged himself more upright on the bed. It was clear that he felt disadvantaged by his prone position. Aubrey leaned forward on the chair, his face expressing disbelief, yet without contempt or indifference. He appeared, half-shadowed from the overhead light, like a priest taking confession, weighing the moral nature of an unexpected and peculiar act of sin. The posture and appearance were intended.

'I do not know why, or whether they eventually intend to release the information,' Wei said. He looked at his opened pack of cigarettes, but did not reach for them. Aubrey cursed the impassivity of oriental facial muscles. Wei's hooded, expressionless eyes were similarly of no help. He felt he could never know the man as he must. 'I am using the information, Mr Aubrey, for my own benefit, as no doubt my government will do—in time.'

'Who interrogated Zimmermann in Wu Han?'

'General Chiang.'

'And in Shanghai?'

'Chiang again—and others. A special team.'

'One of your so-called Harmony of Thought units?'

'Exactly.'

'Drugs, hypnosis.' Wei nodded. 'Your motives for leaving China—what were they?'

'We have already discussed them.'

'It won't bore me. Explain once more.'

'I was, very briefly, connected with the Shanghai People's Commune, in the days when the Gang of Four ruled Shanghai. I—there was evidence against me, being compiled by my enemies, which indicated arrests I had made, certain methods of re-education I had used on peasants. I—had hidden the evidence as well as I could. I had—removed the witnesses. But families of—

35

of peasants and intellectuals who had undergone re-education continued to press for investigation, for knowledge of the where-abouts of those they regarded as missing. When Deng——' Wei's face crumpled into something virulent for a moment, then smoothed itself to a bland mirror once more. 'When Deng finally replaced Hua as Chairman, and the trial of the Four was complete, Deng's people turned on others. I would have become one of those others.' He looked into Aubrey's face when he ended his recital. 'For personal reasons, Mr Aubrey, it was not safe for me in Shanghai, or anywhere in China.'

'I see. You worked in the Anti-Revolutionist Department of the ministry?' Wei nodded. 'Which section?'

'Rice Bowl.'

Aubrey shook his head. 'Vietnam, Kampuchea, Thailand. Not a great deal of use to us, Colonel Wei. As I suggested earlier, you *need* this story about Zimmermann for us to regard you as a prize worth having. You have a rank greater than your abilities or your entrustment. I am inclined to disbelieve the whole matter.' Aubrey stood up dismissively, moving his chair away from the bed. His face was harder in the direct light from the ceiling. Wei studied his expression. 'We'll talk tomorrow. Perhaps your story will have improved. Dig for the bedrock of facts that alone will convince me, that's my advice to you. Good night.'

David Liu lay pressed flat against the pebbles and shingle above the tide on the narrow beach. The rowlocks of the dinghy that had brought him to the water's edge still sounded in his ears, though he knew by now that the faint squeak was out of earshot. Its betraying memory remained with him, vivid and jumpy like a live wire beneath his hand. Deep Bay stretched away from the shore behind him, and he was lying on a narrow beach that was part of the Kwantung province of the People's Republic of China. A different world.

The lights of Hong Kong and the New Territories glowed softly behind him, dimly mirroring from a low, heavy, thunderous cloud cover. The lights of the town of Paoan were dimmer, more diffused and less assertive ahead of him, beyond the narrow, shelving beach.

He lay until his breathing had returned to normal, and the clothes he had adopted on the launch no longer itched and seemed unfamiliar. He lay still until his ears no longer heard the

36

tiny, rat-like squeaks of the rowlocks, and heard instead only silence. He lay still until the impression of clinging to a ledge at the edge of an unknown and dangerous world left him. The darkness ahead of him had been as palpably ominous as threats in an unknown language.

He stood up and dusted down the shapeless grey Mao-suit he wore, his hands running over remembered denim, recollecting mohair and wool. He took the baggy, small-peaked cap from his pocket and donned it. He patted his pockets for his papers, and then began walking up the beach onto the rocks. The stretch of coast where he had been landed was deserted, the fishing port of Paoan the only real settlement, except for temporary homes and a few farming communes. The coast was patrolled, but to prevent potential escapers rather than to deter illegal immigrants. Liu was, however, mindful of light and noises as he clambered over the low rocks.

When he reached the grass beyond the rocks, he looked out to sea. Deep Bay lay in darkness, pricked by the navigation lights of freighters and fishing vessels. There was no sign of the launch, nor had he expected to see it. Hong Kong, another alien world, lay alight with the deceptive familiarity of San Francisco. He turned away from it quickly.

The rolled, coiled barbed wire that had been laid along the verge of the rocks had been damaged on numerous occasions and never renewed. Escapers, holiday-makers, Party officials objecting to the effort required to reach the beach. His hand closed over the wire-cutters in his pocket as he moved swiftly, half-crouching. It was no more than a minute or so before he found the wire lying like the shed skin of a snake rather than the serpent itself, and he began stepping gingerly through it, lifting his feet high in an exaggerated, comic walk. He was aware of his ungainly appearance. It did not seem fitting at his first act of penetration into the People's Republic. He paused at the edge of the wire, regained his breath, then bent to study the strip of bare earth, recently dug and flattened. A compromise between convenience and security. Someone had decided to place anti-personnel mines opposite the largest gaps and rents in the barbed wire. Yes, there was the warning notice. He picked it out in the thin shaft of light from his small torch, then flicked off the light. He moved slowly along the edge of the wire until he reached scrubby grass again.

The glow of Paoan was less than a mile north of him. He knew the road lay mere hundreds of yards inland of the wire. He began to move towards it. He would be on a night train to Kwangchow, and by morning on his way to Shanghai.

It happened suddenly.

There were lights, and yells, and the noise of whistles. No dogs, for which he was momentarily grateful. But figures moved like shadows around him, until one rushed into him, knocking him sideways. He staggered, blinded by the searchlight mounted on a truck which swept over him, hovered, then returned, then began pursuing the fleeing, half-naked figures who scattered in the hollows and folds of the land to avoid it. It was like some frenzied poolside party, everyone drunk, whistles instead of laughter. The truck's engine roared into life, and the searchlight bobbed towards him, as if to swallow him.

It was a trap. He felt the irony of its having embraced him accidentally. They had known about these potential escapers. Someone had betrayed this party of ten, twenty, thirty swimmers before they reached the beach and the bay, and they had waited for them with lights, a truck, guns . . .

Shots, now. Liu looked about him, panicking, yet unable to move. More shots, cries and screams; panic and injury.

It was a joke, a cruel joke. Boo, and we jump out on you, wearing demon-masks. Too bad.

He threw himself prone on the grass, felt someone blunder onto him and stumble over his body. The whistles reached a climax of enjoyment, there were a few more shots, and then there were the voices giving orders, the pushing around, the slaps across the face, the turning over of the bodies . . .

He was turned over with a rifle butt in his ribs. The man with the torch, who was dressed in the uniform of a Border Defence unit, seemed surprised to discover he was still fully clothed. Liu was kicked and ordered to his feet. He raised his hands above his head and began trotting towards the small, frightened herd of bare-chested men who huddled in the glare of the searchlight. It had taken him less than fifteen minutes in the People's Republic to become its prisoner.

Patrick Hyde jumped from the deck of the launch onto the jetty inside the typhoon shelter flung out like a cradling arm into the bay from the glittering Kowloon waterfront. Buckholz himself threw the mooring rope to him. It landed heavily across Hyde's shoulder, and he looped it over a bollard. The launch bumped against the jetty and its row of car tyres. The engine cut out, and the sounds of Kowloon swilled into the momentary silence. Buckholz came heavily up the wooden steps from the water, Godwin moving more lightly and swiftly behind him, ahead of the two CIA locals who had crewed the launch.

Lightning blared across the water, seemingly dimming the lights of Kowloon and the tall bright stalks of the new hotels. The wind rushed against Hyde's face like a rough, damp flannel. He helped Buckholz onto the jetty.

A second flash of lightning was accompanied by the thunder from the first. A flat, eerie, dead light lay across sky and water and town for a moment, then it was black again. Hyde, turning away from Buckholz, saw the white face at the corner of a low warehouse at the end of the jetty. It was as if a grubby spotlight had been turned upon the man, so much so that Hyde was easily able to recognise the KGB man that Godwin had called Vassily, the man who had been on the observation gallery at Kai-Tak that morning.

Hyde's hand clamped over Buckholz's arm as the rain began, a sudden emptying of the clouds accompanied by the second roll of thunder.

'I've just seen one of the KGB locals,' Hyde announced in a conversational tone.

'What? Where?'

'Over there, by the warehouse. You want me to take a look?'

Buckholz was silent for a moment.

'Anything wrong?' Godwin asked. His cream-coloured suit was being stained black across the shoulders by the rain. A car engine started, and they heard the noise diminish in the distance.

'Leave it,' Buckholz murmured, then he snapped out: 'Damn! Did anyone see him when we left?' He turned to Godwin and his own men. 'Anyone see a guy tailing us when we came down here?'

No one had. Hyde shook his head.

'That's you and Mr Aubrey they've seen in Hong Kong,' Hyde remarked. 'I think they'll become very interested in what's going on here, sport, don't you?'

'Damn.'

TWO:

Border Country

'Too much hurry, Mr Aubrey,' Hyde warned. He was standing at the foot of the stairs, and Aubrey, ascending, turned to look back at him. A gritty, irritating tiredness assailed Aubrey's eyes and skin, and he felt a vast reluctance to continue up the flight of stairs to Wei's room.

'You think so?' he snapped.

Hyde sipped at his beer. 'I think so.'

'You assume the right to tell me, too.'

'Look, Mr Aubrey, I haven't got a tan suit on and a blue shirt, and I haven't got steely blue eyes.' Hyde grinned. 'If you want the strong silent automaton type, get in touch with the CIA or the KGB.' He sipped again. Then he pointed his glass up the stairs at Aubrey. 'The KGB know you and the deputy-director of the CIA are both in Hong Kong at the same time. They may know you've mounted a penetration operation against the People's Republic. I don't think that's top-drawer security, do you?'

'No, I don't. Damnation,' Aubrey added softly. 'You're right, of course,' Aubrey shrugged. 'There's nothing that can be done now. Except to keep all the doors closed in future.'

'You going up to see old slit-eyes?'

'I am.'

'Good luck, mate.'

Aubrey reached the head of the stairs, crossed the landing, and moved along the corridor to Wei's room at the back of the house. A young man, whose name Aubrey could not recollect, was seated tiredly on a hard chair outside the door of the room. Aubrey berated himself for his precipitate disbelief. It is because you did not believe in the importance of these matters, he told himself. He had given the debriefing of Wei the codename *Wild Goose*, and now the name mocked him. He had deliberately employed that name, the feeling of futility increasing within him almost from the moment in his garden when he had decided to fly to Hong Kong. It was a futility that had reached its apotheosis during the first interview with Wei.

Wei, he had concluded and still believed, was a frightened man clutching at the straw of notoriety. He was a materialist buying his ticket to America with an inflated currency. He did wonder, as he nodded to the young man who opened the door to Wei's room for him, whether his judgment of Wei sprang in any sense from an old man's tiredness and bouts of inadequacy; frailty of perceptiveness. Then he quashed the idea. The story about Zimmermann was a fabrication, and he would prove that it was.

Wei was reading a newspaper. The grilled square of the window was a black hole above and to one side of his head. Two moths and some unidentifiable insects lay on the sill between the mesh and the glass, exhausted into death. The fan turned slowly, asthmatically. When Wei looked up from his reading, Aubrey saw a flicker of calculation as bright as greed in his eyes, and the assumption of defiance about his lips and jaw.

'I have decided,' he said, 'that I have nothing further to say to you. I will talk only to the Americans now. Please arrange for my transfer to American custody.' He folded the newspaper casually and laid it on the rucked, creased counterpane.

Aubrey drew the single chair in the room close to the bed. He was puzzled by Wei's attitude until he resolved it to his satisfaction as a further species of bluff. The man had absolutely no cards in his hand.

'I don't think we can do that, Colonel Wei.'

'Why not?' Wei, like most English-speaking Chinese, lisped and hissed slightly as he grappled with an alien alphabet, barbaric phonetics. His accent was faintly American. 'I am quite certain that Mr Buckholz would welcome my company.'

'The problem is, the CIA do not operate harbour patrols. If you wished to be rescued by them, you should have chosen another method of entry. Besides, a European interest, shall we say, would have intrigued my service more than the Americans. Which is why you came to us.'

'But I am no use to you. You do not believe me . . .'

'I think your story is a complete and utter fabrication.' Davies, *Davies*, he told himself. The one reason why you cannot abandon this man or this investigation. Davies, who is trusted by Latymer, heard Zimmermann talking Russian, saw the interrogators . . .

Damn.

'You seem to doubt your own words,' Wei observed sharply.

'Not at all.'

'Ah.'

They listened to the fan, to the hum of the city below the house, to the retreating thunder. The air was already losing its freshness outside as the humidity climbed once more. An airliner swung over them, roaring towards Kai-Tak.

'Tell me everything,' Aubrey said finally. 'Everything you know about Zimmermann.'

'I could not see the files, of course.'

'I understand.' Wei seemed puzzled, guarded rather than disarmed by the paternal tone Aubrey employed. Infinite patience, infinite wisdom; compassion for shortcomings, for failure. 'You tell me again what you heard, what you guess.'

'Very well. May I walk about the room?'

'Of course.' Aubrey stood, and moved his chair against the wall. He would be able to watch Wei's face, his body. Then he gestured for the Chinese to stand. Wei nodded briskly.

'Much of my information comes in the form of rumour, and gossip,' he explained, beginning to pace the room immediately.

'I understand.'

'Chiang received a report from the hospital in Wu Han, and left Shanghai immediately—that began the rumours. The German had been taken ill, possibly food poisoning.'

'That was the official explanation,' Aubrey remarked. 'It is what Zimmermann and Bonn believe to this day.'

'It may have been true—I have never heard a different story. Whether a mild delirium or a maladministration of drugs caused the first concern, I am not sure, but the gossip was that Zimmermann had begun speaking in Russian, rambling. There was no one in Wu Han who spoke it, except for one of our low-grade officials. He was summoned, and then he summoned General Chiang.'

'And Chiang summoned others?'

'No. Chiang had doctors recommend that Zimmermann be transferred to Shanghai. That is when the German underwent Harmony of Thought techniques, in Shanghai.'

'How was this concealed from German consular officials, and from members of the trade mission from Germany?' Aubrey's voice was unfailingly gentle. His eyes, when not studying Wei, cast about on the threadbare carpet and the linoleum that appeared at its borders, as if he searched for runes of comfort or conviction.

'Drugs are advanced. You do not use them?'

'There are occasions—I am not an expert, Colonel.'

'I see. Zimmermann was permitted visitors, but he was always sedated. Our doctors reassured enquirers.'

'What was learned?'

Wei shrugged. 'Here,' he explained, 'I enter the realms of half-gossip, third or fourth hand.'

'Proceed, nevertheless.'

'Zimmermann had been an agent of the Soviet revisionists since before the war—since his time in Spain.'

'Zimmermann *was* in Spain, with the Condor Legion.'

'It was there—Republicans captured him, he was persuaded of the truth of Marxist-Leninism, persuaded by infidels, as it were,' Wei smiled, 'and from that time he never deviated in his loyalty to his masters in Moscow.'

'A road to Damascus, then?'

'I do not understand.'

'It doesn't matter. Zimmermann went all through the war fighting on the wrong side, a side which must have been repellent to him?'

'Presumably so.'

'And after the war?'

'Presumably, he remained a sleeping dog.' Wei shrugged. 'It is all in Chiang's file, I expect.'

'But what did you hear?'

'That he was not an active agent.'

'Never?'

'I cannot say. I did not hear so.' Wei paused in front of Aubrey. His hands were in the pockets of his too-large trousers. 'I can tell you very little more, Mr Aubrey.'

'You know nothing about contacts, about his Moscow control?'

Wei shook his head. 'They exist. The usual, but very discreet, periodic contacts. Mr Aubrey, I have given you sufficient indications of good faith. I can do no more to convince you. Of course I wish to impress you. That is why I give you this story. I knew, when I heard it, that it could be my passport to America. Now my fate rests with you. You must establish the truth.'

Davies, Davies, Aubrey's mind chanted to him in an insistent, maddening whisper. He was there, he confirms part of this. The damned Chinaman may be telling the truth. Aubrey entertained a vision of a long ugly concrete wall tumbling to the ground, raising dust. On the other side of it, people were cheering in Russian. He shook his head.

Zimmermann, so high, so influential. The shape and contours and fate of the West might be in his hands. The Berlin Treaty . . .

He could not afford to dismiss Wei or discount the story. He had to establish the truth of the man's story. He *had* to elicit the truth about Wolfgang Zimmermann.

David Liu was pushed in the back, and the wooden, barbed-wired gate of the small compound was shut and locked behind him. There was laughter from the guards, the sniggering of anticipation. He hardly attended to it, grateful still for the lack of a body-search. The carelessness of superiority, of imposing humiliation. Clothed among the half-naked, yet he created little individual attention. The guards classed them all as captives, as failed escapers. As butts, dolts, animals. His wire-cutters and papers were still in his pockets.

He was soaked through from the downpour soon after they were captured. The night air was warm, but his teeth chattered from tension, from the effort to absorb his changed circumstances and alter them once more. The men around him, most of them young, crop-headed, thin, cowed, brushed against him or huddled aimlessly. Their teeth chattered, they rubbed their arms. Fear also made them cold.

The compound was part of the nearest commune. From the gouts of old manure scattered on the bare earth, it evidently served as an animal pen, and perhaps also as a punishment enclosure, as at present. A small wooden dais had been erected on one side of it, presumably for some official to mount and berate the occupants. One of the guards, a platoon commander, was indeed on the dais, but there was no crowd of peasants from the silent, dark commune beyond the searchlight to witness the scene. They would not be lectured, then, on their treacherous revisionism, their heinous desertion of the People's Republic. Two guards dragged something like a flat snake into the glare of the light. Liu recognized it, and slipped behind the bodies of a group of the others. A hose. They would be humiliatingly drenched with water, the compound would be turned into a quagmire, for the amusement of their captors. They had abandoned all humanity with their clothes.

44

The hose spurted, trickled, then sprayed at them. Men scattered, to raucous laughter. One slipped, then another. The hose washed them across the rapid new mud of the compound floor. More laughter, high and almost hysterical, from the border defence unit who now surrounded the barbed-wire compound. The jet of water jabbed at Liu's shoulder, washed his flanks, punched at his chest and back, flinging him off his feet, skidding him across the compound. His hands instinctively protected his pockets containing his cutters and his papers, as dearly as he might have clutched his groin against injury. He lay still. The water licked over him, then pursued others. He climbed slowly to his feet, knowing that to remain lying still would attract further attention.

The border guards and their platoon commander jeered and yelled, shaking their fists. Cultural Revolution images flicked in his mind as vividly as on a screen; rioting mobs of students, flags, the tearing down of posters, statues, buildings, people; the chanting, the fist shaking, the book-burning—the ritualised, formalised hysteria unnerved Liu.

The water jetted over him again. The noise, the humiliation, the mud covered him. The prisoners, too, were screaming. He felt himself splashed, washed at, eroded by the sea of noise and movement. It was as if the nightmarish scene focused upon him, had been created specifically for his anguish.

He cowered on the floor, hands over his head, clutching his ears, oblivious to the water and the mud, uncaring with regard to his papers and his cutters. Like elements of his identity, the noise was sluicing them away. Louder, louder . . .

Then, like a climax achieved, the light had disappeared and the noise had stopped. He was in darkness as close and complete as that of a cupboard, hunched into his own senses. The guards were gone, the searchlight was gone. Silence rang in his ears. Small, snuffling-animal noises nearby. The sucking of sodden mud like some reminder of a trench war. Men groaning, stirring, accepting humiliation. Personality soused and sluiced away. Unpersons. A dramatic foretaste of the remainder of their lives.

The mud was repellent as he crawled across it, hand extended in front of him, eyes still blind from the glare of the searchlight. He touched men's bodies, and his hand shrank from the contact. Then he grazed his fingers against barbed wire. He lay exhausted and paralysed of will. Dimly he could hear the

45

border unit still enjoying the huge, hysterical joke in the distance. Behind him, the prisoners were gathering into a huddle in a far corner of the compound, whispering softly in tones bereft of comfort.

Eventually, as the noises of the soldiers diminished further, he was able to reach into his pocket and check his papers. They were contained in a plastic envelope, and were still dry. Then he took out the wire-cutters and examined the stretched, ugly pattern of the wire.

The first snapping click of the wire sounded horridly, betrayingly loud. He listened. Only the defeated, impotent whispers behind him. He cut again, then again, and peeled back the barbed wire gingerly. Then he eased himself with a dancer's sinuosity through the gap he had created. He paused, and listened once more. A raucous laugh little louder than a whisper. The platoon might well be billeted in the commune, just as the local police, civil servants, and suppliers would all be contained within the perimeter of the commune. A town in miniature.

Liu moved rapidly away from the compound. There were lights, one or two weak and scattered streetlamps, or lamps hanging from the eaves of low buildings. The smell of brackish water was stronger than the scent of the sea. Paddy fields. He had glimpsed them from the truck. He estimated they were perhaps a mile or so inland of the road, perhaps two or three miles from Paoan and the railway station.

A soft rain began to fall. His footsteps sucked and pouted his presence. He began to shiver with relief, and with anticipation. He needed dry, clean clothes. He was moving through a hostile country, a hostile town. Teachers, doctors, soldiers, peasants—anyone might open a shutter, open a door, and light would fall on him.

He had no idea of the arrangement of the commune, nor its extent. The clothes of a doctor or a teacher would be best, but the buildings between which he now walked, heading in the general direction from which they had entered the commune, were long, low, shed-like. Peasant workers' dormitories. Too many people too close together for him to take the chance. And there might be others already at the hole in the wire behind him, eager to escape, making noises of relief and speed that would attract attention.

He entered a wide space which might have constituted the equivalent of a town square. He pressed against the wooden wall

46

of one larger building, and removed his torch from his pocket. He flicked its light over the nameboard. The dispensary, and the doctors' names. Luck. It made him shiver. Luck had entered the arena and demanded acknowledgement. Liu was fatalistic about luck. It shortened the time-scale, it had its own momentum and logic. It ran out. He crept along the wall of the dispensary, then down the alley between it and the next building, looking for an open window. The soft rain insinuated depression, a sense of failure.

An open window. It made him swallow. More luck. Time was running out.

He reached up over the sill and gently touched the frame, dabbing his fingers over it. Caked with drying mud, they were insensitive. He inhaled, and then pushed at the window. It slid up almost without noise. He hoisted himself to the sill, and pushed his body halfway into the dark room. A slight smell of disinfectant and medicines. The shadowy outline of a long room with a low ceiling. Beds, empty, against the far wall. He ducked his head back out, and levered his legs over the sill. He sat for a moment, and then dropped into the room. His hand touched something that moved, something cool and metallic which shivered, then wobbled. He grabbed for it, making it squeak, felt it fall, cupped his other hand, clutching the object to his chest. Then he crouched beneath the window, his breath roaring in his ears and chest.

He examined the object in the faint light coming from the lamp at the corner of the next building. A kidney bowl, chipped white noisy enamel. He returned it to the table on which it had been resting, and stood up. He moved to the centre of the room, straining eyesight to perceive impediments. There was what appeared to be a door at the end of the room. He moved, well clear of the beds, towards it.

Slowly, he opened it. His blood ticked away the seconds in his ears. His chest thumped with anticipation, his thoughts were alive, as in the light of a flickering fire, with images of recapture. A corridor. He closed the door behind him.

A narrow, wooden-walled corridor, without plaster or paint, smelling of disinfectant. Doors without names or numbers led off the corridor. Light coming from beneath one of the doors. He listened, but there was only silence beyond the chorus of his own tension. He tiptoed past the door which leaked light, on down the corridor. Bedrooms, he supposed and prayed.

He listened at each one. The sound of snoring encouraged him, and he tried the door handle. It eased silently open. A scent of soap, and possibly of perfume. Mothballs, too. A small high window, an outside light filtering through the thin curtains. A narrow bed beneath the window. Drawers, a wardrobe, a dressing-table reflecting the square of the window's dim light.

He moved towards the wardrobe, the sleeper accompanying his tiptoed steps with noisy inhalations and exhalations. A sub-conscious protest or grumble at his intrusion. The form of the sleeper was small, but fit was a luxury. Dryness of clothes the only imperative. The wardrobe door opened with a jerk, and he stilled it with his other hand. Then he reached into the mothballed darkness, touching clothes swiftly, carefully. A smock? He bent and sought shoes. Sandals, very small, not a man's . . .

Silence in the room. Then a stirring noise from the bed. He waited, sitting on his haunches, feeling a tremor begin in his thighs and calves. Sitting up? He did not dare to turn and look. Mouth-clearing noises, the slapping of tongue against dry gums, roof of mouth? The noises maddened him with their sinister anonymity.

Snoring. Like an engine stuttering to life. Regular snoring. He controlled his breathing, quashing the jumping of his heart. He got shakily to his feet and left the room, closing the door with exaggerated slowness. A woman, snoring.

He listened at the adjacent door. Silence. No light. He opened the door, passed into the room, shut the door. He took one care-less step before his eyes picked out the contours of the room, and he jarred his shin against the frame of the bed. The same small high window, the same furniture, but the bed near the door.

'Uuuh? What?' The word if not the noise was formed in wake-fulness. A light sleeper had come quickly and totally awake. A doctor, used to interruptions to his sleep. 'What is it?' Then, as Liu's training analysed the information that the man spoke in northern Min dialect as opposed to his own expatriate Yue dialect, a piece of clear, professional irrelevance, the orbit of the man's thoughts changed. 'Who is it? Who is there? Speak.'

An upright torso, a hand extended towards what must be a light cord above the bed. Liu was frozen for a moment, realising that the man was bigger, paunchier than himself, then he moved, and struck his stiff forearm across the man's nose. An escaped bubble of pain gurgled in the man's throat, and his head banged back against the thin partition wall. Liu groaned softly at the noise, even as he dragged the pillow from beneath the man's body, pressed the man flat on the bed, and thrust the pillow over his nose and mouth. Claw-hands scrabbled across Liu's forearms, drawing blood in diminishing protest. Then stillness, one arm hanging down by the side of the bed, the other folded in death across the man's chest. Liu released the pillow, and his hands were shaking with a palsy.

Over-reaction, over-reaction . . .

He had been wrong, even under the weight of his cumulative tension and the steady growth of desperation. It had been wrong, stupid to kill. It created enemies, a pursuit, it was like fingerprints or a note. *Professional*.

He hurried to the wardrobe, dragged out a Mao-suit, measured it against himself, then stripped off his own clothes in the now hot darkness. Airless room. He thrust his legs into the rough cloth trousers, pulled on the too-big jacket. Belt, belt . . .

In one of the drawers, he found a narrow belt. He tightened it around his waist, then buttoned the jacket. He removed his papers and torch and pocketed them. Then he bundled the sodden jacket and trousers under his arm, and opened the door of the room. No one in the corridor. He hurried down it, entered the long room with the beds, crossed to the window, swung his legs over the sill, and dropped to the ground. Later, when he could pause, he would strip off the lining of his jacket and remove the twenty high-denomination notes and the second set of papers. Not here, though. Outside the commune.

The streets of the commune were deserted. Speed now was a comfort, the plaster holding luck together, the child's hand pulling luck out longer like chewing gum. After the narrow alleys and the wooden huts and barns and store-houses was the smell of the paddies. It had stopped raining. A thin, weak, watery moon indicated the paths along the banks above the level of the water. The lights of Paoan were dim to the north. He glanced at his cheap watch.

One-thirty. In half an hour he could be at the station in Paoan. He hurried on, the dead man behind weighing on him, heavy not on his conscience but on his sense of safety.

Aubrey, in a half-sleep, the bedroom fan stirring the humid air that moved over his face and arms, dreamed vividly. The tem-

49

perature would not allow him to achieve real sleep, and he was sufficiently conscious, as the past claimed him, to resist belief in the vivacity and the detail of words and appearances and events that had happened more than forty years before. The thin cotton pyjamas restricted and enveloped him, and for almost all the moments of the dream he was aware of the single sheet lying heavily on his limbs with the weight of numerous blankets.

When Zimmermann had been disarmed and body-searched by Henri and Philippe, they hurried the German officer through the woods on the Marfée Heights, along winding, climbing tracks, past French outposts and patrols, through the French artillery lines away from the Meuse. Aubrey was regarded with a certain admiring futility by the French soldiers who inspected their papers. The *sale Boche* was the occasion of numerous remarks and much contemptuous spitting. Zimmermann, Aubrey now recollected clearly though he would not have claimed to have attended to it that night, was amused by the reactions of the French. Aubrey, in his dream, where many of the images achieved a point of view not his own, as if he were watching a film of the events, saw Zimmermann as the archetypal Prusso-Nazi, his manner and movements a swagger. He distrusted those images especially, as he mistrusted the sounds he heard of disturbed animals and birds in the trees, the night-scents that could have no place in the foetid air of the Hong Kong bedroom where he dreamed. The noises of bats, of nocturnal monkeys and even a domestic dog impinged upon his semi-awareness, but they were distinct and distinguished from those Ardennes noises. The heavier, more corrupt scents of tropical flowers were also distinguishable from the smell of grass crushed beneath their hurrying feet.

After more than an hour of interrupted travel, they arrived at a farmhouse near Flize which was owned by a distant cousin of Henri and Philippe. Aubrey had failed to enlist the man, but the occasional and unspecified use of one of his barns had been grudgingly contributed to the intelligence service. While Philippe went up to the farmhouse to announce their arrival and to obtain food, Henri and Aubrey directed Zimmermann into the barn. Henri lit an oil lamp, then returned it to its bracket near the door. One old horse stirred in its stall at the light and noises. Two Friesian cows grumbled and stamped. Aubrey, lying on his bed and standing again at the door of the barn, was assailed by the warm smell of dung and hay. The scene was lit by a localized shadowy, Rembrandt light. Henri pushed Zimmermann down onto a bale of hay, as if deliberately to erase the elegant posture of the German.

Again, Aubrey the old man saw his younger self from an impossible, filmed point of view, as if he looked into the Nativity painting of the barn's scene. He felt, very vividly, at a loss, traced with a finger-like recollection the remark that had passed through his mind, *First catch your German* . . .

'What do you want of me?' Zimmermann had enquired conversationally and as if reading Aubrey's indecision on his face. 'Do you mind if I smoke?' His hand patted the breast of his tunic.

'Of course. Be careful where you throw your matches.'

Zimmermann smiled. 'Naturally.'

Aubrey seated himself opposite Zimmermann, his hands on his knees, while Henri remained at the door, the big gun tucked obviously into his waistband.

'Now, we have time to talk,' Aubrey announced.

'Certainly. What is it to be?' Aubrey had spoken in German, but now Zimmermann demonstrated his fluent, almost accentless English. 'Literature, painting, music, current events?'

Aubrey's eyes narrowed. 'I think current events, don't you?' He glanced at Henri. A suitably menacing presence, soon to be reinforced by the return of his brother. Yet the German officer seemed relaxed, at ease, confident; as if the guns were in his possession, they his prisoners. There was no sense of isolation, of being cut off from help. Training had emphasised that as an important factor to exploit. The person undergoing interrogation always feels cut off, isolated.

Aubrey realised, quite suddenly and with an insight he suspected but which the dreaming old man on the bed approved forty years later, that this German officer, despite his motorized infantry regiment *waffenfarben* and his standard Wehrmacht uniform, was something other than a common-or-garden soldier. A kindred spirit; someone like one of his instructors in SIS, even his recruiting officer at Oxford. Intelligence. *Abwehr*.

A dog barked in the tropical night; Philippe caused the barn door to protest on its hinges as he opened it. The two noises were concurrent, and distinctly heard by the dreaming Aubrey. The satisfaction of the moment of recognition replayed itself in his mind, was held in focus even though he had attended to Zimmermann's reply almost in the moment of recognition.

51

'Ah,' the German had said, exhaling smoke, watching Philippe and the food he brought with a bright, intent gaze, 'precisely what kind of current event? Perhaps you really mean fortune-telling? A little crystal gazing?'

The old man heard Zimmermann's words and regarded the feat of memory as impossible. Imagination, rather. Yet he wanted to prompt the young self. *Crystal Night*. The pun would have been a thrust, would have helped Aubrey forty and more years later, would perhaps have exposed the Nazi, or the Russian agent. But the youthful Aubrey did not play elegant mental games like his older self.

'I think so. Yes, Philippe, give our guest something to eat.'

Philippe slapped a rich, lumpy stew onto a plate and thrust it at Zimmermann, who courteously thanked the Frenchman. Then Philippe served Aubrey before carrying the pot and the last two plates to his brother. Zimmermann ate eagerly, complimenting the meal again and again.

'Excellent, excellent . . .'

'What is the campaign strategy?' Aubrey snapped, textbook-like. 'How long is the front to be? What is the timetable?' Henri, reacting to tone of voice like an alert hound, drew the Mauser from his belt and laid it in front of his plate, across his knees.

Zimmermann stirred the air in front of him with his fork. 'Ah,' he said. 'I see.' He did not, however, so much as glance in Henri's direction. 'Your men here would, of course, kill me. I do not think you would. We are of an age, but you are very young in this work, I think. It is my judgment that I am safe from harm with you.' Aubrey struggled to keep his expression neutral.

'You will answer my questions, Herr Hauptmann.'

'Oh, I don't say you would not have me beaten up a little. But you will not kill me, I am certain.'

'You're Abwehr—correct?'

Zimmermann's features snapped shut on an expression of surprise.

'Nineteenth Panzers,' he replied with studied evenness. 'I'm sorry to disappoint you. Perhaps I would be dressed more like you if I were a spy.' He laughed softly. Aubrey flushed, unable to prevent expression of his embarrassment.

At the laughter, Henri growled. His fork rattled against his empty plate like a warning. 'Fucking Nazi pig!' he snapped.

Zimmermann coloured. 'Nein!' he snapped back, then pressed

his lips tightly together to prevent the escape of more words. He smiled then, his face relaxing into an habitual, engaging self-confidence. 'Infantry,' he explained to Aubrey.

The dream had followed chronology, had moved at an even pace, edited in some professional and slick way, highlighting instants of drama and interest. Yet Aubrey was warned as the moment approached, as if he knew he had reached the climacteric of some involved plot. *Fucking Nazi Pig*, that was it, snapped out in French, snarled almost, and the hurried, definite, contemptuous cry of denial from Zimmermann. The scene instantly retreated, the film in Aubrey's dream snapped, and he came hotly, sweatingly awake in the bedroom in the house on Peak Road, overlooking the city of Hong Kong.

He had *not* imagined that, he told himself, and smiled as he sat up and switched on the bedside lamp. Three-thirty in the morning. Half an hour or so before the quick dawn spread like mercury across the harbour. The purpose of the dream had been revealed. His half-sleeping, half-waking mind had worked towards that point with the detail, chronology and care of a writer. Zimmermann had vehemently, deliberately denied he was a Nazi, in May 1940.

What had he been? What did he believe?

Aubrey threw back the sheet and got out of bed. He felt hot, but now his temperature was the effluent of excitement. He removed his spectacles from their case and the file Buckholz had given him from its folder. He sat himself in the room's one armchair, adjusted an anglepoise lamp on the dressing-table, and switched on its white light. Sighing with a kind of happiness, he began to read.

Zimmermann had been captured, with the survivors of his unit, in a pocket of German resistance to Patton's US Third Army east of Frankfurt. He had by then become in fact as well as in pretence an infantry officer. The date of his capture was given as 5 April, a month before Hitler's suicide and the German capitulation. Charles Buckholz was then a very young intelligence major in command of a G-2 unit attached to the US Third Army. Zimmermann had fallen into his hands by virtue of his rank of colonel in the *Militaramt* of the RHSA, which had absorbed the Abwehr in 1944.

The inner folder of the file was stained—old rings from coffee mugs, smeared cigarette ash, even a thumbprint. Aubrey recognised on its label, as well as on most of the tied-in pages, a bolder, more confident version of Buckholz's handwriting. It was the transcript of Zimmermann's debriefing, which had been conducted by Buckholz himself and a lieutenant called Waleski, who seemed, from the outset, to have acted as the darker side of the interrogation team. Much of his colourful language had been preserved in the record, which had obviously been typed on an old, heavy American portable by an inexpert typist. There were numerous mistakes and corrections, the spacing and blocking were erratic. For the most part, it was a simple question-and-answer transcript, with occasional conclusions or inferences which had been dictated later by Buckholz, more occasionally by Waleski.

Aubrey hurried through the transcript. There were no evocations from the text. If he envisaged Zimmermann at all, it was in the terms of his own dreaming recollection of 1940. This was his second reading, and he arranged and selected the material on which he focused in terms of his dream. Most of the subject matter of the interrogation—local conditions, Werewolf units, SS and Gestapo individuals' whereabouts, local atrocities, mined roads and buildings, attitude of the local German population, the fate of local Jews—was irrelevant in content, except where it revealed Zimmermann himself, in inner lights and shadows. These Aubrey plucked from the text.

Zimmermann was tired, defeated, cynical. Resentful of defeat, too. Question: *You fucking Nazis are all the same, uh?* Aubrey drew in his breath sharply. Waleski was the questioner. Henri's epithet applied to Zimmermann five years later. Answer: *I said, if you wish. As you wish.* Question: *Major, the guy admits it. This one admits it.* Answer: *I am a German, isn't that enough for you? German equals Nazi.* Question: *You admit to being a member of the Nazi party?* Answer: *I was never a member—but, you see, there is at once disbelief on both your faces, when I deny this.* Question: *You're going to tell us you're a Red, right?* Answer: *I am not a Communist.*

Aubrey smiled, and flicked a number of pages over swiftly. Question: *What did you think when the bomb plot against Hitler failed?* Aubrey realised the changed circumstances of the conversation. After a meal, perhaps, and drinks? Buckholz and Zimmermann alone. Aubrey realised that the conversation must have been recorded rather than taken down in shorthand. Answer: *Oh, that. It was bound to have failed.* Question: *You did not*

54

support the plot? I find that strange. Answer: *Strange? Romantic fools.*
Aubrey had ignored this conversation the previous day when he
had read the file. Later, he recalled, the conversation became
almost metaphysical. Yesterday, these general speculations, the
evidence of Zimmermann's *weltschmerz,* even his nihilism,
appeared of little significance. Now, they loomed larger. They
went beyond defeat, beyond failure. Question: *You would have
advocated doing nothing?* Answer: *It failed, didn't it? Like all the other
attempts to get rid of that lunatic.* Question: *You thought the Führer mad?*
Answer: *I thought Germany mad to follow him.* Question: *Explain that.
You fought in Hitler's army.* Aubrey nodded unconsciously at Buckholz's adoption of the persona of an opponent in debate. Answer:
*I did not wish to go to the camps, or be shot, like the Jews and the Com-
munists and the gypsies and all the others.* Question: *You felt this way
ten years ago?* Answer: *Yes. But a war is worth fighting when you're
going to win. My father was in the army, so I went into it.* Question:
After university? Answer: *Yes.* Question: *You felt no attraction to
Nazism in university?* Answer: *No, nor to the Communists, either.*
Question: *The Communist party was illegal by that time. Why do you
keep insisting you were not a Communist, are not a Communist? Is it
important?*

Aubrey laid the file across his lap. Buckholz had pencilled into
the transcript a reference to the fact that Zimmermann had
merely shrugged and given no answer. Buckholz led him back to
plots against Hitler and anti-Nazism in the Wehrmacht. Aubrey
admired the foresight of Buckholz, beginning his career in post-
war intelligence, gathering these insights like a commodity that
would leap in value once hostilities ended.

Aubrey rubbed his eyes. *Is it important?* he read on the dark,
red-flaring screen behind his closed, pressed eyelids. Was it? He
recollected other instances—many, now that he considered it.
Zimmermann had expended a great deal of effort convincing
Buckholz, and through him the Americans, that he was not, had
never been at any time, a Communist. More time than he had
spent persuading them he was not a Nazi.

Strange. Emphasis after emphasis, almost at every possible
opportunity. Strange. Simply one of Gehlen's protégés with an
eye to the main chance, hoping to be enlisted in intelligence work
by the Americans? Aubrey shook his head in answer to his own
question. Unlikely. A cover-up, a chance to place on record his
political purity? Possibly.

1940 and 1945. Poles apart. The same intelligent, subtle, experienced intelligence officer. Letting be known only what he wished to be known about himself. *I am not a Communist.*

'Are you?' Aubrey's voice surprised him. 'Wolfgang Zimmermann,' he added dramatically, 'what, precisely, are you?'

Kwangchow station, on Huanshi Road. The city's old name of Canton, the one most familiar to the American segment of himself, kept running through Liu's head. What was it in *Hanyu pinyin*, the official system of transcription of Chinese characters? Guangzhou? Yes. He had found that one of the most difficult hurdles to clear, the transposition of names and spellings and pronunciations that he had regarded as traditional and correct, had grown up with, into some other and alien system. It had made him feel less Chinese, less than Chinese. Just as the Cantonese dialect which, though his own and familiar in San Francisco among friends and their parents, was now a further alienation. He felt like a tourist, a foreigner, his version of Cantonese stumbling, slurred, changed by his being the grandson of immigrants to America. His Mandarin, too, which his cover as a Political Department officer required him to speak—the language of Peking, of officialdom, of the police—felt furry and unused and stale on his tongue.

He felt unprepared, and he could not dismiss that feeling as mere reaction to having killed the doctor or medical ancillary or whatever he had been in the darkened bedroom. Admittedly, he had not buried the shock of it with a weighted stone at the same time as he had rid himself of his sodden, mudstained clothes in one of the paddy fields. Under the moonlight, he had hurried along the raised earth banks between the paddies, the landscape of rice-fields laid out under the strengthened, pale moonlight like frozen, formalized ripples on the surface of a vast lake or sea.

Paoan had been almost empty, yet his arrival at the station had caused little interest. He had shown his railway warrant at the ticket office, and the man's eyes had widened in respect and an anticipatory nervousness, but Liu had left him with a nod. He had reached Kwangchow on a slow, nearly empty train in a pearly, soon-lifted cloudy light. The train moved out of the unrelievedly cultivated countryside, dotted with the wooden and stone and concrete buildings of communes, into the south of the town, through factories and warehouses and chimneys belching smoke

56

into the increasingly blue sky; the fingers of concrete blocks of flats seemed to remark the smoke and fumes of industry, advertising progress and the Four Modernizations. Liu observed the People's Republic like a tourist. A small inner part of him regretted the absence of any sense of homecoming. He had to admit to himself that his racial identity survived only as part of an American minority. He was not Chinese *here*, in this place, among these people.

Kwangchow was going to work as he crossed the town by bus to the main railway station to Shanghai. The city was almost carless, and yet deafeningly noisy with the horns of trucks and the bells of bicycles. The thousands of cyclists on Chiefang Road, the main north-south thoroughfare, created in Liu a sense of the backwardness of the new China, and its huge and scarcely tapped energy. Thousands, perhaps hundreds of thousands, of limbs pushing at the pedals of bicycles. Unsmiling faces bent over handlebars, shoulders bowed. A curiously unreal and yet perceptive moment. China was raw human energy. That was its brute fact. Numbers.

The station received the waves of a human tide. Liu ate a breakfast of rice gruel and salted fish from a breakfast stall on the station concourse. As soon as he began eating it with the spoon supplied—he had almost expected chopsticks—and the first raw, strong, appetising mouthful was swallowed, his stomach rebelled, expressing the tensions of the night in a ravenous hunger. He offered the stallkeeper one of his own grubby ten yuan notes for a second bowl of gruel. It satisfied his hunger, and staved off the hollow sense that was more metaphysical; his gradually, inexorably increasing sense of loneliness.

Liu sat finishing his rice gruel on a rough wooden bench against one wall of the station concourse. The roof arched over the concrete expanse like the ribs of a whale. The grimy glass roof let in a diffused, smoky sunlight. The station was headily scented with the unfamiliar smoke of steam engines. Liu watched a man in railway police uniform approach the line of breakfasters of which he was a member and, beginning at the far end of the row of benches, initiate an inspection of papers. Next to Liu a man in the uniform of an artillery captain, his newly reintroduced badge of rank stitched brightly onto the four pockets that formerly would have distinguished his status as an officer, belched loudly, and grumbled. Liu, glancing at the older man's eyes, saw that he had been drinking. A smell of rice gruel, salt fish and what might have been wheat wine hung about him.

'Bloody papers,' the captain muttered, patting his breast and side pockets. 'Here somewhere.' The captain spoke in Mandarin dialect, but probably because he was from the north rather than because of education or official status. He grinned. 'Mou tai,' he explained, dropping his army passbook and travel warrant at his feet, scrabbling them up. Liu smiled. Wheat wine, almost pure alcohol. His grandfather had once given it to him as a child, out of devilment he had always suspected. It had made him violently ill. 'Here he comes.'

The railway policeman stood in front of the captain. The army officer leaned back, staring into the other's face. There was a subtle sense of hierarchy and challenge about the two uniformed men. The railway policeman would be Public Security Bureau while the officer was merely army. Yet he was evidently senior in rank. A draw was declared by a cursory inspection of the papers and a slight nod on their return. Then the policeman was holding his hand out for Liu's papers.

Liu was acutely conscious of the army officer—the shuffling feet, the quiet burping, the exhalations of salt fish and wheat wine on his breath—as he withdrew his papers from his breast pocket. He was aware, too, of the too-baggy suit he wore, even of his physical smallness inside the belly of the whale-ribbed station. The railway policeman took the papers, and turned the yellow Political Department of the PLA card over in his hand. The army captain coughed. Liu felt him lean slightly towards him, his interest caught and held.

'Thank you,' the policeman said, returning the ID card and the travel warrant. He nodded with a less perfunctory politeness than he had employed with the army officer. Liu hurried the papers back into his pocket.

'Political Department, eh?' the captain said slowly. 'Shanghai district?'

'Yes. Twenty Corps.'

Liu attempted to analyse the officer's reactions to the discovery he had made. There was caution, of course, as well as surprise. Yet there was almost amusement; perhaps, too, a self-contained sense of superiority. This captain existed as an army officer, before he was aware of himself as a finger of the Party.

'I'm Feng Yantai,' the captain said, offering his hand. 'I'm with Sixty Corps, at Nantung.'

'Liu Kuan-Fu.'

'PLA Political College in Peking?'

'Yes.'

'War College,' the captain explained of his own military education. It was evident he regarded himself as socially superior.

'Congratulations.'

'A long time ago.' Feng shrugged. 'You've never seen action, I suppose?'

'No.'

The contempt was evident, just for an instant. Liu felt himself moving into a dangerous jungle area, mined and full of snipers and other forms of sudden ambush. Feng, drunk or sober, was more than competent, probably clever and shrewd. How to get rid of him?

'Not to worry,' Feng said good-humouredly. 'You people have your work, we have ours.' He belched again, then rubbed his lips. 'Mou tai leaves you dry as dust,' he observed, then: 'I've been in most of the hotspots. Mm, along the Amur now, there's fun there with the Russians.' He laughed. It was evidently an intimidatory biography. Liu had considered Feng might be cowed—at least made respectful—by his political status within the People's Liberation Army. Evidently, this was not so. Feng was strangely Western, a military man belonging to his own elite, some obscure and stereotyped universal brotherhood of arms. He was self-confident, boastful, contemptuous—and therefore more dangerous. 'Yes, Tibet for a spell—too cold—and Vietnam a couple of years ago.' He tucked his thumbs into his belt. 'Yes. Shanghai's a dull posting.'

'Of course,' Liu murmured, and Feng looked at him sharply, his mind turning over the stone of the words, looking for a biting insect beneath.

'We'll have a talk, on the journey. Get drunk, eh?' He laughed again. Liu inwardly shuddered. It was worse than he had imagined. Feng had become attached like a burr. How could he shake him off? Liu smiled weakly. 'Don't look so frightened!' It was obvious Feng had not the least nervousness of him. He was to become Feng's butt for the eleven-hundred-mile journey to Shanghai. 'Come on, we'll board the train now, get them to serve us drink.'

'But——'

'Forget the regulations. Throw your weight about. We'll be allowed on the train early, they won't refuse your papers when you order a drink. Come on!'

Liu stood up unwillingly.

'Very well,' he said.

'Where's your luggage?'

Liu pointed to a cardboard suitcase near his feet.

'Is that all?'

'Yes.' Buckholz had had the suitcase, with a change of clothing inside it, deposited by one of his people in Kwangchow in a left-luggage locker at the station. It now appeared, under Feng's scrutiny, a very feeble additional disguise. Feng picked up his own suitcases.

Liu trailed Feng towards the platform and the Shanghai train. He might have to spend thirty hours in the man's company. The thought unnerved him. Feng was clever. Liu could not believe that his cover could bear thirty hours of close, drunken scrutiny.

'Godwin?'

'Yes, Mr Aubrey?'

'Get a signal off to London right away, would you?'

'Sir.'

'Shelley. Ask him to dig out the files of my 1940 interrogations of Wolfgang Zimmermann—if he can find them. Tell him he may have to go down to the warehouse at Catford. And tell him it's urgent. He'd better send me the complete post-war biog on Zimmermann, too. *All* the background.'

'Yes, sir.'

'I want it as quickly as possible.'

'Sir.'

'Good tucker,' Hyde observed, and Aubrey became more convinced that the Australian had booked their table on one of the floating restaurants in Aberdeen Harbour in part for the anticipated amusement of watching Aubrey eat Cantonese food with chopsticks. However, those morsels of crayfish that he had managed to convey to his mouth persuaded him to be lenient towards his subordinate.

'Indeed,' Aubrey murmured, reaching towards the bowl containing the crayfish more in hope than expectation.

'Sir,' Godwin murmured. 'Perhaps if you held the sticks in this fashion?' He held out his own hand. 'Bottom stick tucked tight into the joint there . . . that's it, sir.' Aubrey glanced into Godwin's face. His eyes daunted the florid young man, who added: 'This one pivots, sir, like this . . .'

'Thank you, Godwin,' Aubrey replied huffily, and waggled the chopsticks, gradually adopting a more correct rhythm and a snapping-puppet movement unlike his former feeble attempts to imitate knitting needles. He rescued a piece of crayfish, wobbled it in the sticks, placed it in his mouth. 'Thank you, Godwin—like this, mm?' Sudden bonhomie, the sticks snapping like jaws at the younger man. Godwin smiled with relief.

'Yes, sir.'

'An excellent idea of yours, Hyde. Splendid food.'

'Chicken next,' Hyde observed. Aubrey, after two more morsels of crayfish, looked at his surroundings. Splashes of light on the dark water of the harbour on the southern coast of Hong Kong island. Other floating restaurants, rich with coloured lights and paper lanterns; beyond these splashes of colour and affluence the dimmer, strung-out, faltering smudges of light from the hundreds of sampans and junks that housed the floating population of the harbour. Colourful, crowded, noisy poverty by day had become a dim, staining light which uncomfortably reminded, insisted its presence. After a moment, Aubrey studied the moving firefly lights of water taxis, then closer, the lamplit faces of his fellow diners on the deck of the sampan that was a restaurant. Near-sightedness induced well-being.

The crayfish was cleared away, fresh plates supplied, and then the chicken was served. As soon as Aubrey and Godwin began to serve themselves from the bowls, Hyde stood up, finishing the beer in his glass.

'Just going for a pee,' he explained, and moved away from the table. 'Shan't be long.'

Hyde ducked his head and descended the stairs. He passed quickly along the corridor beneath the deck, the odours from the kitchen assailing him like a vivid, complex emotional experience. Then he climbed another stairway leading to the stern part of the deck, where other diners crowded around small tables and other waiters glided between them as if on castors. He paused for a moment in the shadow of the awning over the deck, red lamplight spilling over him from a lantern, and then he walked along the companion way to the jetty. The island's hills loomed over the town of Aberdeen, dotted with house lights. The harbour's shops and restaurants and cafés were a gilded strip of gleaming lights ahead of him. He hurried into the shadow of a small warehouse at the end of the jetty.

Hyde removed from the pocket of his windcheater a small, slim pair of binoculars, almost a child's version of field glasses. With his back to the wall of the warehouse, lounging as if he had little business and much time, he began to scan the harbour front. In the narrow field of vision of the glasses, the scene was enhanced with an eerie, orange-red light. Cars that were only shadow took on shape, semblance of colour, passengers. Hyde knew that any watchers would be in cars rather than on foot. He felt no sense of danger, merely curiosity and a restlessness prompted by inactivity.

Café windows—oriental faces, the occasional white. Men and women, leaning towards one another over café tables, or more intent upon their food than each other. White males, oriental women. Ubiquitous yellow-brown skin more scorched, darker in the enhanced, false light of the glasses. Shadows moving beyond the lanterns and lamps overhead or on the tables. Hyde pried upon fifty tables, a hundred and fifty people. No one attracted more than a cursory, dismissing inspection.

Then the cars. Most of them empty. Then bored taxi-drivers, loiterers, pimps—dark, shadowy girls' faces in doorway, profiled against lighted, gleaming windows, explained the pimps—a face wreathed in cigarette smoke, another shadowed by a girl's raven hair. Car after car, along the harbour front, until he saw, at the point where clarity was beginning to seep away and the eerie light was itself as substantial as the faces and forms, the two men, one of them with a sniperscope employed as a telescope. A jump of the heart at the instrument that should have been mounted on a rifle, and then he began moving.

He crossed the street, avoided the blandishments from a dark doorway and the child-like face that emerged into the streetlight for a moment, and began strolling in the direction of the car. Rock music jarred against him like a blow from an opened café door, car horns engaged in some unseen quarrel. He paused fifty yards from the car leaning back against an unlit shop window, and trained the miniature field glasses again. Two men, one with a thick neck, both with clipped haircuts, their profiles turned to him, eyes looking slightly back behind them towards the floating restaurant. Hyde swung the glasses, and Aubrey jumped at him from behind the dark straight hair of a Chinese woman. He was using, firelit in the glasses, his chopsticks with dexterity. Godwin, side-on to Hyde, seemed to be looking for his return. On the table, the chicken that had been served had diminished in the bowls in the centre of the table.

When he swung his glasses back to the car, the man with the thick neck was using a camera with a telephoto lens and presumably with infra-red film. The sniperscope remained trained. Hyde saw the squinted-up cheek of the man using it, and the movement of the man's lips, as if he was talking.

Little danger, then. Too far off. He swung the glasses again. No immediate danger. But they were interested. The arrival of Buckholz and Aubrey in Hong Kong in the same period of twenty-four hours had acted like a distress maroon, riveting their attention. It was time to consider moving Wei. Aubrey's face was now in the glasses again, animatedly talking, brushing his chopsticks to one side in a gesture of disagreement. His face was thoughtful, and peremptory with authority. Godwin was making a point forcibly. Glasses back to the car. Sniperscope man's lips moving. Back to the restaurant. Aubrey arguing, making a point with the drum-like emphasis of his chopsticks on the tablecloth. Car again, the man's lips moving in the same methodical, hesitant, robotic way, without any increase in tempo. A recitation rather than a conversation.

Car, restaurant, car, restaurant, car. He could almost hear the words, hear their repetition inside the car. Lip-reading. Difficult, not impossible. Time to get back.

Light rain. He shrugged his shoulders and looked up. The long-range microphone protruded from the upstairs window of the un-lit shop like a gun barrel. Hyde drew in his breath, felt his frame tremble with alertness. He trained the glasses on Aubrey. Still talking, still laying down the law. At that distance, the microphone would be picking up a morass of sounds, yet it could be filtered and enhanced later. They might be able to isolate Aubrey and Godwin's voices, their words, the task made easier by the fact of their speaking English in a background mush of Chinese. He studied the microphone protruding from the half-open window above him, then he began running.

Godwin appeared relieved to see him, but Aubrey noticed the

63

wetness of his shoulders and hair and the heightened colour of his complexion.

'What is it?' he asked as Hyde sat down, his back to the camera and the microphone.

'There's a lip-reader using infra-red, and there's a long-range directional mike, both of them trained on you,' Hyde replied. 'Don't react, just listen. If you've been talking about our friend back at the house, then they may have been able to learn the name of the game. Understand?' He had gabbled in a hoarse whisper. 'I see you have. Shit.'

Godwin had gone pale, his mouth opening slowly like that of a fish. Aubrey lowered his head in admission.

'I see,' he said. A piece of chicken remained clamped in the chopsticks, which quivered slightly.

'Then you could have given the whole bloody game away!' Hyde blurted out in the same hoarse whisper and broader Australian accent.

'Yes,' Aubrey said, not looking up.

THREE:

Shanghai

The station lamps at the end of the platform were haloed and diffused by the soft, rain-misty night as the Shanghai train stopped at Nanchang in Kiangsi province, almost halfway to its destination. The platform along which Captain Feng walked was gleaming darkly with the rain. David Liu watched him go, ostensibly to buy something to read, and felt his stomach quickly empty and become hollow with an enteritis of foreboding. His cover had not been good enough, he had not been able to sustain it during thirteen or fourteen hours of conversation with the army officer, cramped into a small compartment with four others, Feng's unchanging glance upon him, his voice eroding the pretence of himself as an officer in the army's Political Department. It was a cover designed to discourage scrutiny, not to bear it.

Feng—he must find out what Feng was up to, where he was going. He opened the door of the carriage and stepped down onto the platform, glancing up immediately at the damp night sky, knowing that Feng would see and remark the wetness of his hair and clothes when he returned to the compartment. He scampered for the shelter of the station roof. Feng, fifty yards away, had passed the still-open bookstall and seemed to be heading for the station exit.

Nanchang station possessed a small, partial concourse like that of a railway terminus, but most of its traffic was heading for Shanghai, Wu Han or the north and its proportions were those of a provincial railway station. The platforms seemed short to Liu, almost empty, exposed. Feng had only to turn to see him. There was nowhere Feng could logically be heading, unless he had decided to leave the train—an impossible, silly hope that Liu immediately quenched. He was certain Feng was suspicious. There had been too many hesitations, too many evasions in his answers, too little offered in his conversation. Over all these hours, he knew he had made mistakes sufficient to alert Feng, who was no longer drunk.

Do you know. . . ? What do you think of. . . ? Aren't they a strange lot at headquarters? Liu had no army experience to rely upon, and his briefing had not been deep enough. *Ever been on the border? Tibet? Vietnam? Kampuchea? Thought you might have been a political adviser there? No?*

The questions reiterated themselves in a harsher, more incisive voice than Feng had used.

Feng paused, and looked about him. He had reached the small concourse which abutted the platforms for local trains. He stood with his hands on his hips for a moment. Liu halted and pressed back against the political daubs that occupied the spaces where he might have expected commercial hoardings. A stylised, dignified, almost Westernly-handsome Chinese, out-of-focus next to his cheek as he leaned against the poster, gripped the staff of a People's Republic flag and exhorted him to devote himself to the Four Modernizations and directed him forward to the second millennium. He felt his heart pumping with wasted adrenalin. Feng, apparently satisfied, crossed the concourse swiftly towards the office of the railway police. Liu cursed the arrogance, the presumed immortality of his Californian self. Because Feng was boorish, in uniform, slurred in his speech, he had kept slipping into contempt for the man. Feng was in command of the situation, and had been from the beginning.

A railway policeman in green jacket, dark-blue trousers and peaked cap was standing at the doorway of the office. Feng approached him, and at once began a hurried and evidently emphatic explanation. He was explaining Liu, it was obvious. Liu could not bring himself to move closer. Feng and the policeman were perhaps sixty yards from him. It was as if he could hear them, or lip-read their conversation. He remained beside the handsome, exhorting Chinaman in his Mao-suit, horridly fascinated, a rabbit with prevision or a sensitive imagination regarding the snake. He expected Feng and the policeman to move back towards him at every moment.

The policeman's attention was caught. His head kept flicking towards the Shanghai train, declaring the subject of the conversation. Feng pointed towards the door of the office, and the policeman shook his head and stiffened his carriage. It was evident that he possessed sufficient authority to deal with the matter. Then the policeman made as if to move towards the train, but Feng restrained him and then proceeded to dissuade

66

him from action. Liu was puzzled. The lips of the Chinaman on the hoarding now appeared to be shouting a warning. Feng kept his hand on the policeman's arm and talked quickly and urgently for some minutes. Liu began to be aware of the gruntings and breathing of the steam locomotive just behind him. The train would depart in a few minutes' time. Feng laughed, and the sound carried. He made a sweeping, dismissive gesture with his arm, and his hand closed into a tight fist. The policeman nodded, nodded again, replied. Feng commented. They had reached agreement. Then Feng glanced towards the locomotive.

A whistle sounded, startling Liu. Feng stepped away from the policeman, who made vigorous assertions to him. Then Feng hurried back towards the train. Liu felt weak, almost pushed himself away from the hoarding. The handsome face on the poster gleamed with pleasure and triumph. Liu turned and ran back along the platform, climbing into the third carriage so that Feng would not see him.

He hurried down the carriages towards his own compartment. There was a yell of steam following a second whistle, and when the train lurched into motion he felt as disorientated as if the earth had moved; as if some tectonic plate in his personal continent had groaned and moved.

Shanghai. Feng had arranged matters. He would be arrested for questioning when they reached Shanghai. He hurried on, trapped on the train, pushing through passengers who seemed intentionally to restrain and impede him.

Chancellor Dietrich Vogel looked out of the window of his suite in the Hotel am Schlossgarten, down at Stuttgart's main railway station, then altered the direction of his unseeing attention towards the Schlossgarten, its concrete paths whitened against the darkening grass that submitted itself to the sunset. Shadows lay across the grass, and rush-hour traffic crowded into the station square, along the Schillerstrasse. The tower of the railway station flung itself towards the darkening gardens. Behind him, Wolfgang Zimmermann's voice insisted on the emphases of that evening's election speech in the Rathaus.

'Yes, yes, Wolf,' he murmured, sipping at his whisky and sensing only the separation of glass between himself and the people of Stuttgart below him. Zimmermann did not need to remind or rehearse him. He knew he could not falter or be in error now. The mood in the Federal Republic, in Germany, was the mood he felt himself. He was at one with the German people.

He smiled inwardly. Too grandiose, he thought. Too like others who have claimed to speak for the German people. But true nevertheless, he reminded himself. He was going to sweep back to power in this election, and he was going to do it precisely because of his *Ostpolitik*.

'Don't be impatient, don't be too confident,' Zimmermann said in what might have been a hurt tone. Vogel turned away from the window and its darkening scene, and confronted his chief political adviser and oldest friend.

'Sorry, Wolf,' he said. 'Listen, you must have sensed it, mm? Even in Bavaria, where we might have expected a rough ride. We have a *winner* here, Wolf. The people want what we offer— they want the Berlin Treaty.'

'Perhaps.'

'You're so cautious, Wolf!' Vogel crossed the room and sat down in the spilled light of soft lamps in a chair next to Zimmermann. Zimmermann's handsome features expressed doubt; expressed, too, the nervousness of a man on the verge of some momentous act or triumph. His look struck Vogel. 'You believe in it more than any of us, don't you?' he said softly. 'You've worked harder than any of us. Sometimes, I almost feel as if you hypnotised me into this *Ostpolitik* thing.' Zimmermann's face narrowed with what might have been conceived as spite, dislike. 'It wasn't my political priority at one time, you know. After poor old Willy Brandt's failure, it looked like a dead duck.' He patted Zimmermann's arm. 'You lit the torch again, Wolf. I'm grateful to you.'

Zimmermann shrugged. 'It's your work,' he replied diffidently. 'Your work.'

'My salesmanship, your work. Or your salesmanship, perhaps?' Vogel's eyes glittered with amusement. He lit a cigarette, inhaling deeply. 'God, you even taught me to trust the Russians! Because you trust them.'

Zimmermann nodded, his face grave, yet closed. 'Yes,' he said. 'I trust them.'

Already the morning freshness had gone from the air and the brazen sky seemed to press down on the white house on Peak Road. Aubrey looked down over the Happy Valley racecourse, then towards the tiny, whiter-than-white toy buildings of Government House and the smudges of green of the zoological gardens already softening into a haze. His mood was angrily, recalcitrantly guilty. Hyde had, of course, been right. He had been remiss, even lax, in discussing Wei with Godwin the previous evening. The young man's questions had been energetic and flattering, and Aubrey had displayed his knowledge and his assumptions out of little more than a complacent sense of self-congratulation.

He had mentioned Wei by name, many times. He had referred to Zimmermann, also on numerous occasions. He had expressed his doubts, beliefs, theories, insights. He had been—*insecure*. The word rankled in his thoughts like a nagging, worsening headache. Just as his temporary surrender of the process of decision to Hyde, the field agent, distressed him.

Walk on the terrace, Hyde had said. *With Wei. Keep the conversation bland.* The look in Hyde's eyes as he gave those instructions had mortified Aubrey, rubbed against his pride. Simple instructions for an old man.

Thus, with Godwin acting as minder, seated on the low wall of the terrace, his face discomforted by the bulge of the shoulder holster beneath his linen jacket, Aubrey walked in a conscious, instructed parade with Colonel Wei.

'The open air to your liking?' Aubrey murmured, glancing at his watch. *Make it ten minutes, no more, no less*, Hyde had instructed.

Wei appeared nonplussed. 'It is thoughtful of you,' he replied.

'Your early career,' Aubrey said. 'You were loyal, of course. You grew up in the Party?'

'This is necessary? I would have imagined these matters would have come later.'

Don't let him get onto the subject of Zimmermann.

'I am conducting this debriefing,' Aubrey replied huffily.

'Where is your running dog?' Wei asked, nodding in the direction of the florid-faced Godwin. 'This is not this one's real game.'

'Running dog? Oh, I see. On an errand.'

'Ah. Yes,' Wei continued, returning to the subject of Aubrey's question, 'I was, of course, loyal to the Party. In the People's Republic . . .' He spread his hands. 'It was impossible not to grow up in the Party. Créche, school, military service, all of them

69

form a fine net.' He linked his fingers, twisting them tightly together. 'One does not escape, there is no thought of escape.'

'Under Mao?'

'It is still the same. The objects of revulsion have changed, as have the objects of belief. But we are all totally as we were, the creatures of the *People's Daily*.' Wei smiled enigmatically. 'There is a cliché cupboard, rack after rack of trite and most-used Party phrases, at the offices of our great newspaper. It is as full as it ever was. Some of the phrases have changed, that is all.'

Aubrey studied the man carefully, stopping in mid-stride. Modulations, a singing voice, hypnotic like that of an actor. The sentiments were sophisticated and clever, established disillusion very effectively. But something about the tone of voice struck Aubery. Was he being played upon? Wei's eyes watched him as if for a reaction.

'I see. Disillusion is your keynote. Not avarice?' The sounds of the city ascended to them, enfolding them like a cloud of insects drawn by their body heat. Aubrey waved one long-legged hovering insect away from his face dismissively.

'Avarice, yes,' Wei admitted. Then his lips shaped themselves in a bitterness which Aubrey could not but accept as a genuine emotion. 'The Great Leap Forward and the Four Modernizations are not thought. They are artificial, pre-packaged items.' Wei turned the Western colloquialism easily. 'Do you understand? A man of intelligence can accept only so much, and only for a certain period of time.'

'I understand.' There was an evident appeal to Aubrey's own intelligence, a subtle flattery there. He glanced at his watch. The ten minutes had passed. 'Shall we go in now?' he asked, ushering Wei towards the house.

'As you wish.' Wei turned with him. Looking at the man's narrow back and neatly clipped hair as he moved ahead of him, Aubrey felt himself baffled by Wei. Hyde's instruction to keep their conversation away from sensitive areas had only increased the sense of mystery surrounding Colonel Wei.

Aubrey glanced back once, across the hot flagstones of the terrace, before he passed through the doorway. Hyde's task was perhaps easier than his own. He did not doubt that Hyde would have learned what he desired to know, somewhere on the slopes and the road below the house.

*

Hyde studied the house, the two figures on the terrace, then swept the glasses over the bush-strewn, rocky slope that dropped gently away from the house towards Peak Road. There was a car on the road, parked as if to sightsee the city spread out below and the shimmering white towers of Kowloon across the pale bay. It was empty, and was the same car that had been parked on the harbour front at Aberdeen the previous evening. Hyde grinned when he spotted it, opening his lips and inhaling the superiority of the unseen watcher like oxygen. His skin prickled with awareness, his mind raced, his frame was compact, reliable, employable around his senses. The gun pressed against his back in a hollow that might have been designed to absorb its shape and dimensions. The glasses swept back once more, examining each bush, each outcrop of rock, each fold of the slope.

The house that was Hong Kong Station for the SIS perched on a flattened area of the hillside which stretched greenly up to the peak of Mt Kellett and fell away to his left towards Magazine Gap. The best vantage points for any observer were on a level with the house, before the slope dropped away to the road. The cover was thick in places where bushes had grown back across the gouges of excavation made when the house was built. Rocks, too.

A glint of momentary light? Bottle top, broken shard of glass, gunsight? Hyde focused the glasses, and waited. Perhaps fifty yards below him and to his left. He shifted a leg that was becoming cramped, and a small fall of dust and pebbles slid away from his suede shoe. Glint again. The barrel of a telephoto lens rested on the flattened surface of a rock, protruding from a thick, spiky bush that leaned out towards the road. The barrel-image made his heart pump for an instant, until its photographic innocuousness was established. He grinned again. Same car— same men?

Where was the mike?

He lowered the glasses and looked towards the terrace. Wei and Aubrey patrolled it almost self-consciously. He looked at his watch. Three minutes gone. These men would wait on after Wei and Aubrey retreated into the house, but they would be more alert, less focused in their attention, more available to the information of moving earth, disturbed vegetation. He stood in a low crouch and moved to his left, treading warily but still disturbing little showers of rock, little puffs of dust. He remained above and behind the watchers until he found a shallow dry gully. He dropped into it and began to wind down with it, sliding his body like a dancer through its narrow course. He raised his head twice, the second time finding himself slightly below the position of the two men, and twenty yards or more behind them. Bright shirts, cropped heads, thick necks, concentration in their hunched shoulders.

Camera and binoculars. A slow voice speaking quietly into a microphone. Small recorder lying on the flat earth behind the lip-reader. Hyde craned his head, listening. A murmur, with hesitations and pauses. Large silences. Click, wind-on, click; the whirring of the camera as a succession of pictures was taken.

Hyde ducked his head and continued down the gully. When he was only a few yards above the level of the road, he climbed out of the gully into the shelter of a small, stunted, drunkenly leaning bush. One of its thorns scratched him. He studied the miniature contours of the lower slope. The cameraman and the lip-reader above him were invisible to him, he to them. He moved rapidly now, after glancing at his watch and discovering that another three minutes had passed. If the long-range mike was here at all, it would be on the other side of the house.

Dust and pebbles skittered away, his breathing became more rapid and uneven, his back ached as he continued to move in his adopted crouch. If he was seen, he was seen. But it was unlikely while Aubrey and Wei held the stage of the terrace.

He paused and looked up. Rain gullies, scattered bushes, dry yellow earth, rocks. A head moved within the camouflage of a low bush, bobbing up and down. Hyde began to climb again, hurrying. When he was no more than fifteen yards from the bush, he slid behind a rock and waited until his breathing calmed. Then he rose on his haunches and looked over the rock.

Glint of the lens from the other side of the house. Nearer, the back of a man's head, a white shirt stretched over broad shoulders, a darkened patch between the shoulderblades. A sunhat pulled forward to shade the eyes. The cigar shape of the microphone protruded ahead of the man like a grey loaf of French bread. Voices, tinny and unsubstantial that might have been coming from the microphone, reached Hyde. Evidently, Aubrey and Wei had reached this side of the terrace in their patrol. The grey submarine of the mike rose from the bush, titillated by the voices, seduced to attention. At that range, with no mush except the dim whispering of the city below, every word would be clearly recorded.

Hyde looked at his watch. Ten and a half minutes gone. The voices vanished, merged with the city. The microphone withdrew. The man's head appeared above the bush, watched the terrace for a moment then dropped down again. Then the KGB man's voice crackled out in Russian, and there was a furry, treble reply. Walkie-talkies. *Da, da . . .*

Hyde retreated, guessing the next move. He used the shadow of the rock until he reached another rain gully, and began to hurry down it towards Peak Road, skipping almost as surely as he might have done down the steps from the house. The gully bent towards the tarmac drive from the road to the garage at the rear of the house, and he climbed out of it and dropped down onto the hot, sticky tarmac. A grey, dented VW Beetle nestled in the drive. Godwin had borrowed it from an acquaintance at Government House, a Foreign Office official with respectability. As far as Godwin could ascertain, the KGB office would not suspect it.

Hyde got in. The air in the car stifled him, despite the fact that the windows were open. He slid down in the driving seat, and waited. Three minutes later, the microphone operator passed across the entrance to the drive, glanced once at the apparently empty VW, and walked out of sight, whistling softly with a self-congratulatory descant. Hyde sat up, grinning. His hand touched the ignition key. He listened.

He had seen, when he first climbed the hillside behind the house, that a second car was parked further up the slope of Peak Road, as if it belonged to visitors to another house. He had expected any of the watchers to return to the KGB office the moment Aubrey and Wei disappeared. The business was evidently urgent; the Rezident was evidently concerned. Outside the timeless, indolent scenario of Aubrey's interrogation of Wei, other people and other plots were moving more quickly. Aubrey had underestimated, ignored, was in error. These people were like flies around a jamjar.

The engine of one of the two cars fired, roared, and then the tyres protested as the car was turned round on Peak Road. Hyde turned on the Beetle's ignition, then edged the car out of the drive.

The dusty black saloon was already moving away up Peak Road, ascending into a haze, its exhaust shimmering behind it, seeming to melt the car, allow the tar of the road to absorb it. Hyde accelerated after the black car. Victoria Peak and the tramway loomed to his left as the road twisted and began to

73

descend towards the central district. The two cars, Hyde keeping a hundred yards behind and allowing two other vehicles to slip between them, slid into the thronging cars and bicycles and motor scooters and rickshaws of the central district. The Botanical Gardens promised coolly to Hyde's right, and then he plunged the car into the congealed traffic of Caine Road.

He was hot, edgy, and tired of negotiating the traffic by the time the black car pulled up onto the pavement of Tung Street in the Sheung Wan district. The KGB office, behind its facade as an antique shop, looked unprepossessing. The KGB man got out of the car, locked it, and went in. Hyde drove on down the narrow street, but found nowhere to park. Irritatedly, he circled the block and entered Tung Street once more. On his fourth circuit, he edged the Beetle, with a hideous scraping noise, between two other cars only twenty yards or so from the antique shop. A Chinese, presumably the nominal owner, stood in the doorway, demonstrating the decoration on a vase to two evidently American tourists.

Hyde picked up his camera from the passenger seat, and settled down to wait. He looked at his watch. Ten-forty. In the narrow, shadowy street the rich odours of food tugged at his stomach, and the temperature became like heavy, hot clothing around his body. Sunlight spilled between blind buildings in molten slabs of light emerging from a furnace.

Customers. He photographed even those who created no sense of suspicion; the ones with slung cameras, straw hats, striped shirts, shorts, mini-skirts, denims. Older than possible, younger than likely. He reloaded the camera, considering there were only two possibles in thirty-six frames. The ubiquitous and titular owner of the antique shop appeared in perhaps half the shots. Eleven-fifteen.

Another possible. He adjusted the focus with more care as the man weaved between the rickshaws and bicycles. A pause, as if to be photographed with clarity, then he entered the shop. He did not re-emerge. Then another, then the little man Vassily at the airport. The suspicion grew that Godwin would not know all the faces, that these men were new arrivals, drafted in. The scenario that enclosed them was accelerating, had moved into another gear. It did not matter what Aubrey wished, planned or performed. The initiative was swinging towards the KGB. They had the fish on the slab, and the gutting knife was poised.

Another one, click, wind-on, click again as he ducked his head into the narrow dark doorway. Eleven-thirty.

And then, stepping out of a taxi, with a small suitcase and one piece of cabin baggage, his face pale and unexposed to the Hong Kong sun—Petrunin. The shock of recognition caused a sharp, coronary pain in Hyde's chest. His breathing was difficult. The man had tried to have him killed, less than two years ago. Eighteen months ago, on Cannock Chase. Petrunin.

His hands were shaking, the shots would be out of focus, but Petrunin had already paid off the taxi and had turned to the building. A smile of amusement—click—a moment of hesitation, his eyes drawn by a slim, small, elegant Chinese girl—click, the girl out of focus, Petrunin grinning ruefully—then he walked into the shop, body disappearing—click . . .

Hyde put the camera thankfully on the seat beside him. Tamas Petrunin, formerly Rezident at the Russian embassy in London, forced to get out when an operation blew up in his face. Tamas Petrunin, who had been promoted to a new job in one of the geographic departments of the KGB's First Chief Directorate—was it China, or the rest of Asia? Hyde could not remember.

Wei was a target. In that moment, at eleven thirty-six in the morning, Petrunin's arrival in the Hong Kong KGB office made Wei a target. The scenario was now in top gear, and Aubrey no longer had any control over it.

Petrunin.

He saw, immediately, a station cleaner who brushed diligently and whose head moved continuously like that of a feeding, nervous bird; the last sigh of steam from the locomotive was like a sound that might have escaped from Liu's tight chest, an expression of his tension. A railway policeman—perhaps, but he was not certain, the bulge of an unfamiliar gun beneath his uniform jacket—strolled with care and deliberation past the carriage window, turned on his heel and came back down the platform as the train finally stopped. Liu avoided looking at the man, and tried to smile the smile of an arriving passenger at journey's end towards Captain Feng, as the policeman passed the grimy window again. Across Liu's mind flitted images of factory chimneys belching smoke, of green parks with small, robotic figures engaged in martial exercises, of temples and hotels and modern concrete towers; as if the last minutes of the train's journey had been left imprinted on the coloured slide of the window. He tried to push the images from his thoughts, but it was as if his mind was trying to retreat back down the line to Canton, out of the crowded, sprawling city.

Shanghai, and they were waiting for him. He was expected. End of the line. A clipped, laconic defeat possessed him. When Feng stood up, merely to reach up to the luggage-rack for his suitcases, Liu's body jumped.

'End of the line,' Feng said, grinning. He looked tired, and wary.

'What?'

'End of the line—thankfully.'

Their two remaining travelling companions, an old man and his plain daughter, squeezed past Feng out of the compartment. The old man had been silent for most of the journey, sleeping as uprightly as he sat, except when querulously demanding food. The woman, who might have been twenty or forty, had read assiduously hour after hour. To Liu it had seemed as if they were aware of the conspiracy against him, and had chosen deliberately to ignore him.

Lui stood up, pulled down his one small case from the rack, and turned back to Feng. The man's black, raisin-like eyes studied him. They were red with tiredness and drink. He swayed slightly, but more like an attacker than a drunk. Liu's own head was clear, but unable to grasp and hold. Images of anticipated arrest flitted through his mind and fell across his concentration like cobwebs might have fallen across his eyes. He could not think. He was jumpy, aware, unnerved.

'After you,' he said.

'After you.'

Liu led Feng along the corridor to the carriage door, already realizing that he should have debouched as soon as the train stopped and worked himself into the first rush of passengers to the barrier. The old man was climbing with painful slowness down onto the platform. The platform sweeper's face was beyond the old man and his daughter. *Come on, come on . . .*

Liu felt a rush of adrenalin overwhelm him, and fought to control it, dampen it until he might need it. His body prickled with tension, jumped and twitched with the need to act. The old man tottered away on the woman's arm, and Liu stepped down. Feng's hot breath on the back of his neck as they had waited revolted him. The platform sweeper became more assiduous. The railway

76

policeman was further down the platform now, talking to a second policeman. Feng hurried at Liu's side, both suitcases held in one hand, his left. The fact and the implication registered. They passed the two policemen. Liu sensed them fall in behind himself and the captain. Perhaps—no doubt—the man with the broom was there, too. Liu accelerated slightly, and he and Feng drifted slowly into the last of the crowd. Liu worked himself through, burrowing with arms and elbows. Feng remained at his side.

Four more handsome Chinese, mounted on a flying horse, raced towards the year 2000 on a poster they passed. Overhead, smoky steel carved and perhaps once gilded flung itself in a series of narrow bridges on which pigeons perched. The crowd flowed towards the barrier. The adrenalin accumulated, waiting to be employed.

The platform sloped slightly upwards to the ticket barrier. Beyond it, over the heads of waiting relatives and friends, Liu glimpsed the ornate station concourse, its green plants and fountain, its carving and statues, as a park-like apparition. It seemed a freedom he would not reach; rather, be hustled through to the waiting police van. He could not see the girl who was supposed to meet him, and he could make no move until he did. She had to see him, see what he did, where he went. And she had to be professional when he did move; watch and wait, be ready. If she lost sight of him, or lacked the expertise, if she panicked, then he was lost. He would be alone and running in a city more than two thousand square miles in area, amid eleven million people. The girl had to see him, and understand . . .

Feng's right hand was sharp, end-of-finger-like in the hollow of his back. A gun. More handsome Chinese on a poster, racing forward under the wise leadership of Deng, banner-bearing, grinning with gleaming eyes at him; mocking him now. As if the gun had been a signal, Liu saw two, three railway policemen move down from the barrier towards him. The figures on the poster now stared into a far perspective unlike his own immediate future; they ignored him. He and Feng had paused, the gun nudging his spine. He envisaged the damage and pain possible from the officer's Type-59 nine-millimetre pistol with startling, unnerving clarity. The crowd straggled away from him, reaching the policemen. Feng was too close, it would be easy . . .

The girl, the girl . . .

The foremost policeman was a matter of thirty yards from him now, arms at his chest, buffeting like a swimmer through the turbulence of the crowd. The railway policeman and the platform sweeper might be closing, or merely blocking his retreat. His eyes frantically searched for the face of the girl. There was no way in which she could have been wearing something distinctive, all they could instruct her to do would be to . . .

Wave the *People's Daily* like a flag, and there she was, her stick-like arm aloft. *No, no*, another woman, older, similarly waving, then embracing someone. His confidence ebbed. Twenty yards now.

'Don't do anything stupid!' Feng instructed, his breath hot on Liu's cheek as he leaned forward, the alcohol tangible. The man was in the perfect too-close, off-balance position—*where was the girl*? She was afraid to wave, because of the police. She'd given him up already . . .

Feng moved back—now he might step too far away. The nearest policeman was ten yards away with a second drawing level with him. Then the thin arm, the newspaper, waving twice, quickly and covertly; a small, dangerous, ashamed gesture. Confusion and near panic on her face. *Imperialist lickspittle spy*. The words closed on his mind, images of the hysterical accusations of the televised trial of the Gang of Four flickering in the sudden hopeless dark that confronted his reason. Feng was still slightly too close, slightly off balance . . .

Liu turned quickly, his hand reaching behind him, grabbing the barrel of the gun, twisting it upwards; he felt the shudder of the first shot and a scorching sensation in his hand. The explosion was loud and deafening; Feng's now confronted face showed a surprise which turned to rage almost at once, the alcohol wiped aside like sleepiness. Liu brought his knee up hard into Feng's groin, tugged the pistol free by the barrel and thrust Feng aside with his foot.

A hand grazed his clothes, he heard yells and demands. The platform sweeper raised his broom like a tufted lance, the two policemen near him began to move as if their boots were weighted. He shouldered aside a light frame then jumped down onto the tracks of the empty platform opposite the train from Canton. Liu stumbled slightly, hopped to save his ankle from twisting, aware of the fragility of his limbs and torso and of the metal of railway tracks and bullets, then began running.

Whistles and cries. The scorched sensation in his right hand

78

diminished, and he thrust the pistol into his belt. The small suit-case banged against his knee and thigh. He threw it onto another empty platform, and hoisted himself up from the tracks with the ease of a gymnast, the adrenalin making his whole body fluid, graceful. He grabbed up the suitcase. Porters stared at him, and retreated. A distant railway policeman began to run. The first pursuers were on the tracks behind him. Feng was still lying where he had pushed him.

The heartbeat of another train, drowning the cries and whistles. He crossed the platform and jumped again. The locomotive was in front of him, and he could see the driver's startled face in the porthole of the cab. The brakes squealed louder. He heaved him-self onto the opposite platform, knelt, then rose into the flurry of steam that was the locomotive's protest at his intrusion. Then the slowing carriages masked him.

A standing train, empty. He opened the door of a compart-ment, passed through to the corridor, then opened the door down onto the tracks. He was suddenly aware again of the fragility of the bones and muscles and sinew and cartilage in his ankles, so that he lowered himself awkwardly from the carriage, wrenching his arm as he did so. His shoulder burned; heat spread across the back of his neck.

Another platform, this time with a few passengers waiting for some local train. No police. He climbed as purposefully as he could onto the platform, crossed it at a walk, business-like, then climbed into another standing carriage. The train was filling up. He opened the carriage door on the other side, reached out and twisted the door handle of a newly arrived carriage which was still shedding passengers, and stepped across into its corridor. A man turned his head in suprise, but Liu ignored him.

He hurried out behind the man into the crowd heading for the barrier.

No police at the barrier—no, one policeman, hands clasping his uniform belt in complacent self-importance, head turned to gaze down the line of ticket barriers, ears alerted by the whistles. Liu passed through the barrier, his one piece of luck the fact that, as with his own train, the tickets from these passengers had been collected before arrival.

And then the girl was hurrying towards him, pushing through the crowd, small, pretty, alert. Professional. She studied the faces that passed her avidly, as if she might have been searching for a

79

lost child. She collided with him; surprise and relief contradicted each other on her features. Liu felt weak, and embraced her with relief rather than in pretence of recognition.

'Quickly,' she whispered in his ear as she returned his embrace.

Light spilled down through the glass roof of the huge station concourse, onto the ornamental fountain. Dragons and gilding. Green bushes and ferns. Liu thankfully walked into the illusory garden towards the exit and the bus stop, the girl's small hand on his forearm as if she were guiding a blind man. The last traces of adrenalin evaporated, and Liu felt desperately tired. Fear, too, began to come back insidiously. His hand shook as he pushed open the exit door, and stepped out into the midday sunlight.

Hong Kong's noonday gun. Aubrey was too distant to see the small, ceremonial puff of smoke, but the gun's report ascended to Peak Road like a whispered shout, inserting itself into a silence between himself and Hyde. A single gun, firing on China across the bay, Aubrey thought with irrelevance, until Liu's features entered his mind and the ceremony of the gun achieved an allusive importance he disliked. Liu, attacking China single-handed.

Hyde's mood was sullen, disturbed. Evidently the Australian disliked being on the terrace of the house, despite the fact that both Aubrey and Godwin had assured him that their watchers had departed, presumably summoned back to their headquarters because of the arrival of Petrunin.

Petrunin . . . The man obviously worried Hyde.

A heavy, damp wind had sprung up. Cloud was filling in the spaces between the hills like a grey dough. Kowloon thrust a dense crowd of white fingers upwards against the heavy, slow-moving cloud. A cyclone on the way, Godwin had said. The sun had vanished like an illusion.

'Hyde, what is the matter?' He had given no reply to Aubrey's last question.

Patrick Hyde was remembering his childhood. Squatting against the sun-leaking, hot wooden planks of the cramped, car-less garage behind the house, his breath still audible from his haste, the air stifling. The *Beano* annual open on his grubby, bare knees. He had found it on top of his mother's wardrobe with the rest of his Christmas presents. Auntie Vi had brought it from London with her. He had only ever seen the *Beano* comic once, a tattered copy for which he had swopped a broken penknife. Now, magically, he had a hundred pages of Lord Snooty and Biffo the Bear and Dennis the Menace. And he had not been able to wait until Christmas Day. He had seen the book's title through the thin wrapping paper that contained it, and had been consumed with a possessive impatience until able to retrieve it from the top of the wardrobe.

And then, as Dennis the Menace in his striped jersey and impossible shock of black hair was about to receive yet more just punishment, he had looked up, giggling, and seen the funnel-web spider emerging from its abode beneath the shelf above his head, the shelf where the old paint cans were stored. Knowing that the spider's bite would kill him, he had sat in rigid, mortified terror for thirty minutes before the spider entered its woven funnel once more and he could force himself to move. He had wet his shorts by that time. His mother and Auntie Vi, returning at that moment, saw the shorts and the *Beano* annual. His spanking was a relief, affirming life and health.

'What?' Hyde said, looking up suddenly. Tamas Petrunin was his own particular funnel-web spider. Eighteen months before, the man, then KGB Rezident in London, had almost killed him in England. And now he was here, in Hong Kong, and he would doubtless already know that Hyde was here, too. Hyde suppressed a new shudder.

'What is the matter?' Aubrey asked, not unkindly.

'Nothing.'

'Petrunin?'

Hyde's left shoulder ached with the memory of a wound. 'No,' he lied.

'You know him?' Godwin asked, surprised. He held in his hand the new, still-wet prints of airport shots of Petrunin, taken that morning. He seemed to be offering them to Hyde, who turned away.

'Slightly,' he murmured.

'Formerly KGB Rezident in London,' Aubrey explained. 'He was recalled, and surprisingly promoted. A clever man. He's now believed to be heading the First Chief Directorate's Sixth Department.'

'China,' Godwin said.

Hyde turned on them.

'It's very bloody important, all of a sudden, isn't it?' His eyes seemed to accuse Aubrey, remind him of his indiscretions.

'It *is* important,' Aubrey replied coolly. 'Made more important by what the KGB has recently learned.' It was almost an apology. On the Boxing Day, all those years ago, Hyde had gone back to the garage with a burning rolled-up newspaper and fired the web and its occupant. The paint tins and bottles of white spirit had also burned. The fire brigade had put out the fire, eventually, leaving the garage a ruin.

'OK,' Hyde said grudgingly, beginning to accommodate himself to the idea, and the threat, of Petrunin. 'OK.'

'It means that Wei is no longer safe here,' Aubrey observed. Godwin appeared crestfallen, as if he had failed some stern examination. 'Suggestions?'

'Extra men,' Hyde replied, his hands in his pockets, the heavy wind distressing his hair. The dampness in the air was as tangible as a facecloth.

'We can borrow them from Government House—police?'

'Yes, Mr Aubrey.'

'Mm.'

'Why not move him down to police headquarters or even Victoria Prison?' Godwin suggested. 'Then he'd be safe.'

'It might very well affect the progress of my interrogation, young man.' Aubrey rubbed his cheeks, as if laving them with the damp air. The wind ruffled his last remaining hair, making the grey wings stand out from his temples like horns. 'Hyde?'

Hyde scuffed at a stone, kicking it along the terrace. Then he looked up challengingly at Aubrey.

'It's bloody important. They know who Wei is, and what he's offering for sale.' The skin of Aubrey's cheeks darkened momentarily and he frowned, but Hyde ignored the signals. 'If they're suddenly so interested in Wei, then perhaps they're moving to protect Zimmermann?'

Aubrey appeared dubious, but he said: 'Go on.'

'If you want further proof, then discover how much they want to get their hands on Wei.'

'How?'

'Easy as picking up the phone. Tell police headquarters you want provision for a special prisoner, to be delivered tonight. The KGB have drafted in more men—Godwin's snaps tell you that, Petrunin didn't come by himself—and it might just be the opportunity they'd like.'

'A trap, you mean?'

'A both-ways trap. Smuggle Wei to prison, but appear to take him down tonight, in technicolor. A decoy. Find out how much they want to shut Wei up. It might tell you something about your German mate.'

'Telephone?'

'Don't tell me they won't have tapped this place by now.'

'Agreed.' Again, Godwin looked as if he had been accused of failure. 'Decoy, mm? You?'

Hyde nodded. 'Me.'

'You'd take on the—task?'

'It's what I'm paid for.'

'Very well.' The wind was scouring across the terrace now. 'Weather?' Aubrey asked Godwin.

'This cyclone is well out to sea. It will do.'

'Let's go inside. There are details to clarify.'

Hyde walked away from Aubrey, and leaned out over the terrace, his shirt flapping loosely on his back in the wind. To Aubrey, the Australian appeared vulnerable, small, unmuscular. It was a new and unusual glimpse of the man.

Hyde came back towards them. 'The car's back.'

'What about——?'

Hyde shook his head. 'They're still inside it. Just arrived. Interested, aren't they?'

The girl was silent during their trolley-bus ride from the station through the centre of Shanghai towards the Bund. They crossed Suzhou Creek near the Shanghai Mansions, a thirties-style skyscraper hotel that would not have been out of place in some parts of San Francisco or downtown Manhattan. The very familiarity of its red-brown appearance sent a shudder of isolation through Liu. The girl merely tapped him sharply on the arm when they reached their destination. The trolley-bus stopped on Zhongshan Number One Road East, opposite the small Huangpu Park. One old woman descended from the bus with them. Liu breathed deeply, as if for the first time since leaving the station.

The girl guided him across the busy road, weaving them between buses, motorized trishaws, cars. As they entered the park, even though it was crowded with lunchtime pedestrians and the benches were fully occupied, there was a sense to Liu of fugitive peace. The city's incessant noise was veiled, the city's unrelieved crowds thinned, weeded. Movement was slower, the trees bent

83

over slow-motion figures engaged in the shadow-play of *tai ji chuan*, the gentle martial art: an aid to digestion. Hands moving like those of actors in a mime: mimed violence. The harmless images of attack, grasping, damage amused David Liu. There were Westerners, too, engaged in the exercise: businessmen, diplomats, tourists.

'He is there,' the girl informed him, touching his arm and leaning to him.

Against the perspective of the river and the modern blocks of offices and flats, its crinkled-sailed junks and sampans and ocean freighters and derricks and cranes, a tall man who could only have been American—grey suit, blue shirt, wide tie, a sleek, groomed presence—was engaged in the shadow-boxing. He stood head and shoulders above the shapeless-capped Chinese men around him. The butterfly wing of a junk's sail moved behind him, a backcloth to his profile. Frederickson, the CIA case officer assigned to him in Shanghai.

Liu looked from the man to the girl at his side. 'Thank you,' he said.

'Can you practise *tai ji chuan?*' she asked.

'Yes.'

'Then join him.'

Liu sensed himself as a manipulated puppet, a delivered parcel. And superfluous to requirements. He had nothing to say to the girl; she resisted intimacy of any kind, confirmed in her role as a courier.

'Very well.' Liu crossed a strip of grass towards the river, gleaming like steel in the sunlight. He put down his suitcase as casually as he could, and edged towards Frederickson, who gave no sign of having seen him. Liu raised his hands, palms outwards in front of his chest, lunged slowly forward, swayed to one side, bent his knees, slid and insinuated his hands through the air. No one remarked his arrival.

'Welcome,' Frederickson said. 'Glad you made it. Any trouble?' The American was glancing towards the girl, who had taken a seat on one of the benches, next to an old woman in a light blue jacket and black trousers. The girl was reading her newspaper.

'Some.'

'Yes?'

'An army captain on the train became suspicious.' Liu did not mention his arrest after crossing the border. It seemed too distant, and unrelated to Shanghai. 'He called ahead, to the railway police here . . .' Frederickson's reactions as he boxed with the hot, humming air of the park seemed to have increased in intensity. He jabbed and cut and stabbed with his hands as if he faced an opponent.

'What happened?' he snapped.

'I got away—the girl got me away. There wasn't any pursuit, if that's what worries you.'

'OK, OK. They don't have your papers?'

'The army captain knows my cover.'

'OK, go to your secondary papers, I'll get you a new back-up identity and cover story prepared. Meanwhile'—Frederickson looked carefully around him; the vigour of his shadow-boxing had subsided—'we'll get right to it—your briefing.'

'Yes?' Liu traced patterns in the air with his hands. A butterfly seemed concerned to evade his grasp. The horn of a river barge boomed from the far bank of the Huangpu. 'I begin to wonder why you need me.' He had not, he remarked to himself, meant to make that observation. It did, however, seem true.

Frederickson grinned. Lines around his pale blue eyes appeared as he did so. The grin was twisted, but handsome.

'They're professional, our people here, yes. But they're not trained agents, not trained to look after themselves. They're just agents in place—ministries, factories, communes. They're monitors, that's all. And *I* can't make a suspicious move—I kind of stand out, you know.' Again the twisted, charming grin, disarming Liu. 'They have no freedom of movement, I have less. That's your job.'

'OK, what have you got for me?'

'A medical orderly, they think.'

'Think?'

'One of my people thinks one of the orderlies at the East China Hospital, right floor, right duties to know about our German pal, might be open to a bribe. They haven't done anything. That's your job.'

'Might, might, might . . .' Liu observed.

'Right. It's all hazy. Everything's been rushed. Langley and Buckholz want too much too soon. So, I've gotten you one orderly who was working when Zimmermann was in the East China Hospital. And now it's up to you. I can't go near him. He won't talk to a Westerner—at least, not one of my colour.' Frederickson looked down, as if disapprovingly, at Liu's short figure and his complexion. Liu felt himself weighed. 'You'll make it,' Frederickson said.

'When?'

'Tonight. You eat at the Clean and Delicate Restaurant, near Fu xing Park, at nine. The table's booked under your second cover. The girl will pick you up there when you've eaten.'

'Where am I staying?'

'Shanghai Mansions. You're booked in under the same cover.'

'OK.'

Frederickson ceased shadow-boxing, and turned briefly and directly towards Liu.

'This is urgent. Do what you have to, but get the information Buckholz wants. Clinch it here in Shanghai if you can—it's going to get more difficult if you have to go upriver to Wu Han. Contacts and back-up are thin on the ground. Understand?'

'Yes. And if I get something tonight . . .?'

'You'll be in luck.' Again, Frederickson grinned. His hands wafted in the air now, like parts of a machine running down. 'The girl will know how to reach me.'

Frederickson straightened his knees, adjusted his jacket, and walked away. He waved to a jogger in bright shorts and a University of Minnesota sweatshirt who weaved through the crowd engaged in shadow-boxing. Frederickson's back-up, Liu presumed. Liu picked up his suitcase. The girl had already disappeared from the bench.

Liu could taste, even after the glass of *pi jui* beer and the green tea which followed his meal, the spices and pimento that had been used abundantly in the Si chuan regional cooking of the Clean and Delicate Restaurant. He felt tense, but in control of his circumstances. His papers and reservation at the Shanghai Mansions had been accepted without demur. He had become a railway inspector, by implication rather than statement an inspector of railway security. It elicited a tangible, though understated, deference, and a larger room than he might have anticipated. He had dozed with ease. In the restaurant, too, a corner table at which he ate alone had been the result of the appearance of his identity papers.

As if the wiping of his lips on his napkin had been a cue, the

86

girl entered the restaurant. Her hair had been done in a fuller, softer Western style, and her jacket was a bright red, above black silk trousers. She caused some heads to turn, and the waiter's glance indicated that such a companion was only to be expected for a Party official involved in matters of policing. Liu went through a mime of asking the girl to sit, but she indicated, pleasantly, that there were other matters at hand, and Liu settled the bill and they left.

'Where are we going?' he asked as he stood on the pavement, his arm crooked to hold the girl's hand. The Fu xing Park's dense, heavy trees loomed against the warm stars. There was a distant chatter of monkeys from the small zoo in the park. Motorized trishaws puttered along the street. Warm streetlamps, the occasional car, bicycles. The city had a feeling of well-being. Liu felt strangely at home, anonymous, safe.

'It is in the Old Town—a shanty.'

'Transport?'

'Bicycle, of course.' The girl smiled. She indicated two bicycles standing together in the rack outside the restaurant. 'A friend brought yours,' she explained. 'Are you ready?' She seemed to be gently mocking him.

'What do I call you?'

'Liang will do.'

'Very well. Lead on.'

Liu mounted and followed the girl, with a more unsure and wobbling action of the bicycle, to the junction with Fu xing Road. More lights here, the noise of the city conducted along the street as if it were an air duct, hundreds of bicycles and dozens of motorized trishaws. An old-fashioned city, bustling, crowded, noisy; yet humming rather than yelling with life and vitality. Eventually they crossed the circular Zhonghua Road, the perimeter of the Old Town. Then Liang led him into the rabbit-warren of blind, narrow, softly lit streets, beneath overhanging upper storeys of richly carved wooden houses, past rows of whitewashed, thatched shanties, winding and twisting all the time so that within minutes he knew he would never find his way out of the area without the girl's help. The district was no longer a festering slum; it was bright, almost aseptically clean, thronged, even light-hearted.

Near the Yu Gardens, the girl slowed to a halt outside a still open shop selling carvings, lanterns, even birds that still sang in the artificial day of the streetlamps. Fish drifted through weed and fern and bubbles in great tanks, mouths opening and closing with a philosophical slowness. Liang pointed ahead, to a low white shanty with a new thatched roof.

'There,' she said. 'He will be at home now.'

'You'll come in?'

'If you wish.'

They approached the door of the tiny, one-storey shanty. The girl knocked. Almost immediately, as if he had been waiting behind the door for their signal, a young man with quick, wary eyes opened the door and beckoned them inside. They pushed their bicycles into the narrow corridor. The house was scented with a mild, sweet incense. The place had a familiarity for Liu: friends' places, relatives' homes when he was a child. The whole of the crowded, cramped, vivid Old Town seemed familiar, as if transplanted from America. Any Chinatown, anywhere.

'Please come in, please come in.' There was a quick, guessing, acquisitive intelligence behind the bland courtesies. 'Welcome to my home.'

The young man waved them through a door which he opened. The scent of something more than incense. The young man was bribable. Opium. The scent of Shanghai's past, the city's former wealth, power and corruption. The incense was intended to mask the smell of the opium. Old men in his childhood had smoked it, the smell had been everywhere. The young Chinese used a needle in America; here, old traditions remained alive. The smell explained the quick bright eyes, the searching glances. The man had a habit that was expensive, and difficult. The Party disliked opium addiction; it demanded addiction to itself, its propaganda-fixes. He had been left above the high water mark by politics and history, without Tongs and Triads and connections to feed his habit easily. The hospital would be a useful source, but he was probably greedy.

He might lie, then . . .

The young man indicated cushions on the polished wooden floor. A woman brought in tea, bowed and left. Liang seemed to dislike the old-fashioned, subservient courtesy the woman expressed. Liu drank the proffered tea before he spoke.

'I am led to understand,' he said easily, 'that you could be of help to me.'

'Perhaps. My name is Xu Bin, by the way.'

'My name is not important,' Liu replied. 'You work as an orderly at the East China Hospital? Is that so?'

Bin nodded. 'Yes.'

'Well, Bin, you had a visitor—a patient—at the hospital some time ago, one you might not have expected. Is that not so?'

'We have many.' Liang sat cross-legged and silent. Both men ignored her. Liu felt a small pulse of excitement begin in his temple. The bright eyes caught the light of the single lantern above them; preternaturally bright, opium-bright. Clever and greedy, too.

'Ah, yes, but this one was not Chinese.'

'We have many Westerners, also.'

'Germans?'

Bin sighed. 'Ah. Not important Germans, perhaps.' He shook his head. His hands clasped his shins as he sat. They quivered slightly. 'You wish to know about this man.' It was not an enquiry.

'I do.'

'You are prepared . . . ?'

'Why would you not talk to the American? I am American, though not white. What difference is there?'

'I do not want . . .' The young man made a sweeping gesture with his hand. 'You smell something?'

'Yes.'

'That would be only the beginning, yes?' He smiled. 'I am not ready.' He looked darkly towards Liang. 'This is something I may do, for money. But I do not wish to become an *employee*, you understand. They might offer me—something in kind, something to smoke, and I would take it, and then they would control the supply, and the habit. This way, with you and with money, they do not have control.'

'The habit must be hard, here?'

'I inherited it. It is, perhaps, genetic. My family have been addicts for generations. Once, I thought myself cured. But that was untrue. I—manage. A little more money would be welcome, however.'

Liang's face was creased into lines of contempt, but she said nothing.

'Of course. How much?'

'One hundred dollars.'

'Impossible.'

'Ask, then. I shall provide some information, as a sign of worthiness.'

'This German—his name?'

'Zimmermann.' Liu recognized the name, despite the difficulties of Chinese pronunciation.

'Describe him, please.' Bin did so. 'Good. Then, you saw him?'

'Many times.'

'What illness was there?'

'Food poisoning.'

'What visitors did he have?'

'What have I earned so far?'

'Five dollars.'

'Ten at least.'

'Seven.'

'Very well. Visitors—there were many.'

'All Chinese, all Western?'

'Both.'

'What shift were you working?'

'Night shifts.'

'He had visitors at night?'

'Many. How much have I earned?'

'Twenty dollars.'

Bin nodded. Liu noticed that the opium scent had been swallowed by the incense. Bin seemed to perceive, and regret, its departure. 'That is good.'

'Visitors at night?' Liu prompted. 'Who were these visitors?'

'Police.'

Liu controlled his sense of excitement, keeping it from his face and eyes. 'Police? Chinese police? What nonsense.'

'It is not nonsense,' Bin protested, now firmly determined to accelerate the accumulation of dollars. 'Chinese police. I know them, their type, their manner. And doctors——'

'In a hospital, of course——'

'Not from the hospital—brought in especially.'

'Why?'

'To administer drugs.'

'What kind of drugs?'

'To make him answer their questions, I suppose. There are such drugs.'

'You *know* this?'

'How much have I earned?'

'Fifty dollars,' Liu snapped impatiently.

'Good. I know this—I have seen. Every night, all of the night. Our doctors and nurses not allowed into the room, and not willing to speak about it. Questions, all night.'

'I see——'

'Have I earned my hundred dollars?'

'Perhaps seventy. You can, however, earn the other thirty, and one hundred more, tomorrow.'

Bin appeared cheated, then suspicious, then avaricious. He said in a small voice: 'What do you want?'

'The files. I want to see the files—*all* the files—kept on Zimmermann by the hospital. Temperature charts, diet, all the medical records, including X-rays if there are any.'

'I can't——'

Liu stood up, confident, dismissive. 'That is up to you. A total of two hundred dollars.' He reached into his wallet, and counted out the equivalent in yuans of seventy dollars. Bin's face twisted in rage. 'I know that US dollars buy more. Tomorrow I will give you, in exchange for these notes, real US dollars. Two hundred of them—if you have what I want.'

'I can't——'

'That is your concern. My gratitude for your hospitality. Good night.'

Liang followed him to the door. Bin made no protest or attempt to prevent them leaving. Liu assumed that he was already engaged in computing the risks against the reward. If it was possible, he would bring the files out of the East China Hospital.

'Will he do it?' Liang said with evident distaste when they had wheeled their bicycles out into the street and the silent woman had closed the door behind them.

Liu rubbed his eyes, suddenly weary. The lantern-soft illumination of the narrow street seemed sharp, hard. Noise from a restaurant, singing; the mutter of crowds funnelled towards them.

'I think so.' He smiled. 'We shall see.'

'You're tired.'

'And satisfied. Will you guide me back to the hotel?'

'Of course.'

They cycled slowly through the twisting, crowded streets until they emerged onto the Renmin Road, another part of the perimeter of the Old Town, of the ring of roads that enclosed it. Liang pointed northwards along the well-lit Henan Road.

'When you reach the Suzhou Creek, turn right. Shanghai Mansions is ahead of you then.'

Liu nodded. 'You're going home?'

'Yes.'

'You'll report to Frederickson?' The girl nodded. 'Tell him I shall want to meet him the day after tomorrow—with good news, I hope.'

'Good night.'

Liang pedalled off, and was soon lost in the throng of bicycles. Liu began cycling up the Henan Road, past the Museum of Art and History, a dark and lowering building, his growing impression one of being in the middle of a pack of riders in some road race. He was eminently satisfied. Most of all, he no longer felt alienated and alone. He was anonymous, and confident in his anonymity, here in Shanghai. The interview with Bin had been fruitful, more than he had hoped.

The flash of sparks from an overhead cable as a trolley-bus passed on the opposite side of the road startled him. He wobbled his bicycle back under control, and shook his head to clear the mood of satisfied reverie. He could smell the river on the warm night air, even before he reached the creek and turned right. The lights of shipping lay ahead of him then, anchored in the river. A string of lights revealed the presence of a bridge, and he saw the random pattern of room lights from the Shanghai Mansions.

He slowed outside the hotel, and left the cycle in the hotel park. He turned to look back at the creek and its bridges, at the train of barges hooting and sidling beneath it, at the crowds and their dense, inexorable sense of movement.

The man had evidently not expected him to turn back at the hotel entrance. He was standing beneath the globe of a streetlamp, a camera hanging on his chest. He was leaning against a car. He made no attempt to use the camera, and turned unsuspiciously away from Liu, bending his head to speak to the car's driver. Two men, then.

Car, camera, two men . . .

Liu felt chilled as he hurried into the Shanghai Mansions. Evidently he was being followed. He was under surveillance.

FOUR:

In Harm's Way

Chancellor Dietrich Vogel handed the laboratory coat and white safety helmet he had worn during his swift tour of the chemical factory to one of his aides. Zimmermann smiled at the practised ease, the sense of confident relaxation that the man exuded. Always, he was able to suggest he was among friends, creating warmth and respect. Here, in an industrial suburb of Frankfurt, engaged in a handshaking tour of one of the I.G. Farben factories, he encountered management, unions and workforce with the same unshakeable good humour.

A second aide handed Vogel his check cap and raincoat, which the Chancellor draped loosely over his shoulders.

'Can I smoke now?' he asked, smiling.

'Not until we leave the building, Herr Chancellor,' he was informed with a note of genuine regret by the managing director who had conducted him on his tour of the factory. 'I am so sorry.'

'I am sorry I haven't given up the habit,' Vogel replied, clapping the man on the shoulder and laughing. The businessman allowed himself a moment of amusement, moved to it by Vogel's manner.

'You have time for coffee, I hope?'

Vogel glanced swiftly at Zimmermann, who nodded.

'Naturally—a pleasure,' Vogel replied, almost thrusting the managing director in front of him towards the doors of the building and towards the executive offices. 'But if I sit down, I may not want to get up again!' The managing director did not seem any longer self-conscious about his laughter. His staff, and that of Vogel, chorused their approval in smiles and guffaws. Vogel turned to wave at overalled and white-coated workers as he reached the doors. Many applauded; among them, Zimmermann imagined, many who would not vote for him. Vogel only occasionally encountered hecklers; always, he dealt with them brilliantly and without offence or humiliation, but much of the time he disarmed criticism by his presence, his behaviour.

The late afternoon sunlight was breezy, grass and concrete

patched by clouds pushed across the sun. It had rained that morning. The neat lawns and banks that surrounded the factory and its office block still retained a freshened scent. Sprinklers were already at work, reinforcing nature. Vogel waved to faces at office windows, to lorry drivers, security guards, trailing his entourage and the management of the factory behind him like gulls in the wake of a fishing vessel.

Zimmermann watched what might have been a royal progress from the factory doors to the office block. Vogel fascinated him, even after all these years. So little of it was pretence, too. Most surprising of all.

Zimmermann disliked Frankfurt. The past stirred too easily to life whenever he visited it. Capture, weeks of interrogation by the Americans, the vision from the back of an army truck of a city that had virtually disappeared. He had been, while enduring that long journey to a detention camp, forced to a discovery of the horrors to which Germany had brought herself, allied to a lunatic, himself the leader of a gang of thugs and sadists. The journey, which had seemed to last for weeks rather than days and to have been an endless succession of encounters with the displaced, the bereaved, the homeless, the fleeing, had begun in Frankfurt, and for that he could never forgive the city. Its energy, brightness, urgency now expressed as well as any German city—perhaps better than most—the new order, the recovery, the miracle. Zimmermann never regarded Frankfurt in that light. To him, it was always the first image of his own vision of damnation. He, in uniform, had been a part of the order that had truly destroyed Germany; not the Allies and their bombs and tanks and men, but the Führer, the Wehrmacht that had sworn an oath of loyalty to him, the Abwehr that had been ingested in 1944 by the secret police. By the time he reached his place of detention, he was sickened by his wartime silence, his acquiescence; and he was ashamed of his uniform.

Frankfurt. Gleaming, bustling, handsome Frankfurt. The beginning of that journey which had really never ended.

Wolfgang Zimmermann saw the correspondent from *Pravda* make as if to approach him. The entourage had been whisked into the office block by Vogel as if it were his factory, they his guests, and Zimmermann in his mild reverie had lagged behind. A couple of correspondents stood on the steps up to the glass doors with him, perhaps expecting a sidelight upon the Berlin Treaty.

Zimmermann recognized them both, one from *Bild Zeitung*, the other from *Frankfurter Allgemeine*. The newspapers' senior correspondents were still in tow behind Vogel, these two were bright, quick, younger men. He smiled at them almost absently as he ascended the steps lightly, but his eyes were still on the *Pravda* correspondent.

Vogel had encouraged the Soviet and East European press corps in the Federal Republic to involve themselves in his election campaign, lifting travel and access restrictions to aid them. Thus the man from *Pravda*, usually based in Bonn, had travelled with the rest of the pressmen accompanying Vogel. The man at his side, festooned with camera equipment, Zimmermann did not recognize. He recognized the gesture, however; the restraining hand placed upon the *Pravda* correspondent's arm. He recognized, too, the urgency of the man's instructions, just as he understood the seniority of the second man over the correspondent. He saw the hand-waving gestures in his own direction which the man either could not, or did not bother to, disguise. He realized, instinctively and completely, that the man was no mere photographer, because he recognized the type. God, he should be able to. Police. And not German police, either. The two German reporters seemed to hesitate in their approach, perhaps recognizing his distraction. Zimmermann, for no reason he could name, felt chilled in the warm, breezy sunshine.

The *Pravda* correspondent nudged his companion. The policeman looked up, towards Zimmermann. Even at a distance of perhaps thirty yards, Zimmermann could clearly see the urgency on the man's face; and an expression of baffled anger and suspicion. Only then did he seem to remember his cover. He raised a camera to his eye, pointing its telephoto lens at Zimmermann. Zimmermann turned away, rejecting the pretence.

Why now? he asked himself. Why now, of all times, was the KGB watching him? What did they want with him?

The lamplit room was hot, despite the stirring of the sluggish air by the fan above Aubrey's chair. The windows were closed and shuttered. The cyclone, venting its full power on the South China Sea, roared around Hong Kong's hills. When he had shuttered the windows in the lounge, with Godwin's help, the wind had seemed like a solid force outside, pushing at the house. Aubrey had found the impression unnerving.

He laid the file aside and rubbed his eyes, then looked at his watch. Twelve-forty. He had arranged over the telephone that Wei would be transferred to Victoria Prison at one that morning. A car would arrive to collect him. Meanwhile, the senior police officer who had arrived at the house that afternoon had received instructions that Wei, under McIntosh's supervision, would be in reality collected by another car thirty minutes after the departure of the decoy saloon containing himself, Hyde, and Godwin, and escorted by a second police car. If the telephone had been tapped and the instructions overheard, then that car and its escort could expect to be intercepted. Thus ran Hyde's gloomy reasoning, and Aubrey did not have the confidence to refute the argument.

Aubrey was pricked by the realization that it was he who had created the situation which now endangered Hyde. It was for that reason that he insisted on travelling in the car with Hyde and Godwin; insisted on putting himself in harm's way. Atonement; apology.

The wind howled and thrust at the house. A shutter, loosened somewhere, banged distantly. The noise of the wind swamped the cassette-recorder on which Hyde had left some jazz piano music playing quietly when he went upstairs to begin the process of turning himself into a replica of Wei by dyeing his skin. Superstitiously Aubrey left the music playing, despite his dislike of jazz.

He was impatient for events to unfold and impatient for the arrival of the Zimmermann files from London. Buckholz's interrogation he had read and re-read; files he had brought with him from London on the German's post-war career, which were now on his lap, had become familiar and dull and unrevealing. Both sets of documents, separated by nearly forty years, revealed a man he did not know. Aubrey, whether from instinct, superstition or vanity, believed that revelation would come from his own interrogation of the young Abwehr officer in 1940. He needed to re-understand *that* man. The seeds of his later life would have been there.

Aubrey clenched his hands into fists in frustration and ignorance. If he recalled every word, relived every moment, he would know Zimmermann. Then Wei and the 1945 file and the general files and Liu's journey and the Berlin Treaty would all exist in a clear, revealing light.

He waved his hand in a dismissive gesture. The fond illusion of an old man, he told himself. He stood up, stretching, hearing the old muscles and sinews protest, the old bones and joints creak and crack. He regretted his determination to accompany Hyde and Godwin in the car, but knew he could not now withdraw. He looked across at the stairs leading out of the lounge. Wei. Twelve forty-five. Perhaps . . .

He climbed the stairs and passed along the landing to Wei's room. As he went, images of Zimmermann's career flickered through his mind like the quick life on the surface of a pond; but in shadow, meaninglessly, to no purpose. Business success, local political office, family, widowhood, appearance in certain Nazi trials in the Federal Republic during the sixties, some journalism of a portentous and semi-philosophical kind, without humour; wealth from the sale of his business interests, his attachment to Vogel when the Chancellor was no more than a junior minister; *Ostpolitik*, television and radio interviews which were no more than declamations under Erhard and Brandt and Schmidt of his support for a united Germany; opposition to NATO, his roving commission as a publicist for *Ostpolitik* and for Vogel; visits to the Soviet Union, Eastern Europe, America, China . . .

And the younger man, the brilliant schoolboy, the army intelligence officer attached to the Condor Legion during the Spanish Civil War, his capture by the Republicans, his wartime career in the Abwehr, his high estimation in the opinion of Gehlen, his chief . . .

A man Aubrey did not know. A web of nerves and shadows and clues. Aubrey could not decipher the symptoms presented to him. He pushed open the door of Wei's room, pushed Zimmermann's files from his mind.

He received an immediate impression of the sardonic smile on Wei's face. Then a mirror-image, dispelled in an instant but nonetheless disconcerting, as a head turned to him: Hyde, face dyed to Wei's colour, wearing the same bright shirt that the Chinese colonel had exhibited on the terrace that morning, the same colour slacks. Godwin grinned at Aubrey's momentary discomfiture, while the young duty officer simply watched Wei from his chair against the wall.

'Well?' Hyde asked. 'You likee?'

'What does this pretence signify?' Wei asked languidly. Aubrey recognized an effort to appear casual, unconcerned. It suggested the possibility of nerves, the beginning of fear. As if on cue, Hyde removed, checked and replaced the eighteen-round magazine of the Heckler & Koch VP 70 pistol with which McIntosh had issued him. Wei's eyes were immediately attracted and held by the gesture and the weapon. Hyde thrust the pistol into his waist band at the small of his back. 'What is this?' Wei repeated.

Aubrey did not look at Hyde. 'Yes, indeed, Colonel Wei, this man is intended to pass for yourself—in the dark, of course, and in a car.'

'I forgot to tell you that there might be certain—um, impediments?' Wei nodded. 'Ah, forgive me. This charade is merely a precaution.'

'Against what and who?'

'Certain interested parties, shall we say.'

'The ministry?'

'No Revisionist elements would be nearer the mark.'

'KGB?'

It was Aubrey's turn to nod. Hyde watched Wei's face twist in surprise, then grow livid with an undisguised fear. The man's eyes assessed the room in quick, darting glances, as if the walls had suddenly grown transparent, glass-like. He evidently felt unprotected. The sensation devoured his confidence, his reticence.

Aubrey smiled. Excitement was like an appetite about to be sated on a fine meal. 'Yes, I'm afraid so. They've become very interested in your arrival.'

'How? Why?'

Aubrey shrugged. 'I couldn't say, old chap. Don't worry, though. I doubt any harm will come to you.'

'This is some kind of——'

'Danger? It is not a bluff—at least, not one for your benefit.' He transferred his glance to Hyde. 'Yes, Patrick, I think you'll do.'

'All Chinamen look alike,' Hyde observed. 'Especially to a Russian.'

'This is preposterous!' Wei protested, swinging his legs off the bed. Sensitive to Aubrey's intentions, Hyde drew the pistol and motioned the colonel back onto the counterpane. Wei retreated, drawing up his legs, sitting upright against the headboard of the bed. 'Preposterous. I demand to be handed over to the Americans immediately.'

'Please, Colonel, do not interrupt me. Matters are—time is running out. Excuse me. Hyde, come with me . . .' Aubrey turned to leave the room.

'Schiller!' Wei called at his back.

'Not one of my favourite German poets,' Aubrey replied. 'However, I'm surprised you're familiar with his work, Colonel. Do you read Rilke?'

'Schiller is the man's name,' Wei hissed, his face creased and small and venomous.

'I'm sorry?' Aubrey appeared bemused, and irritated at the delay. 'Whose name? What man?'

Wei's voice rose to an exasperated shout. 'There was an officer captured with Zimmermann in Spain! *His* name was *Schiller*! Now do you understand?'

Aubrey crossed swiftly to the bed. His face appeared angry.

'How much do you really know, Colonel? How much could you really tell us if you tried?' A car horn tooted dimly from the drive outside. A swift frown of anger crossed Aubrey's features. He had established the circumstances and now had to abandon them. In Victoria Prison, Wei would have time to rebuild his defences before their next meeting. 'Of what importance is Schiller, pray?' he asked icily, contemptuous of Wei's information. He could see Wei already beginning to reconsider, as if the car horn had been a warning to him to remain silent. He did not answer. 'Very well, I leave you to consider matters . . .' He turned his back on Wei once more. Hyde and Godwin had now joined him at the door. The car horn tooted for them again. Aubrey cursed it under his breath.

'They were in the hands of the NKVD in Spain!' Wei snapped out, abandoning whatever comfort he had derived from the noise of the car. Aubrey turned on him. The man looked as if he were being deserted.

'NKVD?'

'Zimmermann was in the hands of the NKVD—a Colonel Aladko, one of those NKVD people with a passport that belonged to a dead volunteer in one of the International Brigades, I forget which one. Zimmermann and Schiller were both under the close supervision of this revisionist Aladko . . .' The words had emerged in a flurry; the desperate display of identity documents.

The car horn tooted, impatiently.

'Where is Schiller?' Aubrey asked greedily. 'Is he alive?'

Wei shook his head. 'I do not know. Hans-Dieter Schiller. That is all I heard . . .' Wei subsided into his fears. Aubrey clenched his fists, then said: 'You will be taken care of, Colonel. You have nothing to fear.' Wei seemed not to hear, but to be engaged in some renewed, and fiercer inward debate.

Aubrey left the room. McIntosh was waiting impatiently in the lounge, like a host anxious to see the last of his troublesome guests.

'The car's waiting . . .' he began unnecessarily.

'Take the greatest care of Wei,' Aubrey replied. 'He's far from played out.'

'Of course.'

The cassette tape on the recorder increased in volume. Aubrey turned his head. Hyde was standing by the recorder, listening. The piano floated a pretty, high melody into the room, delicate, ethereal, syncopated. The pianist provided a grunting, breathy, unintended accompaniment. Hyde's eyes were closed. Then, savagely, he ejected the tape with a loud click like the magnified cocking of a pistol.

'For luck,' he said. 'OK.' He breathed deeply, shrugged his shoulders, and followed Aubrey through the hall and kitchen of the house to the rear entrance.

Two cars. Two peaked-capped policemen in wind-flapped shorts standing by the empty car. They seemed relieved to see Aubrey.

'Get in the car—and you, Godwin,' Aubrey fussily instructed. Then he turned to McIntosh. 'In case I have an accident,' he said above the wind's noise, 'get a signal off to Shelley at once. A full check, pre-war, wartime, post-war, on a Condor Legion officer named Hans-Dieter Schiller—presumably Abwehr like Zimmermann—captured with our German friend. I want to know whether he's alive, and where he is. Soonest.'

'Very well. I'll do that right away.'

Aubrey felt reluctance grip him like a great weariness, then he merely nodded, and crossed to the car. Godwin was seated next to the driver, Hyde in the rear. Aubrey slid in next to him. A police officer bent his head to Aubrey's window.

'Everything's arranged, Mr Aubrey. You'll be the second car. We won't be far ahead, and we'll keep our eyes and ears open. Your driver will call us on the radio as soon as there's any sign of trouble.' He paused, then added: 'You're sure you're being sensible, sir?'

'No, I'm not. Nevertheless, I'm here.'

'Very good, sir. You think there will be trouble?'

'I don't know. We shall see.'

The inspector hurried off to the escort car and climbed in. Aubrey wound up the window, and the booming, howling wind above which the inspector had had to shout lessened its protest. Its rage seemed conveyed to the chassis of the car, as if the police saloon was being buffeted by some large animal. Aubrey brushed his remaining hair flat, irritated at his dishevelment. Hyde had the Heckler & Koch across his lap. Aubrey heard the click as Godwin cocked his Walther, before the noise of the car engine increased as they turned in the drive to follow the escort car. Hyde seemed audibly engaged in breathing exercises. Aubrey felt the hot water of a potential field engagement with a meta-phorical elbow; aware, unusually, of his seniority, of his signi-ficance within SIS, of his age, of all the mouldering and mint-new secrets in his old head—aware, perhaps most evidently, of the unfinished business to which this escapade was no more than a sideshow. Uncomic relief. He disliked the manner in which the chessboard always seemed, finally, to resolve itself into the killing-floor, the arena, the bullring. Papers, microfilm, micro-fiche, codes, signals, instructions, operations, missions, objectives; all in the end becoming a matter of living, killing, dying, wounds and pain. He had no business here. He had the wrong adrenalin—for this kind of business . . .

The stars seemed to be moved by the wind, motes of bright dust. Mount Kellett loomed to Aubrey's left as the road began to drop away towards the scattered, strung-together lights of Hong Kong. Across the dark strip of the bay, beyond Hyde's dyed profile, it seemed that the lights of Kowloon were dimmer, failing. The wind was opaque, light-absorbing. Aubrey was surprised at his increased, almost hallucinatory awareness.

Victoria Peak to Aubrey's left, another humped, shoulder-turned mass protecting itself against the cyclone. The lights of the car escorting them disappeared as it rounded a bend. Their driver accelerated slightly to catch up.

The black, lightless car rammed into the side of their vehicle, emerging suddenly from the white-walled drive of a house on the bend, a house without lights, like the car. Aubrey's driver wrestled with the wheel as their car was slewed across Peak Road towards the steep slope below the road. The black saloon drove on like a bull-dozer, a heavy American sedan with a big engine. Aubrey's driver managed to slow their car, halt it with its nose jutting into darkness over the stones at the verge of the road; the force of the other car expended itself in rending the metal of the wing and door. Aubrey felt the plastic of the door lining bulge against his knee. He could see the face of the driver of the American sedan as the car's nose slid along the side of their own vehicle. The wind howled against Aubrey as Hyde pushed open his door.

'Down!' Hyde yelled, dragging at Aubrey's elbow. 'Radio!' he yelled to the driver, who was clasping his shaking hands together to still them. Then Hyde was gone, rolling out of the door of the car.

Hyde rolled away from the car and rose to a sitting position, the pistol held stiffly out in front of him. The driver, almost lost in the howling wind, was radioing the escort car. Then there were two distant shots, and then only the crackling voice from the radio, creaking through the ether and the storm. The wind jolted him in the back. He knew Godwin would be unable to get out of the car with the American sedan jammed up against the door. He was, effectively, alone.

The battered radiator of the sedan jutted out behind the police car. He waited. Beyond it, the whitewashed wall of the house was like a backcloth, a sheet against which might be played some improvised children's drama, full of high voices and shouting and stiff, unreal poses. He remembered them from his infants' school days, his own attempts at characterization much like the stiff-armed pose he now adopted, holding the pistol.

We have followed the star to Bethlehem, to bring gifts of gold and frank—frank—frankissence . . . In a nervous, heavily-accented, piping voice, his mother in agonies, unable to prompt him, on the front row.

A shadow against the whitewashed wall, moving out from behind the American sedan. Hyde fired twice, and the shadow—*myrrh*—flicked aside, leaving the wall whole and clean once more. Hyde rolled again, then got to his knees. The lights of the city behind him would outline him, so would the wall across the road. He got to his feet, swaying like a drunk in the wind, the rough wine of adrenalin coursing through him. Bent almost double, he began running.

Shouts, whipped away by the wind. Shots, a high whine near his head, then he had reached the steps that climbed up to the house with the white wall. He turned back in the darkness and saw two, then three figures detach themselves from the massed lump of the cars. Someone was trying to climb through the sunroof of the police car—Godwin's light suit. Two stabs of flame, almost no noise, and one of the figures stumbled and fell.

A second car roared round the bed and screeched to a halt. They must have passed it without seeing it, back up Peak Road. Men debouched from it immediately, two of them firing in the direction of the crash. Godwin's light suit slipped back into the interior of the car, and Hyde could not tell whether the man had been hit or was merely taking cover. He felt chilled to the bone and turned, racing up the steps, then thrust himself into and through the bushes that flanked them. He emerged into the open space of an ornamental garden. He felt water on his face, the wind flicking the spray of the fountain across the garden. The moonlight was faint and low, and he crouched in the lee of the fountain.

Voices, shapes that might have been illusion or only shadows; no noise of a car arriving. The pretend-urine from the penis of the boy's stone statue on top of the fountain was funnelled up and away from him in a fine spray. A dark shape was altered by the flaring of a blown overcoat. Hyde fired. The figure dropped to the grass. His fire was returned from others. Chips flew from the stone boy, grazing his cheek. He fired again, and the figures scattered. He wondered, with an excitement that threatened to topple into dread even as he experienced it, whether Petrunin was one of those illusory shapes. He doubted it.

How safe was he? Alive, or dead? Did it matter?

Then the shadows seemed all around him, perhaps five—no, six?—becoming visible and solid as the rising moon peered above the peaks; a slender nail-paring, but enough to cast shadows.

'Give up.' He did not know which shadow spoke. 'Chinaman,' it added. The shadows moved closer, flapping, bulging, changing in outline at the wind's demand. 'You understand? Night-sights, you understand? Night-glasses? We can see you. By the fountain.'

Hyde listened for the noise of a car. If they had taken out the escort car? Twenty seconds or more was enough time. Where was it?

They'd kill him when they discovered the dye, the lack of slanted, almond eyes. In rage and frustration, they'd kill . . . Car engine? No lights in the house. Siren?

The shadows moved closer.

'Stay away!' he yelled. 'Stay back!' The shadows paused. Engine, siren? Voices? Running boots, lights? 'Stay away from me!' he yelled against the wind, a high, panicky protest.

Siren running down, running footsteps, cold running water on his hand from the fountain. The shadows dispersed. Stabs of flame in the night, sparks from a policeman's boots as he skidded into stillness on the steps, yells, more shots . . .

Then only the wind. Hyde rose to his feet, the policeman's hand supporting his forearm and his weight.

'Thanks, mate. How's——?'

'Hyde? Hyde, are you all right, man?' The querulous voice of an old man whose occupation or leisure had been disturbed. A bent black figure on the steps up to the house, the police inspector standing beside him. 'Hyde?'

'I'm all right.'

'Thank goodness.'

Hyde walked unsteadily, not because of the wind's buffeting, across the garden to join Aubrey. Relief became aggression the moment he reached the steps.

'You won't want any more bloody proof, will you?' he snapped. Aubrey stared at him in surprise. The inspector seemed personally affronted. 'They'd have killed a bloody dozen to get hold of Colonel bloody Wei, wouldn't they? Because you told them about him—because you're here in person to talk to him!'

'Hyde——'

'You want more bloody proof? You've had a copper killed, and one of your own people——'

'Godwin was merely grazed,' Aubrey remarked icily. 'He'll be all right.'

'Wei's telling the bloody truth, though, isn't he?'

'They wanted you alive, did they not?'

'Y—yes . . . Why?'

'If they *knew* already everything there was to know, perhaps they would simply have killed you? Perhaps they know as little as we do?'

'Balls! They're panicking because Wei's told us about their precious sleeper!'

'Perhaps they're panicking because of the Berlin Treaty? Perhaps that is important enough to justify the interference of Petrunin, the capture of Wei?' Aubrey was shouting now, both of them battling each other and the wind. The police inspector had walked away from them and was engaged in inspecting the dead constable further up the moonlit steps. 'I'm sorry, but we know only a little more than we did this afternoon, Hyde.'

'Then I got shot at for nothing?'

'To protect Wei, I'm afraid.'

'Christ! You're wrong, you know. Wei's genuine, and the Russians think they're up shit creek.'

'I am *not* convinced——'

'I bloody am, mate! Zimmermann's as guilty as hell! He's a bloody KGB agent!'

'No,' Liu said, shaking his head reluctantly. 'It's not enough. These files have been washed, I'm afraid.'

'My money? I have done as you asked. I have earned my money.'

'You'll get your money,' Liu assured him, handing back the files, letting them slip out of the pool of white lamplight under which they had lain as he studied them. They became shadowy in the room's lantern light—the electricity supply for the block of workers' apartments had failed an hour earlier, and they had had to climb fourteen flights of stairs to this flat—and their shadow-nature seemed high-lighted to Liu. He had learned nothing from them.

Except that, on the assumption they had been washed, there must have been a serious reason to tamper with hospital files. Unless the tale was untrue, all of it. Wei's story in Hong Kong, the orderly Bin's story here in Shanghai . . . The suspicion had insinuated itself, sneaking up on his awareness, like the attribution of an unworthy motive to a friend.

There were four of them in the room, apart from Bin. Himself, the girl Liang, and the young couple who occupied the flat and who were part of the loose federation of individuals that the CIA described as its cell in Shanghai. For security reasons, Frederickson had instructed Liang not to take Liu to Bin's house in the old city again. Instead, he had been brought here to a newish concrete block in a northern suburb of the city, and the young man's wife had brought Bin.

David Liu stood up, stretched casually, then crossed to the window of the small living room. He tugged back the thin curtains. The afternoon was heavy with cloud. A trolley-bus passed along the tree-lined avenue fourteen floors below him. Beyond the road, the suburb came to an abrupt, neat end. Tiny figures were watering the year's winter wheat crop on the flat green expanse of a commune, a sulky, hesitant wind whipping the hosed jets into tendrils of spray like peacocks' tails. Beyond the green were the pylons and wires and transformers of a power station. Specks in white shirts moved on bicycles along a distant road near the power station.

Liu felt himself in control of his situation, even though frustration at Bin's purloined files thrust itself into his awareness, made his skin prickle with a desire for action, for results. He turned back to study the occupants of the room. A look passed between Liang and Bin which he could not identify, but which seemed to possess a familiarity, even an intimacy, their supposedly slight acquaintance would not have engendered. The residents of the flat, the young man and his wife, also seemed enclosed within the circle of the glance and smile, both of which winked out like lamps as he turned to face them. Liu suddenly felt isolated, alone—confronted?

It was an almost feline sensation, something to distrust, not based on fact. Mood, insight, feeling? Mistrust of his companions asserted itself, and he did not resist it; surprised, nevertheless, at its appearance. He endeavoured to control his features.

'My money?' Bin requested sullenly, holding out his hand, gripping the files on his lap with his other hand. Liu withdrew his wallet and carefully counted out ten notes, each of twenty dollars. Bin fished the yuans out of his pocket, and offered them in exchange. Liu watched his face carefully.

'Keep those,' he said. 'You did your best. Here.' Bin's enthusiasm hesitated beneath his skin for a moment, then bloomed on his features.

'Thank you, thank you.' It sounded rehearsed. Liu felt himself adrift in a mass of contrary emotional, physical, and subconscious information. He had to leave them, get away somewhere and consider, reflect, analyse.

'There's nothing more you can tell me?' Liu's inclined head indicated the files.

'No. None of it is here, is it?'

'No, it's not. Pity.'

'You believe me? I was telling the truth.'

'Yes, I believe you,' Liu replied levelly. He turned back to the window, his eyes seeking out the distant power station, then the road and the white-spot cyclists, then the green wheat fields being watered with peacock's-tail sprays, then the tree-lined avenue and . . .

A car. Parked on the opposite side of the avenue from the block of flats. He could not tell whether or not it was occupied. With a sure and chilling instinct he knew it was a surveillance car.

That morning he had been certain he was being followed. The car had been parked outside the Shanghai Mansions all night—he had checked on it periodically. Foot-surveillance all morning by someone who followed him even into the restaurant where he had lunched. Then, perhaps half an hour before he was to meet Liang, nothing. Surveillance withdrawn—or only dreamed in the first place, figments of stretched, raw nerves. Now, another car. He would note whether it returned to the city centre in the wake of the bus he would have to catch.

What did they want? They had to be PSB or MPT—the department did not matter. He was the object of their attention; perhaps the girl, and now himself as a contact? Perhaps, too, the people in this flat, perhaps even Bin?

He turned back into the room. No, it would have to be Frederickson who answered his questions, not any of these people. These he did not know, could not trust.

'We must go,' Liang informed him, as if deliberately breaking a tension of which she was subtly aware.

'Yes, of course.' He had to get away from the girl now. The car in the street, and the medical orderly. His mind focused on those three objectives. How? How could he wait around, without the girl? 'Thank you,' he said once more to Bin. 'And thank you.' He had not been introduced by name to either of the flat's residents. They stood and bowed formally. Liu returned the gesture. Bin appeared in no haste to depart. 'We'll leave first,' he said, for Bin's benefit—for the benefit of all of them.

'Yes, yes.' Bin now seemed eager to see him gone. He had folded and pocketed the two hundred dollars. The yuans, however, lay carelessly on the floor by his chair, as did the files; theatrical props that had served their purpose, Liu could not help reflecting.

Why had the young man drawn the curtains? The flat was not overlooked. Had it been a signal? It had seemed natural at the time, covert, properly secretive. But there had been no need. Had the room been bugged?

They descended the stairs. Suspicion gripped Liu, fear assailed him like waves of nausea. He imagined or guessed no motive for his suspicions, simply entertained the doubt itself, the subtle, corrupt aroma of the set-up, the mantrap. The meat being used as bait was beginning to smell. The girl, descending flight after flight in front of him, seemed unaware of his tense and altered mood. Her slight back and narrow shoulders became objects of revulsion to him. He wanted to beat the truth from her.

Outside, the wind flapped and billowed the girl's thin cotton trousers. It searched his drab suit. He forced himself not to look across the avenue at the parked car beneath the trees as they walked the few hundred yards to the bus stop. An old man and two children waited for the trolley-bus. Liu held himself under control with an increasing effort, answering the girl's few innocuous comments as casually as he could. The car was occupied, he observed. Two men. They were too distant to betray whether they were watching the bus stop.

He did not know what he could do, even at the moment when the trolley-bus arrived and its door sighed open. He helped the old man onto the bus, indicating to Liang that she should board first, with the two children. The old man's wisp of beard bobbed his feeble gratitude. His lips worked as if he were chewing the reassurances Liu supplied thoughtlessly, his mind racing, the beginnings of action occurring to him as a sketchy, grainy film of physical activity.

Bus stop, pneumatic doors, shelter, flats, car, trees, Bin . . .

'OK,' he called to the driver further up the bus. The doors immediately began to sigh shut. Liu stepped nimbly backwards, onto the pavement again. Liang's face moved through surprise, then shock, then a narrow and enraged suspicion. As the doors closed, masking her features momentarily until she moved her head to keep him in sight, Liu admitted that he must surrender to his suspicions. The realization chilled him. The trolley-bus moved away down the almost deserted avenue, beneath the trees.

The parked car did not move. Liu watched it from the shelter of a tree, craning his head furtively round the bole to keep it in view. He felt foolish and inadequate; he fought to keep his sense of isolation under control. It was too raw and potent to be ignored. He did not have much time. Liang would get off the bus at the next stop, come running back . . .

He studied the block of flats, counting the floors up to the fourteenth, but he could not satisfactorily locate the window of the room which contained Bin and the married couple. Would Bin come out, and soon?

The medical orderly emerged from the flats. Liu immediately glanced behind him and saw that the distant blue speck of the bus had stopped. His heart pounded. Bin glanced towards the bus stop, then immediately crossed the avenue to the parked car. Even though it was the evidence he desired, Liu could not believe what he saw. His mind, for its own peace, attempted to reject the information. Bin leaned into the car, handing the files to the passenger.

Liu turned his head and looked down the perspective of the avenue. A single distant figure. He sensed it was running in his direction. Liang. Perhaps no more than a minute away. Bin and the police. Doctored files. The girl was part of it, too. The whole of Frederickson's Shanghai cell? How many others were there?

Bin climbed into the back of the car. Carefully, assessing that the trees masked him from the car and from the flats, Liu began to walk towards the running figure approaching him. It was the girl, and she was running. He strolled, composing his features and his lies. He had to talk to Frederickson.

The girl slowed as she saw him coming towards her. He grinned, and held his arms out in a gesture of helplessness, apologetically. The girl's face was bland, out-of-breath, her eyes searched his face, then looked beyond him towards the car.

'What were you doing?' she asked in a tone of reprimand.

'Sorry. I was fazed.' She appeared puzzled. He tapped his forehead. 'Not thinking. Helped the old man on, forgot I wanted the bus myself.' He broadened his grin. 'Sorry. Mind on other things.'

'Oh.' She evidently did not believe him. Her eyes kept straying between his face and the car. She seemed, however, to decide to accept the transparent fiction of his excuse; no doubt, Liu concluded, that would last only until she received orders. 'I thought you might have forgotten something.'

'No. There's nothing more to be learned here,' he said lightly.

'No, I suppose not,' she agreed.

'What time's the next bus?'

'What? Oh, another ten minutes.'

'Let's walk on to the next stop, then.'

'Yes,' she agreed eagerly.

Liu took her arm, and they began walking. Somewhere behind

him, he heard the noise of a car engine starting, then the retreating sound of its engine as it drove off.

Frederickson, he thought. I have to talk to him.

Strangely, he did not feel endangered, not in any immediate
sense. For some reason, they were letting him run. These people
were . . . misleading him, yes, that was it, for a purpose. He could
not imagine why. Misinformation. Presumably they were covering up the Zimmermann business. They were the smokescreen
around the subject. They contradicted Wei.

He kept a tremor of excitement under control as he held the
girl's arm. Wei could be right, then. *Was* right? There *was* something to hide. They were trying to lead him by the nose.

Frederickson. He would have to talk to the CIA man himself,
but not via the girl.

'You have heard, of course, of the unfortunate events of this
afternoon?'

'Right. Your people messed up.'

'I do not think that your accusations are justified. Perhaps your
man is not as naïve as you suggested.'

'He's suspicious now.'

'In what way, precisely?'

'I don't know. He hasn't called.'

'He will. I suggest a smokescreen, a diversion.'

'Like . . .'

'The arrest of the whole cell, everyone he has met. To take
place when he is present. A convincing arrest, perhaps with one
or two wounded, even dead. That is not important.'

'Wait a minute——'

'Conviction is of the essence, my friend. Liu must be persuaded
of the truth as Wei has told it.'

'Give him the truth, then.'

'Not yet. He must work for it. Then he will believe it. In Wu
Han, perhaps.'

'OK.'

'You must make arrangements for Liu to reach Wu Han.
Please inform me of his report, when he makes it. Then I shall
make the necessary arrangements for our smokescreen.'

'If he's too suspicious, if I can't persuade him——'

'Then he, too, will become the responsibility of the ministry.
But please try to avoid that.'

'I'll work on it.'
'Please do so.'

In the darkness, Frederickson was no more than a shadow, a reassuring yet mysterious bulk. Couples, hand in hand or with their arms around each other, strolled past the bench on which Liu and Frederickson sat in Huangpu Park. A breeze moved the smell of the river and its noises towards them. The boom of a barge's horn, the creak of wood, the slapping of water against concrete and vessels. Navigation lights sidled past them like low constellations. The lovers, hundreds of them, were like a formal, erotic garden, or another elaborate mime. Vertically, they imitated coition, suggested an organised, ritualised privacy tolerated by the State. The murmuring hubbub of their conversations imitated the dialogue between himself and the American, suggesting a community of secrets. Somewhere, a transistor radio played approved music.

'What does it all amount to, Liu?' Frederickson asked bluntly, his profile just discernible against the warm stars. 'What exactly do you suspect?'

Liu had telephoned the consulate and cryptically arranged the meeting without identifying himself. Now, hours after the bus doors had shut and he had seen Liang's face, hours after Bin had leaned into the car, he was uncertain, hesitant, inclined to disbelieve his own senses.

'I—am not sure.'

'You think this guy Bin was bait?' Frederickson listened to the silence from Liu, realizing that he might have voiced a point of view that had not occurred to him.

'Bait? How do you mean?'

'It's not impossible they know who you are, why you're here. Bin was a risk—he's not one of our people. You think he was planted on you?'

'But he confirmed Wei's story, at first.'

'To gain your confidence, maybe?'

'But the girl . . .'

'She never trusted Bin.'

'I don't mean that. I mean, on the bus—she panicked when I got off.'

'She told me. She was worried, about you. You're her responsibility, man.'

'I see . . .' Liu sounded hopefully thoughtful to Frederickson. The American was glad of the darkness. Murmuring lovers strolled past against the lights of a small freighter. 'Then Bin is hiding the truth?'

'Wouldn't the Chinese like you to go home and disprove everything Wei's telling them in Hong Kong?'

'Of course, but——'

'Then maybe that's the name of the game? You were there, Liu. Do you trust Bin?'

'He's an addict. If they have him by that rope, he's theirs all the way down the line . . .'

Frederickson hesitated before he spoke. Liu's quiet voice sounded as if he were on the point of convincing himself; taking the hook.

'Well?'

'Perhaps.'

'OK. We'll wrap things up here. Get you to Wu Han tomorrow, or the day after.'

'Won't they be expecting me?'

'I'll get you a new cover. Things are too tight in Shanghai. Maybe up-country they've been more slack, or people may be readier to talk.' Frederickson stood up. 'I'll be in touch. And Liu——'

'Yes?'

'Watch your back, uh?'

'Yes.'

'South Australia? You're certain?' Aubrey glared at Hyde, who had guffawed with surprised laughter. 'Near Adelaide?'

'I never liked Adelaide,' Hyde murmured into his beer.

'Shut up, Hyde,' Aubrey snapped. Godwin smothered a companionable grin, an expression which turned to one of discomfort as the plaster on his temple tugged at entrapped hairs.

'You can't drink the water,' Hyde added.

Aubrey looked up from the signal pad that McIntosh had brought with him from the cellar of the house where the communications equipment was housed. McIntosh seemed to hold himself responsible for the information from London. He appeared guilty and evasive.

'That's what it said, Mr Aubrey. That's Shelley's signal.'

'And the 1940 files?'

'I've sent through another request. He doesn't mention them.'

'I see that. I *must* have those files.' Aubrey looked at Hyde, slumped on the sofa, the headphones he had been using to listen to the stereo system lying like a dark crab on his lap. 'Hyde?'

'Sir.'

'Does all this sound likely to you? I know absolutely nothing about Australian wines, but I find it difficult to imagine a former Abwehr officer inheriting a vineyard in South Australia. Do you?'

Hyde shook his head. 'You've missed a lot that's worth drinking,' he said.

'Forget the salesmanship, Hyde.'

'Adelaide's surrounded by vineyards—it's the capital of the Australian wine business. Where is this vineyard—Barossa Valley?'

'Yes. How did you know?'

'It used to be a German settlement, in the old days. They brought the vines. There's still plenty of Krauts speaking pure Strine up there.' Hyde grinned. 'A relative died, Schiller fancied a change, packs his bags and goes off to grow grapes. Why not?'

'This wine is of good quality?' Aubrey asked ingenuously.

'The best is really good.' Then Hyde's eyes narrowed. 'You'll get the chance to taste some, won't you?'

'I—haven't decided.'

'You want to talk to Schiller?' McIntosh asked in surprise. 'In person? But, sir, what about Wei?'

Aubrey passed a hand over his eyes. He had spent most of the day at Victoria Prison. He was weary of Wei, prepared to flee the man's intractable company. 'I cannot break him,' he admitted. 'He has retreated again, just as I foresaw, now that he believes himself safe. Perhaps Buckholz . . .' He looked at the signal again. 'A fresh approach, for two or three days.' He cleared his throat. It appeared to be Hyde that he wished to convince, unless the Australian was no more than a mirror in which Aubrey was carefully arranging his features. 'Everything we have learned goes back to Spain, and to 1938. It was there, if anywhere, that Zimmermann was recruited by the NKVD. This man Schiller was with him. I think it's worth the journey—worth the distraction.'

'I agree, sir,' Godwin intruded.

'Yes,' Hyde added.

'Very well. McIntosh, I shall want two tickets for Adelaide, for tomorrow. Understand this, however. Mr Buckholz is to have full access to Wei, but he is not—I repeat, he is *not*—to remove Wei from Victoria Prison.'

'Don't worry. The Yanks will have to wait.'

'If he interrogates Wei, it is to be with one of you two present, and everything is to be recorded.'

'How much do you think Wei knows, sir?' McIntosh asked.

Aubrey shrugged. 'Everything? Nothing? I don't know. To him, information is wealth, and he has become miserly—until he sees we are doing something for his future. No, at the moment, I am more interested in what Hans-Dieter Schiller, late of the Abwehr and now of the Barossa Valley, has to offer in the way of information.'

'Will he talk?'

'If he doesn't, I think he will encounter all sorts of problems with the Australian authorities.'

'Sir?' Godwin asked.

'Yes?'

'What about Petrunin and his friends?'

'As long as they do not find out, then they're not a worry.'

The dead Russians had, improbably, all been carrying Irish passports bearing the proper stamps and visas. Aubrey had ordered that close surveillance be kept on the antique shop, and then had chosen to ignore the KGB in Hong Kong. Wei was safe, and that was the end of the matter.

'I see, sir,' Godwin murmured dubiously.

'Make sure they don't find out. Whatever measures are required, Hyde and myself must leave Hong Kong secretly.'

'Yes, sir.'

FIVE:

Trapdoor

'I am afraid there can be no quibbling with regard to your people.'

'Look, when we agreed to make them known to you, for the purposes of this operation, you guaranteed their safety.'

'That is true. It is the safety of the operation, however, which is paramount. Would you not agree?'

'Of course I have to agree——'

'Then Liu must be convinced. If your people have to die, then that is regrettable, but necessary.'

'I can't see it that way——'

'As agents, they became inoperative as soon as we were told their names. You cannot use them again.'

'That's not the point——'

'Isn't it, my friend? Well, in deference to your Western ideas of the value of human life, I will see what can be done. But if it is necessary, then you will have to mourn them. Their families, no doubt, will be taken care of. Very well, instruct the girl to contact Liu.'

Liu had slept badly, a twisting, perspiring repository of anxieties, fears and expectations. His clarity of thought had been gradually eroded by his sense of isolation and dependence. Frederickson's explanations and answers had not been satisfactory, but he had no solutions of his own upon which he could depend, and the CIA station head in Shanghai was the only person he inclined towards trusting; his senior officer, his case officer. David Liu could not rid himself of the sense of being entirely alone. He was an American with a yellow face in the middle of China's most populous city; the police were tailing him and his confederates seemed engaged in betraying him.

He eventually got up, shaved and washed, and took up a stance at the window, gathering strength to go down to the hotel restaurant for breakfast. From his window, he could not see the police car he knew must be watching the hotel. What he did see, however, was the girl walking on the road below him, beside the

Suzhou Creek. Red tunic, black trousers. As he watched her, his body masked by the curtain and the window frame, she periodically glanced up as if searching for his window. Her walk, her pause, her upward looks, all conspired to enrage him. What did the girl want? What could she possibly have to say? How would she explain . . .

Buttoning his jacket, he left his room and took the lift to the ground floor. He strode through the hotel foyer, oblivious of any police surveillance, and swiftly jostled his way across the crowded pavement, then whisked alertly like a matador between the rush of cycles, until the girl was no more than a few yards from him. At that moment, she saw him approaching.

'What do you want?' he asked coldly. The hesitant smile slipped back inside her mouth.

'Frederickson sent me,' she said hurriedly. 'I have your papers —your new cover.' She seemed to wish to lead him out of the throng. Liu followed her. Papers, cover? Frederickson still trusted her, then.

They walked down concrete steps to a narrow towpath beside the creek. Here the bustle diminished and the age of the pedestrians increased dramatically. Old people engaged in *tai ji chuan*, shadow-boxing, moving slowly and aquatically in deference to ageing sinews and muscles, or sitting calmly on the benches, watching the river traffic. A train-like convoy of barges sidled towards the bridge and the Huangpu River beyond it.

'My papers?' he demanded, his hand held out to her. Their pace was slow, imitative of the other inhabitants of the towpath.

Liang reached into her red tunic and removed a small package wrapped in clear polythene, secured with elastic bands.

'Here,' she said.

'What are Frederickson's instructions?' He slipped into the habit of trust. The papers were like securities, bankers' drafts on her loyalty to the CIA.

'Why do you not trust me?' she asked. 'Bin was a mistake. Bin was not my fault—everything was so hurried . . .' She appeared hurt rather than angry. Her crumpled, expressive features were appealing. 'It was a risk. He must have told the police.'

'Perhaps,' Liu replied, not unmoved. He scanned the towpath for surveillance. Unless it was one of the grandparents here, there was none. A barge horn sounded a dragon-like bellow, startling them both. Liu grinned.

'I ran back to you,' she said, 'because Frederickson made you my responsibility . . .' she explained lamely. Her very hesitancy implied amateurishness rather than deceit, and Liu accepted it as such.

'OK,' he said. 'Bin's scrubbed out. Are the police still watching the hotel?'

'When I arrived, yes. Then the car left.'

'I wonder why?'

'Perhaps a change of shift?'

'Maybe. OK—Frederickson's instructions?'

'You leave for Wu Han tomorrow on the morning train. Your tickets are with your papers. Your cover is as a minor Party official being transferred to Wu Han from Shanghai—promotion.' She smiled. 'Frederickson himself will be there—there is a US delegation of businessmen travelling to Wu Han by air tomorrow from Peking. Frederickson, as Trade Attaché, will accompany them during their visit.' Liu felt absurdly, overwhelmingly comforted by the knowledge that Frederickson would be on hand. 'You will be met at Wu Han station. You must, however, ensure that you are not observed boarding the train.' Liu nodded. With the pale blue sky behind them, the figures walking across the bridge over the creek looked like mechanically swimming ducks in a shooting gallery. It was an unnerving unbidden image.

'Anything else?'

'There will be a suitcase at the station—here is the locker key.' She handed it to him, and he pocketed it as swiftly as if it had been stolen.

'A gun?' he asked involuntarily.

'No.'

Liu recovered. 'Of course not.'

'Do not book out of the hotel here.'

'Naturally. Anything else?'

'Tonight . . .'

'What about tonight?'

'We have someone for you, to make up for Bin.'

'Who?'

'A policeman.'

Liu appeared stunned by the information. 'What?'

'No!' the girl cried as if he had struck her. 'One of our people, one of *Frederickson*'s people. He is a police clerk, no more than that. He is not often used, he has little access . . .'

Liu recovered himself, and prompted her when she faltered. 'Go on. A police clerk?'

'Frederickson put him to work as soon as Bin became suspect. He may have something by tonight . . .'

'Is he known to be one of your cell?' The girl shrugged. 'It's important. Through Bin, you're known, so are the couple in the flat. Who else?'

'I cannot tell. No one has been near him since—since the error with Bin.'

'What information?'

'Who visited the German, how many times, perhaps what records were kept, I do not know. It will be dangerous for him, but he will try. Will you meet him?'

Liu hesitated, then he said: 'Why can't this clerk feed his information through you or one of the others?'

Liang appeared shamed. Looking at her feet, she said: 'Frederickson does not trust us—we are not trained agents. Who knows if this man is secure? He wants you to judge, not us.'

Liu nodded. 'Very well. Tonight. Where?'

'The Yu Garden, in the Old Town. Directions are with your other papers.'

'What time?'

'He will finish his shift at ten. Ten-thirty will give him time to reach the meeting place.'

'OK. Now, leave. I don't want to be seen with you again, not today. You, keep off the streets, keep away from your flat. Understand?'

'Frederickson, too, has given me the same instructions.'

'And me—I'll try not to get arrested.' The girl looked fearful, but Liu grinned. 'Don't worry, somehow I don't think they're ready to pull me in yet. They don't know enough. After all, if they keep close to me, I could lead them to every agent Frederickson's got in southern China, couldn't I?

Aubrey, like a child with a new comic delivered with his father's morning paper, could not resist glancing through the record of his interrogation of Zimmermann in 1940 as he ate his late breakfast. The files had arrived in the Bag on the day's first flight from London. Pineapple, boiled egg, toast and marmalade, fruit juice, coffee. He bit and swallowed each mouthful of his meal without noticing what he ate. His eyes, alert and gleaming though they appeared, were not focused on the breakfast table, even on the dining room. Hyde, with the previous day's *Daily Telegraph* propped against the condiment set, was enjoying his fried meal and the complete county cricket averages on one of the sports pages. He had already, wistfully, read the racing page.

'What time are you expecting Buckholz?'

'What? Oh!' Aubrey's damp blue eyes cleared and narrowed their focus. 'Americans seem to have invented an atrocity called the working breakfast. He should have been here by now. I postponed the meal-time as much as I could.' Aubrey's look of ironic amusement vanished, and weariness possessed his face. Hyde wondered whether the journey ahead daunted the old man, or if Wei dragged at his optimism. He was locked as tightly as a cuckolded, worshipping lover into the unsatisfactory relationship with the Chinese defector. Whatever Aubrey learned in the Barossa Valley, it was to Hong Kong he would have to return, and it was that relationship he would have to take up once again.

He attended to the buff folder and its closely typed, grimy-edged sheets of paper. There was a musty smell of age and blind alleys vying with the smoked bacon in front of Hyde.

'Schiller may have the answer, you know,' Hyde suggested, slicing his fried bread then neatly apportioning a slice of bacon and egg to it before opening his mouth. 'He could say, yes it happened, or no, it wasn't like that.'

'Do you think I could believe him if he said no?' Aubrey asked in irritation.

'Then why ask him?'

'As you remarked, he might say yes. Or I might be able to tell he's lying if he says no.' Aubrey sighed. 'I *have* to ask him.' Aubrey looked up. Buckholz entered the room, ushered in by Godwin. Aubrey, almost furtive with haste, closed the folder on the table and slipped it beneath his copy of the previous day's *Times*. 'My dear Charles!' he exclaimed, with a bonhomie that was transparently false to Hyde, as he stood up to welcome the American.

'Kenneth.' The two men shook hands. Aubrey indicated a chair. Buckholz acknowledged Hyde's presence with a slight, though not dismissive, nod.

'What would you like?'

'Just coffee.' Buckholz appeared on edge, undecided whether affability or bullying would serve his purpose. Hyde ate attentively, the *Telegraph*'s close print blurring as he pretended to study it. 'Kenneth——'

'Yes, Charles?' Aubrey poured coffee for Buckholz and himself. 'What can I do for you?'

'It's about Wei——'

'Yes?' Aubrey was at his most ingenuous. 'What about Wei?'

'I think it's time we got our hands on him.'

'But you have. It's your interrogation, from today.'

Buckholz watched Aubrey, his grey eyes alert, his cropped, whitening hair and broad shoulders implicitly threatening the small old man. 'You know what I mean, Kenneth. Wei is, in all but name, our responsibility already. He wants asylum in the States, it's us he really came to. China's our sphere of influence. So is Germany, for that matter. I want him, Kenneth. Transfer him to my custody.'

Aubrey's eyes narrowed. His cheeks seemed more lank. His brow was furrowed, as if he was inwardly debating the administrative difficulties involved. Hyde knew he was gathering defiance.

'I'm sorry, Charles, it just isn't possible.' Buckholz's face coloured slightly. 'You have complete freedom of access to him——'

'In company with one of your people! What's the matter, Kenneth? You don't trust me?'

Aubrey's lips pursed in displeasure. 'It is not a matter of trust, not at all. Wei was fished out of the harbour by members of the Hong Kong police force. He is, therefore, my country's responsibility. Quite definitely, and quite properly. Until my investigations are completed, he remains in Victoria Prison where, incidentally, he is more secure, under the closest supervision.'

'And that's your last word?'

'It is.'

'You're making a mistake.'

'I hope not.'

Buckholz shrugged, and grinned slowly and reluctantly. When he spoke again, his voice had lost its cutting edge. 'This guy in Australia, Zimmermann's old team-mate. You think you'll get results?'

'I really don't know.' Aubrey was mollified by the American's change of tone. 'I hope for clues, at least. If Wei is lying, then we will have to establish *why* he is lying.'

'Simple anti-Soviet smear campaign.'

'Quite likely. If he is telling the truth, and this man Schiller helps in any way to confirm the story, then Zimmermann will have to be exposed.'

'Which would bring down Chancellor Vogel's government, and stop ratification of the treaty. Vogel's opponents wouldn't sign it.'

'I realize that. That is the decision of politicians, not intelligence services. They must make up their minds in London and Washington on the basis of the facts—the *full* facts.'

'And, hell, you're going to supply those facts,' Buckholz said with a grin.

Aubrey smiled deprecatingly. 'I hope to do so.'

Buckholz stood up. 'OK, Kenneth. I'll read the files you sent over on Wei's story so far, then I'll meet with him. It should be very interesting.'

'As soon as I have anything—*if* I have anything—I'll be in touch with you, Charles.' Aubrey stood up, and the two men shook hands once more. Buckholz left the room with an easy step that in no way lessened his bulk.

Hyde looked at Aubrey enquiringly. 'What was that all about?'

'Probably irritation at sitting on the sidelines, nothing more.'

Aubrey poured himself more coffee. McIntosh entered the room.

'Mr Aubrey, it's all arranged.' Aubrey indicated that he should join them at the table. 'You and Hyde will board the aircraft thirty minutes before the other passengers. To all intents and purposes, you'll still be at the prison interviewing Wei when you're on your way to Australia.' McIntosh seemed genuinely delighted with his arrangements.

'Good. You're certain no details of our journey will have reached our friends in the KGB?'

'Not unless they've got taps and ears in places we don't know about.' McIntosh shook his head. 'No, I think you can be assured they know nothing about your little jaunt to the colonies.'

'Why is Aubrey booked to fly to Australia this afternoon?' Tamas Petrunin demanded. Vassily, perched respectfully on the edge of a hard chair on the wrong side of what was normally his own desk, looked crestfallen. 'Sydney, and then Adelaide? Why on earth should he leave Colonel Wei to take such a holiday?'

'I do not know, Comrade General,' Vassily murmured with abject respectfulness. Petrunin, as Vassily glanced at his face from beneath drooping eyelids, did not seem flattered by the use of his rank. 'We have been unable to ascertain from our sources— *any* of our sources—what connection this might have with the Englishman's investigations.'

'Australia?' Petrunin muttered, as if to himself. 'This matter concerns the Chinese, the Germans, the British, the Americans. It does *not* concern the Australians! You've signalled Moscow Centre?'

'Yes, Comrade General. Requesting priority time on the central computer. That was three hours ago.'

Petrunin looked at his watch. 'Aubrey will be leaving in two hours. You have the reservations held for Singapore?'

'Yes, and through to Perth, then Adelaide.'

'Disposition of forces?'

'Sydney embassy will be organizing support in Adelaide for you——' He paused, as if he had blurted some embarrassing secret. Petrunin smiled.

'You guessed?'

'Your personal interest, Comrade General, your very great interest . . .'

'Yes, yes. I shall go, if the game seems worth the entrance fee. The man Hyde—he, of course, I know of old. A very good operative. Aubrey would not chase off to Australia on a wild-goose chase, oh, no . . .'

The telephone rang. Vassily's hand reached out automatically, then he hastily withdrew it, as if he had been burned. Hand and figure seemed to Petrunin, as he picked up the receiver, to retreat into the shadows of the hot, airless office above the restaurant. Petrunin had retreated from the antique shop which was now under close police surveillance. He expected no more provocative action from Aubrey. The smells of cooking from below were omnipresent. The fan whirred and grunted and sighed over their heads, making no inroads on the room's midday temperature.

'Comrade General?'

'Yes, yes.'

'A reply to your signal, from Moscow Centre.'

'Yes?'

'They've come up with a name—Schiller, that's S-c-h-i . . .'

'Never mind the spelling! Who is this man?'

'Another Abwehr officer, one who served in Spain with the repressive forces of Fascist capitalist imperialism . . .'

'The Condor Legion?' Petrunin asked with affected boredom. 'Skip the ideology and get to the point. With Zimmermann?'

'Same unit—and captured in 1938 with him.'

'Remarkable. And . . .'

'Schiller is now an Australian citizen. He lives in South Australia——'

'Near Adelaide?'

'Yes, Comrade General.'

'You have a precise address?'

'Not yet.'

'Signal Sydney—get them to find him at once. And send up the full text of the signal. Thank you.' Petrunin put down the receiver. 'So,' he murmured, 'Aubrey thinks this Schiller is worth the journey. I wonder, precisely, what Herr Schiller's importance is in the scheme of things. Don't you, Vassily?'

'Of course, Comrade General.'

'Hm. Very well, hotel reservations in Adelaide. Sydney must arrange support. I want Schiller before Aubrey finds him.'

'Why, Comrade General?'

'Why? How should I know? Schiller, perhaps, will tell me.' Petrunin leaned forward across the desk. His eyes were bleak. 'Zimmermann *is* the Berlin Treaty. Moscow feels—and I agree with Moscow—that whatever is going on, it threatens Zimmermann's position. Therefore, it threatens the Berlin Treaty. And therefore it threatens *us*. The Soviet Union. The Chinese certainly don't like the Berlin Treaty—perhaps they want to ruin matters by ruining Zimmermann? But what tale they could spin about him, I have no idea. Schiller might.' He leaned back in his chair, then added: 'Well, get on with it! There isn't much time if we're to be first past the post.'

The clouds below the aircraft were lit by the full moon. There was no real downward perspective, and they floated like sandy islands on the glimmering sea thirty-five thousand feet below. Aubrey dozed, replete with champagne and a lobster dinner on the 747. The film being shown in the first-class section seemed demented and banal without its sound track, and created no desire to use the uncomfortable headphones. The sea below possessed more attraction, moonlit like pale lace, especially around the coastlines of the Philippines and then the Moluccas.

The record of his interrogations of Zimmermann in 1940 was

123

locked once more in his briefcase. Zimmermann's face and voice, however, still occupied his half-sleep. Once again, Aubrey returned, in a strict chronology of recollection, to the farmhouse near Flize and the remainder of the first night of the German's capture.

He had persisted in questioning Zimmermann, even though the man refused to admit the Abwehr connection of which Aubrey was now convinced. Zimmermann had an armour composed of quick-wittedness, humour, and courage. Aubrey, reluctantly and amid his growing frustration and self-criticism, was forced to grant the man a grudging admiration. Some impersonal part of himself, which in reality was the kernel of his future talent as an interrogator, recognized the professionalism of his prisoner.

'You are not an infantry officer, you are an officer in the Abwehr, German military intelligence,' he persisted once again. On the humming aircraft, his lips moved in union with the inwardly-heard statement, and his facial muscles reproduced their twist of dislike which was his reaction to Zimmermann's easy, relaxed, patronizing smile and the shake of his blond head.

'Nineteenth Panzers,' he replied.

Aubrey the old, dozing man shook his head vigorously. The laughter of some other first-class passenger at an episode of the film almost roused him. Then he slipped back to the smell of dung and hay and the oil-lamp. Rembrandt again, the little group of himself, the German and the two French brothers—both of them asleep—like a secular Nativity, lit by a warm light, with shadows gathering around them. The stamping of a cow made the two horses shuffle in their stalls. The half-dreaming Aubrey thrust himself back into the past.

'You persist with your story?'

'Of course. It is the truth.' Zimmermann waggled his identity tags at Aubrey again.

'I've seen those before.' Aubrey, acting by instinct, had stood up at that point and moved to the edge of the pool of light from the lamp. 'Frankly, I think they're fake—but fake or not, you're here and we have the guns. I can't say I think much of your experience, your cleverness, your superiority, you know.' The young Aubrey drawled and postured, imitating a debating society contempt for an opponent's argument. Some instinct guided him, indicated he should irritate the German, unsettle him. 'You're my prisoner, whether you talk or not.' He turned and smiled. 'I'm quite pleased with myself, really, you know. First time out, and all that. A *real* German officer!' Then he had laughed softly.

'I seem to be captured quite often,' Zimmermann replied, seemingly unmoved. 'I must tell you that I'm used to it. I've been interrogated before, by experts.'

'Captured before? Dear me, how clumsy of you. How inexpert,' Aubrey mocked.

'It may be foolishness, or foolhardiness, or bravery, I do not know. I should warn you, however, that I do usually manage to get back to Berlin in time to collect my medal.' Zimmermann was smiling easily. 'Still,' he added, 'you are beginning to learn the game.' Aubrey walked back into the lamplight, his face expressionless. On the face of the old man in the aircraft, there was an amused smile.

'What game?'

'The interrogation game. You are very young.'

'You'll be here long enough to teach me, I'm sure.'

'I doubt it. Yes, but you are learning. It is a craft at which we must work hard.' He grinned. 'Ignore the plural, I am only an infantry officer,' he added easily. 'I remember,' he went on quickly, before Aubrey could interrupt, 'being held in Spain, in Aragon, when I was a young officer with the Condor Legion . . .' It seemed to Aubrey that the far-sighted look that entered Zimmermann's eyes at that point was not assumed but real. He was looking back to some better, cleaner time, his mouth suggested as it pouted with regret. 'Yes, I was interrogated by a Russian then . . .'

The old man, his head leaning near the window, his face gilded by the moonlight so that he was the colour of the pale clouds, the silvered sea, sensed the excitement he had experienced earlier. Not forty years or more before; then he had felt only a kind of envious curiosity towards the German's story. No, it had been just before dinner was served, when he had been reading through the files as if they had been a novel, beginning at the beginning, immersing himself in that first night of his acquaintance with Zimmermann. He had felt his heart pound, his breath become short. A steward had enquired after his health. He had requested champagne with a quite conscious sense of celebration. He had *known* Zimmermann had spoken of his capture and of his Russian interrogator, but he had needed the proof that lay in the record of that night and the subsequent days and nights.

'Go on,' the young Aubrey had prompted when Zimmermann had paused at that point. Zimmermann had nodded, seeming to agree with some other part of himself that the tale had no military or intelligence significance . . .

The dozing Aubrey admitted that his recollection had been interrupted by dinner. His stomach had betrayed him, the gastronomic part of his imagination had greedily flooded his mind with images of lobster, a kind of imaginative mouth-watering. He should have pursued the moment, brought it back, *seen* it . . .

Zimmermann's face now, how was it? What was its exact expression? The old man's face was puckered and contracted in the gleam of moonlight from the window. Zimmermann had paused. 'Go on,' Aubrey had said, hardly noticing the pause or understanding it simply as a moment used to weigh the pitfalls and traps of telling it. Then the German had said:

'Yes, I remember the Russian. Aladko, he called himself. I presume he was a Soviet intelligence officer.' Zimmermann shrugged. *There, there*, the old man told himself in his dream. *The very name that Wei supplied.* Zimmermann had passed over the name, mentioning it only once. He had gone on to talk of the man's beard, his smell, his bad German, his brutality, his cunning as dark and narrow and enclosed as his small black eyes by his inflated cheeks.

His face, his hesitation? the old man asked, rousing himself to an upright position in his seat. He concentrated his newly awake mind upon that moment of hesitation and attempted to see the German's expression. He had continued because there was no cause for retraction, for hesitation or caution. The story had emerged naturally, and seemingly in full. Zimmermann's eyes had been full of recollection, not calculation.

Aubrey looked out of the cabin window at his side, down at the bulk of an island slipping through the sea like an unlighted vessel. Then there was only the gleaming flat sea again, and pale islands of cloud. He was no further ahead. In fact, he was more confused. It had happened then, according to Wei's story. Zimmermann and Schiller and a small unit, on a reconnaissance, had been captured by Republican forces. During the few days before they made good their escape, Zimmermann had, apparently, become a Soviet agent.

Yet he had recounted the incident without hesitation, without secrecy?

The narrative had been interrupted by the arrival of a major from an intelligence unit of the British Expeditionary Force. He had been like the turning out of a bright white light. He instructed Aubrey that he and his prisoner should move north, at first light, to the BEF's intelligence headquarters at Louvain.

The recollection of the major fully awakened the old man. He shook himself like a hound, sat up and rubbed his eyes. The vivid memories faded and paled, became sepia prints of dead grandparents on a lounge wall. Aubrey yawned. A nagging curiosity had begun to develop like hunger in his stomach. He knew that he had to talk to Schiller in Australia. He suspected that Schiller held the key to Zimmermann.

Spain. The Condor Legion, 1938, Aladko of the NKVD . . . Schiller held the key, of that Aubrey was certain.

In the warm, gathering dusk David Liu walked into an old and vanished China. The Yu Yuan, the Garden of Leisurely Happiness, was like the recreation of something from a dinner plate. The last of the light rendered the garden in the blue-black and cream of the willow pattern on bone china. However, his knowledge that it was the basis of the pattern's design did not reduce the sense of surprise, even wonder, that he experienced. Pleasure subdued tension. For a few minutes he was alert only to the shapes of buildings, the last sunlight held in calm water, the whisper of man-made waterfalls, the hum of late insects.

He crossed the zigzag Bridge of Nine Turnings, past the ornate teahouse whose lights glowed in the dusk, and observed the heads of customers at the windows. The gardens were still crowded, but emptying with a regularity that was disciplined and somehow depressing.

He was an hour early for his meeting with the police clerk. He had returned to his hotel room to inspect his papers after leaving the girl, then he had gone out, not to return. There was a new surveillance car, but he lost his tail by plunging into the crowded, rabbit-warren streets of the old city, using the morning to inspect the Yu Garden, memorize its lakes and halls and towers and trees. It was an intricate trap, and there were a hundred trapdoors. He was satisfied.

For the remainder of the day, he had walked the streets or spent the time in restaurants and teahouses.

He had no idea whether a trap had been set. The exact

meeting-place was the Hall that Looks Up at the Hills, at the northern end of the garden. He walked towards it beneath trees hung with lanterns. If it was staked out by the police, then he would know it. As yet, they would not be fully alert, fully concealed.

He spent fifteen minutes inspecting the surroundings of the hall, and its shadowy, warm-lit interior. Banners, lanterns, heavily-carved furniture in the rooms, ornate beamed ceilings. It was alien, and familiar; alien to his experience, familiar to a wistful, deracinated part of himself. Beneath the upcurved, elaborate tiled eaves of the hall, he wished, for one fleeing moment, that he was not an American.

No one. It was not a trap, then. He found a bench which gave him a clear view of the hall and the small lake and Rockery Hill beyond them, and seated himself to wait for the arrival of Liang and the clerk.

The garden was almost empty by ten-twenty. The flow of people out of the Yu Yuan had become no more than a trickle, individuals loitering like raindrops sliding down a window. There had been no remotely suspicious activity in or near the Hall that Looks Up at the Hills. Then he saw Liang, following the main path. He would be shielded by bushes from her view when she passed him. He enjoyed the moment of secrecy and concealment. Then he saw the couple from the flat, and picked out in the next minutes two more people he did not recognize but whose patterns of movement were familiar. All four of them were engaged in surveillance.

Back-up. Frederickson was looking after him. Perhaps all the Shanghai cell was here, protecting him. He watched them post themselves around the building, and continued to wait. Liang went into the hall, and a few moments later appeared on the carved railing of the first-floor balcony, standing beneath the glow of a lantern, alone.

Still he waited, his breathing light and quick, his senses alert for noise, his eyes, accustomed to the darkness, picking out each moving shadow. By ten twenty-eight, there appeared to be no one in the garden other than Liang and those who formed the security screen around the hall.

Then a man joined Liang on the balcony. They greeted one another. Liang immediately began studying the paths around the hall, presumably for him. He stood up and stretched the tense cramp from his limbs, then began walking slowly towards the hall. In a pool of lantern light, the young woman from the flat nodded to him reassuringly. He smiled. He entered the building and climbed the stairs to the first floor.

'There you are.' Liang greeted him like a friend rather than a co-conspirator as he appeared on the balcony. Directly below them, the lake gleamed with reflected light, as if luminous paint had been flung into the water. Further from them, the water was dark, pinpricked by the reflections of the lanterns adorning Rockery Hill. The hill, surmounted by a tiny pagoda, loomed black against the stars like a child attempting to imitate a giant. 'This is Huang.'

The police clerk nodded politely. His nervousness was evident to Liu, as was his sense of the importance of the occasion.

'Huang,' Liu acknowledged. 'Thank you for coming. Have you any information for me?' Liu's senses and mind were alert, tuned.

'Let us look at the lake,' suggested Liang, with an insight Liu admired. Movement, slow, deliberate movement, might calm the clerk, loosen his tongue. They began to stroll around the balcony, out of sight of the path leading to the hall.

'It was difficult . . .' Huang began almost immediately.

'I understand that,' Liu replied soothingly, encouraging conversation.

'Some things I have discovered——'

'Yes?'

The lake seemed larger at night. Rockery Hill was decked with lanterns, its pagodas at summit and base like huge paper lanterns themselves.

'The records were, you understand, not available. I had to use subterfuge, purloining the keys . . . I did not have much time to examine them . . .'

'I suppose not,' Liu murmured.

'It was my good fortune to have the small camera that Mr Frederickson supplied on my person when I obtained the keys.'

The path below the hall was empty, except for the woman from the flat who was keeping watch.

'You have photographs?'

'Yes. I left my duties early, claiming that I had contracted a cold.' Hung sniffed in amusement. 'I have developed some of the film. Mr Frederickson taught me to do this.'

'Yes, yes.'

'You will understand that I had time to take very few of these photographs, but I selected the documents I imagined would be of most interest——'

'Show me,' Liu demanded like a greedy child being offered sweets.

Huang bowed slightly, and reached into his jacket. He brought out three stiff, folded sheets. Liu carried them to the light of a lantern while Liang and Hung stood in silence a few yards away.

He unfolded the three stiff enlargements and inspected them, turning them in the light in order to read the Chinese characters and figures they presented. Dosages of drugs, were they——? It seemed like. Pentathol, he translated, excitement plucking at his heart. He examined the second photograph. The sheet had been laid out under a bright lamp. The writing was almost bleached away by the glare. Assignments: a requisition for men with medical and psychiatric qualifications. The names meant nothing to him. The third photograph was of a letter, written by MPT General Chiang to a senior member of the Politburo in Peking. A progress report on the rehabilitation of the German's raked-over, scrambled, drugged mind; pasting over the cracks so well that he would not recall, even in dreams, the interrogations he had undergone. The Harmony of Thought unit's repair work after they had finished with Zimmermann.

He pocketed the photographs and turned to Huang, who appeared relieved, even happy. Liang opened her mouth as if to speak to him, but the first whistle from the other side of the hall drowned even her intention of speaking. Other whistles answered, there was a shout and a single shot from close by. It had been a woman's voice raised in warning. The girl from the flat . . .

Liang appeared stunned, betrayed. Huang could not move. Panic had locked his muscles—no, he appeared almost relaxed. More shots. When Huang fell forward against the carved railing of the balcony, his face exhibited a vast and final surprise. Liu, even as he concentrated on survival and escape, registered Huang's final living posture, his last strange expression, and the sprawl of his body across the balcony rail.

'No, no, no . . .' the girl was murmuring over and over again as she stared at Huang's body. 'No . . .' She had been damaged by shock, unable to move, unable to act. Liu moved towards her, his hand outstretched, before self-preservation motivated muscle and sinew and brain and he backed away.

Whistles, shots, commands uttered in a magnified voice. 'Keep still! Do not move! Police! You are all under arrest!' The shutter of an automatic weapon, the slither of something heavy on gravel.

Liu looked over the balcony. Feet pounded on the wooden stairs to the first floor of the building. The lanterns illuminated the water. The silvery glide of a carp's body distracted him momentarily, and then he climbed onto the railing and jumped, praying that the lake was deep enough.

He hit the water, it cushioned his fall, and then his feet and ankles jarred against the slippery bottom of the lake. He struck out underwater, disorientated and blind, the lantern light above him shimmering and diminishing, the blood pounding in his ears, his lungs straining for relief. He grazed a rock, his hands slipping on weed. He clung to the rock and climbed it to the surface.

He drew in lungfuls of air and looked back, flicking his wet hair from his eyes. Racing figures were surrounding the hall, the girl Liang's bright red tunic was visible among them as she was herded away; two policeman were carrying Huang's corpse between them, head and arms lolling.

Torches flickered over the water, seeking him. A few hopeful shots plucked at the calm dark water. Liu submerged again, swimming towards Rockery Hill and the boundary wall of the Yu Garden. When he came up for air again, he was on his knees on a ledge of rock.

The pagoda's lanterns cast deep shadows along the base of Rockery Hill and the white boundary wall curved away behind it, the recumbent form of a sleeping dragon lying along its top like a guardian. Liu crawled up the slippery rocks towards the base of the wall. He reached it, and touched the surface of the wall with gentle, enquiring fingers. Rough, pock-marked, chipped. It would have to do.

He let his breathing slow. The white wall was a screen against which he would perform his small, desperate mime of escape. Eight or nine feet above the base of the wall, another six or seven feet below the sleeping dragon, were upcurved carved scrolls and boughs together with regular, tusk-like protrusions. He stood upright, and jumped.

His hand rubbed against one tusk, but failed to grip it. Immediately, as if he had touched some electronic alarm, whistles and shots could be heard across the lake. Brick and whitewash dust spat from the wall. He jumped again, held on with one hand, wrenching his arm in its socket, then flung his other arm upwards, grabbing the upcurving tusk. His feet scrabbled violently, then he found purchase and heaved himself level with the tusk. The dragon slumbered above him. He felt the bullets striking the wall, heard them whining away. He rolled his body sideways and over the tusk, sweating profusely, driven by panic. Then, pressing himself against the wall—he could hear orders and running footsteps now—he stretched his body like a cat until he stood upright on the tusk of stone. His hands, reaching blindly above his head, encountered the folds of the dragon's stone scales. He tested his grip and heaved, drawing himself up until his eyes were level with the empty basilisk stare of the carved dragon. Gratefully, he slumped over the dragon's neck.

The poorly lit street outside the garden was almost empty. He swung his body weakly over the wall, straddling it, then lowered himself. On that side, it was no more than ten feet to the pavement. He let his body lengthen against the wall, then dropped.

He stumbled, staggered with exhaustion, but then the whistles prompted him. He began running away from the Yu Garden, the three incriminating photographs water-damaged, sodden, still inside his jacket, their information now safe in his head.

Gradually the whistles faded behind him.

1940: 13—15 MAY

13 May 1940

At first, the noises were part of Aubrey's fitful sleep. After the effort of making precise and detailed notes of his long conversation with Zimmermann, the reverberations and duller, heavier detonations seemed only to serve to underline the disconnected words and phrases that belonged to the German and his own unanswered guesses and questions.

He awoke. The voices faded, the noises were amplified. Artillery fire. Bombs. Eastwards, towards the Marfée Heights and the river Meuse. He rolled onto his side and found Zimmermann, handcuffed and guarded by a soldier, watching him wake. The German smiled. The major from military intelligence had supervised the making secure of the prisoner. Aubrey seemed to remember his heavy eyelids falling to the accompanying click of the bracelets on Zimmermann's wrists.

The barn door was open. Sunlight spilled across the straw, and cool, sweet air seemed to follow it. Aubrey smelt coffee brewing. He patted his jacket pocket, touching his notebook. Zimmermann's smile broadened.

The major entered, purposeful, long-striding. He was almost as tall as Zimmermann, and powerfully built. Aubrey wondered whether his dislike of the man related to his physical impressiveness or to the hardly concealed contempt that the officer had displayed towards him, his methods of interrogation, even his civilian clothes and status.

'What's happening?'

The major paused in front of Aubrey, who proceeded to brush straw from his jacket and trousers. 'I was just about to ask Fritz here the same question.' His stick tapped lightly against his creased trousers. The soldier appeared immensely efficient, thoroughly competent. And experienced. Aubrey realized the major had become an object of envy on his part.

'Yes,' he replied, nodding. The soldier turned away from him. 'Well, Fritz?' the major asked, standing in front of Zimmer-

135

mann. Aubrey was unable to see the German's face. 'What *is* going on?'

Aubrey saw Zimmermann's shoulders heft in a shrug. 'I do not know.'

'Don't give me that. Our friend here'—he indicated Aubrey with a small, dismissive motion of his stick—'may believe that rubbish about your infantry status, but I don't. You're Abwehr all right, and you *do* know what's going on. Eh?' The stick tapped his thigh, predicting the future. Aubrey found the display distasteful, but enviable. Authority, as expressed by the major from intelligence HQ at Louvain, cast an unflattering light on the inexperience and youth of Kenneth Aubrey. 'Come on, Fritz, what's up? What's the game across the river?'

'I cannot answer your question. What is happening out there? I have not seen it. You have.'

'Corporal, get him outside. We'll give him a look at what's going on. Quickly!'

The corporal thrust the butt of his rifle into Zimmermann's back, jolting him off the bale of straw onto his knees. Aubrey saw pain distorting the German's face, then Zimmermann rose lightly to his feet and faced the major. They appeared well-matched opponents. Zimmermann was shoved towards the door of the barn. Aubrey, still brushing his coat, followed the three soldiers. As soon as he reached the door, he saw in the distance smears of smoke against the sunlight and the pale blue sky. Above the smoke wheeled what might have been birds, black and quick. Henri and Philippe were standing with two soldiers, watching the aerial display. There was an ominous freedom about the swooping black specks. Stukas protected by Messerschmitt 109s.

'I see,' Zimmermann murmured, turning to the major. 'It appears the French are being attacked on the Marfée Heights.'

'You arrogant bastard. Is Guderian going to attempt a river crossing?' The corporal thrust his rifle butt into Zimmermann's side. The German gasped with pain. 'Is he?' Thrust. Zimmermann's knees buckled, but he did not fall. 'Where else are they going to cross?' Thrust again, a quick, heavy jab. 'How many crossing points?' Zimmermann staggered from another jab in the back. 'What is the timetable? How soon? What units? Come on, you German bastard! How soon? How many? *Where*?' The corporal jabbed downwards at the prostrate Zimmermann, who groaned at the force of the blow, but said nothing. Aubrey brushed at his clothing with a furious desire to ignore and escape. Wisps of straw dropped from him like innocence. 'Very well, corporal, that'll do for now.' The corporal appeared relieved to step away from Zimmermann. The major turned to Aubrey, his face livid with frustrated anger and something that might have been self-contempt. 'We'd better get this hero back to Louvain at once,' he remarked in a tight, choked voice.

Aubrey nodded slowly like a halfwit. 'Yes, yes,' was all he managed to say.

'Breakfast first. Keep an eye on him, corporal.' The major strode back into the barn. The black birdlike shapes wheeled and swooped like vultures against the painted blue of the sky.

It was well after eight by the time they were ready to leave. Aubrey was placed in the rear of the second of the two open cars in which the major and his unit had arrived at the farm. Zimmermann, lowering himself gently into the seat and being careful to keep his arms away from his ribs, was next to him. Aubrey, in compliance with the major's instructions, ostentatiously displayed his pistol on his lap. Henri, on Zimmermann's other side, was similarly posed. Philippe sat next to the driver. The corporal and the three remaining members of the major's unit were crowded into the leading car with their officer. Aubrey was grateful for not having to travel with the major.

They followed the farm track down to the main road. In the market town of Flize there were anxious faces, some cheering at the sight of British uniforms, an abiding impression of attention and concern and even fear directed towards the oily-clouded east. Smoke hung like a thickening curtain less than twenty kilometres ahead of them. The major had decided to view the situation at the Meuse before heading north along the river towards Louvain, east of Brussels, where the British Expeditionary Force under the command of Lord Gort had its GHQ.

The hamlet of Dom-le-Mesnil seemed full of people talking, moving slowly, forming groups, waiting. Zimmermann studied the faces of the French they passed. The sight seemed to gratify him, to lessen or make worthwhile the pain he had suffered. The breeze of their passage blew his fair hair off his forehead. Aubrey decided there was something irresistible about the man; he represented a superior, overwhelming force. The essence of what he knew could be discerned on his features. Victory. The impression chilled Aubrey. He felt himself a child playing at hide-and-seek, who had dug into a heap of autumn leaves or pulled back the branches of a bush only to discover some hideously mutilated corpse or some act of obscene violence in progress. In Zimmermann's face, the war expanded, enlarged, lengthened through years ahead.

Two slow, lumbering, underpowered Morane-Saulnier 406s in French air force colours droned overhead, heading towards the circling black specks. Zimmermann, looking up, watched them with a fascination Aubrey could only imitate. The aircraft moved ahead of them, losing feature and colour. Three or four black specks seemed to detach themselves from their attentions to the rising ground ahead and move towards the French intruders. It was a matter of seconds before they encountered the two Moranes, and then only seconds more before each of the newcomers was spiralling towards the hummock of the Marfée Heights, trailing thick black smoke. The German specks returned to their flock.

'Useless bloody Frogs,' the driver murmured, oblivious of the presence of Henri and Philippe or perhaps ignoring them through some process of adoption, 'just the same as the last lot. We only 'ad any time for 'is mob,' he added, tossing his head to indicate Zimmermann.

Aubrey looked at Zimmermann. The German shrugged, then pain squeezed his face into narrow contour lines. The shrug indicated superior planning, equipment, men. Irresistible.

The cars began climbing through wooded countryside, up towards the heights. The narrow road twisted and turned, climbed and dropped. For a moment or two, until the whine of the Stukas and the drone of Messerschmitt engines insisted their presence, Aubrey could imagine they were engaged in some pleasant social outing. He lost sight of the aircraft.

Aubrey let his awareness smear the distinct sounds of the attack ahead into a general loud insect-like buzzing, hearing the explosions much as he had done in the moments before he woke. He felt drowsy as if with heat. Strangely, as the car climbed again and he was pressed further back in the cracked leather seat, the drone of engines became louder, as if he were lying in tall grass and bees were buzzing very near his head. The insect-noises grew louder and louder, became like the ceaseless ripping of cloth. It began to hurt the ears . . .

Then he realised that Zimmermann had moved. His hand-cuffed hands were over the driver's head. Aubrey snapped awake, only to realise that Henri and Philippe, instead of struggling with Zimmermann, were staring behind the car, faces mirroring the same growing expression of fear. Zimmermann was yelling.

'For God's sake, get the car off the road!' The driver was struggling to retain control of the steering wheel as Zimmermann wrenched at it. Aubrey fumbled with his pistol, opened his mouth to warn Zimmermann to sit down . . .

The Messerschmitt behind them opened fire, its four smaller machine guns and one 20mm cannon tearing at the engine noise, ripping and stuttering like cloth torn in a fury. The sound deafened Aubrey as he turned to watch his own death leaping upon him.

Leaves flickered and dissolved, the road coughed dust and chippings. The three-second burst pursued them, leapt after them. The mottled camouflage of the Me 109, its black propellor hub, white belly and painted shark's teeth grinning, filled Aubrey's vision. The car swerved wildly out of control and lurched at the edge of the road, dropped its bonnet, began to roll down a shallow slope. White belly after shark's grin, tailplane; the flash of flame, a distinctly heard scream from the other car—then Aubrey's world was shaken and flung upside down as the car overturned. He dropped his pistol, grabbing the yielding substance of Zimmermann's body and uniform to him like an eager lover.

They spilled from the car together. Aubrey, winded, watched the car right itself with a shuddering bump, and stop. The driver lolled ominously over the door, his head at an impossible angle. Philippe lay prone and groaning a few yards behind them. Henri was on his knees, near the road, clutching his reddening shirt at one shoulder, his head hanging like someone vomiting. Aubrey held Zimmermann, his hand gripping the chain between the two bracelets of the handcuffs as he levered himself to his knees. He had fallen on top of Zimmermann, who seemed unconscious.

'Philippe, Philippe! Quickly!'

The younger Frenchman sat upright with a quick, jerky motion. His gun was still in his hand. He looked around at Henri, and appeared about to move in his direction.

'Henri——'

'Philippe, I'll look to Henri. *You* watch the prisoner.' Zimmermann opened one eye. He smiled, presumably at his continued existence. Aubrey staggered, regained his balance, and began running towards Henri. A pall of smoke belched up into the branches of the trees that overhung the road, to be masked by the greenery before emerging like a signal into the sky. 'Henri, how is it?'

'It hurts, M'sieur. It hurts a lot.' Henri groaned. Aubrey studied the wound. The bullet had passed directly through the shoulder.

'Hang on, I won't be a moment,' Aubrey murmured, climbing the last few steps onto the pockmarked road.

The leading car had stopped burning. A few flames flickered from the upholstery and from some dark and foreboding lump heaped in the rear seat. The thin trail of smoke was moved by the slight breeze into twisted, anguished contortions. Aubrey approached the car slowly, reluctantly.

They were all dead. The smell of scorched and burned flesh was hideous, making his stomach heave. There were bullet holes in charred flesh and uniforms. The major, the corporal, the driver and the remainder of the unit: all dead. His nerveless hand touched the sill of the driver's door. He withdrew it, yelping with pain, sucking it furiously as if to absorb himself in a lesser, physical distress. He felt his stomach revolt once more, and hurried back down the road towards Henri. He helped the Frenchman to his feet, cradling his larger frame as he assisted him to their car. Philippe had ordered Zimmermann, hand-cuffed though he was, to remove the driver's corpse. It lay reposefully on the grass beside the car.

Aubrey searched the car for its first-aid kit. Zimmermann, ignoring the protests of the two brothers, examined Henri's wound.

'He's losing a lot of blood,' he commented. Henri's face was pale and drawn. 'Give me that,' he added, as Aubrey held up the tin box bearing a squat red cross. 'And unlock these.' He held up the bracelets on his wrists. Aubrey freed Zimmermann's hands without hesitation. Then quickly and expertly, Zimmermann bound up the red-lipped wound that gushed on Henri's shoulder.

'Thank you,' Aubrey murmured when he had finished. 'For——' He shrugged expressively.

Zimmermann shook his head. 'Self-preservation. The pilot couldn't see my uniform. I regret the driver. Perhaps not the major or his corporal quite so much . . .'

'Can he travel?'

'Yes, but he must receive attention soon.'

'Very well. I'll leave him at the nearest field hospital.' Aubrey turned and explained the situation to the two brothers. Strangely he felt more intimately bound to Zimmermann; perhaps the man's coolness and his expertise was something to cling to. Aubrey was confused by his feelings.

'Where are we going?'

'To Louvain, I suppose,' Aubrey replied. 'GHQ.' The cryptonym had a comforting ring to it. Solidity. The immovable object confronting the irresistible force represented by Zimmermann and the Me 109. That swooping, shark's-grin death . . . charred, withered flesh . . .

His stomach revolted again and he fought to control it, feeling his body shake, change temperature as if each part were some separate climatic region. Zimmermann placed a steadying firm hand on his arm.

'I remember the first dead body I ever saw,' he said quietly, 'in Spain, three years ago. A peaceful appearance, like someone sleeping. A child. When I got closer, it was like a broken eggshell. One side of the head had gone . . .' He gripped Aubrey's arm, and shook it almost fiercely. 'Welcome to the war, Englishman.' There was sufficient scorn and mockery in the tone of his voice to diminish Aubrey's horror. He shook off Zimmermann's hand.

'Get in the car!' he snapped.

'It will start, by the way,' Zimmermann drawled. 'It is no more than dented and shaken—like us.'

'Philippe, Henri, in the car.' Aubrey was almost officiously precise and clipped in his tone. He bustled in imitation of efficiency, expertness. 'We'll continue. Do the major's job for him. Philippe, keep an eye on the prisoner.'

Aubrey started the car. Mud churned from beneath the wheels, then they moved, climbing the bank slowly until they reached the road. Aubrey steered with exaggerated, narrow-focused care around the burned-out car and its bodies, then accelerated as soon as they were beyond it. The smoke from the wreckage was now the thinnest of grey streamers, without the spirals that suggested a human frame in anguish.

Within an hour, they had reached a point only half a mile from the place where they had captured Zimmermann the previous night. Their progress had been slow, threading their way through units of the French 55th and 71st divisions of the 10th Corps of General Grandsard which occupied the Marfée Heights and the defensive positions on the left bank of the Meuse. Zimmermann had been alert and absorbed. He studied faces more than dispositions, the atmosphere more than the defences. And his confidence of mien steadily increased. He appeared sunny, unconcerned, almost amused. The divisions were composed almost entirely of elderly reservists with limited training. To Aubrey, they now appeared an illusory counter-threat to Guderian's Panzers across the river. It was as if daylight had turned a powerful dream into a pale ghost of itself. Guderian, Aubrey now believed, would cross the river that day, at his own choosing and almost on his own terms.

Ammunition in short supply, Aubrey heard. Untrained, unskilled units. Fat and flabby troops. The front, twenty-five miles long, was too thinly defended at any and every point. Many of the pillboxes along the river were unfinished, unarmed. The concrete wouldn't withstand the Stukas' bombs. Troops slaughtered in their trenches . . .

The bombardment had already lasted for three hours. It was unceasing, terrifying. And the German artillery hadn't even opened up yet . . .

Aubrey wanted to flee the Marfée Heights, as from the scene of a disaster that had already occurred. Instead, he remained in the immediate area for perhaps an hour, making furious, continuous scribbled notes. The major's persona occupied him, pushed away the recollection of the man himself, and his charred body. Zimmermann, with amusement, pointed often across the river whenever a gap in the trees allowed them a view of the field-grey tide waiting on the right bank, the concentrations of armour, the silent artillery, the numbers of troops.

Aubrey became charged with a sense of mission. It was like some swift religious conversion. He wished the truth to reach Louvain, not the reassurances he knew would be passed by telephone and coded signal. The front at Sedan was about to erupt, bulge back, be broken. He must get that news to the BEF . . .

Zimmermann seemed reluctant to leave; a spectator for whom the main actors were yet to come on stage. Aubrey drove the car as recklessly as he could away from the ramparts of the Marfée Heights, away from the smoke above the town of Sedan.

They drove north, following the river towards Charleville Mezieres. The town was filled with people, its approaches beginning to clog with the Belgian refugees driven before the German advance through the Ardennes. Carts piled with possessions, upturned chairs and mangles, small pianos and waif-like, empty-faced children who already predicted the future in unequivocal terms. Dust, the smell of petrol on the air that had gone sour with fear and uncertainty. Zimmermann, seated in the rear of the car, an army raincoat draped over his betraying grey uniform, passed through the scenes with a lordly, comprehending, satisfied in-difference—or so it seemed to Aubrey. The Englishman dis-covered himself hurled into an adult, irrecoverable world. His espionage career had been little more than a game by comparison with what he now witnessed. He felt diminished and inadequate; ashamed of himself. Pipesmoke, scarves wreathed beneath un-shaven chins or wrapped over women's heads. Countless, endless grey faces. These people were prophets, forerunners. They had already witnessed France's future.

By lunchtime, they reached Montherme, where the French 102nd division had prevented the Germans from crossing the river. Aubrey was delighted.

'No aircraft,' Zimmermann observed laconically.

Above them, through the trees and over the fields to the west, French aircraft circled and droned and waited. The Luftwaffe had not arrived. Artillery crumped and wailed, but no Stukas howled and terrified.

'It isn't going to be as easy as you thought,' Aubrey remarked with an irritated bravado, munching on some sausage and bread that Philippe had managed to obtain in Charleville. Henri was being fed by his younger brother in the car. Aubrey and Zimmer-mann had carried their food and wine some yards down the slope towards the river. A picnic above the battle. Units of the French division were dug in on the slopes around them: casual, confident, relaxed. Below them, on their side of the river, German units were pinned down, protected only by the guns of the tanks drawn up beneath the trees on the opposite bank. Cigarette-smoke as-cended into the trees in company with the smoke of rifle fire as the French enjoyed their advantage. Zimmermann, frowning as he studied the dispositions, seemed nevertheless undeterred.

'Perhaps not,' he said. There was a note of pity in his voice.

'I shall leave Henri with the medical unit of this division,' Aubrey announced. 'That shoulder needs treatment.'

'I agree.'

'You claim you are not a Nazi,' Aubrey said suddenly, swallowing a lump of bread and sausage. Rifle fire crackled around them, followed by cheering. The cannons of the tanks drawn up on the other side of the river were evidently conserving ammunition. The sky above them was silent except for the occasional French fighter.

'I am not.'

'This is a Nazi war—you are a German, brought up under the Nazis for the last seven years. A veteran of Spain and the Condor Legion, fighting with the Falangists and Franco. Those are impressive credentials for a non-Nazi, wouldn't you say?'

Zimmermann studied Aubrey carefully, then he nodded. 'My father was an army officer. I am an army officer. It is a family tradition. That is all.'

'Where were you born and brought up?'

'Wittenberg.'

Aubrey smiled. 'Is that propitious, Martin Luther's city?'

'I doubt it. I went into the army when I was seventeen. I am now twenty-three. It seems a long time between. I fought in Spain because soldiers are trained to fight. That is why I am here now. The Wehrmacht is full of non-Nazis. It is why France and England have no need to worry. Gestapo and SS—you have heard of them?' Aubrey nodded. 'They are not everywhere or all-powerful, you know.'

'Organizations like them have a way of becoming so—at least, history seems to indicate as much. You were captured in Spain, you said?'

'Yes. By one of the International Brigades, in Aragon. The 15th, I remember—Yugoslavs, French, British, Americans.' Zimmermann smiled. 'And Russians, of course. Certain Russian officers operating on American passports, attaching themselves like limpets to idealists and materialists alike. If you wish to make pronouncements, perhaps you would like to apply them to the NKVD. That is the sort of organization that even the Wehrmacht could not control.'

'Mm. You're talking about an ally of Germany.'

'The honeymoon will be short—as soon as Stalin is ready, he'll change sides.'

'Interesting. Where in Aragon?'

'I was on patrol—reconnaissance. In March. East of Saragossa, behind the Republican lines. Much as now.' He spread his hands

144

and grinned. 'Even though they were in retreat, they still managed to take and keep us for a few days.'

'And you met this Russian officer?'

'Russian secret policeman. Aladko. He was quite open about his real name and identity.'

Zimmermann had begun massaging his ribs.

'Sore?'

'Memory makes the bruises worse. Aladko liked inflicting pain. Not like your major this morning, working himself into the right sort of rage before he could give the order.'

'Beatings?'

'He had plenty of cooperation. Russians, one or two Americans, even local Communists enlisted in one or other of the Aragonese units. Especially the local Communists . . .'

'And?'

'I kept my mouth shut. Others didn't.'

'After that?'

'Courage or cowardice made no difference—the Republic was already beaten and they knew it.'

Cannon shells whistled overhead, burying themselves beyond the lip of the hillside; presumably to discourage reserve units from moving up. It was strangely unreal as a war. The refugees in Charleville had been more real than this. This was a kind of war-game. The ground shuddered for a moment beneath their feet. The trees at their backs remained unmoved.

'Go on,' Aubrey prompted, swigging at the wine before passing the bottle to Zimmermann.

'Oh. Then came the softer approach. The idealism. I made no secret of my dislike of Nazis—officers in the Legion, visiting generals and policemen and politicians. Boot-stamping, salutes, bullshit. Grubby little men without education, without background. And some soldiers who should have known better than to have been taken in by it. Aladko tried to recruit me, would you believe?'

'Did he?'

Zimmermann shook his head. 'Of course not. I am not a Communist.'

More shells whistled across the river, smashing into the French positions below them. It was as if events had suddenly been orchestrated to impress Aubrey. Screams, smoke, flying earth and stone. It was not a game, just a period of waiting before the full

145

fury of the storm broke. Men groaning; the lower slopes obscured by flame and smoke. Ammunition exploding.

'Come,' Aubrey said, remembering the pistol as he got to his feet. 'We'll get Henri to the field hospital.'

It was another hour or so before they returned to the road that paralleled the Meuse. Philippe was now driving, apparently relieved at leaving his brother. They headed north once more, towards Dinant, forty miles away. As the afternoon advanced and their progress, though slow, remained unimpeded, it became more and more evident to Aubrey that the Germans now overlooked the Meuse from Sedan to Dinant. A great flood behind a dyke wall. One crack, and the Panzers would pour across the French plains towards Paris and the coast. It was an enervating, depressing journey. The confidence, the good humour of the French units they encountered seemed empty, wilfully blind to reality.

South of Dinant, the Meuse's sharp meanders and thickly wooded, high escarpments improved Aubrey's grim mood. Here, at least, the Germans could be held. To the south, well . . . But here, yes. It could be done.

'Colonel Aladko,' Aubrey mused. 'Not a likeable man, then?'

'No.'

'How important was he? The information may be of future use if, as you suggest, we become allies of the Russians.'

Zimmermann smiled. 'Before then, the war will be over.'

'Nevertheless——'

'I would say he was an important officer in the NKVD. Not by his bearing or manner, but by his experience, his shrewdness. If he was not important, then his skills had neither been recognized nor used. While he dragged us north with him as they retreated, I studied him. Learning the craft, as it were.'

'The craft of the infantryman, naturally.'

'Naturally.'

'Aladko had all the correct credentials. He was with Lenin and the Bolsheviks in Petrograd, later he distinguished himself in the Civil War—*their* civil war, Red and White. The Party relied on him greatly, giving him a roving commission to check on the loyalty of unit commanders in the field.' Zimmermann's smile broadened. 'He was boasting about the number of people—of all ranks, even up to Commissar or general—he'd had shot. That was an occasion where he was threatening me, rather than trying to enlist me.'

Philippe turned the car off the road, down a country track. The road beyond the turning had been bombed. It was torn and holed. The car bumped along the rutted lane.

'I see.'

'I suspect Aladko was very important, and still is. In Moscow, or wherever he is now, he will have an influential post. Do you know what he once said to me? *All power springs from the nape of the neck.*' Zimmermann made a pistol of his right hand, and pointed his finger at Philippe's neck. 'Pfff. That's all there is. I think he was joking.' Aubrey shuddered involuntarily.

Black smoke hung over the river behind them, now that they were away from the wooded escarpments of the Meuse. It seemed denser, heavier, more pall-like. Artillery fire was omnipresent; the black bird-shapes in the distance were Messerschmitts and Stukas. It was too like Sedan, and broke Aubrey's confidence in topography.

'Philippe, head north as soon as you can,' he said.

'M'sieur.'

Philippe skidded the car into a narrower lane, jolting his passengers between the tall hedges. The lane twisted through blind corners; the ruts of tractor and wagon wheels flung Aubrey and Zimmermann into constant physical contact. Ahead of them, at the end of their green tunnel, there was smoke hanging over the town of Dinant. The track rose gradually, and the cornfields sloped away from them in bright sunlight towards Charleroi to the north-west. An unsmeared sky. A farm tractor chugging audibly in one moment of artillery silence, a breeze moving the fields in a slow, soporific rhythm. All of France beyond those fields. Aubrey regretted the vision as mere illusion, turning away from it towards the real sky, heavy and oily with smoke.

14 May 1940

Aubrey had awoken in the shabby hotel room in Dinant experiencing an image which remained vivid even after he had opened his eyes. The south coast of England, the previous summer; distant specks that had been German aircraft, patrolling the Channel —practising for war. He had seen so many of those ominous specks the previous day, in earnest. As he dressed, watched by Zimmermann who was handcuffed to the bedpost, the illusions of 1939 left him.

147

A scrappy breakfast in the almost deserted hotel dining room was followed by an hour which they spent searching for petrol for the car. It was as if events had already overtaken Dinant, that the Germans had already passed through it leaving a bereft, provisionless, dazed town in their wake. Eventually Aubrey was able to fill the tank and the two jerry-cans in the boot, and with Philippe driving they headed north once more along roads that seemed perpetually clogged with Belgian refugees, wagon-trains of people already purposeless and defeated. Yet the allied armies became more evident and unscathed. Discipline, equipment, uniforms were still burnished, pressed, polished.

'Why did you choose that hotel instead of a more secure army unit?' Zimmermann asked soon after they had passed the village of Anhée and the road had become a disciplined, orderly artery down which units of the Belgian army flowed. The sight heartened Aubrey, even impressed Zimmermann.

'I——' Aubrey paused to consider. 'I think I was reminding myself I was a civilian.'

'There aren't any civilians any longer,' Zimmermann observed drily. Aubrey looked down at the pistol held loosely on his lap. His grip upon it tightened involuntarily, a reaction which disturbed and disheartened him.

Aubrey felt he had stepped perhaps two or three days back in time. Troop movements and dispositions, unblooded divisions, a stillness over the country, while further south at Sedan and Monthermé the Germans were poised to cross the river, attacking fiercely, beginning to win. Here, nearing Namur, the front was entirely secure, settled, quiet. He began to wonder whether this quiescence was not somehow to the German advantage. Zimmermann, he suspected, would know the answer.

'We have it wrong, don't we?' he snapped. 'It isn't here that the main brunt will be borne, is it?'

Zimmermann's face clouded, then cleared into a look of denial. 'I don't quite understand——'

'Yes, you do—and so do I!' Aubrey snapped.

Zimmermann shrugged. 'If you say so.'

'I do!' Aubrey's knuckles were white where he held the butt of the pistol. His other hand gripped the barrel, as if to prevent him pointing it into the German's side. Zimmermann appeared to be awaiting the outcome of Aubrey's inward conflict. 'Oh, yes, it's in your face—at least it was for a moment—you *do* know. You understand the whole strategy, don't you?' Aubrey felt a clarity of mind he had not previously experienced. Obliquely, scenes and impressions had conspired with his curiosity to provoke the sudden question.

Zimmermann looked at his watch. 'It's too late,' he said. 'Everything I have seen, yesterday and today, tells me it is too late.'

Philippe slowed the car and pulled onto the road's grass verge. A French unit, armoured cars in the lead, light tanks close behind, approached and passed them. Aubrey saw Zimmermann tug the British army raincoat up over his uniform. The dust choked them, obscured the faces of the tank commanders. The armoured unit was moving south towards Dinant. In a matter of a few minutes, the road was empty again in front of them. An industrial haze hung over Namur to the north as the dust of the tanks' passage settled in the warm air.

'Too late?' Aubrey asked as Philippe drove off.

'That was a reserve unit, being deployed at leisure. This road, *all* roads south, should be choked with military traffic.'

'Sedan?'

'Yes. You know the German word *Sichelschnitt?*'

'*Sichel*—sickle?'

'Scythe. The sweep of a scythe.' Zimmermann moved his arms, imitating a scything action towards Aubrey. 'It has begun, it cannot be countered.'

'But we captured most of your *Fall Gelb* invasion plans in January——'

'They were revised. Bock's Army Group B is waving the red flag. He has only twenty-eight divisions. Do you know how many Runstedt has in the south? Forty-four, including seven Panzer divisions.' Zimmermann smiled gently. 'At least, that is my understanding of the plan.'

'So we're wrong?' Aubrey asked wildly, looking behind them back down the road to Dinant.

'I am afraid so.'

'My God!'

'If I had told you two days ago, it would not have mattered. The French are inflexible, believing in the Maginot Line, even in trench warfare. If I had told your major yesterday, it would have made no difference. There is nothing that can be done. There is no remedy. What I have told you is valueless now.'

Aubrey was silent for a moment, then he snapped: 'Philippe,

put your foot down. Drive faster! I want to be at GHQ this afternoon. It's fifty miles or more. Hurry!'

Zimmermann's face was almost saintly with the sad patience it expressed.

15 May 1940

Aubrey held out the packet of Gold Flake cigarettes to Zimmermann, dismissing the guard with a curt nod of his head which encompassed the German, the army represented by the guard's uniform, and the preceding twenty-four hours. Zimmermann, who had been lolling on the bed, sat upright, stretched, then took a cigarette. Aubrey lit it, then his own. Blue smoke curled to the damp-stained ceiling. It was a narrow, high, attic room in the three-storey building temporarily commandeered by the intelligence units of the BEF's headquarters in Louvain.

A tank rumbled along the cobbled street outside.

'How are you?' Aubrey asked solicitously.

Zimmermann inhaled, exhaled noisily. 'Quite well,' he replied frostily. 'Very tired, of course.' He shrugged. When he continued, his voice was more pleasant, less acrimonious. 'Ah, there is no point. Before this war is finished, interrogation methods will have improved dramatically. Then there will be no hope for any of us. Your people—bright lights, a hard chair, no sleep—but no beating.'

'You told them everything?'

'Everything that mattered. Precisely what I told you. What one or two reconnaissance aircraft could now tell them. Forty-four divisions can't be kept secret.'

'No.'

Zimmermann lay back on the bed once more, cradling his head against the wallpaper with one crooked arm. Aubrey sat in a chair whose horsehair stuffing was beginning to thrust like some tough weed through its shabby, worn upholstery. The room was shadowy in the pale light from the single, high, narrow window that sloped above their heads. The bare floorboards were rough and dusty.

'And your day—how has that been?'

Aubrey smiled. There seemed to be an amicable conspiracy between them. 'Much the same as yours. Without the bright

150

lights, of course. A hard chair, and ceaseless questions. Going over and over the inevitable.'

'Today the order for retreat will be given. Now that the strategy is perceived and has begun to work, there is no alternative. Your BEF will be ordered to pull back.'

'How far?'

'Perhaps the Schelde. I cannot say.'

Aubrey rubbed his smooth chin. Zimmermann had evidently not been issued with shaving tackle.

'I—you're transferred back to me, by the way. To SIS, that is. You're my responsibility again.'

'Ah. Soon, then, I shall attempt to escape.'

'Perhaps. I convinced them that you had information of general interest to SIS, apart from your military knowledge. They did not appear reluctant to let you go.'

'I don't know any more. I am not familiar with the tactics, only the general strategy. Apparently, they have become persuaded of that.'

Artillery fire made the window above them rattle. A slight dusting of plaster drifted slowly to the floor.

'Yours or ours?' Aubrey asked.

'Ours.'

'Army Group B on the move?'

'Perhaps. If so, it means that all three bridgeheads across the Meuse have been secured—as you will have guessed.'

'Yes.'

The shells landed at some distance from the buildings, making deep, hollow crumping noises, rattling the window again, making Aubrey flinch.

'I shall take you back with me,' Aubrey remarked almost casually.

'Where?' Zimmermann was alert, though apparently he was staring sightlessly at the ash on the tip of the cigarette.

'London.'

'London?'

'I'm sure you can tell us a great deal about the workings of the Abwehr—about agents in England, et cetera, et cetera.'

'You are learning, Mr Aubrey. Yes, perhaps so.' Zimmermann's frame was rigid with tension. Aubrey opened his jacket to reveal the pistol stuck in his waistband. 'I understand,' Zimmermann murmured.

'Incidentally—to return to Aragon and your last period of captivity—would you be prepared to talk about this Russian, Aladko, and his interrogation of you? His attempt to enlist your services?'

'Of course. As you said, you may well have such an ally one day. It would be well to be prepared.'

'Thank you.'

The artillery had become a constant deep rumbling, like rippled hollow drumbeats in a quick pattern, interspersed with the closer explosions of the shells they fired. Lighter, closer noises could also be discerned.

'Ours again,' Zimmermann explained before he was asked. 'Tanks. Our Panzers. Less than half a mile away.'

Aubrey felt frightened, yet detached. An observer in a high room, enclosed and unmindful. It was as if the war had been drained from him during his long night of questioning. Zimmermann, too, appeared to relapse into a state of half-alertness. Aubrey watched him carefully for signs that he was bluffing.

'Did you consider his approach to you to be the only one he made?'

'No. Everyone captured from my unit was put through the same thing. The hopeless cases, the ones who believed in Hitler through thick and thin, they were taken out and shot on Aladko's orders. In the nape of the neck. They could look at the snow on the high Pyrenees, the smoky cold air out of which the forests loomed, as they knelt to receive the benediction of the pistol.' Zimmermann's face twisted in contempt. He evidently envisaged himself in the identical situation, but Aubrey had no idea whether the contempt was for Aladko or some future image of himself. 'I stayed alive, so did Schiller and the others, by playing Aladko's game. Even then, it didn't save everyone.'

'How extensive was Aladko's authority?'

'In the woodsman's hut, in the clearing, amongst the members of the Brigade we saw—absolute. Life and death, as I said.' More plaster drifted like snow from the ceiling, coating the backs of Aubrey's hands and Zimmermann's stained and crumpled uniform jacket. Zimmermann watched the last motes of plaster and waited until the rattling of the window had subsided. 'Absolute. And his real purpose was recruitment, not execution.'

'We're aware of the Communist involvement in Spain.'

The drone of aircraft became an increasing whine that in turn became a howl. It seemed to originate directly outside and above their single window.

'Stukas!' Zimmermann's face revealed a genuine, unexpected fear. He rolled off the bed, then beneath it. Aubrey hesitated, then crouched against the wall, the tired, sagging chair in front of him. He could see Zimmermann's pale face beneath the bed, saw his lips moving, but he could hear nothing except the hideous howl of the bombers and his own blood beating in his ears as he clamped his hands over them.

The building shook. Plaster rained down. A vivid, snakelike crack whipped its way across the wall above the bed. The window shattered, flinging glass into the room.

The dust settled. Aubrey got up. His shoes crunched as he moved. He picked two pieces of glass from his hand. Zimmermann emerged from beneath the bed. Whether from relief or rage or his own and Aubrey's temporary deafness, he was shouting. Gradually, as a background to his words, the noises of the German artillery returned to the room.

'You don't realise their real purpose—they're looking ahead, always ahead.'

'Who?'

'The Russians, the NKVD. To this war, then to after this war. Long-term. Aladko and the others had a chance to encounter so many people from so many countries during that war!' Realizing that his own hearing had returned, Zimmermann lowered his voice. He went on talking as he brushed lumps of plaster and shards of glass from the bed's coverlet. 'Americans, British, Spaniards, French—a royal hunting forest of different people. They were recruiting madly. Of that I am certain. I think they knew the war was lost almost from the beginning—once we arrived, perhaps. Their main purpose was—agents. Long-term agents.' Zimmermann looked up and smiled. 'One day, you may thank me for that information.'

Artillery closer now.

'Ours,' Aubrey said with a grim smile, brushing plaster dust from his hair. 'And you—did he succeed with you?'

After the deafening ripple of the BEF artillery barrage, in the silence before the explosions which only seemed to emphasize Zimmermann's own silence, a ruffled, disturbed bird chirped in protest somewhere in the eaves of the house. The snake-like crack behind the German's head had put down spindly, spider-like legs towards the floor, becoming some giant stick insect instead of a serpent.

Then Zimmermann shook his head with a slow smile. 'No,' he said, 'he did not succeed with me. I was not available for purchase.'

The explosions shook the house. The door opened, as if flung wide by the blast, and the guard-corporal put his white-dusted head into the room.

'Everything all right, sir?'

'Yes, thank you, corporal.' Self-consciously, Aubrey brushed his jacket and trousers. 'We're both fine.'

Another violent ripple of artillery fire seemed to buffet the house.

'Monty's giving 'is lot what for,' the corporal explained, tossing his head in Zimmermann's direction.

'What's happening, corporal?'

'Jerry launched an attack, sir. Third Division's in the process of booting 'em out again.' He grinned, his teeth discoloured by nicotine, his expression satisfying to Aubrey.

'Thank you, corporal.' The guard shut the door once more. 'Well?' Aubrey asked Zimmermann.

'A temporary setback, I assure you. I suspect you're fighting for a town you will be leaving tomorrow.' There was something narrow and calculating about Zimmermann's expression that Aubrey failed to notice.

The plaster dust stirred on the floor and furniture as lighter, more distant shellfire was answered by the closer, heavier British artillery.

'Aladko—did he recruit British agents?'

Zimmermann shrugged. He seemed intent upon brushing his counterpane clean of dust and creases. He moved slowly to the foot of the bed.

'Possibly. I would not know. A lot of English would have been sympathetic to his approach, I suspect?' He glanced at Aubrey assessingly for a moment. Once more his hands brushed the coverlet at the foot of the bed. A lump of plaster crackled beneath his boot, another thudded on the floorboards.

'Perhaps,' Aubrey admitted thoughtfully, his mind filled with unexpectedly lurid images of Russian agents within his own organization. Zimmermann might know, Zimmermann could point the way . . .

'Sorry,' Zimmermann murmured, and then his clenched fist struck Aubrey on the temple. At the same time, his left hand grabbed the barrel of the pistol, twisting the weapon out of Aubrey's grasp.

Aubrey saw Zimmermann's detached, calm face, saw the gun held up like a prize, saw the stick-insect marching frozenly across the wall, heard the protesting bird in the eaves drowned by artillery fire, then his head was tilted back by a blow to the jaw. His eyes perceived the broken skylight rapidly darken. He felt the floor against his body without the sensation of falling. He dimly heard the door open, the guard's surprised challenge. The noises of a struggle—slipping, grinding boots, grunted breaths, a cry of pain —faded and disappeared. He entered a silent, close, warm darkness.

PART TWO

THE TORTOISE AND THE HARE

The tortoise goes round once how slow,
Twelve times as fast the hare will go;
But watch the tortoise, watch the hare,
At twelve o'clock you'll find them where?

—old rhyme on a child's clock

SIX:

In Vino Veritas

Liu's clothes had dried quickly in the warm night and because of the heat of tension and relief his frame exuded. In the crowded streets of the old city he lost himself and any pursuit for two slow, endless hours. Eventually he felt able to enter a teahouse and eat something, drink dry white wine and smoke two *tai shan*, miniature cigars. He choked back his coughs and tried to let the aromatic smoke and its taste and inhalation finally calm him.

It was after midnight when he crossed Suzhou Creek, passing Shanghai Mansions, and headed for the railway station. Surprisingly, the hotel did not present itself against the warm, starlit night as a refuge or a burrow into which he wished to run. It was simply an empty room, shed as lightly as his last persona. Now he was a Party official; the papers in his breast pocket, still wrapped in polythene, were a portable safe house. When he shed the crumpled, stained suit he was wearing, he would leave Shanghai and its dangers. It would be a fresh start.

The station was crowded with people waiting for the first trains of the morning. The police seemed more in evidence than on his arrival, but not especially alert. He hurried to the luggage lockers, used the key the girl had given him—pausing for a moment with it in his hand to indulge the new sadness and regret with which he could now regard her—then took the small suitcase of scuffed mock leather to the toilets. He changed quickly, put the crumpled suit and underclothes back into the case, then washed and smartened his appearance. The two small wads in his cheeks fattened his features. The padding beneath his jacket gave him a slight but noticeable paunch as he studied himself in the mirror. He parted his hair on the opposite side. A new man smiled with mild, resigned sadness out at him. He picked up his case and made his way back to the station's main concourse; the illusory gardens were made more artificial, almost plastic, by the hard lighting in the roof.

He sat on a bench near the fountain. Its mild noise made him feel drowsy. His paunch was visible as he slumped more comfortably. It amused him. His companions on the bench also seemed sleepy. Liu settled into rest, his suitcase held in front of him between his feet, hands resting on the unfamiliar paunch. His papers, unwrapped and ready for inspection, served him like a shield and comforter.

Idly, he looked at his watch. A little more than four hours until his train to Wu Han. The girl . . .

What she could tell them, might tell them? The fountain whispered, an out-of-sequence drip making the sound less than perfect, reminding him of the mechanics involved in the swish of water. What could she tell them?

His papers, his new identity?

Not unless she had looked. And the girl was sufficiently professional not to have looked, not to clutter herself with information that would damage, hurt, betray. Liang assumed a new and beatified reality in his thoughts. Her capture hurt him. He repressed the shudder that accompanied images of her interrogation.

No, he was safe. In Wu Han there would be no delays, no time lag. Swiftness, contact, extraction of information, escape. He would keep ahead.

The drip subsided into the distant, general noise of the fountain and the whispers of waiting passengers. Liu slept.

The Ansett Boeing 727 from Sydney via Melbourne floated above its own drifting shadow towards Adelaide. Aubrey, at the window seat, watched that shadow slide across the low, green-stubbled sand dunes of the Coorong and ripple across the wrinkled water trapped between the coast and the Younghusband Peninsula. The bright midday sun glinted off the sea, making it as polished and terrain-like as a dented shield. Then they were crossing the delta at the mouth of the Murray River, and the heights of the Lofty Ranges were hazily before them, looming out of the heat.

The memory of the blows to temple and jaw that had been inflicted on him more than forty years before were as vivid as a current physical sensation to Aubrey. Time had not distorted the physical images. Yet he doubted the recollected days of May 1940. He could recall the sensations, the activities, the locations of that journey from Sedan to Louvain, but he was uncertain as to what Zimmermann had said, the expressions his features had revealed, the implications of his opinions and his narrative.

Sydney Airport had been a confused, half-perceived experience, his awareness fogged with tiredness and memory. Hyde had left him like a parcel while he collected their luggage, and Aubrey had drifted back through the years noting, like a signpost unseen when he first passed it, the prophetic nature of many of Zimmermann's observations concerning the NKVD's recruitment of agents in Spain. He had interrogated some of the people, the 'moles', that were the fruit of the International Brigades. It was only from Zimmermann, however, that he had heard the name Aladko.

Doubt, however, had strengthened on the crowded Ansett aircraft from Sydney. What game had Zimmermann been playing with him? Any game at all? Was the man telling him the truth? *I was not available for purchase*. Was that true? Had he even said it? To an awakened Aubrey, taking in the landscape that slipped green and blue and brown and gold beneath the belly of the 727, the words had a suspiciously familiar ring. It was like something he might have said himself. In the files, the account of Aubrey's tussle with Zimmermann and the German's attempted escape made no reference—except in generalities—to the conversation that had immediately preceded the two blows to Aubrey's face.

The Boeing banked, its shadow melting and sliding and becoming as fluid as oil as it rose against the slopes of the Mount Lofty Ranges. Then the land dropped away again, and Aubrey was immediately struck by the sight of vineyards. Their regular green patterns on the lower slopes and spreading towards the coast of the gulf shocked him, and he felt his body itch with a fierce, younger man's anticipation. *Schiller*. Yes, Zimmermann's friend. Zimmermann had referred to Schiller being interrogated and bribed by Aladko, without success. He was, perhaps, the key.

The aircraft turned north. Adelaide lay ahead of the port wing, submitting to an envelope of visible heat. As the Boeing began its descent towards the city's airport, the haze revealed trees and parks, beyond which like a bastion stood the white towers of office buildings. The northern suburbs extended until they vanished in the heat. Aubrey experienced a sense of the illusory, as if he were pursuing the city, never to reach it; never to obtain his answer. The Barossa Valley lay somewhere north of Adelaide, in what appeared to be an impenetrable haze.

The sensation depressed him.

Hyde collected their luggage, then the key of the hire car from the Avis desk, once more depositing Aubrey in the passenger lounge like an elderly, geriatric relative until he had completed his chores. He used the locker key he had been given at Sydney airport, and collected the pistol that had been left for him. Another Heckler & Koch VP 70. Three spare magazines. He slipped it into his suitcase. Ten minutes later, they were threading through Adelaide's noonday traffic towards their hotel.

Aubrey remained silent for several minutes, as if Hyde had been no more than a cab driver, then he said: 'I must call Shelley when we reach the hotel.' It sounded like an order to a member of some imagined entourage.

'Welcome back to the world,' Hyde replied. 'I thought you'd gone walkabout.'

'No,' Aubrey remarked in a pinched, offended little tone that admitted the half-truth of Hyde's observation. 'Far from it.'

'Anyway, welcome to Adelaide.'

White, windowed columns, palm trees lining the street, the strikingly cloudless sky; spring becoming summer almost as Aubrey watched.

'The 15th International Brigade, was that it?' he murmured.

'I was in the Scouts, not the Boys' Brigade.'

The hotel was opposite the Cheltenham Racecourse. Hyde turned the car off the road and into its drive.

'Shelley can verify that. I remember that number, the 15th. Locals. Spanish volunteers. The Aragonese units in the area . . .' the old man muttered with increasing excitement. 'There must be survivors, perhaps still living in the area. Madrid station could check . . .'

'We're here. You just carry on dreaming, I'll register.'

'Thank you, Patrick,' Aubrey replied icily.

Once ensconced in his room, Aubrey, tie loosened against the open-windowed heat and the humidity, dialled Shelley direct. Absent-mindedly, he emptied his pockets onto the bedside table while Hyde, slumped feet-up in a chair, sipped beer from the room's refrigerator. He stirred the collection of coins with his hand while he waited for Shelley to come on the line. He held up two British one pound coins.

'I told the Secretary to the Treasury, when these were first issued, that it was the experience of the Weimar Republic that a barrowful of notes was easier to push to the bakery than a barrowful of coins,' he remarked. 'He did not seem to appreciate the advice.'

'I never even saw a white fiver,' Hyde replied, staring at his can of lager. Aubrey waved him to silence, snapping into a more upright posture, old eyes brightly alert.

'Shelley—can you hear me?' A slight delay, then Shelley's voice was close enough to have come from the adjoining room.

Hyde stood up and walked to the open french windows. He stepped out onto the narrow balcony. Adelaide basked like a mottled animal in the sun. Aubrey's voice murmured behind him. To the north and west of the hotel, the city merged at the edge of shape and contour into the glittering, hazy sea. He breathed deeply, and closed his eyes.

It was some minutes later, when he had ceased to distinguish Aubrey's voice from the general murmur of traffic and insects around the potted plants on the balcony, that he was jolted into wakefulness by Aubrey's impatient voice at his side.

'I think we'll set out at once, don't you, Patrick?'

'You don't want a rest first?'

Aubrey searched Hyde's features for irony, and seemed satisfied. He shook his head. 'No. I must talk to Schiller as quickly as possible.' He paused, then: 'I'm unhappy with the momentum of events so far. Cut off from our Chinese friends—Wei and David Liu—and quite as ignorant and confused as I was whole days ago.'

Wittenberg.

'What is it?' Hyde asked, lowering the empty lager can from his lips. 'What's the matter?' Aubrey's face had contracted, his eyes become vague. His lips were pursed.

Wittenberg. Zimmermann was born and bred in Wittenberg. He had not imagined that. It was in the current profile dossier Shelley had included.

'Wittenberg,' he said.

'What about Wittenberg?'

Aubrey looked out across the landscape of Adelaide, his hands gripping the balcony rail, and saw the city retreating into the heat. Beyond the veil was Schiller. Was he any longer important? Was it 1938, or 1940 or 1945? 'Wittenberg is in the German Democratic Republic, Patrick.'

'Yes?'

'Zimmermann was born and lived in Wittenberg until he joined the army in 1934. His family, if they survived the war, would have found themselves living in the Russian Zone, and then in East Germany, after the war. Is that the most important fact about our German friend?'

'Christ!'

'He could have fallen into their hands *after* the war. Because of Wittenberg which is now called Lutherstadt. I must talk to Shelley again at once. He must get onto this . . .' Aubrey retreated into the shadows of the hot room. Hyde closed his eyes again, leaning against the window frame. He heard Aubrey dialling, the telephone purring like a cat as the dial returned after each digit. East Germany? Then Zimmermann could be KGB after all.

Wolfgang Zimmermann watched the rain running in mercury-swift tracks down the window of his hotel room, leaving orange, wriggling traces where the streetlamp shone blearily through. His room was in darkness. He had awoken with the decision to make the telephone call. He had moved to the telephone without thought, and begun dialling. It was one in the morning, but the number he had would enable him to reach Petya Kominski of the Bonn embassy staff in his flat.

Halfway through dialling the number, he paused to consider, and heard his heartbeat amplified in the lightless room, and his ragged breathing. Grinding his teeth, he continued to dial the remaining digits.

He heard the number ringing. He could picture the small, neat flat in Bonn, almost watch Kominski get out of bed, cross his bedroom, enter the hall, reach for the receiver . . .

'Yes?' Kominski said in German. 'Can I help you?'

'Petya—it's me, Wolfgang.'

'Wolf—what do you want? You woke me up.' The voice sounded almost peevish.

'I'm sorry. I want you to do me an important favour.'

'Oh?'

'Yes. You owe me a great many favours, Petya.' Zimmermann

could not decide whether his mounting irritation was with himself or the mildly truculent young Russian.

'All right. My promotion is largely due to you, I agree. What is it you want?'

'All the years, Petya. All the secret meetings . . .' Zimmermann reminded Kominski.

'Yes, yes,' Kominski replied, sounding bored. 'What do you want?'

The young Russian was actually *indifferent*. Zimmermann found it hard to believe. He said: 'I want you to find out which of your people are following me around. *That's* what I want.'

'What? You're joking.'

'I'm not. Think I can't recognise the type after all these years? There're two who are KGB, and there may be more I haven't spotted, dogging me night and day. Posing as *Pravda* people. Who are they?'

'No one. There's no one——'

'Don't give me that, you young puppy! I've *seen* them!'

'Don't get uptight, Wolf.' Kominski's slight American accent, his Moscow Radio newsreader's tones, had always rankled with Zimmermann. Now, expressing amused indifference as they did, they enraged him.

'*I am not uptight.* Don't you realize how dangerous this could be? *Now*, of all times? Within ten days of the Treaty being ratified. If it came out now that the KGB were in close proximity, if *anyone* suspected it, the newspapers on the Right would have a field day. Springer's press would blacken me, and our precious Treaty.'

'All right, calm down.'

'You don't seem to understand what I'm saying. I've been as good as accused of working for the KGB a hundred times. If those people on my tail were even suspected for a moment, the case would be proved. Get rid of them. Find out who they are and get rid of them!'

At the other end of the line, Kominski chuckled softly into the tense silence. His voice was relaxed, soothing, when he replied.

'You're working too hard, Wolf. You're over-tense. I tell you there's no one. *You?* Why should anyone need to follow you?'

'Tell your masters——'

'No. Sorry, Wolf, but you're imagining it all. There's no one following you, no one investigating you. I can assure you of that. Now, get a good night's sleep.'

'Kominski——'

The line crackled with ether for a moment, then clicked and purred. Zimmermann, taking the damp receiver from his cheek, stared at it as if he could not believe that Kominski had put an end to the call. Just like that, without listening, without believing a word . . .

He crashed the receiver onto its rest. The telephone fell onto the carpet. Zimmermann ignored it, striding across the darkened room, ignorning the pain from barking his shin against the metal edge of a coffee table. He squatted on his haunches before the door of the bar. He opened it. His face was twisted and male-volent in the pale light that the interior emitted. His still hand-some features became gaunt and hunted in the glow. He removed a miniature whisky, then another, and poured the contents of the two small bottles into a plastic glass. He angrily twisted ice out of a polythene rack into the glass. Then he swallowed almost vio-lently at the drink, making himself cough.

He could not believe it. He simply could not believe the manner of Kominski's reaction, his lack of concern, even interest. Every-thing depended upon the next ten days, everything. If he became suspect now, if any mud attached itself to him before the Treaty was ratified, then Vogel would lose the election, he would be ditched unceremoniously, and the Berlin Treaty might be aban-doned. Couldn't those clowns see that?

He paced the room, sipping at his drink, the ice setting his teeth on edge.

Now, *now*, he kept repeating to himself, increasingly afraid. After all this time, now? Now? Why *now?*

They drove north-east through Salisbury, Elizabeth and Gawler on Highway 20. The suburbs of Adelaide straggled, as if limp and dehydrated by the heat, abashed and daunted by the utterly cloudless sky, towards the foothills of the low Barossa Range. At Gawler, Hyde turned the car onto the Sturt Highway, and they began to climb through a tidy, neat landscape of orchards and small farms before the slopes became neatly, rigidly ornamented with vineyards. Buildings too ornate and large to be farms squatted amid the dark-green trellises of vines; the wineries of the Barossa Valley.

Aubrey sat impatiently next to Hyde like someone forced to divert his course. The refreshment of a shower and change of clothing had already evaporated. The air blowing through the open windows of the car was hot and dusty. His short-sleeved shirt was already beginning to stick to his body.

Hyde turned off the highway at Nuriootpa and headed for Angaston. In his impatience to settle a matter he no longer thought important, Aubrey had not even bothered to telephone the winery. They would arrive like casual visitors. mildly interested. For Hyde, the lack of concern seemed inappropriate. Schiller might still hold the key—at least, one of the keys—to the puzzle. He had known Zimmermann then, after all. The hills rose ahead of them, smokily-blue.

Schiller's Winery was a large, three-storey building surrounded by palm trees and lawns. Sprinklers dazzled as the sun caught their revolving spouts and columns. The winery and vineyards that Hans-Dieter Schiller had inherited had been built and planted and developed in 1851—there was a carved date above the door, in the cool deep shadows thrown by the verandah that ran along the second storey of the building. Aubrey could just make out the date as Hyde brought the car to a halt beneath a palm tree. Attached to the main building was a smaller, two-storey wing of late nineteenth-century design; presumably the house rather than the winery. There was a sense of wealth, quiet but evident, and pride about the two unequal wings. The larger winery indicated the source of the wealth, the house one of its fruits. Huge, merely ornamental, white-painted hogsheads stood beside the door of the winery like a medieval craftsman's guild symbols.

Hyde got out of the car. Aubrey watched a tall, fair-haired young man in rolled-up shirtsleeves and neatly-pressed shorts and white stockings stand for a moment in the doorway of the winery, then come towards them. Aubrey was shocked. The young man reminded him forcibly of his own memories of Zimmermann. Germanic, almost arrogant, at ease and assured.

'G'day, can I help you?' he asked Hyde, merely glancing at Aubrey. His voice and accent were undoubtedly Australian. The image of Zimmermann dissipated.

'Wonder if we could have a word with the owner?'

'Mr Schiller? You're out of luck, mate. He's gone walkabout. Sorry. What did you want him for?'

'My boss here'—Hyde indicated the car and Aubrey—'wine correspondent for the Diner's Club magazine. Know it?' The young man shook his head.

'Use American Express myself,' he remarked.

'He's in Australia on holiday—been drinking a lot of your stuff. Wants to interview the owner. Bloody shame he's away.'

'What do you do? Same line?'

'Stringer for a few European magazines—you know the sort of thing. Trying to get the Poms and the rest of 'em to find out where we are.'

'Oh.'

Aubrey was amused at Hyde's exaggerated, hard-boiled accent and manner. He nodded as the young man inspected him, then crossed to the car and held out his hand. Aubrey shook it.

'Name's Peter,' he said. 'I'm the office manager. I could help— or Mr Schiller's daughter?' He leaned closer to the window of the car. 'Matter of fact,' he confided, 'she runs the place these days. The old man's taken up photography. He's on one of his trips right now.' Aubrey controlled the disappointment he felt leaking into his expression. 'Had a book published last year. Big job, all colour. Cost almost twenty dollars to buy it.'

'I see,' Aubrey murmured. 'I really had no idea . . .'

'You're a real Pom, all right. Look, you want to talk to Miss Schiller? She's over at the house, going through the accounts for the week. She won't mind being interrupted.'

'Yes, certainly,' Aubrey said with forced enthusiasm. He opened the door and climbed out. The sunlight lanced down through the blade-like leaves of the palm tree. 'Thank you. If you'd be so good as to introduce us—my name is Kenneth Aubrey.'

Hyde was grinning at Aubrey's affected pomposity.

'Sure. Follow me.'

Peter left them standing in the shade of the first-floor verandah that ran along the house wing of the building. They heard knocking, then voices. A chair creaked, then they heard footsteps. Aubrey negligently held the back of a cane chair that stood to one side of the door, one of four arranged around a white-painted metal table, intricately patterned. Hyde shuffled his feet like a visitor of dubious social standing, hands behind his back.

The woman was about thirty. Her fair hair was scraped back from her forehead, and her eyes were pale blue. Her skin was unsoftened by make-up, except for lipstick, and appeared more

168

tanned than merely suntanned. It seemed incongruous that she should be emerging from indoors. She wore a check blouse and slim blue denims. Aubrey held out his hand. She took it in a cool, firm grip.

'Mr Aubrey? I'm Clare Schiller. *Signature* magazine?' Aubrey nodded. The woman seemed doubtful rather than flattered. 'Peter, bring us some '81 and '82 bottles of riesling. The *qualitats* through to—*auslese?*' she asked, turning to Aubrey again, who nodded once more. 'And some of the '77 cabernet.'

'Sure.' Peter re-entered the house.

'Make yourselves comfortable,' Clare Schiller said, indicating the table and chairs beside the door.

Once they were seated, she seemed to await some utterance from her guests. Her eyes were clear, sharply-focused, and the faint lines around them might have been caused as much by inner amusement as by sunlight. Peter returned, wheeling a wine-cooler and opened it, to display a number of tall bottles. Then he brought the glasses and the bottles of red wine.

The woman poured glasses of pale Schiller's Rhine Riesling for them. Aubrey sipped in an informed, birdlike manner. Hyde, in persona, swallowed half the glass in a gulp.

'Very pleasant,' Aubrey remarked.

'And if you're a wine correspondent, I'm Ned Kelly's sister,' the woman commented. She seemed unruffled. Hyde laughed, and wine which went up his nose made him cough. 'And your mate's a real connoisseur, I can see that. What do you want with my father?'

'I—um,' Aubrey began.

'Look, you're drinking one of our poorest years in the last ten. Can't you tell?'

'Unfamiliar . . .' Aubrey murmured.

Clare Schiller threw the contents of Aubrey's glass towards the sunlight. It glittered, then became a brown wet spot on the drive. She opened a second bottle, and filled his glass.

'Try that.'

'Delicious,' he said, recognising its superior quality. 'The '82, I see.'

'Young and beautiful. Now you're drinking the good stuff, tell me what game you're playing.'

'Ah.' Aubrey reached into his pocket and handed Clare Schiller a folded piece of paper. 'You can ring that Canberra number now, if you wish. In turn, to confirm what you might be told, they will put you through to—shall we say the police?'

'Police?'

'Or you can listen to my story now and confirm it later.'

She was thoughtfully silent for a few moments, sipping absently at her own wine, then she said: 'Tell your story. You——' she added, turning to Hyde.

'Yes?'

'You can go on drinking the '81.'

'Right.'

Aubrey launched into his explanation. He was frank with the woman, though not entirely. He spoke for perhaps five minutes, sipping from time to time at the wine, the woman filling his glass once while he spoke. Aubrey provided no background concerning the nature of the doubts regarding Zimmermann, merely the necessity of talking to her father about the man's Spanish experiences. Aubrey had decided that a cover story would be inappropriate. It was as if he were already talking to her father.

When he had finished, she remained silent for some minutes. Her eyes moved over an internal ledger, balancing his account. Then she looked up, and nodded.

'I realise you've told me a lot less than half, but I guess what you've said is something like the truth. My father's on a photography trip. Before I tell you where, I'll ring this number.' She stood up and went into the house.

'I'll bet she asks directory enquiries what the number of the British High Commission is,' Hyde remarked. 'What's wrong with the '81, anyway?'

'I'd be disappointed if she didn't,' Aubrey replied. 'Well, what do you think?'

'What do you want to do? You want to chase after him?'

Aubrey looked over his shoulder, as if back towards Adelaide and its airport. 'I'll be out of touch with Shelley,' he fretted. 'And yet . . . ? The girl gives me confidence. If she's like her father, he'll have forgotten nothing, he'll be shrewd. He may have a good idea . . .'

'Give Shelley a bloody chance! You only gave him his orders an hour or so ago. You've got—what, a couple of days?'

'I have less than ten before the Treaty's signed . . .'

170

Clare Schiller emerged from the shadows inside the doorway.

'That extension number you gave me? I spoke to a Mr Price, a Third Secretary or something at the High Commission. He seems to think you're straight. Quite polite, he was.' She nodded mockingly, then sat down. Behind her head, pendulous fuchsias added to the exoticism of a kookaburra's ringing laugh. Hyde's head snapped up, and he grinned. 'Welcome home, cobber,' the woman drawled with evident irony and amusement.

'Miss Schiller, where is your father?'

She was clutching a large book on her lap. She held it up by way of explanation. *Hidden Australia* was lettered above a photograph of a bird with a small snake in its mouth. The picture was sharp, vivid, keenly alive. The photographer was H-D. Schiller.

'That's what my father does these days. He's quite good, too. Good job I'm as good at running his bloody winery for him, isn't it?' The remark was made with only the slightest tinge of bitterness.

'Where is he now?'

'Cooper's Creek.' She looked at Hyde, whose face fell.

'Is that far?'

'North through the Flinders to Lake Eyre, turn right,' Hyde said. 'Maybe five hundred miles. Trouble is, the Creek's two hundred miles or more long, just in South Australia.' He turned to Clare Schiller. 'Can you be more precise? Can you get in touch with him?'

Aubrey appeared sunk in some private and disappointed reverie. He paid no attention to Hyde's questions, or the girl's reply.

'He's working the Creek west to east. He calls in every couple of days.'

'When did he leave?'

'Last week.'

'Is he going through the Flinders first—taking snaps there?' The girl nodded. 'Where's the last place he called you from?'

She frowned. 'Day before yesterday. Um, Wilpena—no, that was the time before. Nearer Leigh Creek.'

'Got a map?'

'Yes.'

'Get it. Please.'

Clare hurried into the house. Hyde watched the silent, meditative Aubrey and had no idea what decision the old man would make. The girl was back with the large-scale map of South Australia within seconds. She unfolded it on the table.

'Here,' she said.

'Then he was almost out of the Flinders Range two day ago. Mm.' He looked up at the girl. 'When will he ring again?'

'Today, tomorrow . . .' She shrugged. 'He'll ring some time. He always does. Pretends to ask after business.' She shook her head with a smile. 'You really do want to talk to him, don't you?'

Hyde nodded. He studied the map. His finger traced a black line north. 'Birdsville Track. We might be able to head him off, if we get a bloody move on.'

'If you go like a bat out of hell you might,' Clare observed.

'Too right. I'll need a Land Rover, supplies, the whole bloody shooting match.'

'What about the wine correspondent?'

'Mr Aubrey—*sir*.'

The woman's eyes widened in surprise.

'Yes, Patrick?'

'Say the word—do we go or not?'

'I——' He paused, then shrugged. 'I must *do* something!' he suddenly snapped. 'I am at the other end of the world from the epicentre of this disturbance. Yes—we must go.'

'Right, then we'd better head back to town. There's a lot to do, and not enough time to do it in.' He looked at Clare Schiller. 'Love you and leave you.'

'Tell me something new,' she remarked with surprising bitterness.

'You asked around?'

'Yes.'

'And?'

'The owner of the vineyard, Schiller, is on a photography trip up north.'

'Where, precisely?'

'Cooper's Creek.'

'And Hyde and Aubrey must be about to follow him in the Land Rover they have hired. Good, then we must follow—by car and by aircraft, just to be certain. Schiller was a wartime comrade of Zimmermann. Evidently that acquaintance has become vitally important to Aubrey. As it has to ourselves. We'd better find him first.'

'Yes, Comrade General.'
'Don't call me that! *Mister Jones*, understand?'
'Yes, Mr—Jones.'

SEVEN:

Outback

From his vantage point on a wooden bench near the Dingdao Temple, David Liu watched the small, neat man emerge from the door of the hotel which overlooked the East Lake. Behind the hotel, the buildings of the three municipalities of Wu Han reached into a late summer, humid, smoggy sky. Inside, in one of those rooms where the windows were shaded by overhanging, ornamental eaves, Wolfgang Zimmermann had first fallen ill during his visit to the city. And the small, neat man—Liu glanced again at the snapshot in his hand—was the hotel doctor who had first attended him.

The doctor strolled towards the trolley-bus stop near the lakeside. He dabbed lightly and fussily at his forehead with a very white handkerchief, doubtless regretting the absence of the hotel's air conditioning. He walked along the water's edge, seemingly amused by the approach of glossy ducks and the wading intentness of bright water birds.

Liu left his seat, patting his breast pocket to assure himself once more that he carried the details of his cover: his means of questioning the doctor.

Liu's journey from Shanghai to Wu Han the previous day had been uneventful. He had booked into the Sheng Li hotel on the other bank of the Yangtse River, in the Hankou municipality. It was a sufficiently good hotel for a minor government official to use. His room overlooked the river and, beyond it, the dykes and the water country that surrounded the city. Factory chimneys belched smoke, power stations fumed, steel plants—some of which the West Germans had helped to finance and construct, hence one of the motives for Zimmermann's visit—flared and erupted between himself and the green flat plains. The first hills of the distant Tapieh Shan were hidden in humid smog.

He had slept for much of the journey from Shanghai. His papers had been inspected three times while he was still at Shanghai station, and another twice on the train; and had held up.

Then they were scrutinized at the barrier of Wu Han station, then once more at the hotel desk. Each time they had been greeted by a perceptible deference; at the least, with a recognition of equality. Fleeting, half-seen impressions of the journey remained with him, particularly the lowering, dark, smog-haloed monster of an industrial city that seemed to have settled on the fertile green plain of the Yangtse.

He had rung the East Lake Hotel but had not spoken to the doctor, merely affirmed his duty shift. He had no idea whether or not Frederickson had yet arrived in Wu Han, his industrialists in tow. Strangely, he did not concern himself. Leaving Shanghai, he had left many things: the girl, Bin, Frederickson, immediate danger. In Wu Han, he was beginning again, and beginning effectively, properly. First this doctor, then the specialist who had treated Zimmermann at Wu Han's Hospital of October 1911. He would question them both. He possessed an unexpected and welcome confidence that either or both of them would provide the answers he sought.

The doctor held his bag in front of him in both hands as he stood waiting for the trolley-bus. Beyond him, the East Lake and the low wooden hills of its surrounding parks belied the industrialization of the city. It might, except for the temperature, have been an early morning mist that hazed the air. Liu joined the small queue for the trolley-bus, three places behind the doctor.

Their journey took them out of the parkland around the lake, down the wide and tree-lined Wu luo lu Street towards the huge Changjiang Bridge swooping over the Yangtse. Liu watched the freighters and barges. The rumble of a train on the lower level of the bridge was apparent through the soles of his shoes. Cyclists and pedestrians crossing the bridge lent the city the same sense of urgency possessed by Shanghai. Hoardings exhorted the population to continue the semi-sacred work of modernization, promising them television sets and dreamed-of-cars as their reward for even greater efforts. Liu was stimulated and enervated at the same time by the messages the hoardings offered.

The trolley-bus trundled beneath the rounded hump of Tortoise Hill, then crossed the Han River towards the orderly, wide boulevards of Hankou municipality. Liu watched the doctor as they neared the residential district off Zhongshan Boulevard. When the doctor stood up and eased his way through the standing passengers towards the doors, Liu rose and followed him. Events were moving his way. The doctor evidently lived near the Sheng Li hotel. Keeping fifty yards behind, having paused to retie a shoelace, Liu followed the doctor towards the river. Modern apartment blocks flanked the quiet street. The leaves were beginning to turn brown and gold on the trees, as if the humid, hot air was somehow roasting them.

Liu followed him up the steps of an apartment block, now only a few yards behind. The doctor, turning his head at the sound of more urgent footsteps than his own, saw Liu instantly approach him, a card in his hand.

'Doctor Tai?' Liu asked, his voice carefully official. The doctor assented with a careful nod of his head which might have been an embryonic bow; an anticipation of rank. 'My name is Liu— Public Security from Shanghai.' He flashed the card at Tai, allowing him to recognize the small official photograph and read the rank and status of the stranger. Tai nodded his head once more; the bow was more evident. The metamorphosis of the promoted Party official into a minor policeman had been effected. Liu's authority had increased, required deference.

'Yes?' Tai asked, seemingly untroubled. He, too, was a Party man, and wore his membership like a protective carapace. 'What is it?'

'I wish to ask you some questions.'

'Concerning myself?' Worry flickered for a moment in his dark, tired eyes. Tai was perhaps no more than forty. He felt himself secure—unless the Party had somehow changed the parameters of criminality. Deng's uncertain, fearful China stared out at Liu for a moment.

'No,' Liu assured him, shaking his head. 'You may be in possession of knowledge we require, that is all. May I come in?'

'Certainly.' For a moment, the seemingly-solid structure of Doctor Tai's life and position had been threatened by a distant tremor. Now that he had established that the epicentre was well away from himself, assurance leaked back into his features. 'Please follow me.'

They ascended to the top floor of the apartment block in a creaking, slow lift. Tai ushered Liu down a narrow, thinly-carpeted corridor to a dark wooden flush door. He unlocked it, showing in his unexpected guest. The plain bare living room informed Liu that Tai was a fastidious, unacquisitive bachelor.

'Tea?' Tai asked.

'Perhaps later.'

'Sit down, please. Tell me why you have had to travel up from Shanghai to see me.' Only some of the assurance was adopted; much of it derived, presumably, from Tai's competence, his secure and unruffled past. Liu felt he might need to shake that confidence. On the other hand, Tai seemed prepared to be helpful.

Liu removed a notebook from his pocket, and a pen. He pretended to consult notes. The room was airless, dry. 'My enquiries concern the German diplomat, Zimmermann,' he began.

'Yes?' Tai replied, genuinely puzzled. Was that a quick flicker of suspicion, secrecy there? Liu could not be certain. 'What of him? That was some months ago. As you know, he was transferred to Shanghai soon after he entered the hospital here. I merely attended——'

'Yes, you attended him when he first fell ill.'

'I was on duty at that time. My report is with your superiors in Shanghai, I am certain.'

'Yes. I have read it,' said Liu slowly, allowing an ambiguity of tone to possess his voice.

'Well, then . . .'

'I am not necessarily concerned with the medical details, Doctor. My superiors are interested in other matters.'

'I see. Am I permitted to know——?'

'Of course,' Liu snapped. 'Otherwise, you could not help me.' Liu leaned confidentially forward. 'The illness was most embarrasing, you understand . . .' Tai nodded cautiously, as if he felt himself being drawn towards the admission of some unspecified guilt. 'Anyone responsible for that embarrassment to the People's Republic and to the leadership would be in serious trouble . . .'

'Responsible? How responsible?'

'I believe you diagnosed food poisoning?' Tai nodded. 'Your report does not indicate how many other cases of food posioning occurred at the same time, in the hotel.'

'I——'

Liu felt an inward relief. His briefing by Buckholz had indicated Zimmermann was alone in his induced illness, but the report was based on hearsay, on second and third-hand accounts gathered over more than a month. Yet it had been true.

'There were no others?'

'No.'

'Strange. What caused the illness?'

177

'Snake—I am convinced it was the snake,' Tai said hurriedly. 'Perhaps the fish, but more likely the snake.' Tai essayed a smile intended to charm. 'Westerners should not be so adventurous when first coming to China.'

'Did any of his party have the snake?'

'I—do not think so. Officer Liu?'

'Yes?'

'What is the purpose of this enquiry? IIow important is it that the food he ate is known?'

'If it *was* the food that caused the poisoning . . .' Liu said, enunciating carefully. Tai's features paled, then he coughed and again attempted the smile.

'I am certain it was the food—so were the doctors at the hospital here. I was never told what they diagnosed in Shanghai.'

'Does food poisoning usually cause delirium?'

'Any fever may, depending on its severity—why?'

'Do you agree, doctor, that there are elements present in our society who wish the failure of the Revolution, who wish to undermine Chairman Deng's glorious Four Modernizations? Who would like to tie China's legs together in the race to the year 2000?'

Tai looked appalled by the jargon and its message of treachery. The ripples he had seen coming in his direction had become a wave buffeting against him, with rougher seas behind it.

'I—suppose so . . .'

'Here, in Wu Han, scene of the first victorious battle of the 1911 Revolution,' Liu continued, his voice mounting, his eyes increasingly, deliberately glazed, 'home of the National Peasant Movement Institute, scene of key battles with the Guomindang which paved the way for our final victory . . . In *this city*, there have been revisionist plots, trouble fomented among the peasants and workers by filthy lickspittle counter-Revolutionary elements!' Liu had half-risen from his seat. He settled back into it. Tai's face was white, his hands rubbing each other in distress on his lap. His knees were pressed primly together. 'You understand me, Doctor? There are elements who would have delighted in the embarrassment to the leadership, to Noble Steersman Deng . . .' Liu flung in the *People's Daily* epithet which always accompanied reference to the Chairman, further establishing his conformist fanaticism to Tai. 'Would they not?'

'I—I suppose it is possible . . .' Tai kept looking towards the window as if seeking escape.

'It is very possible. That is my mission, Doctor.' Liu leaned confidentially forward in his chair. 'Can you say that this Westerner was not poisoned deliberately?'

There was a silence then, long and tense. Liu saw the conflicting emotions on Tai's face with a sense of disappointment. It seemed that Tai perhaps had suspected a deliberate act of poisoning, had suspected there was something unusual, not even logical, about Zimmermann's illness, but he knew nothing. He was certain of nothing, possessed no facts. Liu decided to pursue the line of questioning no further as soon as Tai shook his head.

'To me,' the doctor said slowly, his voice diminished and small in the plain, bare room, 'there was nothing unusual about the case. You are privy to matters I know nothing about. I am afraid I cannot help you. I know nothing. I merely examined this man, relieved his distress as much as I could, and summoned an ambulance. His symptoms were consistent with food poisoning.'

'I see,' Liu replied with an evident disappointment which indicated belief in Tai's statement. The doctor appeared relieved. Liu shrugged. 'Well, there are no more questions.' Tai's relief flourished. 'You will, of course, report nothing of this conversation.' Tai obediently shook his head and rose unsteadily to his feet. He was taller than Liu, but diminished by his sudden encounter with what he regarded as police authority, police suspicion. Greater authority, confidence and assurance than his own had knocked on his door, demanding entry.

'No, of course not,' he said quietly.

Liu was disappointed. Considering Tai, he had believed the line of questioning was right; brutal, sinister, surprising. Yet it had opened no doors for him. Tai knew nothing, was in no way privy to any suspicious circumstances regarding the illness of Zimmermann.

'How did you talk to him? Do you speak his language?' Liu asked.

'An interpreter accompanied me to his suite. Also, one of his staff was there, who spoke Mandarin well.'

'I see. Delirious, wasn't he?'

'Not when I treated him, no. Disorientated, in pain—but when conscious, quite lucid.'

'I see. Thank you, Doctor Tai. Good day.'

'Good day.'

As Liu walked towards the lift, it seemed to him that Tai

slammed the door with a vast feeling of relief. Or perhaps nerveless fingers could not control the force they applied to closing the the door. The echo of its slamming followed Liu down the corridor.

The sky was cloudless, uniformly blue except where it was rendered a brassy colour around the noon sun. Aubrey sat in the shadow of a canopy which was fastened to the side of the Land Rover and supported like a shop awning by two thin metal poles. On his lap Buckholz's transcript of the interrogation of Wolfgang Zimmermann went unregarded for a moment as he attended to Hyde's restlessness.

'What's the matter, Hyde?'

'I—I want to check we're not being followed.'

'What?'

'Just to make sure.'

'You suspect something?'

'One car—been with us since we left Hawker. Keeping more or less to our speed, well back behind us.'

'I see.' Hyde was rubbing his bare arms as if, impossibly, he felt cold. 'Very well. Where is it now?'

Hyde shook his head. 'It passed when we pulled off the road. If it's interested, it won't be far away.' Dramatically, and perhaps for self-assurance, Hyde removed the pistol from the small of his back, and checked the magazine. 'OK,' he said.

'I gather you were looking for bugs under the car just now?'

'I didn't find one. But they don't need one, do they? This isn't London. There aren't too many places to go to on this road.' He waved his arm to indicate the country around them.

Hyde had stopped for their midday meal and rest within the boundaries of the Flinders Range National Park. They had already driven more than a hundred miles north of Port Augusta, where they had spent the night in a motel after arriving late from Adelaide.

'Very well. I'll keep alert,' Aubrey promised.

'Your gun?' Aubrey patted the briefcase beside him on the blanket on which he was seated. 'Right. See you.'

Aubrey watched Hyde move away from the shade of the Land Rover, his upper torso bisected by the line of the open bonnet. Almost the moment he was gone, Aubrey felt the heat assail him, making him immediately drowsy. It was as if the heat aided their pursuers, if such pursuit existed. Reluctantly, Aubrey got to his feet and put his straw hat on his head, stepping out of the shade into a fierce heat that might have been emitted from one of the foundries of Whyalla that had flared into the hot night as they drove north towards Port Augusta. All Aubrey recollected of that drive was a fleeting, neon-lit, star-bright landscape and sky which had followed the hiring of the Land Rover and purchase of supplies in Salisbury. Aubrey had telephoned the hotel and the British High Commission in Canberra while Hyde obtained water, food, petrol, emergency equipment.

When Aubrey had climbed into the Land Rover, he had been struck by its air of expedition, the prophecy it suggested of desert and wild place. It had seemed unreal. In a way, even deep into the Flinders Range, it still seemed unreal except for the heat. St Mary's Peak was steel-grey a little to the south, the river red gums in full dark leaf surrounded the campsite; the hills south of the Brachina Gorge were dark and glossy with vegetation. There was grass as well as dust and stony, flinty creek beds. After the farming country on the edge of the southern extent of the mountain range, this place still did not unnerve or appear alien. Thus far, Aubrey had moved north through seemingly familiar landscapes.

He moved about slowly, watching Hyde as he became a speck of shirt and light slacks climbing the slight incline back towards the road. Then a rock obscured him, the shadow of a group of heavy-boled gums caused him to vanish.

At that moment Aubrey did feel isolated and alone, until he saw Hyde again, climbing slowly up the slope of a shallow, sun-crowned cliff. Presumably he was taking some kind of shortcut. He topped the cliff, and disappeared. Unsettled, conscious of the silence which the noise of insects and the laughter of a bird did nothing to lessen, Aubrey returned to the shade of the canopy and to the somehow real companion of their journey: Zimmermann. He remembered lines he thought belonged to Eliot. *Who is the third who walks always beside you?* And again, *There is always another one walking beside you . . .*

He attended to Buckholz's file. Memories of Zimmermann's escape from that attic room in Louvain pricked his consciousness for a moment. Waking with a painful jaw, seeing groggily the chair balanced on the bed, beneath the damaged skylight; the door open where Zimmermann had, for some reason, re-entered the room, to attempt escape via the roof. His own tottering climb onto the shabby chair, its crazy tilting, his effort to heave himself through the skylight and the chair slipping away from under his feet so that he was left hanging above the bed, elbows bent and the perspiration beginning to break out on his forehead and beneath his arms. Then he had heaved his head through the skylight and looked around, his face cooled by a mild breeze. Zimmermann was crouching at the edge of the sloping, green-tiled roof, Aubrey's pistol still in one hand, his face slowly displaying the familiar smile. Aubrey had scrabbled unathletically onto the roof and inched his way down its slope towards the German. At no time did Zimmermann point the pistol in his direction; it was as if he had forgotten the gun. When Aubrey reached him, the German had shrugged and simply handed it over. They had retreated back up the roof to the skylight to the accompaniment of artillery fire, answered now more hesitantly and distantly, like the shouts of an unsuccessful bully making empty threats, by the German tanks. Zimmermann, pausing at the attic window of another empty room, looked back at Aubrey with no trace of regret or disappointment on his features.

Memory had almost tricked him into sleep. Shaking his head to lighten its sense of numbness, Aubrey conscientiously quartered the scene in front of him, squinting into the hard glare and the shadows thrown by cliffs and gum trees. No one. He attended to the files open on his lap.

It was quite easy now to take up Buckholz's interrogation of Zimmermann like a familiar book. More than a narrative, it had become a drama in Aubrey's imagination. He saw GIs moving armed and unfamiliar and often helmeted, khaki ghosts, through the panelled rooms and flagged and pillared halls of the castle that Buckholz's section of G-2 had commandeered as their headquarters; the stamp and click of boots, the out-of-place accents, the combination of awe and disrespect.

Aubrey read a passage that had intrigued and troubled him earlier. Only Buckholz was present; Lieutenant Waleski was engaged in a separate interrogation, presumably in his inimitable style. There was brandy and cigars, a civilized atmosphere. Notes in Buckholz's familiar handwriting set the scene like a careful dramatist.

Zimmermann had been open, even indiscreet, with the American. There were the phrases—*I would have supported a plot even before the war . . . Stauffenberg's only error was to fail . . . Yes, my superior, General Gehlen, has always been loyal—it's where he and I disagree . . .*

It seemed evident to Aubrey that Buckholz's mind had already turned towards the possibility of recruiting Zimmermann for some post-war intelligence work for the Americans, for the questions proceeded to the Soviet Union in an obvious manner. Zimmermann's answers, too, were clear and pointed. An insect buzzed near Aubrey's head. He brushed it aside, finding his temperature rise even from that small effort.

No, I accept that Stalin made mistakes . . . I don't think you Americans have much to boast of—what about your Negro population's freedom? . . .

Aubrey flicked over the page.

You must rememger that the Revolution attempted, is still attempting, to drag Russia into the twentieth century—of course there have been mistakes . . . Yes, there is much to admire . . .

Aubrey turned another page, then another, as if anxious to reach the resolution of some dramatic, fictional crisis. He felt his temperature mounting steadily as he searched the pages.

Socialism—Hitler? Incompatible . . . Aubrey smiled. He could hear the words on Zimmermann's lips. *Lenin says . . .* Aubrey let his eyes roam the succeeding pages. *Marx says . . . Lenin says . . .*

He looked up with a jerky movement of his head. The sunlight beyond the canopy glared at him. The landscape swam into a haze, reformed. The bald light and inky shadows hurt his eyes.

He closed the transcript after noting that an army stenographer had been present. It was a faithful account made at the time, not a later recollection. He sighed with dissatisfaction. Zimmermann? A Marxist-Leninist mouthpiece, devoid of originality of mind or expression?

Was Zimmermann playing a game—avoiding any possible recruitment by the Americans by pretending socialist sympathies? Was this really Zimmermann, after five years of war and on the verge of defeat, beaten, captive, weary?

Aubrey patted the transcript, almost smiling. It was as if he anticipated pleasures to come from an entertaining, enthralling narrative. Yet he was troubled, also.

Zimmermann was a German, not a Russian. Zimmermann had encountered the NKVD in the person of Aladko, in Spain. He had been under no illusions then. He had not swallowed the conformism of National Socialism—would he have been open to

183

persuasion now? If he was at pains to impress his lack of persuasion by Aladko in 1940, why was he so remiss as to indicate Russian sympathies in 1945? One record contradicted the other.

Aubrey shook his head. Anticipation, yes. But not of pleasure or amusement. The file beneath his hand was somehow dangerous—suspicious and unreal . . .

Unreal?

The word returned, even though he tried to banish it. It was, somehow, unreal. Untrue?

Hyde huddled in the cleft in the rocks overlooking a neat, ordered campsite with its barbecue pit and wooden toilet hut. He might have been no more than twenty miles from the outskirts of Sydney or Melbourne or Adelaide. The shade of a narrow-boled blue gum fell across Hyde's place of concealment. A moment before he had reached it, a pair of rock wallabies had bounced away across the cliffs, causing the men below him to look up. Seeing the moving wallabies, they had laughed and taken no further interest in the rocks above them.

Three steaks on the barbecue grill, sausages enough for three. Only two men, however, in shorts and bright shirts were standing near the van; which meant that there was a third man watching the Land Rover just as he was watching the Volkswagen. He needed to get back to Aubrey.

He studied the two men through his field glasses. He recognised neither of them. Their voices floated up to him, quiet but distinct. Their Australian accent disturbed him as a species of treachery rather than mere danger. He could smell the steaks, see the blue smoke ascending from the grill in a thin, straight line. A kookaburra laughed in the tree above him.

Three men, then. No sign of Petrunin. Even the thought of the man made him chilly. The Russian had achieved the significance of a destiny, a fate that lay ahead even as it pursued him. He did not intentionally enlarge or dignify Petrunin in this way, but his shoulder ached with the old wound whenever he thought of the man. He knew, with a fine and chilling clarity, that Petrunin would be happy to see him dead; not even beaten or outboxed, just dead.

He levered himself back among the rocks to the bole of the gum. A bright spider bobbed and wobbled along a thread of its web, spun around a tiny clump of yellow wild flowers. They had been secure, come all the way from Hong Kong to the South Australian outback, and Petrunin was, at least his people were, still no more than a step behind them. Apparently, he was inescapable.

Hyde brushed the spider's web and the tuft of flowers deliberately as he rose. The spider bobbed violently, but clung onto the thread, upside down. The flowers stilled, the thread quieted. The spider continued. Hyde, despite himself, grinned. Then he scuttled his way down the opposite side of the cliff, making his way back to Aubrey and the Land Rover as quickly as he could.

The low wooden bungalow which was the home of the hospital specialist who had examined and treated Zimmermann during his confinement in Wu Han was on the outskirts of the municipality of Wu Chang, part of a privileged development for important professional and Party men near the East Lake. There were other such developments in the conurbation of Wu Han, especially where the banks, offices and palaces of colonial days survived in Hankou.

There was space here, and the trees of the parks around the vast lake masked the industrial city that lay to the west, where the low sun was creating a purpled, smoky gold wash of the sky as its rays struck through the industrial haze. Eastwards, the gold was tinged with pink above the advancing dark blue line of night. Skeletal, fragile pagodas rose above low trees. Delicate willow-pattern bridges arched over narrow inlets where moving swans dragged the water into creases behind them. A few small boats were being poled or oared across the smooth, glass-like water. David Liu breathed deeply. The air was almost fresh after the humid day, with even the merest hint of cold and autumn.

He looked at his watch. Eight-thirty. The specialist had been at home for half-an-hour. He had arrived in a small, fawn car, which was itself another token of esteem and importance, just like the bungalow. There was warm light at the window, and music from inside. Liu could hear hedge-clippers clicking from an adjoining property, even the whisper of a lawn sprinkler. Wu Han's privileged, its elite, resided beside the East Lake.

He moved swiftly towards the doctor's front door. This, he told himself, was the significant encounter. This man knew the drugs, the visitors, the medical condition. He would have heard the Russian spoken, known the nature of the questions asked under drugs, the quality of the answers given. The man could prove that Zimmermann was a KGB agent.

Or prove the opposite?

Liu dismissed the question and rang the doorbell. It chimed gently inside the house, like a glass bell. He turned swiftly to look once more at the lake as it slipped into darkness, and then the door was opened. A small old man bowed.

'Sir?' he asked. Liu was transported back through time to the China his grandfather remembered. A servant?

'I wish to see Doctor Meng.' Liu's voice hinted at authority, purpose. The old man's face crumpled into sharper lines, rivulets of old fears suddenly in spate.

'Yes?' He seemed at a loss. Such people did not come to this house; this refuge.

Liu handed him his policeman's ID. It was the first swift, telling blow in the encounter he had determined should take place between himself and Meng. Inside, the sleek-haired, upright, tall specialist might already be wondering who his visitor was. He had no idea what was coming to him, Liu thought with a certain savage satisfaction.

'Tell Doctor Meng I have some questions for him.'

The old man hurried away into the warm shadows of the hall and through a door into a well-lighted room. Soft laughter was silenced for a moment, then there was a murmur of voices, the scrape of a chair, and then a taller figure than that of the old man was coming to the front door.

Meng was wearing a silk dressing-gown in deep golden and brown shades. A dragon appeared at his left shoulder. He was confident, almost amused, slightly puzzled.

'How can I help you?' he asked.

'I—have some confidential enquiries to make, doctor. I believe you can help me.'

'They concern me or my family?' Meng asked loftily.

'Not directly, no.'

'Then you had better come in, officer——?' He looked at the ID card for a moment, then handed it back. 'Officer Liu. Come in. We can talk in my study.'

Liu entered the bungalow. Rich and spicy aromas of a meal greeted him, and the smell of incense. There were deep rugs on the floor of the hall.

Yes, he thought. This man is wealthy, intelligent, privileged.

He will know. Liu recalled the photographs he had seen the moment before the first shots in the Yu Garden. Drugs, treatment, visitors. This man would *know*. He was almost there . . .

'Herr Professor Zimmermann, are you then prepared to categorically deny the insinuations of this newspaper story?'

The voice of the Press Association correspondent, an Englishman Zimmermann normally respected and to whom he might well have been amicable, seemed a laconic, insulting drawl. The press conference was crowded, of course; not unexpectedly, in view of the story carried by the early editions of the *Dusseldorfer Abendzeitung*. According to the members of Vogel's press staff it was also in most of the principal West German evening newspapers. Foreign pressmen, in particular the British and the Americans, were much in evidence and prepared to shout their questions above the hubbub created by the German press corps covering Vogel's campaign.

'Of course I deny it!' Zimmermann snapped, immediately regretting the evident irritation in his tone. The perspective of the Springer press in Berlin and Hamburg, the popular Sundays, then the weeklies, opened before him, daunting and angering him. A field day, it would be called.

'What, precisely, do you refute?' the Press Association man asked. The conference room of the Dusseldorf Hilton had fallen silent. Eyes watched him carefully from behind a veil of cigarette smoke. Hands were poised over notepads. The two press aides who flanked him were no longer real. He was alone on the dais, behind the long table with its crisp white cloth and water jug and glasses and array of microphones like steel flowers.

Zimmermann leant back in his chair, a conscious gesture of assurance at variance with his feelings. 'Everything, naturally. Except the details concerning the Treaty itself—a few of which are correct.'

A few droplets of laughter, insufficient to refresh. The room was hot, eager; not hostile—not yet—but the smell of a story, a possible scandal or at the least a *cause célèbre*, was as redolent as blood.

'There are no secret clauses in the Treaty?' the correspondent from *Die Welt* demanded to know.

Zimmermann spread his hands above the white cloth, and shook his head.

'There are not.'

'What about the accusations of secret trade agreements—huge trade credits?' *Suddeutsche Zeitung* of Munich. Zimmermann's familiarity with, and knowledge of, the press corps now seemed fatuous and redundant. 'The story calls it a massive bribe.'

Of course, they were all furious that their papers hadn't carried the story, which had originated with a so-called exclusive in *Bild* that morning. All the paraphernalia—unnamed sources, classified evidence, more to come . . .

The evening papers had gutted it, built on it, speculated and fantasized about it. Now the dailies wanted their hundred marks' worth.

'That is nonsense. The full text of the Treaty has been public knowledge for months.'

'But it is asserted, Herr Professor, that there is another and undisclosed document, which exacts the price of the Treaty itself?' *Frankfurter Rundschau*. 'Do you deny that?'

'Of course I deny it.'

Flashguns flickered and blinded, as if he had said something which betrayed him. The red lights on the portable TV cameras, perched like ugly pets on the shoulders of their cameramen, attracted Zimmermann's glance. Film cameras whirred at the back of the conference room.

'As for yourself, Herr Professor,' the correspondent of *Bild* and *Bild am Sonntag* began. Zimmermann steeled himself. Springer's man. Others in the room, too, attended to the tall, bespectacled political muckraker. This was the beginning, Zimmermann told himself. This is the source and this is the rabid animal. My enemy.

'Yes? You should know. It's your story,' he essayed. A small trickle of laughter. The correspondent smirked, and bowed.

'Indeed.'

'What is your source—the CIA?' Zimmermann suddenly snapped, irrationally irritated, losing his temper plainly and mistakenly.

'The old smear, Herr Professor?' More laughter. Zimmermann cursed himself. 'Do you deny any contact or affiliation with foreign agents yourself, Herr Professor?'

Herr Professor . . . After selling his business, there had been that brief, enjoyable period as an academic: economic research at Bremen, funded by the German Research Foundation. Now this odious, cynical man made it appear no more than a shabby pretence, a mask of respectability to be torn aside. Vogel had found him, and enlisted him, at Bremen.

'I deny it, of course. It is ridiculous that I should have to deny it.' Zimmermann waited, wary.

'Do you know a man called Kominski at the Soviet embassy in Bonn?'

The silence is going on too long—*answer*! Zimmermann told himself.

He nodded carefully, as if his head was delicately balanced on his shoulders.

'Yes. A member of the embassy staff engaged in preparatory and liaison work . . .'

'Would it surprise you to learn that Kominski is a KGB officer?'

'That is nonsense!'

Then the uproar, the *Bild* correspondent the centre of attention, then Zimmermann. The focus of TV and film cameras swinging like gun barrels between the two men. Unable to prevent himself, Zimmermann nervously brushed his hair with both hands.

He had to leave. He was beginning to perspire. He had to desert the field, or lose in another and perhaps more complete manner. He stood up. The press corps, seeing the movement, bayed at him. A hundred questions, demands. He waved his hands to indicate he had nothing to say. The *Bild* correspondent watched him, smiling; he, not Zimmermann, was the most important man in the room at that moment.

'Kominski——?' he heard a dozen people shout in ragged unison. Petya would, of course, be recalled. Of *course* he was a KGB officer—most of the important people were. Of course they had had to discuss future security with the Soviet secret police and intelligence people. But, how could he explain *that*? He could give no answer.

He walked into the wings of the dais, and mopped his brow. The faces of the two press aides were dark, foreboding. Zimmermann tried to breathe calmly, but he could not; as if his lungs pursued air that was always just out of reach.

'Confirmation, uh?' Buckholz said with a grin, closing the cell door on Wei.

Godwin shrugged. McIntosh's telephone call had summoned him away from Buckholz and the Chinaman for a few moments, but the news from London and Bonn had been more than sufficient to disobey Aubrey's instructions. Presumably Shelley in London was putting it through in a signal to Canberra, thence to Aubrey himself.

'You think so? *Bild*'s a bit of a rag, isn't it?'

'A popular newspaper, maybe. Doesn't have to be wrong, though.' Buckholz gestured over his shoulder with an extended thumb. 'That guy in there's been saying the same thing for a week. Now the Germans are raking over their own ashes. And look what they find!'

They began walking along the catwalk of the most secure wing of Victoria Prison; the warder, having locked the door to Wei's cell, was a pace behind them. Through wired, reinforced, barred glass at the end of the catwalk, the blare and flash of lightning illuminated the doors, stairways and gantries of the prison. Thunder rumbled as distantly as a stomach complaint.

'Sir?' Godwin began with natural deference.

'Yes?'

Their shoes clattered on the stippled metal steps down to the ground floor. The noise echoed.

'London's inclined to play down this story in the German evening papers, you know . . .'

'Sure. London plays everything down. I wonder *London* even announced the start of World War Two over the radio.' Buckholz laughed, and Godwin smiled. 'And now, after the sports news, the beginning of the next war . . .' Buckholz continued in a grossly exaggerated English milord's voice. The warder, a Briton, sniggered behind them. 'I tell you, son, I begin to think that Wei is telling us the truth about our friend Wolfie Zimmermann. I look forward to future episodes, uh?'

Godwin looked anxious, and distressed. 'Perhaps you're right, sir. I can't really say. But *you* think so——?'

'It sure doesn't make his innocence more likely, does it?'

'No, it doesn't . . .'

'OK. Let me get Langley onto this. We got to dig over Zimmermann's background, but good. What's been happening up to now is just rehearsal. *All* the background to this Treaty business—all the negotiations, all the meetings—on and off the record. Come on, son. We have a long signal to draft.'

Buckholz clapped his large hand on Godwin's shoulder. His lips were smiling, but his eyes were glinting with urgency, and with a fierce conviction. To Godwin, it appeared that Buckholz felt he had at last learned the truth.

Outback. During the day, the dry air had brought the horizon in front of the Land Rover almost close enough to press against the windscreen; a telescopic lens of air. Now, in the warm night, the sky was so brilliant with stars that they seemed to drip light, to shed it like ornamental fireworks rather than to be content as pinpricks in black cloth or mere spots of brightness.

The sense of dehydration had lessened. It was only the end of September, yet he had felt it throughout the afternoon accumulating like a fear of illness. Outback. Now, even at night, it was still so silent that he could hear the beating of his heart as he stood near the Land Rover at the side of the road, waiting.

Patrick Hyde was by upbringing a town dweller, by adoption a Londoner. Here, on the outskirts of the township of Marree, less than fifty miles south-east of Lake Eyre, he felt tiny and unremarked. The brilliant sky was vast, the silence was all but absolute, the air like dry paper in his lungs, and the land stretched endlessly northwards ahead of him towards the Simpson Desert. He was one tiny man looking for another mannikin on the surface of the huge blank map that was the Australian outback.

He shivered. He was unprepared for it. No wonder Aubrey had retreated behind the drawn curtains of his motel room as soon as they arrived. Marree had one new motel, to serve the safaris of tourists that visited Lake Eyre and the Birdsville Track and who even ventured into the Simpson or Sturt's Stony Desert during the winter.

Aubrey had called Clare Schiller. Yes, she had spoken to her father. Yes, he would meet them. Where? Lake Palankarinna west of the Birdsville Track, south of Cooper's Creek. Could they find their way there, her father had asked, without getting lost? The knowledge that Schiller had a location, had become a fixed point ahead of them, was no consolation. It was no signpost towards a landmark in the blankness. The scraps of outback and bush that Hyde had known as a boy were as safe and familiar as back garden plots when compared with this immensity.

Aubrey was sleeping now. He had had dinner in his room, reluctant to emerge. He had drunk, strangely for him, a number of beers. Then he had retired for the night, presumably to try to preserve his strength. Hyde, however, knew what he had to do;

for his satisfaction, his self-confidence, and perhaps even to feed his fear. He might yet make it familiar and tame, if he admitted and recognized and faced it often enough.

He had driven the Land Rover out to the dusty airstrip north of the township. It was an appointment rather than a whim.

The airstrip buildings were in darkness, as was the runway. If an aircraft radioed for landing instructions, the runway lights would be switched on. The airstrip was little more than a harder, straighter line across a fenced field of stone and baked dirt.

It was not precisely accurate to assume the complete darkness of the airstrip. There was a light behind a blind in one of the low buildings, presumably the radio hut; a faint greenish glow. And, occasionally, there was the flare of dim light whenever someone opened one of the doors of the Volkswagen van, or lit a match. The three Australians were waiting for an aircraft. Hyde was waiting for the aircraft's passenger. He knew he had to see him, had to be certain; another example, another way, of taking out his fear and confronting it. If he saw him, he might diminish the man's power over his imagination.

It was after two when he heard the small, distant noise of a single-engined aircraft. When he was certain of the noise, he moved swiftly, wriggling under the wire of the airstrip perimeter, then running towards the largest of the wooden buildings, the low hangar. He reached its shelter before any of the three men got out of the van and began watching the night sky. Hyde watched it, too—so intently that when the scattered necklace of runway lights was switched on, it was no more than a faint glow at the edge of his vision.

The noise of the engine loudened. A red star moving, two white stars moving, none of them as brilliant as the still lights behind them. Then the silhouette of the aircraft could be seen against the stars, then its light-painted, sharklike belly was visible in the glow from the landing lights. Dust billowed beneath it as it ran down the track towards the airstrip buildings.

Hyde gripped the wood at the corner of the hangar, feeling its roughness and splinters under his fingers. He waited. The aircraft slowed to a halt, nose-on to Hyde, no more than fifty yards away. Its propeller ran down, emerging into separate blades then stopping. Dingoes quarrelled somewhere in the night.

Then he saw him. Light, tailored safari suit, broad-brimmed hat held in one hand, stepping onto the wing and then jumping lightly to the ground. The three Australians moved towards him. He waited for them.

Petrunin.

It didn't make his fear any the less, any more familiar and capable of being despised. He was here now. The odds were five to two—one and a half, in truth. The tortoise and the hare. They'd been overtaken, overhauled.

Petrunin.

Hyde wanted to kill him now, and knew he would not. He had no order for the man's execution. Aubrey had not ordered Petrunin's death. Hyde wanted, nevertheless, to kill him.

Petrunin.

EIGHT:

For The Record

To David Liu, it had become increasingly evident that the doctor
felt himself to be in command of his situation; unthreatened. His
confidence did not stem from the comparatively lowly rank displayed on Liu's false identity papers, nor from the deference with
which Liu had questioned him. There was something traditional
and unchanged about Meng Chiao, something almost aristo-
cratic—Mandarin—about his height, his bearing, his manner, his
words. The hospital specialist who had treated Zimmermann
was polite, aloof, perhaps a little bored after the conversation
had lasted for ten minutes. Laughter from the next room, dimly
heard through the closed study door, attracted his attention and
his desire whenever he perceived it. He had left a dinner party to
talk to a policeman, and now he wished his unbidden guest gone.

Pieces of jade, pottery, silk paintings, deep rugs, carved wood.
Liu's impression of the study, as warm lantern light fell on the
contours of objets d'art and displayed the highlights in the grained
wood, was of a room trapped in a time bubble, surviving from the
past unaltered, even enhanced. Affluence and privilege pressed in
upon him, demanding acknowledgement.

'I take it that is all, officer?' Meng said finally, after studying
Liu, registering his youth, his lowliness of rank, his manner of
perching lightly on his chair as if to avoid offending the furniture
with the material of his creased, rough suit.

There was another faint gust of laughter from the dining room.
Meng turned his head towards the door. A look of irritation
played about his mouth for a moment. The guests had evidently
arrived long before their host had returned from the hospital,
even before Liu had taken up watch on the bungalow. Long
parties, drink, intimacy, pleasure. Again, the fossil remains of
old China, invested with a new flesh and animation.

'Doctor Meng,' Liu began with a stiff authority. Meng waved
his hand tiredly.

'Please, officer, I have answered your questions. Your speculations concerning the ideological purity of the people who visited this Westerner are not my concern.' He rose upright in his chair, hands on the arms, ready to rise.

'This is important Party business, Doctor,' Liu snapped, a new and disrespectful tone in his voice. Meng's eyes narrowed. 'It is a matter of security. My orders are from Peking . . .'

Meng still affected boredom. 'Really?' he said with acid indifference. 'I see. Well, I can only repeat that I have answered your questions. Now I really must return to my guests, if you will permit me.'

'You supervised the administration of drugs to this man Zimmermann?' Liu asked.

Meng appeared surprised. 'Yes? They *were* pure,' he observed mockingly. 'I will vouch for them.'

'This is not a matter for joking, Doctor.'

'Quite.'

Liu looked down at his notebook, flicking back the pages. He had almost all of it: General Chiang, the Harmony of Thought unit employed on Zimmermann, the Russian spoken, the interrogations under drugs. He had all the dosages and details of the sodium pentathol, and the benzedrine which would have brought Zimmermann back to a dazed semi-consciousness to allow him to be questioned. He knew the techniques of regression employed to convince Zimmermann that he was talking to his Moscow control rather than to Chinese interrogators. It was almost all there, from one man's lips in the space of ten or fifteen minutes. The German *was* a KGB agent, and had been for more than forty years.

Meng's vanity, perhaps, had been the key; even his contempt for the intelligence agents and policemen with whom he had had to cooperate when Zimmermann was interrogated. He had been willing to talk—to amuse himself by playing upon Liu's orthodoxy, his rigid, subservient mentality. He had even revealed the kind of suggestions he had repeatedly made to General Chiang and his staff. Each suggestion had been greeted, Meng had implied, with deference and applause, and put into immediate effect. To illustrate his importance, the information had come tumbling from Meng's lips, accompanied by broad, sweeping hand movements and the persistent presentation of the doctor's profile to Liu.

'I administered the drugs, or supervised their administration, as you say,' Meng mused, his eyes observing the past. 'You do not wish me to repeat what I have already told you?'

Liu shook his head, then snapped: 'My superiors are very suspicious concerning these matters.'

'Suspicious? In what way?'

Liu tapped his notebook with his pencil. 'Your part in this business—your cooperation with elements who are now fallen under suspicion of anti-revolutionary tendencies . . .'

'How can the questioning of this Westerner—the discovery that he was no more than a lickspittle of the Soviet revisionists——' Meng used the jargon with an amusement that masked a faint unsettlement. 'How can that be regarded as anti-revolutionary?'

Meng's eyes were on Liu's chest, as if he sought to examine Liu's papers once more. His former deference and the lowliness of his rank seemed belied by the questions he now asked.

'That is not your concern.'

'Is General Chiang under investigation?'

'No one is above investigation,' Liu answered obliquely.

'Is he?' There was something peremptory about Meng's tone. Liu shook his head. 'I cannot say.'

'Am *I*?' The idea seemed new, strange and unacceptable to the doctor.

Liu shrugged. 'Perhaps . . .'

'The German was an agent of Soviet revisionism!' Meng snapped. 'I and the people from Shanghai served the Party and the Revolution by unmasking him.' Meng evidently despised himself for resorting to popular, unthinking slogans. It was beneath him. Yet he appeared unnerved and suspicious. Or did he? The question floated into Liu's consciousness and enlarged there, opening from a chrysalis into a butterfly shaking its wings. A glitter of calculation in Meng's eyes did not fit his words.

'Perhaps . . .' Liu repeated a confident drawl.

'Perhaps?' Meng's eyes glanced towards the telephone on his desk. 'Perhaps I should talk to General Chiang? Perhaps I should discover what it is you are engaged on?' The threat was evident.

Liu glanced at his notebook again. It was all there; not almost all, everything. He had it. He could get up, apologize for his intrusion, and go straight to Frederickson with the proof of Zimmermann's KGB involvement. It would not do to anger Meng, cause him to check on the police officer from Shanghai. Leave, he told himself.

196

Or did he . . .? He watched Meng's eyes. They were still aloof, almost amused, cold. Untouched by the implied accusations, contemptuous of any danger. Why?

'There is no need to contact General Chiang. In fact, you may have difficulty contacting him.'

A flash of ridicule in Meng's dark eyes. A sense of what could be triumph? Liu was confused. He felt he had played into Meng's hands.

'We shall see. Are you ready to leave? Have you finished with your questions?' Meng dismissed him with a gesture, as if brushing fluff from his dressing-gown. Even the clothes were those of a closet aristocrat, Liu remarked to himself. Behind the bungalow's closed doors, Meng and his family and friends played at ignoring almost a billion people and the system under which they lived. Liu shook his head visibly to dismiss the complications introduced by his dislike of the doctor. 'You have more questions?' Meng asked in surprise.

'I was simply thinking of something else,' Liu explained.

'Perhaps you could do that elsewhere? And I still think I should talk to General Chiang.' Meng got up from his chair and crossed purposefully to his desk. He consulted an address book, the telephone in his left hand. Liu watched him intently. Leave, he instructed himself. Leave before he calls your bluff . . .

What was it? What did the calculation, the triumph mean? Only vanity, arrogance? Something more? Why had it all come tumbling out so easily, so effortlessly, like, like . . .

Something rehearsed.

Liu felt chilled in the warm room. Meng found the number, glanced at him still seated in his chair, and began dialling the first digit of the Shanghai code. His lips were pursed and angry.

Something rehearsed—second digit—something prepared and ready for transmission, like a little play or a public speech or a prepared confession—third digit, fourth—Liu could not rid himself of the imagery of play-acting. There had to be more to it, more to discover—fifth digit, over halfway through the Shanghai number, three more numbers before the telephone began ringing in the offices of the MPT. What more? Get out—*stay*. Ask, find out—sixth digit—Meng glanced at him once more, his finger poised to dial again, challenging him or perhaps giving him another moment to withdraw. It seemed a moment of crisis for Meng, too. Why? Why was Meng bluffing? Why did he *want* his visitor to leave rather than investigate him, humiliate him, even ruin him. Seventh digit, Meng's hand quivering slightly in the pool of light on the desk. Ask, ask . . .

Play-acting: rehearsed, prepared, faultless delivery. Dumb, expectant—*expected?*—audience . . .

Liu's conflicting ideas possessed him.

Stop him . . .

Finger poised, one more number, Meng hesitating once more. He doesn't want to make the call, he wants me to get out, taking his story with me . . .

Liu reached into his jacket and removed the Type 64 pistol that Frederickson had had put into the suitcase at Shanghai station. He pointed the heavy, awkward, old-fashioned and somehow naked-looking Chinese weapon at Meng.

'Please put down the receiver,' he said quietly. 'Return to your chair, Doctor—at once, please.' Liu waggled the pistol between Meng and the chair. The receiver clattered onto the rest. Meng moved robotically to the chair and slumped into it. A naked fear looked out of his eyes. There was no detachment left in them as they stared unwaveringly at the gun.

Yet, Liu told himself, there is a sense of failure, of upset schemes about him. The actor's performance has not been well received. The eyes drew inward, as if retreating from the threat of the gun, and it became evident that Meng found another danger. Others behind him, hidden and powerful, would hold him responsible for the intrusion of the gun, the suspicion of this fake policeman. After a few moments, he felt that Meng no longer saw the pistol, only the bleak future.

Liu forced himself to keep the gun steady, not to glance towards the door. A sense of a closing trap assailed him. He wanted to breathe certainty again, clear his head.

'What . . .?' Meng began, and faltered.

'What do we do now?' Liu supplied in a level voice. 'I think you should tell me the truth.'

Meng shook his head slightly, then rallied. He seemed, by an effort of will, after his eyes had taken an inventory of the room's furnishings and possessions, to straighten in his chair and appear defiant. A shadow of his earlier self emerged.

'I have told you the truth, you stupid individual. Who are you to threaten me with a gun? How have you the authority to interrupt my call? What treachery are you engaged in?'

Orthodoxy became a means of composing himself; playing for time.

'That won't do, Doctor Meng. I don't believe you have told me the truth. I think the truth is something much more subtle and hidden and dangerous. You've been acting a part, that's all.'

'Nonsense.'

'Not at all.'

'Who are you?'

'That doesn't matter.'

'What do you intend?'

'I want the truth.' He waved the gun in threat. Meng glanced at the door.

'I have only to raise my voice . . .'

'In order to be shot.'

'You *have* the truth!'

Illumination glared in Liu's mind like a bright light suddenly switched on.

'You imply that what you have told me, what you boasted of, is what I came for?' he said in a constricted voice. Meng appeared puzzled and suspicious. 'I didn't come for that. I told you my interest was in the people, not the techniques—in the exercise and not in the results. But you'—Liu hurried on, his excitement mounting as he saw Meng's mouth fall open and his hands grip the arms of his chair, as if to fight off dizziness—'you pressed upon me dosages, drugs, techniques, questions, times, dates—everything. You'd have done that whatever I asked you. We began, remember, by talking of one or two of Chiang's team . . .' Meng was now evidently appalled, and very afraid. His eyes darted over the room, seeking escape. 'Minor police officers who might need to be purged. You recalled, in splendid and precise detail, not only those people but everyone else, and *everything* else!'

'No——' Meng protested feebly, as if against the shadows in the corners of the room.

'Yes! You pressed upon me a truth I wasn't seeking—not as Officer Liu of Shanghai Public Security Bureau. You pressed upon me a truth you thought I *really* wanted. Someone else wanted. The man behind the ID card.' Liu pointed the pistol at Meng's stomach with deliberation, and squinted along the barrel. 'You know who I am. Don't you?'

'No!'

'Yes. You acted the part for me, not for the man on the ID card.'

199

'No . . .' Meng rubbed his cheeks with long-fingered hands. His complexion was doughy, colourless. His body, slumped once more in his chair, appeared invertebrate, doll-like. 'No,' he repeated, shaking his head. 'No . . .'

'Yes. You knew who I was, and why I came. You provided everything I needed. Now, tell me why you did it.' Meng looked up, his mouth quivering. 'Now, tell me the truth.'

Aubrey sat in the Land Rover, feeling his clothes beginning to stick to him. Already the unsmoothed wrinkles and tucks that Hyde's haste had helped create in his clothing were irritating. The motel glowed with a grubby, subdued light as he watched the doors, waiting for Hyde to emerge after paying their bill. Overhead, the stars gleamed, highlights from the edge of some invisible blade. The lumpy, half-formed shadows of tumbledown stores, railway houses and the post office emerged from the soft blackness of the night.

He flinched as a black, broad-nosed face appeared just below the window of the Land Rover. The aboriginal child stared at the old man for perhaps a minute with an expressionless face and deep black eyes, then walked slowly away towards the hump of one of the buildings. Aubrey found the visitation unnerving, and was grateful, unreasonably so, when Hyde finally emerged from the motel, walking briskly to where he had parked the Land Rover.

He climbed in, settled himself, and then gripped the wheel. He breathed deeply and looked across at Aubrey.

'Ready, Mr Aubrey?'

'Very well, let's get on with it,' Aubrey snapped. He had been sleeping soundly when Hyde had knocked at his door. He had been rushed into his clothes, then into the vehicle. Only now was there leisure to complain.

'I'm sorry, Mr Aubrey.' Hyde was tense, his shoulders hunched over the wheel as if beneath some burden. 'We have to go now, and we have to move fast. Petrunin is one step—half a step—behind.'

'We've known we were being followed, Hyde——'

'This is *Petrunin*!' Hyde snapped in reply, his lips compressing into a thin line as soon as the words were out, as if he were trying to prevent further admissions of weakness and fear.

'Yes . . .' Aubrey said softly. 'Very well. I hope that Schiller will be waiting for us.'

'We won't have much time with him.'

'What do you mean?'

Hyde turned to Aubrey. 'You want to know why I'm uptight? I'll tell you. I *know* we're running towards violence. It's waiting for us as surely as the sunrise. Petrunin and his goons will want Schiller. They either want answers, or they want silence kept about things they already know very well. Correct?'

'Perhaps.'

'Correct. And there's only yours truly. I'm not running away from anything. Just towards . . .'

Hyde clicked his tongue against the roof of his mouth, then switched on the ignition. He let out the clutch and the Land Rover pulled away from the Marree Motel, down the unlit dusty main street. In a minute they were out of the town. The road forked and Hyde took the right-hand, the Birdsville Track. Immediately the tyres encountered a rough surface hardly distinguishable from the surrounding flat, empty gibber plain. In the headlights the sand and stone moved ahead of them, slipping endlessly away from the beams. Within minutes Aubrey became infected with the isolation, the lonely menace, of the land beyond Marree. He, too, was increasingly aware that they were approaching rather than escaping.

They left the small car parked at the side of the road that followed the East Lake and walked down to the water. Behind David Liu and the doctor, the sky was smudged with an orange glow from the steel mills, as if sunset still lingered.

Meng had excused himself from his guests with a mixture of self-importance and mystery. An important patient, a secret consultation. He had to accompany the officer. He would not be long. Liu, standing in the doorway with an adopted deference, had seen privileged eyes inspect him. He saw that he represented no threat to them. Meng had kissed his wife—a beautiful, languorous, Westernized Chinese—quickly and with an odd sense of self-deprecation, and then they had left. Laughter had already resumed its occupation of the dining room as Meng closed the door behind them with a noise. His face appeared angry. Liu sensed the wife had a lover among the dinner guests. The insight rendered Meng oddly human, diminished.

Meng seemed to study the black, flat surface of the lake as if he sought some secret writing, some explanatory characters brushed on its surface. Liu watched the doctor, his pistol thrust into his waistband so that Meng should remain aware of it.

'Confession is good for the soul,' Liu remarked.

Meng turned on him, his face twisted with rage. 'I *cannot* tell you!' he almost wailed, anger disappearing as soon as he began to speak, to be replaced with an overriding fear, one that he saw he would be unable to rid himself of, ever.

'You must,' Liu said, patting the gun.

'I *cannot*!'

'You have a simple choice.'

'I have *no* choice!'

'Yes, you have. Either I kill you now—or you tell me, and risk getting away with it. Death isn't as certain, following that second course.'

'No?' Meng asked with a scoffing bitterness, tossing his head in profile against the warm stars. Liu smelt heated metal on the breeze, tasted it at the back of his throat. He did not know whether he could kill Meng, if it came to it.

'No. If you don't tell them, I won't.'

'You don't understand . . .'

'What don't I understand? Tell me.'

Something rustled in its sleep in the reeds near them. Meng flinched, startled.

'I can't tell you.'

'Do you want to walk?'

'Yes.'

They began a patrol of the lake shore. A pagoda rose to one side of them like a vast and sinister warrior's helmet. The weak waning moon struggled through a gauzy mist that might have been a night-time version of industrial smog. A delicate, arching bridge lay ahead of them.

Meng's face was pale and grim in the strengthening moonlight.

'Don't you want to return to your wife and fam——'

'Leave my wife out of this matter!'

'You could return in time to prevent tonight's infidelity, surely?'

'Damn you,' Meng snarled.

'You have everything to live for, Meng,' Liu announced in a new and cold voice. 'Respect, position, money, influence. And a beautiful wife who cuckolds you regularly.'

'Shut up!'

'I can end your misery. I can kill you—even cripple you for life. Yes, I could do that, Meng. I could leave you in a wheel-chair for the next thirty years, able to watch your wife's behaviour, never able to rest or forget it. Watch her go out through the door, dressed in order only to undress, perfumed in every place *he* might wish to kiss . . .' Liu's voice, guided by instinct, promised venom-ously. Meng had given himself away. He should have denied his wife's unfaithfulness. He was helpless before it. 'No job, no money, no position or respect—*and* no wife. I can give you a state pension, *now*!'

Meng turned to Liu, his hands grasping for him. Liu stepped neatly aside and pushed the tall doctor. Meng stumbled and slipped, and his hands splashed in the water as he ended on all fours. He sobbed. Liu helped him roughly, companionably, to his feet. Meng hugged his hands under his armpits, as if he had been beaten.

'I, I——' Meng began.

'Yes?' Liu asked, excluding excitement from his voice.

'I—I write poetry, you know.'

'What?' Liu was baffled. Meng's eyes looked inward. His face had an abstract, beatific look in the pale moonlight, and Liu began to fear he had lost the man.

'Poetry. Silly, is it not?'

'I wouldn't know.'

Meng began walking, striding with a more positive step, head up. He appeared once more as a proud and confident man. Liu kept pace with him, at a loss as to his next approach. Meng seemed to have retreated into some private, almost fey world, an unreality where his wife did not impinge upon him. Perhaps somewhere he was safe from questions, too.

'Cold,' Meng murmured. 'I always seem to be writing about cold. A central image, you might say.'

'Yes?'

Meng did not glance at Liu as they walked. David Liu was angry with himself. Somehow, he had triggered a retreat. He had only threat to offer, and Meng had found a way to circumvent it. He was retreating, doubtless, just as he escaped the knowledge and evidence of his wife's unfaithfulness and the pain it caused him.

Now he was reciting in a murmur.

> Keep away from sharp swords,
> Don't go near a lovely woman.

Meng's voice remote. The poetry, to which Liu attended in spite of himself, seemed transmitted from some distant perfect region, somewhere unimprinted with human footsteps. A moonscape.

> A sharp sword too close will wound your hand,
> Woman's beauty too close will wound your life.

They walked on, Liu gradually feeling himself drawn into Meng's chilly, ice-capped dreams.

> The face of the autumn moon freezes.
> Old and homeless, will and force are spent.
> The drip of the chill dew breaks off my dream . . .

Liu looked up at the watery, mist-weakened moon.

'Rather old-fashioned?' he murmured.

'Ah, yes,' Meng replied. 'Perfect reiteration of old forms. Rather out of fashion now, I'm afraid.' He did not seem to be apologizing. His escape was perfect: not simply into poetry, but into the imitation of forms and sentiments perhaps a thousand years old.

'The shock of a gleam, and then another . . .' Liu watched Meng. The doctor had turned suddenly to him. Their feet were on the bridge which spanned some small neck of the lake. Liu felt they were moving further into the dream, but Meng's face was now vivid, palely awake in an intense way. 'Yes,' he said. 'I accept.'

'What?'

'What you can do to me is more certain than what otherwise might happen.' He looked steadily at the black stain of the pistol against Liu's shirt, and nodded. Liu mistrusted this new wakefulness as much as the mysterious retreat of only moments before. Meng nodded again, and cleared his throat. When he spoke his voice was close and narrow and alive to the present moment. 'Yes, you were quite right. You were misled.'

'By whom?'

'The ministry—*your* people?' He smiled wintrily and shook his head. 'No, not yours, of course. The police, the secret police, the spies. Call them what you will.'

204

'How misled?'

'Utterly. As deluded as—as I am myself, perhaps,' he added in a low voice. 'Everything was a forgery—*my* forgery.' A rag of pride waved like a flag.

'Everything?' Liu quivered with excitement. *He had it*! All of it. His eyes darted about, as if he already sought to leave Meng and report to Frederickson. Pride, too, swelled in him. *He* had done it. 'Wei?'

'Who?'

'The defector.'

Meng shrugged. 'The man who caused you to be here? Yes, I suppose so. I was not told how the seed of doubt would be planted.'

'Then . . .?'

'There was no interrogation, no discovery. No drugs, no records, no revelations.'

'And the German, he isn't a KGB agent?'

'That I do not know. He may be, for all I know. All I do know is that he was given something to make him sick, as if with food poisoning, and brought to me at the hospital. General Chiang himself supervised my—forgery.' He turned to Liu, then, and added, arms away from his sides: 'Now you know everything.' His eyes were on the pistol in Liu's belt.

'*Why?*' Liu asked.

'I do not know. I did as I was ordered. I supplied only the medical forgery. I do not know why.'

'Everything—but he spoke Russian!'

'A tape recording, I believe, played in his room.'

'Everything . . .' Liu looked down at the dark, calm water beneath the bridge. Everything . . . he had it now.

> When the evening chimes send off the departing guest,
> The notes I count drop from the farthest sky.

Meng's voice was unearthly again. Liu glanced at his profile as they rested their hands, side by side, on the parapet of the bridge. The stone was soft, crumbly as cheese beneath his grip.

'Thank you,' Liu murmured. He could think of nothing else to say, yet submitted to a pressure to speak.

'What——?' Meng appeared dragged back unwillingly into Liu's world. His face was stained by regret in the moonlight; his eyes were already contemplating his uncertain future before they became once more obsessed with the pistol. Liu closed his loose jacket over it. Meng sighed. 'Oh, yes,' he said. 'I had no choice, of course.'

'No.'

'What now?'

'Now . . . ? Oh. Doctor, you may return to your wife and to your dinner guests.' Flame belched on the horizon to the west as if from a dragon's mouth. A furnace disgorging. Meng rubbed his arms. 'I have no more questions.'

'And—the future?'

'You—may be safe. It will not be my decision. But as long as the police do not know I have seen you, they should not assume your guilt.

'Mm. We shall see. I may go?' Meng's eyes were narrow with calculation. Liu nodded.

'Yes. Go.'

Meng studied the smaller man as if contemplating an attempt at violence, then he turned swiftly and decisively on his heel and left the bridge. Liu watched him moving away, back towards the car.

Liu could not help smiling. It was a long time before the mechanics of his contact with Frederickson and his escape from China entered his awareness, dispelling the satisfaction he felt.

'Wolf, what the hell is going on?'

Vogel was angry. His features, normally disposed to good humour even when not smiling, were darkened with a sense of outrage and betrayal. Zimmermann had been expecting him ever since he left the press conference. Evidently the Chancellor had been checking, weighing the harm done, investigating the source of the newspaper stories. Perhaps even checking on Zimmermann himself, his past . . .

'I'm sorry, Dietrich, believe me . . .'

'That's it, Wolf. Can I believe you? Or do I believe *this*?' In his large hand Vogel held copies of the principal evening papers. He slapped the folded newspapers with his free hand. 'Well? Which?'

Zimmermann did not leave his chair by the window of his hotel room. Behind him, through the net curtains, light filtered from a fine late afternoon. The noise of Dusseldorf's homecoming traffic seeped from beyond the double glazing. To Vogel, it was immediately evident that Zimmermann had been drinking; not too much, perhaps, but certainly drinking. Vogel did not know whether the bottle of Asbach brandy was newly-opened. It was half-empty.

Zimmermann shrugged. 'You know it's all bullshit, Dietrich. I'm sorry it's happened, but none of it's true. God, you *know* that!'

'A week tomorrow—that's all we had to worry about. Another seven bloody days!' He raised his eyes to the ceiling as he slumped into an armchair opposite Zimmermann. 'Couldn't you have given us another week?' Vogel poured himself a brandy. The newspapers slipped from his lap and lay accusingly on the carpet, headlines half-revealed, half-obscured. Vogel swallowed at the brandy, coughing. He pointed the glass, around which his fist was clenched, at Zimmermann. 'There's an avalanche of this bullshit, Wolf.' His voice seemed less loud, but no less angry. 'Secret clauses—what does that mean? Secret meetings—of course there were secret meetings! Your connections with East Germany?' The observation became a question, perhaps even without intention on the Chancellor's part. Zimmermann studied the bottom of his own glass, and shook his head. 'Your past—even the suggestion that you're some kind of magician with a Svengali hold on me! My *God*!'

'What—what do you want to do about it?'

'What? Where's the proof we can use to disprove it. Is there any?'

'It would be labelled a whitewash, a cover story.'

'Don't remind me! I'll have to broadcast—there's no way out of it now. They've all been onto me: radio, TV, every damned company and organization. I'll have to go . . .'

'Do you want me . . . ?'

'*You*? You keep out of it, Wolf. You've done enough damage for the moment.' Zimmermann blushed with suppressed anger, but Vogel ignored his complexion and the fierce light in his eyes. He refilled his glass. 'Another week. It was in our grasp!' Brandy spilled on his knuckles as his hand shook with rage. He licked it off as if sucking a wound. 'A united Germany: a neutral zone in the middle of Europe. Peace, prosperity . . . write your own clichés, it was ours for the signing. My God, they're trying to tear it all down! You go and *I* go, that's their bloody plan. And the Treaty goes with us!' He stood up, as if the chair had rejected his virulent and sudden changes of posture. He went to the window but did not pull aside the net curtain. Then he turned on Zimmermann. 'Don't let it bring me down, Wolf. I've worked too long and too hard for this. I'm not prepared to be kicked out on my backside, and my work with me, by Springer and the right-wing press. Help me squash this rubbish, or—I'll see you in Hell.'

The dry pale air brought the horizon almost within touching distance of the Land Rover's windscreen, yet it never revealed anything other than further expanses of flat, stony desert plain out of which the occasional isolated homesteads rose unwillingly, their low, extensive buildings hugging the ground as if in apology for intruding upon the desert and the silence. Once, an aboriginal stockman looked up from saddling his horse to watch them pass. Lake Harry Station, Clayton Station, Dulkaninna Station—fragments of a human meteorite half-buried in the landscape. A solitary group of kangaroos, a few slow-moving emus, cattle so isolated they might have been deliberately placed and fixed to mark the sparseness of the land. Eventually the stony plain surrendered to the sandhills of the Tirari Desert, which stretched endlessly away around the old stock route that was the Birdsville Track.

They had driven for the remainder of the night, then for hours, it seemed, while the sun climbed out of the pink-splashed desert and up the eastern sky. Dark, mirage-like gums struggled out of the landscape, their shade scanty. Hyde lost the track, found it again, lost it; pursuing it and his future northwards. Or so it seemed to Aubrey, who had already surrendered himself to the passivity induced by the landscape and to the urgency of his field agent. He thought of nothing, spoke only occasionally. From his desultory, vague answers, it seemed Hyde knew as little about the outback of South Australia as he did himself.

Then, just after midday, they came upon water. It was no more than an isolated waterhole, a remnant of some spur of Cooper's Creek, fattened into life by winter rain. Amid claypans and dry gullies and sandhills the Land Rover tipped their horizon downwards as it crested a hill and the grey-sheened water lay unreflectingly in front of them. Willow-like acacias drooped, ghost gums, stunted and pale-boled, struggled into a group, throwing shade like a liberal gift. Some unknown purplish plant carpeted much of the ground. Tufts of grass were astonishingly green against the sand, against the past hours. What might have been a mirage of parkland opened before them.

Aubrey sighed with relief.

'We'll stop here,' Hyde remarked, his lips salty-dry, his eyes squinting behind his sunglasses. 'Give it a bit of a rest. OK?'

'Yes.'

The Land Rover stopped in the shade of the ghost gums, at the edge of the dirty grey water. Aubrey lowered himself to the ground, which was firm beneath the loose, trickling surface sand. Hyde remained in the Land Rover, the door flung wide, studying the map. His face seemed set, cut by the wind or tide of some inner crisis into sharp, fragile planes and surfaces which might crumble at any moment. Aubrey opened the bonnet of the vehicle. Heat radiated, seeming to scorch his hands and face. He filled a plastic cup from the water container and could not rid himself of the misgivings which Hyde's expression had evoked in him.

He wondered how afraid Hyde was, and by how much his efficiency would be reduced by the knowledge that it was Petrunin who hunted him. Despite his experience and his seniority, Aubrey felt his understanding of field agents—the runners and minders and gunmen of his service—was precarious and possibly erroneous. Aubrey understood opponents, defectors, administrators, strategists; but not the men with the guns. What drove them, how they reacted, all their *whys*. He knew them only as functionaries, machines that worked with efficiency whether in victory or defeat. He did not understand the kind of mechanical failure that might overtake them.

He shook his head. The desert leached his mind of insight, sensitivity, quickness. Of course he knew more about Hyde than that. The man was simply . . .

The noise of the aircraft might, at first, have been that of an insect. There were insects, moving about the purplish flowers with a pace that implied pessimism. The noise grew, however, in the clear and silent air until Aubrey realized that it was the sound of a light aircraft's engine.

Almost instantly, Hyde was out of the Land Rover and beside Aubrey, searching the pale sky with binoculars. The engine's note gradually increased, nearing them. The binoculars swept back and forth with what seemed to Aubrey to be a frantic urgency. Then Hyde sighed. Aubrey, squinting, watched the small aircraft drift above the near horizon, then bank towards them, passing low overhead only seconds later. He looked at Hyde as he lowered the glasses.

'Well?'

'Yes. It's the plane I saw last night. Petrunin.' He shuddered. Images of another light aircraft, pursuing himself and a fleeing girl in England, flickered cruelly in his imagination like scenes lit by flame. His shoulder ached. He cleared his throat and said: 'You may just have time to talk to Schiller, if we hurry. After that —I don't know. I just don't know.'

'Davie boy—you're beautiful!'

David Liu was abashed. His grin was awkward and boyish, making him, he realized, appear absurdly young; the wrong man to have brought Frederickson the information. The Shanghai CIA station head, however, appeared delighted. Taken aback, almost breathless—yes. But excited, too. His eyes glittered, his white teeth flashed as he grinned like some fierce hunting animal. He slapped Liu on the shoulder once more.

'Thanks,' Liu shrugged.

'Our thanks to you, Davie. Man, we're all in *your* debt!'

They were standing in the doorway of a dress shop on Zhong nan lu, where the wide thoroughfare climbed away from them and from the Hong Shan Hotel where Frederickson and his party of U.S. businessmen were accommodated. The hills of the municipality of Wu Chang rose behind the hotel. Trees lined the thoroughfare of smart shops and restaurants, new apartment blocks and office buildings. Yet despite the morning crowds, they seemed to be on the verge of countryside. A ten-minute walk would take them to the shore of the East Lake.

'You're surprised?' Liu asked.

'Shocked, David, shocked.' Frederickson rubbed his chin. Liu had summoned him with a telephone call which purported to change his restaurant reservation for that evening. Liu had been certain that he had heard, in the moment before Frederickson put down the receiver, an indrawn breath that might almost have been the warning of a striking snake. Surprise, he assumed. Shock, as Frederickson now admitted.

'It's all a set up, then . . .'

'Man, it's big and it's clever.'

'Why?'

'Why?' Frederickson's eyes narrowed. 'Bring down the German government, maybe? The Chinese wouldn't want a neutral Germany. It would give the Russians time to turn on them. They wouldn't like that, uh?'

'I suppose not.'

Frederickson consulted his watch. 'You get back to your hotel, Davie. Stay there. I have to arrange to get back to Shanghai with this. I haven't got secure communications here. You—you we got to get out of China, fast.' He placed both hands on Liu's narrow shoulders. 'You're a prize, Davie. Stay in your hotel room until you get a call from me. I'll meet with you and brief you on your passage out. First, though, I have to break off my stay in Wu Han. This has to go to Langley, utmost priority. OK?'

'OK,' he replied.

'Good boy. Remember, stay in your room until you hear from me.'

Nodding once, Frederickson left him, crossing the wide, quiet thoroughfare towards his hotel with an urgent, elastic step. A man hurrying towards a satisfactory conclusion. Liu watched him pass beneath the concrete canopy into the hotel's foyer, his own satisfaction still entire and complete.

The photographs would never hold the complete scene. Yes, he could capture the apricots, greens, pinks, purples, golds of the cliff faces, and the slow-moving flock of black swans and their evening shadows; the sandhills and the white sand on the lake shore, but not the noise of the swans. They were hooting as if alarmed at the presence of strangers and intended warning Schiller of their arrival. Nor would the photographs contain the struggling roar of the Land Rover's engine as it crested a long, flat sandhill and dropped down towards his campsite in a shallow dry creek leading into the lake.

Schiller focused the telephoto lens, clicking off frame after frame, studying the dim faces of the two men behind the dirty windscreen. He caught the raised necks of the swans, the dark stain of a rushing flock of blackbirds overhead, as he analysed the two people, absorbing the visual clues, deciphering their characters. One young man, one old. Aubrey, from the British secret service. Clare, when she had told him and suggested he agreed to a meeting place, had not seemed suspicious or frightened. He had faith in his daughter's perspicacity. There was no danger here.

He lowered his camera and waved lazily as Aubrey stepped down from the Land Rover. The younger man, his driver and guard, remained behind the windscreen, rubbing his face as if signalling his weariness.

'Herr Schiller?' Aubrey enquired, holding out a hand.

'Mr Schiller.' The emphasis was sharp, then its edge was blunted by a grin and an assumed Australian accent. 'I'm from Aussie now.'

'I understand.'

'You two eaten yet?' Aubrey shook his head. 'OK, we'll share. Unload your grub. Who's your mate, anyway?'

Hyde was standing by the Land Rover, staring at Lake Palankarinna as if he disbelieved it. Beyond the black swans, whose noise had subsided, blunt-headed pelicans floated on the mirror surface of the pink-tinged water. Sandhills cupped themselves like hands around the water of the lake. Brilliant colours hurt the eyes.

'Patrick Hyde,' Aubrey explained as the younger man joined them. 'My—companion.'

'Hans Schiller.' Schiller felt himself keenly studied. In Hyde, he recognised not an individual but a type. He nodded his recognition, then his eyes briefly searched Hyde's clothing for the gun he knew would be there.

'Mr Schiller.' Hyde shook the man's hand.

'What is it you want?' Schiller asked.

As if at an order, the pelicans lifted from the stillness of the water, becoming white crucifixes which were almost immediately dyed pink by the low sun as they moved overhead. All three men watched them, Hyde as if he anticipated some threatening, further transformation. Their light-aircraft shapes moved westward, into the sun. They turned black as they achieved distance.

'I—wish to talk to you about Wolfgang Zimmermann.' Schiller nodded, apparently without surprise. 'I want to take you a long way back into your mutual past—to Spain.'

'Biography? Ancient history? Why not ask Wolf? He's a little bit closer to England than me. Isn't he?' There was a German accent only in the pronunciation of Zimmermann's name. The Australian-accented English seemed to Aubrey to indicate a lack of reality in the questions he asked, the answers he elicited. 'You haven't come all the way out here to ask me about my Civil War exploits, have you?' There was a barrier, in the voice itself, between past and present.

'Your imprisonment, with Zimmermann.'

'Christ, that's a very long time ago. Why not ask him, Mr Aubrey? You chased me hundreds of miles up from the Barossa to ask me about 1938?' Schiller shook his head indulgently. 'We'd better have some tucker. Give me time to think. Try and remember. Christ . . .'

The noise of the Beechcraft that had shadowed them for most of the afternoon burped into the silence after Schiller's voice had faded into amusement. The brightly-painted aircraft slipped from the cover of sandhills and cliffs and passed over them with a rush, like the pelicans, its noise drowning the renewed trumpeting of the black swans. Some of them scattered and flapped into the sky behind the aircraft, as if it had netted them. It circled lazily, one wing dipped, and came back. Hyde saw Petrunin's face, merely glimpsing it before the plane disappeared behind the low cliffs.

'Where's the nearest that plane can land?' he snapped at Schiller.

'Nearest—what's the matter?'

'Where?'

'Etadunna Station, maybe . . .'

'He won't go there. Where else?'

'There's no water in Lake Eyre these days. Salt crust's firm and flat enough, maybe, plenty of flat sand around Madigan Gulf. Why? Is he looking for you?'

'Yes.'

'Mr Schiller,' Aubrey interposed, 'I'm afraid he's as interested in you as he is in us. I'm sorry . . .'

Schiller's gaze narrowed and hardened. 'Who is he?'

'Russian.'

'What——?' Schiller watched Hyde move to the Land Rover and studied the gun as he climbed back out of the driving seat. 'I see.' He turned upon Aubrey. 'You'd better explain yourself, mate. You've fucked up my trip, and maybe me with it. You'd better have a bloody good reason!'

'You are under arrest.'

David Lui had opened the door to the knock and voice of the maid. He was unsuspecting, his sudden tension only that of expectation, which dissipated as soon as he realised the voice was female and not that of Frederickson. He had spent the afternoon in his hotel room, obedient to orders, waiting for his escape route like a ticket. His satisfaction had not been worn by the waiting, or diminished by the empty isolation of his small room. He had done his job; he was finished with China. *He* had done it.

The door had been shouldered open as soon as he unlocked it, and the force of their entry had flung him back into the room, prone on the carpet. There were four of them, three in uniform and a man in a Mao-suit who possessed authority. His features expressed pleasure even before he spoke.

'What is this . . . ?' Liu managed to form.

The guns were evident. The maid had already hurried away down the corridor.

'You are under arrest: the charge is espionage against the People's Republic.'

Liu's satisfaction ran away like rainwater into a drain. He was immediately and completely frightened.

NINE:

Blank Film

The cliffs behind them held the last rays of the setting sun like the embers of a fire. The rich colours darkened and merged into shadow as Aubrey watched. He sighed, as if someone had removed a work of art he was enjoying and which made all the personal elements of his life and situation seem unimportant.

He turned to Schiller. The German's Volkswagen, his winery advertised upon its dusty flank, and the Land Rover stood between them and the lake. They had moved camp, finding a more easily defensible position beneath an overhanging low cliff, an inlet of the lake to one side of them, a sandy stretch to the other across which any approach would be visible, or audible. Hyde, having climbed the crumbling cliff face, was invisibly on watch above them. They had seen nothing of the three men in the Volkswagen, Petrunin's men who Hyde had last seen at Marree airfield, and the aircraft had not returned to the lake since its first appearance.

'How much more do you remember, Mr Schiller?' Aubrey prompted, sipping the last of the black coffee in his enamel mug. 'It is very important.'

'You still won't tell me why it's important?' Schiller stared into the last few embers of the wood fire.

Aubrey looked up, startled at a sudden howling noise in the distance. 'Dingoes,' Schiller explained.

'I can't tell you, Schiller. I wish I could, but I'm afraid I can't.'

'National security bullshit, I suppose?'

'Yes.'

'How can Wolf's past matter today? To you, and'—his hand waved towards the sky and the lake and the tumbled land behind them—'to the Reds?'

'I repeat, I can't tell you.'

'My daughter vouched for you—OK. You've got bona fides. But . . .' He rubbed his chin. Aubrey heard the rasping sound of his rough hand over his stubble. 'I don't know whether you want to harm Wolf, or help him. OK, you haven't threatened me into helping you—and you could—but that doesn't mean much. I haven't seen Wolf Zimmermann since . . . oh, 1943, maybe. Some party in Berlin. He was just the same as ever. Heard about him a bit . . .'

'You have no contacts with Germany now?'

'Never been back. Read about him occasionally.' Schiller shook his head. 'Wouldn't want to go back. Lost my first wife and kid in Hamburg—British bombs. Nothing to stay for, nothing to go back to. The winery being left to me was a godsend.'

'Post-war Germany wouldn't have been the place for you?'

'You guessed, mm?'

'That you were a member of the Nazi party?' Aubrey saw Schiller nod slowly. 'I guessed, yes.'

'Does it matter now?'

'No. It didn't matter when you came out here because the war had been over for a time and old feelings were being forgotten. And I expect you lied.' Aubrey was almost amused.

'Too right. My relatives out here had been important. *I* was important. It wasn't difficult to get in, become Australian, be at home. Eventually.'

'I mean Zimmermann no harm. He—he once saved my life.'

Schiller looked strangely at Aubrey. 'When?'

'In 1940.'

'Where?'

'In France. He—he was my prisoner.'

Schiller laughed, and slapped his thigh. 'That's him,' he said in delighted recollection. Aubrey was satisfied. Somehow the past had begun to flow in Schiller. It no longer moved slowly or subterraneously like an underground stream. Sunlight gleamed on it. 'Just like him. Full of charm, wasn't he?'

'He was.'

'Saved your life? I wonder . . .' Schiller was silent for a moment, then he said: 'Saved mine, too, in a way—when we got away from those fucking Republicans in Aragon. We both owe him. In trouble, is he? International trouble?' Again, his hand flapped to indicate their surroundings.

'He might be. Whatever danger he might be in, only the truth can help him.'

'That sounds pompous. Is it true?'

'I think so.'

'OK. Ask me.'

Aubrey felt only a momentary disinclination to pursue the past. A dingo called, another answered it more distantly. Schiller almost unconsciously threw more grey, bone-dry sticks of wood on the fire. Their crackling reminded Aubrey of the vast spaces of the night surrounding them, and of the light aircraft and the other Volkswagen. Then his perspective narrowed. They were two old men reminiscing.

'How long——?' he began involuntarily.

'It'll take them most of the night to cover the forty miles or so from the lake. He couldn't put down any closer. Ask.'

'Wittenberg. What do you know about Wittenberg?' Aubrey glimpsed the rope spread round them to keep out snakes who might be drawn by the warmth of the fire and their bodies. Like the cry of the dingoes, as the firelight caught its rough length, it impressed itself vividly upon Aubrey's imagination. Five hundred miles from Adelaide, on the other side of the world . . .

Where was Liu, what did he know . . . ?

'Wittenberg?' Schiller replied ruminatively. 'Wolf was from Wittenberg. What else is there to know?'

'Family, friends?'

'Yes. Mother, father—no, his father was dead, I remember—mother, sister, two brothers. I remember one of the brothers was killed, before '43. North Africa, I think.'

'You don't know how many of the family survived the war, do you?'

Schiller shook his head. 'No. Knowing the Russians, none.' Schiller spat. Aubrey became aware of the hunting rifle that lay beside the flat rock on which Schiller was sitting. Aubrey himself was perched on a heap of sleeping bags and blankets. He sat cross-legged, and his circulation seemed sluggish. He rubbed his thighs.

'Put a blanket across your knees. Night's turning a bit cold.'

'Yes.' As he did so, Aubrey said: 'Take me back to Spain. Your capture. Aladko . . .'

'Him?' Schiller was silent for a time. 'It's him you're interested in, is it? He must have been dead for years. No spring chicken when we met him.'

'Wolf Zimmermann told me—in 1940—that he was NKVD?'

'He was. Nasty piece of work. Very.' Schiller growled in his

217

throat and rubbed his ribs as if erasing old bruises. 'He was a real
bastard. It's recruitment, isn't it?'

After a silence, Aubrey said: 'Yes. Was he?'

'Like hell he was!'

'Think!'

'The bloody Treaty—that's it, isn't it?' Schiller exclaimed
triumphantly. 'What are you up to? Putting a black on? Is that
it?'

'Not me.'

'Someone else?'

'Perhaps.'

'I swear——'

'Don't!' Then, more gently, he added: 'Don't swear—think.
Aladko tried to recruit you, and Zimmermann.'

'Didn't get him far. Got me a few beatings, mind. Kicked shit
out of me because I was a Nazi, then forgot about me.'

'And spent more time with Zimmermann?'

'Wait a mo——'

'Tell me.'

'Christ . . .' Schiller proceeded to rub his large, stubbled jaw
again. The rasping sound might have been the noise of a snake's
skin against the encircling rope. 'Christ . . .' he muttered again,
then: 'Wolf was never a Nazi. The Russian pig would have picked
that up almost at once. He was sharp. But he wasn't a Red, either.
I know that.' Schiller looked into Aubrey's face. 'On the other
hand . . .'

'Yes?'

'The Russian fascinated him. You could see that. Wolf was too
clever for his own damn good, half the time. Used to laugh himself sick every evening, when they brought him back. He'd been
taking the piss out of the Russian all day, leading him on, I suppose . . .'

'He wasn't being persuaded?'

'No, I'd swear to that—I don't think so,' Schiller corrected
himself. 'Wolf was too clever, too arrogant inside his head, ever
to fall for that ideological claptrap. Yes, I'm certain of that.'

The opinions had an unreality. The remained unconvincing
simply because of the colloquial, accented English. A credibility
gap had been opened by the Australian voice.

'How did you get away?'

'Wolf's plan. They were run ragged, retreating. Our boys were

218

close behind. It was easy to slip away.' Schiller shrugged. 'We were found by a Condor unit the next morning, cold and hungry and free.'

'The escape wasn't arranged? Since you say it was so easy . . .?'

'It wasn't. Two others with us, the survivors of our patrol—they were shot. Wolf wouldn't have arranged that for the sake of convincing me. And I wouldn't be here, would I, if it was all arranged?' He spat again. 'The Russian would have shot me to keep any deal secret.' He shook his head. 'No, Wolf didn't go over, not then.'

Aubrey sighed. He could not distinguish relief from disappointment in his feelings. There was no proof, just another opinion. Perhaps there was no certainty anywhere.

Schiller reached for the rifle, turning as they heard a body slithering down the crumbling cliff face. Dust billowed just at the edge of the firelight.

'OK, it's me,' they heard Hyde announce. He walked into the light.

'What is it? Anything?' Aubrey asked.

'A fire. Less than a mile away, as far as I can make out.'

'They've made bloody good time,' Schiller observed.

'If it's them. I'm going to take a look. I came to warn you to keep a lookout. I won't be long.'

'Be careful, Patrick.'

'Don't get lost,' Schiller added in a practical tone.

Hyde nodded. He looked at the rifle for a moment, then walked away. As he began climbing the cliff face again, gagging on the dust, he heard the two old men talking.

'You have no opinions to offer?'

'On Wolf? Oh, he liked secrets and he liked power—maybe in that order. But he'd never have been a Red . . .'

The voices faded behind him once he reached the top of the low cliff. He crouched on hands and knees to recover his breath and his night vision. Yes, there it was, flickering against the wall of what he supposed was a sandhill. Its glow was diffused, magnified, but it was a fire. Perhaps no more than half a mile away. He followed the slope of the cliff downwards, away from the lake. The outcropping rock soon became gritty with sand, then his feet were sinking into it. He slithered down the unstable side of a dune, losing sight of the fire. The sand was soft, not stabilized by grass or trees.

On top of the low cliff he had been able to hear their voices, see the fire reflecting, hear the dingoes. Now there was nothing except the serpentine slither of disturbed sand, and a strange and unexpected claustrophobia. He was hemmed in, within a vast desert; a contradiction that unnerved him.

He rounded a large sandhill, climbed a lower one, hurried down the slope, then followed a small, narrow, dry creek. It wound away, then back towards the distant fire. When it petered out, he climbed another sandhill. The fire was off to his left now. Pale sand gleamed all around him and shimmered between himself and the prick of light ahead.

Another dune rose against the stars directly in front of him. It looked sharp-edged, with a ridge like a whale's backbone. The sand was soft as he scrabbled up its slope. When he reached the top, the fire winked closer than before. Strangely, the claustrophobia had passed. The first chill of the night, seeping through his thin windcheater, alerted and refreshed him. More than that, mere activity, the progress towards and into a defined situation, satisfied him. For the first time since they had left Adelaide, Hyde sensed his own competence like a thin, tough armour around him.

It took him more than thirty minutes to reach and circle behind the fire. As he had encountered no guard, he cautiously climbed the slope of a hill, slithering upwards on his stomach, using knees and elbows to propel himself. He was careful not to disturb the loose, fine sand at the crest of the hill, and then raised his head.

There was no one seated around the dying fire. Retinal images of the fire's declining light flickered in his mind, melding into the knowledge that he had been tricked. Petrunin had shown him a signal, a false light to lure him away from Aubrey. A chill possessed him as he suspected an ambush. He was immediately certain that he was unimportant and that Aubrey and Schiller were the objects of the deception. He careered down the slope of the dune, scattering the last burning twigs of the fire as he began running. The effort drove out recrimination and every other feeling except an almost primitive fear on Aubrey's behalf. It was impossible to believe that Petrunin would not kill Aubrey when he had the opportunity.

His ears strained to hear, in those moments when he checked his direction against the stars or paused to recover his breath, but he never caught the noise of shots or protest or struggle. He floundered on, scraped his hands and knees on outcrops of rock. He stumbled over clumps of tough grass, rolled when he lost his footing down the shallow slopes of fine sand that would not bear his weight. He ran on. The minutes passed.

No shots, no sound of a vehicle; no noise of an aircraft. Nothing louder or more unfamiliar than the noise of his ragged breathing and the beating of his blood in his ears. Against all reason, he began to hope. He stumbled, rolled, picked himself up, ran. The sand became a gritty deposit, then his feet began to make a dull concussion on rock. The starlit blackness ahead of him might have been the lake.

Firelight. Dying embers? No, the fire lively, compact, newly encouraged. He did not heed the warning, because he saw Aubrey stretched out on the sand of the shore—a dark, spread-eagled collection of limbs against the fire-ruddied sand—and scrambled down the cliff face towards him. He stumbled onto all fours only yards from Aubrey, and the first shot whined above his head, burying itself in the loose surface of the cliff. He groaned with renewed effort, perhaps even in protest, and rolled out of the firelight, into the shadow of the Volkswagen blazoned with Schiller's Winery.

Schiller . . . ?

No second body. Aubrey was alone. Two more shots thudded into the flank of the Volkswagen. Hyde, beneath the vehicle, felt their impact shudder in the ground. Night-sight? Aubrey lay only yards from him, his face averted as if in silent disapprobation. The body was still. His collar seemed stained with something dark. Hyde dismissed the image as he reached beneath him and drew the Heckler & Koch from his waistband. The gun, which he gripped tightly in both hands for a steadying instant, composed him.

Schiller . . . ?

They had him. Killed Aubrey, had him . . .

Aubrey moved, stirred one hand, clenching and unclenching it slowly in an underwater, tired way. *Don't*—Hyde's mind cried above his relief. In the same complex instant he realized that Aubrey was the tethered goat, lying almost as if arranged within the circle of renewed firelight. The fire, he told himself, reason catching up with impression. Nice big fire, plenty of light, bang . . .

Another shot, as if he had commanded it, thudded into one of the Volkswagen's front tyres, near Hyde's head. Night-sight? he asked himself, his awareness splitting into fragments. Part of his mind guessed at the accuracy and type of gun and its telescopic sight, another part inspected the Land Rover fifteen or twenty yards away, then a third section picked up, above the crackling of the tinder-dry fire, the roar of a distant accelerator. Petrol which he had previously ignored dripped onto his shoulder. The Volkswagen had been put out of commission. The Land Rover was undamaged and intended as the marksman's method of escape.

A further fragment of awareness watched Aubrey. The hand now clawed very weakly at the sand, drawing it into contour lines. It was as if Aubrey were attempting to climb the horizontal plane of the shore. Was he wounded, dying . . . ?

Petrunin hadn't killed Aubrey, hadn't dared . . . Only field agents were expendable without protest or reprisal. Not deputy directors. Aubrey's head flopped sideways and his body turned onto its back as if the head had moved it like a corkscrew. The marksman would begin to watch Aubrey, listen to him, wonder about his accidentally becoming a victim after all . . .

Hyde rolled from beneath the Volkswagen, on the far side from the fire. Aubrey groaned again. Hyde stood up, shielded by the van. He pressed his cheek against the cold metal, feeling the gritty dust on it.

Fire, body, cliff face . . .

Straight line, shortest distance. He stood away from the van. He could hear the struggle Aubrey was having to lift himself, either to stand or sit upright. Another old man's groan and a cough. The marksman would be watching, would begin to realize that Aubrey was now in the firing line. Hyde hoped Aubrey was sacrosanct, that Petrunin had given a definite order to let Aubrey die in the desert or recover sufficiently to get to Etadunna Station, perhaps. If so, the marksman would be over-cautious, anxious. Hyde had to die, but not Aubrey . . .

Hyde reached the scattered rocks where the small inlet threw the cliffs back into a tiny canyon. Hyde tiptoed with exaggerated care through the shallow water, then began climbing the cliff. When he reached the top, he looked down. Aubrey was sitting, head resting on his knees, hands clasped like those of a prisoner on the back of his neck. The firelight spilled over him. He shivered, then pulled his coat more warmly around him. He seemed un-

222

aware of his surroundings or his immediate past. Too stunned. The marksman would soon begin to discount the danger he represented. Hyde scanned the only possible cover on the beach, the rocks outside the circle of firelight. Unless he was up on the cliffs—no, the angle of all four shots was wrong for that—that was where he had to be.

It seemed minutes before the starlight replaced the glow of the fire in Hyde's night vision. He shielded his eyes with his hands and studied the rocks. The Land Rover had been moved . . .

He hadn't heard it. He had accepted the circumstances of the moment . . .

The pale screen of the Volkswagen, the firelight to illuminate Hyde, the tethered goat of the old man.

Where, then . . . ?

There. The sand smeared and contoured to hide footprints. That rock.

Hyde could see nothing, just the black shape of the rock and its shadow before the sand began again like a gauze spread on the ground.

Patience, patience, he counselled himself. Aubrey stirred once more, tottering to his feet, groaning, his head obviously tender and egglike to the touch of his fingers. He staggered a few yards.

'Patrick . . . ?' he called in a croaking voice. Then, with more immediate fear: 'Schiller? Schiller?'

Aubrey staggered towards the Volkswagen. Hyde, peripherally aware of his movements and his voice, watched the rock. His night vision had caught the reflection of the fire again, and he cursed the involuntary movement of his head when Aubrey called his name.

The fire's glow faded in his eyes, and the pale sand gradually solidified . . . mist, gauze milk, sand. A figure detached itself carefully from the shadow of the rock, rising above it. The rifle seemed at shoulder-level, pointed towards Aubrey. Desperate remedies: Aubrey was in the way, the man would lie to Petrunin, nothing more would be heard . . .

Aubrey turned, staring at the dying fire. His figure was black-etched against the flank of the Volkswagen. Hyde, on his knees, arms stiffly out in front of him, fired four times. The rifle clattered on the rock, the body spun away, gouging itself into the sand like some frantic, burrowing animal. Then it lay still. Aubrey staggered with shock, as if drunk.

Hyde slid and scrambled his way down the cliff-face, loose rocks and stones tumbling ahead of him. He picked up the rifle, then inspected the marksman. One of the two he had seen at the camp-site in the Flinders Range, cooking steaks on a barbecue grill. He lay face-upwards, staring at the stars and seemingly surprised by the sudden change in his perspective. The distress of the sand around him, created by his last moments of pain, was without meaning.

'Shit,' Hyde breathed.

'Is he dead?' Aubrey asked at his side. His voice sounded calm and rational.

'Yes.'

'Now he can tell us nothing.'

Hyde turned on Aubrey, the adrenalin that had remained unemployed flooding into a sudden rage. 'He was about to kill you, for Christ's sake! I'm a gunman, not a fucking surgeon! I *had* to kill him!'

He stepped over the body and walked away from Aubrey. He heard the old man say: 'I apologize. Thank you.'

'OK,' Hyde muttered, waving a hand dismissively. 'What happened?'

Hyde wandered towards the edge of the shallow water. It was dark but bore a sheen of starlight that appeared to gild its sable. Aubrey followed him.

'They were on us in a moment. Schiller had no time even to pick up his rifle . . .'

'That fire was a dummy. They took Schiller?'

'Yes. Dragged him away, hit me over the head.'

'Petrunin?'

'Yes.'

Hyde kicked a loose pebble across the water, and listened to its plopping submersion. It might have been an unidentifiable bird or fish.

'Christ . . .' he whispered.

'Where will they have gone?'

'What? Lake Eyre. Just like Schiller said—the only place they could land the aircraft.'

'We must go after them, Patrick.'

'I suppose so.'

'The vehicles . . .?'

'The Land Rover's OK. That was his escape route.' He gestured over his shoulder with his thumb, towards the body.

'Why—am I alive, Patrick?'

'Too much fuss. You could die in the desert—they'd have disposed of my body, left yours near the Volkswagen. All a terrible accident, isn't Australia a wild place . . . but no one would put a bullet in you. Reprisals. A gang war with SIS. Petrunin wouldn't want that.'

'I suppose not.'

'Why do they want Schiller—can you guess? Do they know, or not?'

'I don't know.'

Hyde shuddered. 'Come on, we've got until morning. That plane can't risk a take-off from Lake Eyre before it's light. Much too dangerous. You all right?'

'I shall have to be. Thank you once more, Patrick.'

'Come on, we're wasting time.'

The dawn seemed appropriately wintry. Misty, chill, damp. The industrial smells of steel, rubber, smoke and oil scented the air. Wu Han assailed him, even at the airport, pressing its reality upon him as if to suggest its freedom was no longer available to him. David Liu registered the unattainable airport buildings as he was marched along the glass corridor towards the gate to the Peking plane. It did not begin to occur to him that the flight might be delayed by the weather. There was not even the hope of postponement in his situation. He was numbed, as utterly and thoroughly as if he had been frozen like a slab of fish or meat; he was no more than a camera lens registering the scene through the windows, and aware of the armed guard on either side of him. He accepted his situation with the passivity of an animal's bloodless carcase emerging from an abattoir. He simply could not think about it. His reason, his imagination, would not function.

He had spent the night in one of the cells at Wu Han's central police station. No questions were asked of him, and no answers supplied to his own questions and protestations. From time to time during the night, a guard had opened the cell door's spyhole. He had not been physically ill-treated. He had been ignored. Everyone seemed certain of him, and of what to do. He was given breakfast—a thin fish gruel—ordered to dress, and then he had been taken to the blind-windowed police van which had driven him to the airport.

His defeat had been so sudden and so entire that the shock of it remained, numbing him. Even the reflection that since his arrest he had seen no one in authority, no one from the MPT or the Public Security Bureau, was something that faded in his mind as soon as he conceived it. He was utterly numb.

The gate lay ahead. The guards were close on either side, almost touching his arm. Both of them carried stubby, narrow Type 43 SMGs, slung on straps across their bellies. Behind him, the detective in the Mao-suit, a pistol in a shoulder holster which Liu had been allowed to see in the police station foyer, accompanied them. There was a lone figure waiting for them beneath the illuminated sign which indicated the gate number and the flight destination. A figure in a light grey suit. A tall man.

The recognition produced breathlessness in David Liu. There was no instant of unreasonable, desperate hope, simply the cold-water douche of recognition which itself was trampled beneath full realization. Images already shaded and altered filled his imagination. Frederickson in the street the previous day, Frederickson shadow-boxing the first time they made contact, Frederickson reassuring him . . .

Frederickson.

The American CIA station head in Shanghai smiled a thin, knowing smile, then nodded curtly at the detective behind Liu.

'Get him aboard,' Frederickson told the two armed policemen. Liu was immediately thrust in the back by the stock of one of the SMGs. His breath emerged in pain and ineffectual protest. 'Go along, David, be a good boy.'

'There will be a delay?' the detective asked.

Outside the glass corridor, at the end of the umbilical tunnel from the gate, a Chinese version of the old Soviet IL-14 transport aircraft appeared grey and chill in the mist. It was decorated with military rather than civil markings. Its two large turboprops were still.

Frederickson shrugged. He appeared indifferent. 'Maybe. Get him on board, anyway.'

Liu opened his mouth as if to speak, but shut it again slowly. Frederickson seemed to enjoy his speechlessness, and nodded. The policemen thrust him down the tunnel towards the door of the IL-14.

Zimmermann sat as if transfixed by the images on the television screen and the voices that came from it. He had drawn a chair closer, and he hunched over his knees as if supplicating the glowing screen and its two doll-like figures. The interviewer was distinguished and formidable—and the single subject of his half-hour programme was the Chancellor of the Bundesrepublik Deutschland, Dietrich Vogel. Whether the interviewer was of the right or the left did not matter. Vogel in an embarrassing, awkward situation—a political minefield—was too tempting a prey to allow any restraint in matters of question, tone and persistence. He was performing close to his best, but the ride was rough.

Zimmermann imagined the millions watching with him. Vogel had agreed to appear and chosen his adversary. It had been unavoidable, but he believed he would have entered the bullring anyway. Vogel, his friend, had courage.

And nothing to hide.

Vogel had chosen the pipe, rather than his preferred cigarettes. Cigarettes might have indicated nervousness; they formed the lips, employed the breathing in a different way. A pipe—an intricately carved Meerschaum with a woodland scene that would deflect the camera's inquisition of his features—implied solidity, confidence, honesty. It enabled Vogel to sit back in his chair, fold his arms across his chest, appear at ease. It was something for his eyes and his hands to employ.

The Americans had taken up the story, together with the rest of Europe, particularly France and Britain. Newspaper digests and ambassadorial and consular breakdowns of news coverage had swamped the Chancellor's press corps during the early part of the evening. Twenty-four and more hours after the story had first broken, the tide was running, the ripples had spread to the banks of the lake.

'Chancellor, there are accusations of secret clauses regarding trade with the Soviet Union and her satellites. Clauses and undertakings for huge trade credits, substantial loans, supplies of advanced technology—perhaps even military technology crucial to NATO—all of which form a massive bribe to the Kremlin. How do you answer those accusations?'

Vogel took the Meerschaum slowly from his mouth and inspected the squirrels who peeped from behind the tree-stump bowl of the pipe. He smiled slowly, then looked up. Zimmermann admired his coolness. The interviewer's spectacles flashed in the studio lights as he waited with impatience for a reply.

'I would answer them by denying their truth,' Vogel announced calmly, careful to exclude bluff or smugness from his voice. 'There are no such clauses. And I know what you mean when you refer to NATO. Germany will not be a part of NATO any longer, but we have made no agreements with the Soviet government to supply them with details of the Panavia Tornado . . .' He smiled again, almost a chuckle. A carved fox peeped engagingly at the camera from the other side of the tree-stump. It did not appear to be stalking the squirrels, each of whom held a large acorn. 'The President of France accepts our assurances on that point, but it appears that the British government does not. This morning's *Times*, and America's *Washington Post*, are both being more than a little hysterical over this issue. I can assure them that NATO pilots will not be flying Tornadoes in combat with Russian Tornadoes!' He laughed, inviting a complicity of innocence. The squirrels faced the camera once more.

'Credits, loans, civilian technology, computers, Herr Chancellor? You did not mention them.'

'My apologies. Trade with the Soviet Union and her allies in the rest of eastern Europe will be continued as before. We have been trading with them for twenty years or more. We will not stop—nor will we become an economic slave state for the Soviet Union's benefit. I think that answers your question . . . ?'

A small pale snail was in the act of climbing the tree-stump. It filled the camera and the screen for an instant—charming, beautifully carved, innocent. A thrush or some other speckled bird watched it, apparently without hunger or desire. Vogel took the pipe from his mouth and mulled over it, turning the pastoral carving in his fingers.

'Your chief adviser and negotiator, Professor Zimmermann . . . ?'

'Yes?' Vogel snapped, face hardening into unpleasant lines in an instant.

'No,' Zimmermann murmured, hands clenched on his knees in the darkened room. 'Stay calm.'

'Herr Professor Zimmermann has been accused——'

Vogel cut him off with a sweeping gesture of his hand. The pipe flashed in and out of camera focus, now a mere object without charm or detail.

'Careful, Dietrich, careful,' Zimmermann whispered.

'The smear campaign conducted against my adviser—and my friend—Wolfgang Zimmermann is one of the most unpleasant occurrences in German journalism for twenty years,' Vogel thun-

228

dered. Something in the tone indicated to Zimmermann that the anger was under under control, being employed rather than employing. Vogel supposed his audience wished to see him angry on Zimmermann's behalf. 'He is *not* a Russian agent—that is patent rubbish, and unworthy of the German press, as well as being libellous—and he never has been. He is a German, and has worked untiringly for the good of Germany, the proper and historic reunification of our country.' Vogel leaned his bulk towards his interviewer. '*Don't* call Herr Zimmermann a Russian agent— don't even suggest it. Not in my presence.'

Vogel sat back, contemplating the pipe once more. Fox, thrush, snail, squirrels. He turned it in his hand, attracting the camera.

Zimmermann accepted that Vogel had thrown his hat into the ring on his behalf. He was on the tightrope, taking the stroll across the chasm or the waterfall at a bull-like rush, headlong. Zimmermann wondered whether it would work. The inertia, the energy, was on the other side.

Zimmermann believed that the Berlin Treaty was doomed, and would not be signed in six days' time. The Russians would not pull down the Wall. All would be as it had been for almost forty years. They would go down fighting—but they would go down. Surely and certainly, they would lose.

Liu studied the green-painted whale's belly of the IL-14, its arching, riveted ribs and intestinal webbing and wiring. It was a bare, half-finished place, and the noise of the two big turboprops thrummed through the fuselage. Frederickson, who evidently wanted to explain, had almost to shout above the noise as he sat next to Liu. Soldiers, machine pistols across their laps, sat impassively on the opposite side of the fuselage. The throb of the engines quivered through the padded steel chair, emphasizing the distressed, watery feeling in Liu's stomach and bowels. It was as if his digestive system had apprehended his condition in advance of his awareness. In mind, he still felt drugged and bemused and without fear.

'You were meant to walk out free,' Frederickson was saying, 'taking the story with you.' His grin became a twisted expression of contempt. 'Then you have to do a Charlie Chan on us, and dig deeper than you should have.'

'Everything was arranged?' Liu asked. His curiosity was detached and academic.

Frederickson nodded. 'Everything. Wei, Shanghai, Wu Han, Doctor Meng—everything.'

'What will happen to Meng?'

Frederickson's eyes glittered in the hard, grubby lighting. 'Meng failed,' he said.

'Everything was arranged.'

'Wise up, Chinaman.'

'The CIA and the Chinese and the British—everyone.'

'Not the Brits.'

'What?'

'In a game like this, there has to be a dummy. You're our dummy, so are the Brits. Someone had to take Wei seriously, besides ourselves. The Brits fished him out of the harbour, dried him off, listened to him . . . wondered about him, and agreed to send you in. And, brother, you had to be ignorant of it all. You just *had* to be convincing when you eventually talked to Aubrey.' Frederickson shook his head. 'It should all have been so neat. Uh?'

'Neat,' Liu echoed in agreement.

'Very neat.'

'Why?'

'Because we don't want the Krauts leaving NATO. Because we don't want a hole in the middle of Europe any enemy of ours can simply piss into and stake his claim. Because it couldn't be allowed to happen. Sure, the Wall coming down is nice for the Krauts on both sides of it—but not for us.'

'Us?'

'We—us—the Chinese and America. Us.'

'America and China?' Liu asked as if he had comprehended nothing.

'For the moment, *us*. The enemy's the Soviet Union, if I have to spell it out for you. Get it?' Frederickson was grinning again. 'We have to have guns and tanks on either side of Russia, to east and west—not some half-assed neutrality, kiss and make up. Don't you understand anything about strategy, Charlie Chan?'

Liu's eyes flickered with rage and hatred for a moment, but the emotions were only embers; or the first sparks of a fire. He shook his head. Now, he was listening more closely. Now, images began to move, the element in his head no longer treacle or wool but a thinner, purer, more transparent medium.

'And everything you want can be achieved by this?' His

gesture took in the aircraft's interior. One of the guards moved the machine pistol on his lap.

'Sure. If Zimmermann goes down, he takes Vogel with him. *And* the Treaty.'

'Neat. What—happens to me?'

'You? You got no worries. You just stay quiet until it's all over, then it won't matter. You got no worries.'

Fear stabbed Liu like a sudden abdominal pain. He did not believe Frederickson. It was too large, too important, for witnesses to survive. He swallowed the thin, acid bile that had forced itself into his throat.

'I see,' he said carefully.

'You almost did a good job,' Frederickson conceded. 'Meng should have kept his mouth shut, is all.' Frederickson's hands clenched into claws in his lap. He studied them with what appeared to be satisfaction.

'Why wouldn't the Germans listen to you? Why do you have to do this?'

Frederickson studied Liu. 'You interested in this?' Liu nodded. It was evident that Frederickson enjoyed the superiority of explanation. It was Liu's education in the ways of the real and covert world. The CIA man was his instructor, his private tutor. 'The Krauts—their only interest is a united Germany. They think about it when they're awake, dream about it at night. You can't reason with them. One united and neutral Germany, that's the name of their game.' Frederickson's face winced, as if he had toothache. 'Bastards,' he murmured.

'So Zimmermann isn't a Russian agent?'

'No. Hell, not as far as we know.' Frederickson laughed, his large, long-fingered hands slapping his thighs. The creases in his slacks were sharp, knife-edged. 'He may well be. We don't really know. Now that would be a laugh. Maybe he is, after all. He's kissed enough Russian assholes in his time. Maybe he is.' His raucous laughter continued.

Liu glanced out of the porthole behind him. A layer of cloud with a pool-like opening revealed green, flat country stretching towards distant grey and brown uplands. Liu felt detached from it, encapsulated in this whale's belly, and in the narrower prison of his new knowledge. He thought of the Englishman, Aubrey, the other dupe. There was no way he could stumble upon the truth. Then he thought of his own silence, and the CIA's method of ensuring that it became permanent, even eternal. The ground seemed a long, long way down, the mountains in the distance hard and sharp and infinitely solid.

The Beechcraft was silent and still on the crust of the saltpan, changing colour from grey to pink to gold in the rapid dawn. Behind it, the salt crust of Madigan Gulf, the south-eastern part of Lake Eyre, gleamed white. Hyde and Aubrey had walked the last half mile, climbing and skirting ridges of hard sand partially covered with canegrass. They made slow time until they found a saltpan before them, beyond which dunes loomed in the last of the night. Beyond the dunes, the dry lake stretched to the horizon. The Beechcraft was parked perhaps a few hundred yards beyond the grass-tufted mud that bordered the lake.

'Can you see Schiller?' Aubrey asked in a weary, tense voice.

Hyde, who had been searching the area of the campsite, where a tent was pitched next to the Beechcraft and the Volkswagen, guiltily concentrated the field glasses on figures other than that of Petrunin.

'No. He must be inside the tent. Poor sod.'

Hyde refocused the glasses on Petrunin. The man was bent over a bowl, and the rising sun winked off the surface of a mirror. He was shaving. Hyde almost rubbed his own stubble in envy. One of the two remaining Australians from the Volkswagen that had dogged them since Adelaide was preparing breakfast. Hyde had seen the other one walking towards the nearest dune to complete his ablutions. The Beechcraft's pilot was, presumably, still inside the tent with Schiller. Hyde lowered the glasses and glanced at Aubrey.

Aubrey, sensing the element of inquisition in the look, prepared his face for inspection. He regretted its unshaven appearance, and the washed-out blue of his eyes, red-rimmed as they were. Strangely, he felt less than weary, despite the night-long journey from Lake Palankarinna through the unchanging, endless sandhill country towards Lake Eyre. To Aubrey, Hyde appeared hunted and driven, his face thinned by some internal hunger. His eyes were red-rimmed, with dark stains beneath them. He had done all the driving from lake to lake, and the strain and effort were as clear on his face as flood channels on the landscape behind them.

'Are you . . . ?' Aubrey began.

'OK? Yes. I was asking myself the same thing about you.'

'I—I'll manage.'

'OK. It's now or never.'

The pilot emerged from the tent, stretching. A murmur of sound reached them, but the words were indistinct. Petrunin looked up from his shaving and nodded, then resumed smoothing his face with the razor. The Australian emerged from behind the sand dune, scattering a handful of birds like black scraps of paper as he brushed a wattle shrub.

'What?'

'Give me the gun.'

Aubrey hesitated for only a moment, then slid the hunting rifle across to Hyde. Without this weapon, he well knew, they would have been helpless. He considered, with a fierce, cold, narrow satisfaction, that the sniper they had left in ambush at Lake Palankarinna had not died in vain. His legacy possessed sufficient stopping power and a telescopic sight.

Hyde adjusted the sight, focusing on Petrunin. The Russian leapt into sharp close-up, bending over his mirror, working the razor across the deep cleft in his chin. The crosshairs met at Petrunin's temple.

'Not Petrunin,' Aubrey warned him sharply.

'What?' Hyde snapped angrily.

'Tit for tat, necessity for necessity. Don't kill a senior KGB officer if you can possibly avoid it. I have other people at risk here, in other parts of the world.'

'Christ . . .' Hyde breathed. 'He's the only real danger!'

'Nevertheless . . .'

'OK, you're in charge.'

'Yes.'

Hyde swung the rifle across the shoreline. The salt crust glimmered, unfocused, behind the scene. The pilot, then . . .

He adjusted the sight, let the crosshairs meet on the pilot's chest, at the V of his open shirt where black hair curled on his breastbone. Slowly, he squeezed the trigger.

He took the rifle from his eye, cursing. In the newly re-established distance, the Australian who had disappeared behind the dune fell awkwardly in front of the pilot and lay still. He had walked into the telescopic sight at precisely the wrong moment.

Hyde refocused the sight, swinging the rifle as the pilot stumbled and began running. He heard distant yells. He lost the pilot, swung the rifle back and found the man cooking breakfast rising from his haunches. He fired. Sand spurted near the fire, then Hyde swung the rifle again.

'They're scattering,' Aubrey said. 'The Volkswagen . . .'

Hyde looked over the sight at the scene of the camp. The pilot and Petrunin were running out onto the salt towards the Beechcraft. The Australian was climbing into the cab of the Volkswagen. The engine stuttered, then caught. Hyde, squinting into the sight once more, sought and found the rear tyre. He fired twice before the Volkswagen jerked out of his vision. He swung the rifle up, towards the aircraft. Two unfocused, running figures. He adjusted the sight until Petrunin's naked back was in focus.

'They're getting away!' he almost wailed.

'They don't have Schiller—*that* is what matters!' Aubrey snapped tersely.

Petrunin climbed awkwardly into the cabin of the Beechcraft. The door slammed shut behind him. Two faces in profile, that of Petrunin preventing a clear shot at the pilot. The Volkswagen was slithering out across the salt out of range, one tyre flat. The Beechcraft's engine started, and the aircraft lurched, swung tail-on to them, then rolled away across the salt crust, gathering speed. The Volkswagen pursued it.

'Shit!'

'Come on, let's get down there. Schiller must be——'

'Is he!' Hyde said darkly, as if intending to mar Aubrey's satisfaction.

They stumbled down the shallow slope of the dune, through its soft white sand onto the level shoreline of baked mud. Hyde ran ahead of Aubrey, pausing only to inspect the dead Australian and smelling the overcooked bacon on the fire, then he lifted the flap of the tent with the barrel of the rifle.

Schiller appeared to be sleeping, but he was dead. He lay staring at the apex of the tent's roof, hands at his sides. His face was pale. Aubrey arrived, breathless, at the door of the tent. Hyde turned on him. The Beechcraft's engine sounded distant now.

'You and your fair play!' Hyde raged. 'They've fucking done for this poor sod, though, haven't they?'

'Hyde!'

'Petrunin is a *shit*! He's killed this poor bugger.' There were blotches visible on the pale, waxy skin of Schiller's face. Marks of violence. Schiller's lips were still drawn back against his dentures, as if grasping at another last, difficult breath. 'Christ!'

Aubrey knelt by Schiller's body for a moment, and shuddered.

'A heart attack, I think,' he murmured, turning to Hyde.

Hyde brushed the flap of the tent aside and studied the lake and the sky. The Volkswagen and the Beechcraft were two retreating specks, inviolable and unattainable. Hyde clutched the rifle in impotent rage, grinding his teeth. The bacon had burned in the battered frying-pan. Aubrey emerged from the tent.

'Will they come back?'

'Like hell they will.'

'What did they discover, I wonder? About *us*? Why beat him up? What did they want to know so badly? *Do* they know what is going on themselves?' He looked guiltily back at the open flap and added: 'I had much to ask him.' His voice had dropped to a shamefaced murmur. Hyde crossed to the flickering fire of salt-bush roots and hickory, studied it for a moment, then kicked the frying-pan away across the mud. It banged against the temple of the dead man, spilling its bacon. A dried-up fried egg sizzled in the twigs and stumps of the fire. 'Hyde,' he heard Aubrey say behind him.

Without turning, Hyde snapped: 'What?'

'Get back to the Land Rover. Use the radio to get in touch with the nearest homestead. Inform them there has been an *accident*.' Hyde tossed his head. 'Get them to inform the police. Tell them we will require an aircraft. I—I'll look after things here.'

Hyde stood still for a moment, as if in disobedience, then he turned, threw the rifle in Aubrey's direction, and began trotting towards the first dunes that lined the lake shore like low cliffs.

235

TEN:

End of the Line

Shoudu Jichang Road, the wide boulevard leading from Peking International Airport into the heart of the city, was lined with trees and midday crowds who seemed as orderly and planted as the vegetation, even though they moved like a tide. Liu's apprehension of China's capital was subject to his mood of profound hopelessness. He had, he knew, been brought here to die. It was a simple, inevitable, unavoidable fact. He would be terminated with extreme prejudice, as the vile euphemism of his service described murder. Thus Peking's buildings, people, atmosphere became menacing and imprisoning.

Soviet. Most of the newer buildings might have belonged to Moscow or Leningrad or Kiev, a succession of monuments, government offices and workers' dwellings lining broad streets or surrounding bare, vast squares. The police car used the middle lane of the boulevard reserved for official and VIP traffic, sweeping past the herds of cyclists moving in their direction.

Terminate with extreme prejudice. This view of Peking was a species of premature burial, flinging him into the whirlpool of people that was China before removing his identity entirely and forever. He shuddered. Next to him, Frederickson grinned in satisfaction at his evident depression. On Liu's other side, an intelligence officer—who obviously knew Frederickson well and who possessed an unmistakable air of authority—stared at the driver's neck. An armed and more junior intelligence man sat next to the driver. Silence pressed in upon Liu with the weight of physical bodies. Since his explanation on the aircraft, Frederickson had said little, breaking his silence only with the punctuation of orders to himself or the soldiers. He had even greeted the two intelligence officers waiting at the airport, their car drawn up at the edge of the taxiway, in silence. Satisfaction and resolution of difficulties was expressed only in the warmth of handshakes and smiles.

It was the beginning of Liu's interment in the cold ground of silence. He shuddered again, uncontrollably.

'Cold?' Frederickson asked sardonically. The Chinese intelligence officer blinked, once. Liu shook his head.

The car passed the huge, ugly block of the Soviet Embassy. Liu saw the secret, triumphant smile on Frederickson's lips, and the slight, superior nod of his head. Then they turned south towards Chang An Avenue. Public buildings, grandiose concrete and steel ideologies, replaced blocks of flats. The avenues and thoroughfares became wider, more and more hoardings exhorted the population towards the second millenium. Chairman Deng stared benevolently and sternly upon cyclists and pedestrians and the drivers and passengers of cars, trucks, even horse-drawn wagons and carts. No representation of Mao caught Liu's eye. He, too, had been obliterated. Red flags draped countless buildings.

The car turned into Chang An Avenue. Streetlights lined the broad thoroughfare, bearing clusters of balloon-like globes. Then, in another minute, they were in the vast Tiananmen Square, the vermilion walls and yellow roof of the Gate of Heavenly Peace confronting the symbol-less, poster-less mausoleum which contained the remains of Mao. Even Deng had not yet dared to order the dismantling of the building. His features seemed to stare across the square at the mausoleum from a hoarding on the walls of the Gate, disapproving, even envying. Around the square, the huge buildings of the Historical Museum, the Great Hall of the People, the Workers' Cultural Palace and others less distinguished or massive, seemed low and diminished by the grey concrete openness of the square itself. People, crowds of them, became insignificant in that vast arena.

The car turned through an archway into the courtyard of an unnamed building. Liu divined it to be the headquarters of the security service, the Ministry of Public Tranquility. Pedestrians had drawn back, their faces suddenly hangdog, as the car turned in. They had watched his face, as if attempting to identify him. The courtyard was filled with black saloon cars and police vehicles. The driver showed a pass to an armed guard, then stopped beside a small, closed door.

'End of the line,' Frederickson said, and then added, without seeming to correct himself: 'End of the ride.'

'Get out, please,' the intelligence officer said quietly. The junior officer held his door open, and Liu climbed out behind the MPT man. He glanced up at the windows around the courtyard, many of them barred.

'It is, isn't it?' he asked.

Frederickson nodded. 'It is. The MPT. You'll like it here.' He grinned again. The windows were blank, row upon row of them. Blank like the American's eyes.

Inside, in a small, cramped office, they removed his belt and shoelaces, searched him thoroughly, taking all his documents, before he was escorted to the cells, below ground level. Frederickson and the senior Chinese security officer did not accompany Liu and his two guards.

The cells were in two rows, facing one another across a tiled corridor. One door was already open for him. He was thrust inside, firmly but without violence, and the door was slammed and locked behind him. The cell was tiny and windowless. A single bulb glowed through reinforced glass above his head. Weakly illuminated within the globe, what might have been the decaying bodies of insects appeared merely as smeared specks of shadow. The bed was thin and hard and covered with a single blanket. There was a latrine bucket in one corner. A bowl of cold water for washing stood on a narrow wooden table. The room had no identity.

Liu subsided on the bed, arm over his eyes to shield them from the light; to hide them from the spy-hole in the door.

Aubrey was in full signals contact with Shelley in London. The high-speed, frequency-agile transmissions were beamed, via the transmitters on the roof of the Mutual Life Centre and a geostationary communications satellite, across the world to be received at GSHQ outside Cheltenham. Then they were relayed, via the receivers on the top of the Euston Tower in London, to Queen Anne's Gate or Century House, wherever Shelley happened to be. In fact, at that moment he was presiding over the operations board at Century House.

The Signals & Administration Section (SigAdS) of the Secret Intelligence Service occupied the top two floors of the largest office block in Sydney, the Mutual Life Centre, even though the SIS headquarters for the Australasian and Far Eastern Geographic Department was situated in the federal capital, Canberra. The Governor-General, the High Commission, even the Foreign & Commonwealth Office in Whitehall, preferred much of the sensitive business of the intelligence service to be conducted in the relative anonymity of the business district of Australia's largest city. The Australian federal government, and the government of New South Wales, accepted the residence of an important SIS section in a commercial building in Sydney as the price of close liaison between British Intelligence and ASIO, the Australian Security and Intelligence Organization.

The previous afternoon a police Cessna light aircraft had brought Aubrey, Hyde and the body of Schiller from Lake Eyre to Adelaide, via a refuelling stop at Quorn. Aubrey's diplomatic status had held a police enquiry in abeyance and enlisted their services in an unsuccessful search for Petrunin's aircraft. The Adelaide police had informed Clare Schiller that her father had been found dead by her two English visitors, apparently the victim of a heart attack. *Was there any history of cardiac trouble, Miss Schiller? . . . Not for some time . . . I'm very sorry, Miss Schiller . . .* Hyde had listened to the polite, impersonal call, and been unable to feel anything more than relief that it was not his task to inform the woman.

Aubrey and Hyde had slept on the Adelaide-Melbourne-Sydney shuttle flight. Now, looking down over Sydney Harbour across the roofs of other skyscrapers towards the oyster shells of the Opera House, Hyde felt weariness lift from him. Somehow, in an unexpected and vivid way, he had come home. Aubrey, across the huge, open-plan communications room, was no more than an insect-buzzing noise, without meaning. Hyde saw only Government House, the Botanic Gardens splashed towards the sea like a spillage of bright, glossy paint, Sydney Harbour Bridge arching towards the north shore, and the darker blue of the sea beneath the hard shell of the sky. And the yachts, tiny paper hats of sails slipping across the glittering water. A hydrofoil ferry dragged its wake towards the Opera House. He was home. Strangely, he was momentarily at peace.

'Peter,' Aubrey was saying, hunched before the console and its slowly revolving tapes. His coffee cup stood next to the microphone he was using. 'I have no clear idea of the state of the Russians' knowledge. I do not know what they learned from Schiller before . . . he died.'

The console operator, taking his cue from Aubrey's nod, dabbed at the keyboard. The tapes behind their clear plastic covers speeded up, whirring dizzily. The conversation was converted into a blur of sound, then transmitted. When Shelley's console received it, it would again be slowed down, and Shelley would hear the voice of his superior much as if he had been using a telephone. The message was incapable of interception, even though not encoded, because the transmission frequency was altered by as much as one hundred times per second following a pattern on a computer card that would be used only once, then scrapped. Effectively, this method of communication had replaced the 'one-time pad' and the 'code of the day'.

A spit of sound like a distant, muffled scream, and then the tapes slowed and began their stately progress once more, revealing Shelley's clear, next-room voice.

'And you feel your dialogue with him was inconclusive, sir? You haven't any definite ideas . . . ? We're putting everything into the computer. We have one correlation already. Zimmermann was a frequent and regular visitor to Wittenberg in the late '50s and for most of the '60s. That would fit in with your idea of a family connection.'

The tape hummed slightly, hissing as if to prompt Aubrey's reply. The operator's fingers tapped the keyboard. The tapes stopped. Aubrey could feel only a profound disappointment. The visits, the blackmail? The rewards for tasks performed, or merely the journeys to make dead-letter drops, meet his control . . .

Everything could be interpreted suspiciously. Everything an agent in place did *was* suspicious, he reminded himself.

He nodded. The tapes stirred sluggishly.

'Peter, I want information out of the DDR, and I want it quickly. If none of our people can move fast enough, then we shall have to send someone in. I want to know all there is to be known about the Zimmermann family *after* 1945.'

Speeded-up tapes, silence, tapes running again after the quick buzz of noise, then the stately unrolling of Shelley's reply.

'I've already put that in hand, sir. I think it will have to be someone sent in. None of our Wittenberg people can move easily or without plenty of notice. Shall I organize it?'

A few seconds later, Aubrey said: 'No. I'm coming back at once. I'll do that. You have that Hercules for me? It can divert to the Federal Republic . . .' Aubrey sensed Hyde staring out of the window on the other side of the room, and nodded to himself. '*I*'ll handle the matter. I'll need you there, of course.'

Pause, then: 'Where in the Federal Republic, sir? It'll take time.'

When the tapes began again, and the recording light appeared on the console, Aubrey said: 'I'll get Buckholz to organize that. Somewhere like their Wiesbaden base. *You* signal our people and put them on the utmost priority schedule. And Peter—did the ending of these regular visits coincide with anything in Zimmermann's own career?'

The tape slowed. 'About the time he sold his business interests, took up the academic life . . .'

'Followed by the political life—damn!' The console operator winced, as if the expletive, though mild, had surprised and offended him. 'He was preparing to go into the political realm, become active. No more incriminating visits to the DDR.'

Silence. The incoming message whirred, then slowed.

'Sir, what about Spain? Your report is pretty vague. *Did* they?'

'I don't know. He might have been ripe, he might not. What have you got for me on Spain?'

'Sorry, sir. Madrid Station haven't come up with a survivor of any of the units we know were in the immediate area. Not one with Communist sympathies, who would have been close to the centre of the action. We're still working on it. Sir, the campaign against Zimmermann and the Treaty is hotting up.'

'No doubt. Have you gleaned anything from it?'

'No, sir. It's mostly speculation and rumour—nothing *we* can use.'

A slightly hissing silence, then the tapes stopped, and began again after a rewind. The small bright red light came on.

'Very well, Peter. I'll talk to you again from Hong Kong. Meanwhile, I want a scenario for a penetration run into the DDR, target Wittenberg. And I want something for the agent to collect when he gets there. Then I want *you* in the Federal Republic. Good luck.'

The tapes whirred, then stopped. Aubrey sighed and leaned back in his chair. His coffee was cold. Sunlight, even though filtered by the tinted windows, spilled hotly into the room. The dust motes swirled. The harbour was dazzlingly blue beyond the Opera House.

'Patrick,' he said tiredly. The frequency-agile transmissions were a tiring form of communication. So much tension, curiosity, anxiety were expended in the silence between the words. He appreciated, and disliked, the technology he employed.

'Sir?'

'Are you ready to leave?'

Hyde turned reluctantly from the window. The sunlight illuminated one side of his face. He nodded.

'Ready.'

'We'll leave for the airport at once, then.'

Charles Buckholz, Deputy-Director of the CIA, watched the tapes above his head begin to roll and the red light wink on. He gripped the microphone in his hand. To his left, the console operator waited, his fingers poised like those of a secretary over a keyboard. The room was hot and humid, even in the middle of the morning, and Buckholz had loosened his tie and rolled up his shirt-sleeves. The US Consulate in Hong Kong was situated near the Botanical Gardens and Government House. The smell of blossom on the hot air was almost illusory as it clashed with the scents of petrol and dust.

'OK, listen to me. Aubrey's returning today. I'll be travelling with him and the Chinaman—and he wants arrangements made for reception at Wiesbaden. That means you have no more than twenty-four hours at the outside to ensure that he's met by the right reception committee when he steps off the plane. I want Wei to become our responsibility as soon as we land in Germany, and I want Aubrey's investigations suspended. That has to happen as soon as we land. It's the only way to stop it. And in connection with our friend Liu, I'll have his bogus report for Aubrey ready the moment he reaches Hong Kong. It won't satisfy Aubrey— he likes Zimmermann, wants to believe in his innocence. And he'll want to see him in person. That he can't do, but maybe the report will help But you—you have to organize it so that Aubrey is stopped, and by his own government. A direct order.'

The red light winked out. The tape speeded up to a blurred rush. Buckholz, while he waited for acknowledgement of his orders, rubbed his smooth chin. Then he sniffed the ends of his fingers for the last trace of his after shave, as if warding off the smells from outside. He shook his head. Only some of the details had failed to work out. The essence of the operation he and the Chinaman had from the beginning called *Jade Tiger* was still intact and potent. It was a pity he could not have entirely fooled Aubrey, and a pity that the bright-eyed, bushy-tailed Charlie Chan they had sent into China had come up with the right rather than the wrong answer. However, he was out of the way, and soon Aubrey would be out to grass.

Buckholz nodded. Everything still held good. It was going to pan out. It would work.

The middle-aged bachelor who lived in the quiet street in one of the grid-patterned, tightly-packed south-eastern suburbs of Melbourne was well known to his neighbours as an amateur radio enthusiast. That fiction enabled a communications base to be established by the KGB outside the confines of any official Soviet building or organization in the city. The cellar of the neat, fastidiously-clean wooden house was crammed with equipment which, though heavier and more bulky than its Western counterparts, performed the same functions of high-speed, frequency-agile transmission. Its relative lack of sophistication, its inability to change frequency with the same rapidity as SIS and CIA equipment and the reluctance of Moscow Centre to employ computer cards on a 'one-time' basis, led to the necessity of concealing the point of transmission more effectively than either the British or Americans would have considered necessary.

Thus Petrunin sat in the cellar of the supposed radio enthusiast, in front of the console and beneath the unshaded lamp and its hard light, waiting for a reply to his lengthy report direct to a Deputy Chairman of the KGB in Moscow Centre. The radio enthusiast had gone to his official employment as an office clerk.

Petrunin had ordered the pilot of the Beechcraft to fly direct to Marree, where they had refuelled, and then to file a flight plan for Melbourne. There, the aircraft was abandoned at the airport and the pilot paid off, before Petrunin came directly to this suburban Melbourne address. Of the driver of the Volkswagen, he had no knowledge and possessed little concern. Others would have to take care of him. Subordinates would have to patch up the Australian operation and get it back into effective working order. He had merely used it as was his right and in what he considered an emergency.

Petrunin had made his recommendation for further action on the part of his service. He had laid before his Deputy Chairman the facts of the case as he knew them, giving special emphasis to the nature of Aubrey's enquiries. Schiller had, unfortunately, suffered a massive heart attack as a direct result of the tension of his situation and the physical beating he had sustained. Yet he had revealed enough to deeply disturb Tamas Petrunin. He hoped Moscow Centre would share his anxiety. Certain procedural understandings, perhaps no more than niceties, would have to be overridden in order to achieve a satisfactory solution.

He looked at his watch. An hour and a half since he had concluded his report. He sighed.

Ten minutes later, the receive light on the console glowed into green life. The tapes rolled swiftly, then stopped. Petrunin operated the keyboard and, after rewind, set the tapes rolling at the normal transmission speed. It was the voice of his Deputy Chairman.

'Comrade General Petrunin,' he began formally. The mode of address indicated that Petrunin had won the argument even though he was on the other side of the world. 'The Operations Crisis Committee has considered your report, and your recommendations . . .' The transmission was unclear, cluttered with the hissing of the upper atmosphere or some decline in power in the satellite's solar batteries. Petrunin clicked his tongue in irritation. 'It is our decision that your recommendation is accepted and put into operation at the earliest possible time. The Politburo has conveyed, through Chairman Andropov, its total agreement with this decision.' There was a pause, then the Deputy Chairman added: 'There is too little time fully to discover, and foil, whatever scheme the Americans and the Chinese have initiated. Therefore the elimination of the principal parties is essential, in disregard of normal operational practice. Therefore you will communicate your operational scenario to the Centre within the course of two hours. Transmission ends.'

Petrunin switched off with a vigorous, final gesture, and leaned back in the swivel chair. He sighed with anticipation, tension and pleasure. Aubrey had been seen at Sydney airport, boarding Qantas flight for Hong Kong, together with Hyde. He would be returning to Wei, the defector, and to Buckholz. Hong Kong, then.

Aubrey dead, Buckholz dead, Wei dead . . . and Hyde, of course. The little personal satisfaction within the shell of the operation. The wet job which would have as its kernel the small, neat, satisfactory revenge upon Hyde.

Kill them all, he had said. Kill them, then, Moscow had replied. Silence them. We can't find out, so—just stop it. Dead.

*

244

The 747 swayed, righted itself, and its wheels met its shadow on the white finger of concrete stretching out into Kowloon Bay. The deep blue water glittered on either side of the aircraft as it slowed its rush towards Kai Tak's buildings. From his window, Hyde had already picked out the olive-drab shape of the RAF Hercules transport plane waiting for them. He nudged Aubrey and pointed to where it stood, isolated from the main terminal buildings. There were three cars drawn up like dwarfish attendants near it, and blue spots of men in RAF uniform guarding the aircraft. Aubrey smiled in satisfaction.

The afternoon heat of Hong Kong assailed them as they left the first-class compartment of the 747 and walked down the gangway to where Godwin, smiling broadly—white teeth gleaming in his pink features—stood beside the black official car. Other passengers, impressed and mystified, watched them climb into the car after shaking hands with Godwin.

The car pulled away across the tarmac towards the Hercules. Aubrey realized that one of the cars was a large American sedan. Buckholz.

'You're both all right, sir?' Godwin asked, turning round in the front seat, his face as solicitous as that of a relative.

'Thank you, Godwin, yes, we are. A little tired, of course.'

'It's all arranged, sir. Mr Buckholz has got clearance for a landing at Wiesbaden Air Base, and Shelley's on his way there to set up station. I'm to inform you that *Wild Hunt* is all but ready to run.'

'*Wilde Jagd*—Wild Hunt. Yes, that operational title is satisfactory,' Aubrey murmured. 'Good. Anything else?'

Hyde stared at the looming bulk of the Hercules with distaste. He did not, at that moment, seek within himself for reserves. When he began his run, he would find them available—or they would remain unavailable, in which case he would undoubtedly fail. The German Democratic Republic still lay over his emotional horizon. At present, he was merely freight.

'I . . .' Godwin had a telling-tales-out-of-school grimace on his features, at which Aubrey clicked his tongue. 'I think he wants to take complete charge of Wei. I think he might be right.'

'Why? What's the matter?'

'I think our chap—*their* chap—Liu has found something . . . Mr Buckholz thinks . . .' Godwin's features became more lugubrious than ever. 'He's sure Wei's right. He seems convinced——'

'What does he know?' Aubrey snapped. The car came to a halt beneath the shadow of the Hercules. Buckholz was at the door, grinning solemnly. 'Charles!' Aubrey exclaimed as the American tugged open the door. Wei's face peered out from the rear of the American sedan, where two Hong Kong policemen in peaked caps guarded him. It was as if the CIA had already appropriated the Chinaman. 'Charles, what news have you had?'

'Good news—and bad, Kenneth.' Buckholz shook his head. 'Good news insofar as it's definite news, bad in that it confirms Wei's story, dammit!' Aubrey climbed out of the car, his squinting gaze searching Buckholz's face.

'You mean . . . ?' Buckholz nodded.

'Zimmermann was interrogated, there *was* something to find out. They went through the mill with him, broke him down and built him up again. Liu has seen the records, talked to people involved. He was fooled into believing he was in Moscow, with his Control. He spilled everything—all the way back to 1938.' Buckholz appeared furiously angry. 'The guy's KGB—has been for forty years! Jesus Christ!'

Aubrey was appalled. 'You're sure . . . ?' was all he could say.

Hyde watched them. He, like Aubrey, felt he had walked into a brick wall, winded and suddenly halted. Everything had been futile on their part; one little Chinaman had all the answers, off pat.

'Where is Liu now?' Hyde asked irrelevantly.

'What? Oh, back in Shanghai. We'll get him and his full report out safely as soon as we can.'

Hyde felt envy creep into his emotions. His risks, his efforts, his danger—all pointless. Someone else had found the answer. Even so, Aubrey's reaction surprised him.

'Get him on board—*now*!' he snapped at Godwin, pointing to Wei in the back of the sedan. 'Get him on board!'

The pilot of the Hercules, after climbing down the ladder from the hatch behind the aircraft's nose, came towards them like someone careful of interrupting a family quarrel. He nodded in salute to Aubrey.

'Are you ready, sir?' he enquired.

'Yes, Squadron-Leader——?'

'Michaels, Mr Aubrey.'

'Yes, Squadron-Leader Michaels, we are ready to leave.'

'This way, sir.'

Aubrey watched Wei with violent animosity as he was led towards the steps up to the fuselage between the two policemen. Buckholz's assertions had stunned him. Zimmermann *was* KGB . . . ? He could not—yet had to—believe it. It was the end of the line. It had all been verified by Liu. End. Finished. Zimmermann had been proven guilty. The Berlin Treaty had been masterminded by an active, long-term Soviet intelligence agent. God alone knew what secret clauses, what secret concessions, had been granted to the Soviet Union in pursuit of the illusion of a united Germany . . .

It did not bear thinking about—had to be thought about . . .

Wei passed out of a halo of late afternoon sunlight into the shadow of the aircraft's interior. Aubrey felt viperish towards the defector, just as he did towards Zimmermann. He felt personally betrayed, which he recognized and admitted sprang from the interest he had taken in Zimmermann. As he had ventured further and further into the unknown territory of the German's past and present, he had come increasingly to wish the man innocent. He could not decide, however, whether his own ego might not have been more satisfied by the disproving of Wei's story rather than by confirming the evidence of the defector.

He dismissed the idea. There was, anyway, the matter of owing Zimmermann his life . . .

He climbed the steps, Buckholz directly behind him.

'I might as well take this guy over,' Buckholz announced almost casually as they passed into the sudden, dim coolness of the Hercules' interior. The aircraft's cargomaster, a WRAF Flight-Lieutenant, smiled at them, indicating the troop compartment aft of the flight deck. Chairs and tables, bolted to the bulkhead, awaited them; a drab, ribbed, hard-lit office without comfort or welcome.

'Thank you, my dear,' Aubrey murmured.

'Coffee, gentlemen?'

'Please.'

The two Hong Kong policemen saluted and left. Two of the RAF guards entered the troop compartment and seated themselves on either side of the disconsolate-looking Wei. The WRAF officer closed the metal bulkhead door behind her as she left.

Buckholz sat, large and clumsy, hands on his thighs, opposite Aubrey, across a narrow metal table.

'I'm sorry, Charles, what was it you just said to me?'

247

'Kenneth, I just said I might as well take this guy off your hands.'
Wei brightened visibly at the words, as Buckholz jerked his thumb
towards the defector.

'Oh. You must give me time to adjust to the new circumstances,
Charles.' Aubrey looked at Wei. Instantly, the pathetic, withdrawn, defeated look appeared on his features once more. Aubrey
was disturbed, as if he had glimpsed a mask, or a face behind a
mask. 'I must consider . . .' he murmured to Buckholz.

'What?' Buckholz asked sharply.

'Everything. Oh, something I meant to return to you . . .' He
indicated the briefcase that lay on Hyde's lap. 'Your files—your
interrogation of Zimmermann. Charles, in 1945 you were a lot
more adept at interrogation than I was in 1940!' Aubrey smiled
winningly, received the briefcase from Hyde, removed the files
and passed them to the American. Godwin watched the little
drama, absorbed, while Hyde stared at the fuselage as if engaged
in counting its panels and bolts. Outside, the sedan drew away,
followed in convoy by the two other cars. Hyde watched them go
with profound indifference.

'The guy was beaten, Kenneth, that's all. He'd had enough.
When you met him, he was on a high. With me, he was careless and
disillusioned.'

'And yet, I would never have thought . . .' Aubrey murmured.

The port outer turboprop started up with a shattering noise,
followed by the starboard outer, then the two inner engines in
sequence. The racket thrummed in the fuselage, causing the
table between Aubrey and Buckholz to quiver. The files twitched,
as if possessed of human nerves. Moments later, the Hercules
moved out onto the taxiway. The cargomaster brought their coffee,
then left them once more.

The Hercules swung its lumbering bulk onto the runway, nose
pointing out into the bay. White concrete, light-sheened glass,
blue water, the white dots, brown spots of sails; Aubrey's last
images of Hong Kong. Why, he wondered, did it so dissatisfy him?
Why did Colonel Wei seem such a burden of undigested matter?
As the aircraft began to accelerate down the runway, picking up
speed, flashing past the bright bodies and great tailplanes of
other aircraft, the scene quivering in the heat as if it would melt,
Aubrey studied Wei.

The Hercules lurched into the air and began to climb, banking
out over Kowloon Bay and Victoria Harbour. Wei sat like a

statue, or a piece of machinery that had been disconnected from its necessary power supply. Run out of steam, or oil—no juice . . .

Green, hazy hills on Hong Kong island swung past the nearest window port, then only the cloudless sky was visible. Hong Kong had disappeared.

Out of juice . . .

Aubrey unbuckled his seat belt and picked up his plastic container of coffee. He sipped at it, and found it drinkable. He continued to watch Wei until the Chinaman became aware of his attention. Wei avoided Aubrey's steady glance, looking instead towards Buckholz as to some protector. Buckholz, Aubrey was increasingly aware, was watching him intently. Each of them was watching the others keenly, even suspiciously; a small, tight circle of guilt . . .

Why guilt? Why did I form that idea . . . ?

'I must meet young Liu as soon as possible!' Aubrey announced breezily. And caught a strange, careful, suspicious glint in Buckholz's eyes for an instant, before an assumed puzzlement masked everything else.

'Meet him?'

'To congratulate him, of course! Splendid job he's done.'

'Oh, yes . . . Sure, we'll have him flown wherever you want, once we get him out.'

'Excellent!'

Aubrey raised his cup in a toast, saluting Buckholz. Wei watched the Englishman with the deepest suspicion. Buckholz's features assumed confidence.

And I saw guilt, Aubrey told himself. I saw it. I wish I had not, and I do not understand its presence, but I saw it. Charles is feeling guilty.

Why?

Wolfgang Zimmermann reached across the coffee table with its headline-displaying newspapers to pick up the ringing telephone. He had returned to Bonn overnight while Vogel continued his election tour north to Bremen and Hamburg. His presence was, it had been made clear to him, an increasing embarrassment to the Chancellor. Low-profile, please . . .

'Yes?'

His office was familiar, but it seemed no more than somewhere to contain him while in transit. He felt he no longer belonged there. Yet, strangely, he had not possessed the courage to return to his apartment; it was as if there he might meet a similar rebuff from furniture and fittings, and be desolated by that diminished image of himself.

'Kominski,' Petya announced with barely disguised anger. It was the private telephone. Zimmermann switched on the scrambler. Previously, trusting no one in a suddenly shifted and corrupted personal world, he had checked that the office had not been bugged during his absence with Vogel.

'Petya . . .' he began hesitantly.

'Cut the crap!' Kominski's idiom was American, like many of his young, English-speaking contemporaries in the Soviet Union. Beyond the window, a grey September noon drew colour from the parkland surrounding the Federal Chancellery buildings, the Schaumburg Palace. 'What's going on? My people in Moscow want to know what the hell is going on?'

'Petya,' Zimmermann pleaded in the tone he might have used to placate an angry lover, 'Petya, listen to me!'

'You have to stop it, Zimmermann, you have to *prove* you're not working for us. Do it!'

Zimmermann's gaze slipped from the window, as if drawn by the opened newspapers on his coffee table. His secretary had brought them in on his orders. The black capitals bellowed at him from the world's best, most serious newspapers. *New York Times*, London *Times*, the *Daily Telegraph*, *San Francisco Chronicle*, *Los Angeles Times*, *Boston Globe*, *Washington Post*—then Europe; Holland, France—*Le Monde* he could read, *De Telegraaf* he could make out—the Spanish, Italian and Scandinavian he could guess at with accuracy, their chorus of denunciation and suspicion.

AIDE ACCUSED . . . A SECOND GUILLAUME? . . . DOUBTS CONCERN-ING RATIFICATION OF TREATY . . . ZIMMERMANN TO RESIGN? . . . TREATY MUST BE RECONSIDERED . . . TREATY MUST BE RENEGO-TIATED . . . TREATY MUST NOT BE RATIFIED . . .

Defeat stared at him, large and black and in clear, bold type.

'How do you suggest I do it?' Zimmermann enquired with sarcasm. Fuelled by the headlines on the table, something rebel-led in him against the tone of the young, cynical Russian. 'You have a scenario?'

'Submit yourself to television interviews, make a strenuous denial in the newspapers, sue for libel—get off your arse and defend yourself!'

'Stop foaming at the mouth,' Zimmermann snapped curtly, his mouth curling in a contempt he wished Petya Kominski could witness. 'Your own masters' anger sounds too violent for you. You need a smaller size—petulance, perhaps?'

'You smug bastard, Zimmermann! You were crawling to me for reassurance last week!'

'I have stopped crawling.'

'Then get up on your feet and shout LIES, for God's own sake!'

'For my own sake—for your sake. For the sake of the Treaty we both so much desire, I will do what I can.'

'Keep me informed.'

'No. It is my problem, not yours, Goodbye, Petya.'

He put down the receiver delicately, as if handling something precious and fragile, or something infected. Immediately he broke the contact, the mood of desperate optimism left him. Courage evaporated without the necessary prop that Kominski had provided in the form of insults and demands.

Whatever he did, he could not save the Treaty. Of that, he was convinced. The chorus was too loud, too like the baying of dogs or wolves. He could not even save Vogel, who had slipped four points in the opinion poll taken the day of the first news story in *Bild*. Both Daedalus and Icarus were plunging towards the sea, feathers melted from the stick-like wooden frames they had thought of as wings. Both of them would fall . . .

Daedalus and Icarus, both plunging to the sea . . .

Even in the rain, and the darkness, there was still some prophetic formality about the two figures under their black umbrellas which warned Aubrey, made him suddenly alert after the long flight from Hong Kong. Wiesbaden Air Base, glossy and busy in the rain, became distanced and instead Aubrey recognized Peter Shelley, devoid of his familiar welcoming smile, and Alex Davenhill, SIS Special Adviser at the Foreign Office. The military officers around them, and the white-raincoated CIA officers, were mere scenery to their drama.

Almost at once Wei's hair was lank in the rain. He shivered with cold, despite his borrowed RAF blue overcoat. Godwin complained about the temperature more volubly. Buckholz moved closer to Aubrey at the bottom of the steps down from the Hercules, and Aubrey almost sensed the man's satisfaction. Hyde hunched into himself at the rear of the group, hands in pockets, bareheaded.

'Sir,' Shelley greeted him curtly. 'Mr Buckholz.'

'Peter, is that Alex Davenhill?'

Davenhill whisked his umbrella aside for a moment, and grinned with infuriating and dangerous youth. 'Kenneth!' he exclaimed, coming forward and holding out his hand. Aubrey took his chilly fingers. 'You look tired, my dear,' he added.

'Australia is no country for old men,' Aubrey snapped, recollecting the desert and Schiller's dead face. Blue around the lips, the eyes only slowly losing the last pain. 'To what do we owe the pleasure, Alex?'

Davenhill indicated Shelley. 'Sir, a letter for you, from "C".'

Aubrey's eyes narrowed, looking up at his aide as the young man held the umbrella over his superior's head. The roofs of the waiting cars shone with rain. A USAF Galaxy transport howled above their heads, lights winking as it lowered towards the runway, and Aubrey had to raise his voice to be heard by Shelley.

'What's going on, Peter?'

'Not here, sir . . .' Shelley appeared to be pleading rather than reminding him of basic security.

'Which car?' Aubrey snapped, and glared at the silent, apparently diffident Davenhill.

'This one . . .' Shelley indicated a large Ford.

'Charles, get my people into the cars, would you?' Aubrey climbed into the rear of the Ford as Shelley held open the door. Shelley then switched on the courtesy light and handed Aubrey the letter. Aubrey read in silence, his lips moving at first with the words then twisting into anger and suspicion. 'What is this?'

'It means stop, sir. No go.'

'I *can* read. "C" has been told, by whom?' Aubrey glanced at Davenhill's slight figure in a leather overcoat, beneath the black umbrella. 'The Foreign Secretary?' he added, almost in disbelief. Then he picked out Buckholz, shepherding Wei towards one of the American staff cars. Furiously, he wound down the window and shouted. 'Patrick, get Wei into *our* car, at once!'

A mime followed in the rain, umbrellas jigging to hand and shoulder movements—Buckholz, Davenhill, Hyde. Then Hyde bundled Wei into the second Ford.

'Sir . . .' Shelley protested gently.

'No!' Aubrey could not prevent himself shouting. 'Is Washington behind this? Is this an order from Washington?'

'Sir, believe me, I don't know!'

Rain spattered on the velour upholstery from the open rear window. Davenhill and Buckholz were still engaged in dialogue; angry and dismissive on the American's part, stiff and restrained from Davenhill. Godwin and Hyde stood evidently on guard by the second SIS car. The CIA officers and the army men hovered at a slight distance from Buckholz and Davenhill.

'Alex!' Aubrey shouted. 'A word with you, if you please.'

Davenhill detached himself from Buckholz, who was immediately surrounded by the other Americans, as if hurt. Davenhill's face was pale with rage.

'My God, Kenneth——!' he began.

'Alex, shut up, and tell me what this means.' The sheet of notepaper was already damp and limp.

'It means what it says.'

'You drafted this?'

'At the Foreign Secretary's request, yes.'

'What does it mean? What is its *precise* meaning? What are its implications?'

'It means you must cease investigating Zimmermann, and you must hand over the Chinese defector to the Americans. No more and no less than that.' Davenhill's suppressed anger was now focused on Aubrey. The umbrella was tilted to one side, and his dark, curling hair sparkled with raindrops. The shoulders of his coat shone.

'*Why?*'

'We have agreed that it is not our proper sphere of interest——'

'*Germany?*'

'We have agreed. We have further agreed to hand Wei over. You have finished with him.'

Shelley shifted guiltily, uneasily, in his seat.

'No,' Aubrey said firmly. 'No. I have not finished with him. The house is prepared?' he added, turning to Shelley, who merely nodded. 'Good. We'll drive there. To discuss this further.'

'Kenneth, no——'

'Yes!'

'You have your orders——'

'I have my judgment still . . . And it tells me that something very unpleasant is happening. Everything is back in the melting pot. Why this order, now? I have been assured that Zimmermann is a KGB agent, by Buckholz's man . . .' His voice trailed off into

253

silence. Rain drummed softly on the roof of the car like impatient fingertips.

'You are not to mount this *Wild Hunt* operation.'

'Why not?'

'You are ordered not to do so.'

'Buckholz? The Foreign Office? What the devil is going on here?'

'Matters of policy.' Alex Davenhill's youthful face looked suddenly guilty, self-condemning, as if he had betrayed a secret.

'Policy?'

'Hand Wei over, Kenneth——'

'Not yet. I want this explained. I was assured of Zimmermann's guilt. Perhaps the German operation is unnecessary, but you have ordered me not to undertake it. Why? What is under the stone?'

'Leave it, Kenneth. Leave it alone.'

Aubrey's anger overrode every other consideration. He knew himself to be acting irrationally, and a cold part of his consciousness despised the heat and quickness of his emotions. But he could not quell, or rid himself of, his fury. Suspicion, too, came in hot, violent moments, accompanied by images. Zimmermann, Wei, Schiller dead, Petrunin, Buckholz . . .

'I—must have time to think. For the moment, Wei will remain my responsibility. I must talk to "C"—to London. Please accompany us to the house. Then,' he added finally, offering Davenhill an elusive hope, 'you can explain. You can persuade me that I am wrong.'

Davenhill was silent for a moment, then he nodded stiffly and turned on his heel. Buckholz awaited him, they talked angrily in whispers for a few moments, and then the American shrugged. Davenhill gave orders. Aubrey smelt the wetness of the driver's raincoat as he climbed into the front seat of the Ford. Aubrey watched Hyde and Godwin climb into the other car to accompany Wei, then he wound up the window once more and turned to Shelley. There was admiration, and fear, in the younger man's eyes.

Buckholz's car passed them and took up the leading position in the small convoy. The Ford pulled away from the silent Hercules, towards the buildings of the airbase and its main gates.

'I—I'm sorry, sir . . .' Shelley stumbled out.

Aubrey patted his thigh. 'Not your fault. You were only following orders.'

'Sir, what will you do?' Shelley almost wailed. In reality, it was a warning. He had asked: *what* can *you do*? Aubrey shook his head slowly, almost dismally. It was as if he, too, regretted his anger and impetuosity.

'I don't know, Peter. I'—he spread his hands on his knees—'I became convinced in Hong Kong that Wei could be lying—not was, but could be. I went to Australia to approach the problem from the other direction, Zimmermann himself. I found nothing conclusive. I have read files which conflict, contain two different men. I returned to Hong Kong to learn that David Liu had been successful in elucidating the truth. Zimmermann, when he fell ill, *was* discovered to be a Soviet agent.' The fingers of both hands played a silent, solemn accompaniment on the stuff of Aubrey's coat as he spoke. 'But it is not good enough. Not to stop there. What if Liu is mistaken, has been lied to?' He looked at Shelley, whose face expressed utter misery and foreboding. 'I have seen no evidence, I have been told nothing conclusive. No, this must be argued out. *Wild Hunt* might have helped, might still help. You know what is at stake here. I cannot—I simply *cannot*—permit Zimmermann to be judged guilty on the evidence so far presented.'

'Oh, sir——'

'No, Peter. My mind is made up. I may sound stuffy and impossibly self-righteous, but my mind is made up. I must talk to Wei again, and I must talk to Liu. I am the disciple who must put his hands into the wounds of this business before I will believe . . .

'And?' Shelley asked softly.

'And, Zimmermann once helped me.' Aubrey's fingers fiddled to no pattern of accompaniment, expressing only embarrassment, perhaps honour. 'I owe him my life, Peter. I owe him my life.' Then Aubrey fell silent, and both he and Shelley peered through the rain-streaked windows at Wiesbaden slipping past like an illusion in the dark.

The SIS house in Wiesbaden, staffed on a permanent basis only by an elderly couple who acted as housekeepers, was in the suburb of Sonnenberg, at the foot of the wooded slopes of the Taunus. It was situated in a quiet, residential street of detached, nineteenth-century properties, most of them painted white and standing withdrawn and coy behind black railings reinforced by thick hedges. The SIS house was office, safe house, communications centre, operational headquarters—but only when occasion demanded. Otherwise, it purported to be the offices of a small, London-based export company. In wealthier times, its cover had included a small staff and a real, if modest, business life. Now, the effects of inflation and economies upon SIS's secret appropriation in successive budgets had reduced that cover to a mottled brass nameplate and two elderly housekeepers.

The gates were open. The street was well lit, but respectably silent after eleven at night. The Ford turned into the short, noisily-gravelled drive behind one of the CIA cars. The light over the front porch was on, illuminating the scene. The rain had lessened, though the cars still gleamed like beetles. Aubrey watched Hyde assist Wei proprietorially from the other Ford. The white facade of the house with its closed shutters was like a backcloth to the small drama of SIS's continued possession of the Chinese defector. Godwin bustled to the other side of Wei, as if to assist some old man up the steps to the front door. Buckholz's broad back straightened as he got out of his car, a raincoated CIA man holding the door open. The four cars crowded the short, semi-circular drive. The CIA officers outnumbered them, as if deliberately to pose a threat of force. Buckholz glanced back at Aubrey's car, his face a tight mask of suppressed anger and urgency.

The door was closed. Hyde rang the bell, which sounded in a muffled fashion deep in the house. Apart from the porch light, the house was in darkness. Instinct surfaced as tangibly as if he had sniffed gas from beyond the door, or heard the crackle of a consuming fire. The hall light was switched on, but he heard no approaching footsteps and no voice. He turned to look back at the cars in the drive.

The orders must have been precise, the targets selected in a strict and necessary order. The rifle was, naturally, silenced, but at that range—probably from across the street in one of the darkened houses, a first-floor room so that the railings and hedge did not impede the view through the night-scope—the slowing effect of the silencer's baffles would not have mattered. Hyde watched Buckholz slump against the American sedan, a white splash of raincoat on the black roof, and opened his mouth to yell. Then Aubrey crumpled and fell to the gravel, resting on his knees for a moment before slumping forward onto his face. Shelley was immobile with shock. White raincoats moved slowly through the glutinous element of incapacitating surprise. Hyde drew the Heckler & Koch and shot out the porch light, while

Godwin, with surprising recovery, dragged Wei to the ground, sprawling over him on the steps. Godwin's body shuddered at the impact of two bullets as Hyde fired at the lock, then heaved the door open with his shoulder.

The hall was empty. He fired twice in discouragement. No shadow moved. A door banged shut at the rear of the house. He turned. White raincoats were spreading out, moving across the street to shouted orders. Lights flickered on in other houses. Shelley was bending over the prone figure of Aubrey, who was no more than a crumpled black rag on the gravel. Buckholz had been turned over and leaned immovably against the sedan, staring sightlessly into the night sky. Hyde dragged Wei and the inert Godwin—a dark stain on the shoulder-blade of his light jacket—across the threshhold, kicking the door shut behind them.

1940: 27 AND 28 MAY

27 May 1940

The German artillery and airborne bombardment of Ypres had continued for twenty-four hours almost without cessation. For two days before that, under Hitler's direct order, the German advance had halted and fallen virtually silent. Zimmermann had informed Aubrey that 'even German armour has to rest' with a smile that was less than mocking and which expressed the German's impatience that his imprisonment end, and with it, perhaps, the whole battle of France. To Aubrey, Zimmermann appeared to have lost interest in and become disgruntled with a war in which he played no active part.

The ceiling of the room scattered plaster dust on them as they lounged, apparently senseless to the outside world, in two arm-chairs on either side of an ornamented cast-iron fireplace. Aubrey presumed the room had once been a bedroom, though now there was no carpet and no bed. A marble washstand remained, with a cracked jug and bowl, and the edges of the old floorboards were darkly stained, indicating the extent of the former carpeting. The ceiling betrayed spars and splinters of lath where the plaster had been shaken off by nearby detonations.

Zimmermann picked dust from his brandy with a fastidious fore-finger. Aubrey removed the hand which had shielded the liquor in his own glass, and sipped. Strangely, he felt comfortable. Zimmermann had been his constant companion for ten days. The guard outside the door did not exist for either of them; food and drink appeared, delivered by unnoticed soldiers. Aubrey slept in a narrow attic room on a camp bed, while Zimmermann's room, guarded every night, was in the cellars of the house. They had become attached to intelligence headquarters and part of the retreat of the BEF to the sea and Dunkirk. Operation Dynamo, the attempt to rescue the BEF, had been put into effect the previous evening. A curiously stale sense of relief had pervaded the building since that news.

During the ten days since they reached Louvain, the headquarters had functioned as a run down, outmoded, even archaic organization. There was no intelligence, and no intelligence function. They acted in the capacity of pessimistic historians recording events that had long overtaken them. The loss of function released Aubrey to talk to Zimmermann uninterruptedly as they moved from Louvain to Oudenaarde to Ypres. They waited, often like two members of the same club in an otherwise empty reading room, and moved westwards when ordered. Aubrey learned tradecraft rather than secrets, skills rather than information and, without any tinge of disloyalty or disobedience, did so consciously. He learned much about Zimmermann's mind, his talents and his background—and something of the state of Germany and less concerning the Wehrmacht. Of the military situation, there seemed nothing useful to learn. The loss of France and the Low Countries was as clear and evident as sky-writing; as if those incessant Luftwaffe aircraft billowed coloured smoke instead of dropping bombs.

Shells exploded near them, perhaps in the next street, with a jaw-shuddering effect. Neither of them flinched any longer at the proximity of danger. Again, plaster drifted down. Aubrey sneezed.

'We should have our movement orders soon,' he remarked, looking at his watch.

'I should hope so,' Zimmermann replied with a grin. 'For your sake, my friend.'

'What do you think of our chances?'

'Poor. It would take days to get this army off—and you don't have days. I'm sorry . . .'

'For the enemy?'

'No, for you. I shall not need to escape. As long as you prevent them from shooting me.'

Aubrey's mouth opened to reply. His hand moved to rub through his hair in embarrassment, then he turned his head to the window as the whine of the descending shells attracted his attention. The sound neared, became louder. Both of them sat in their chairs—Zimmermann had raised his glass to his lips once more in an ironic toast—unmoving, unalarmed. The wail of the shells might have been the distant practice of a choir of boys.

The first crumping explosion was overtaken by the bulging of the outside wall, which seemed to inflate into the room like one panel of a barrage balloon. The window flexed like a blind eye and then disintegrated, showering them with shards of glass. Aubrey's hands prickled and hurt, the back of his neck as he ducked burned with tiny incisions. Then all feeling became subordinated to the dusty, sweet-smelling influx of air, and the simultaneous lurch of his armchair as the floor collapsed beneath them. Aubrey saw the room below—even a lifeless, uniformed body beneath a wooden beam—and then he fell forward into it, tipped out of the suddenly trick chair. He put his hands out in front of him, cried out, fell and felt his body strike the floor below. His unfocused eyes watched the floor and ceiling, and the floor above that, tumbling down towards him. Then he was choking on plaster and rubble, engulfed and immediately unconscious.

Zimmermann heard voices, faint and in a language he felt he ought to understand but which was unfamiliar. He sensed his hand to be cooler than the rest of his body. Afraid, he opened his eyes. Slits of dusty light. The voices seemed to be coming out of the splintered, still-bright light. He coughed. The voices stopped for a moment. What language . . . ? He could not think. His head ached, and there was a pressing, crushing weight on his chest and legs. Instinctively, he tried to wriggle his toes. They seemed to move, but he could not be certain. He opened his mouth. Dust and tiny fragments of brick and plaster filled it. He coughed and spluttered. What language . . . ?

German—*German* . . .

He waggled his hand, as if waving farewell to a loved one, dispiritedly, tiredly. His wrist seemed restrained. The light hurt his eyes, filtering through what seemed like bars and then diffused by the tears that sprang into his eyes.

'Soldaten, zu hilfe!' he called out. The muffled croak of his own voice appalled him. 'Hilfe! Ich bin ein Deutsches offizier! Hilfe!' He gagged on the dust in his mouth, and began coughing again.

Rubble was moved from him. The light grew brighter. He blinked and spat. Weights seemed removed from his chest and legs. He felt exposed, undressed. A featureless face was staring down at him. A gabble of German that seemed too swift to understand went on near him. Someone referred to his uniform.

'Are you all right, Hauptmann?' someone asked in a softer voice. He opened his eyes again, wiping at them with a dirty sleeve. His arm moved stiffly, but freely and without pain. He blinked, and saw the shoulder boards of a lieutenant. His hand fell on the shoulder, patted it roughly. He laughed, and the sound turned into a racking cough. He was helped into a sitting position, and then they waited for his coughing and spitting to subside.

Eventually, Zimmermann looked at the young, blond officer and said: 'Thank you, Herr Leutnant, thank you. All of you,' he added, looking up. The young faces of the patrol grinned in unanimity. 'The British . . . ?' he then asked, looking around him.

'Gone.' The lieutenant grinned. 'Abandoned Ypres this afternoon—looks like they're pulling back to Poperinge.'

'They're making for Dunkirk.'

'Sure. But they won't get there. Can you stand, Herr Hauptmann?'

The lieutenant holstered his pistol and gave Zimmermann his arm. Shakily, Zimmermann rose to his feet and looked around him. The front of the house was open to the street. There was rubble everywhere, one or two khaki-dressed corpses. Smoke rose over the town. A German tank rolled past, its tracks squeaking and complaining on the cobbles. He had fallen from the second floor . . . ?

Somehow, he had fallen into the first-floor room below his own, then subsided more gently after breaking his fall as the whole of the house slowly collapsed. He shook his head gently, expressing a sadness which seemed without cause. His eyes roamed over the rubble, the upturned and smashed furniture, the broken telephones, the smashed bottle, the dead body in the uniform of a sergeant.

Something . . . ?

Nothing. 'Come on, let's get out of here,' he muttered to the young lieutenant.

'Medical unit will be along in a minute, sir, if you'd like to wait here for them? You'll be safe in that uniform.' He grinned again.

'Mm? OK—I'll wait. Legs feel a bit weak.'

'Oberschutze, get the Hauptmann a chair out of that lot.'

A young, boyish-faced senior private nodded, and began wading and clambering through the heaps of rubble, rooting until he found an upright chair with seat intact and back unbroken. He brought it back to the narrow pavement.

'OK, sir?'

'OK,' Zimmermann replied. 'Thank you.'

'You just sit here, Herr Hauptmann, and the doctors will be along in a minute.'

Across the street, other members of the lieutenant's platoon had herded perhaps half-a-dozen wounded British soldiers together on the pavement. They sat or lay as their wounds allowed. The lieutenant shook his head.

'You dug them out?'

'We dug them out. Their war's over.'

'But not their lives.'

'I don't anticipate their gratitude.'

'You have mine.'

The lieutenant saluted, and he and his men began moving up the street, cautiously aware of possible snipers, their heads cocked as they listened for cries or groans. They seemed to Zimmermann, in a sudden flush of relief at being alive, to be curiously merciful in appearance, despite the guns they carried.

Zimmermann felt like an old man, sitting on the pavement, prepared to watch the world pass him. Across the street, the groans of the few wounded British were muted, almost respectful. Perhaps they did feel gratitude . . . ?

The late afternoon sun was reddening, gaining a late evening dullness from the smoke hanging over Ypres. The street was long, straight, cobbled, quiet. Deserted, except for himself, the wounded, and the platoon now moving away from him. He experienced a curious, tired lack of energy and purpose. He simply wished to continue sitting there, emptying his mind, sensing the freshness of the air behind the smells of rubble and burning.

He heard one of the British groan across the street. Dully, his eyes took in the khaki uniforms, the slumped, hurt, defeated shoulders and upper torsoes. He had seen nothing but those khaki uniforms for almost two weeks. He glanced up the street. One of the platoon were dragging a British corpse from the ruins of a house. A child lay there, too, looking like the adult corpse's doll. There were civilian casualties—now he looked more carefully, he saw many of them. Dark trousers, printed skirts and frocks. Collections of rubbery, lifeless clothed limbs.

He returned his eyes to the uniforms across the street. Familiar . . .

The chair clattered over as he stood up, shouting as he did so. The lieutenant turned, his platoon halted. Then the officer and two of his men ran back towards Zimmermann.

'What is it?'

'A man—in there!' Zimmermann explained, pointing wildly into the rubble of the house.

'Who?'

'A British officer—you must get him out!'

'Where?'

'He fell from the same room—he must be close . . . under all that.'

'Why is he special?'

'He . . .' Zimmermann's face clouded, as if he were trying to recall something about Aubrey. 'He will make a very valuable prisoner,' he said eventually. 'An intelligence officer.'

'Very well, Herr Hauptmann—you two, get to work. Quick as you can!'

They moved and dug and shifted and lifted and threw aside for perhaps half an hour. The lieutenant watched them for a time, then, as if embarrassed by Zimmermann's feverish attempts to assist his men, he moved off to catch up with the remainder of his platoon. The two young privates obeyed Zimmermann as an officer—a lunatic officer, but nevertheless a captain in their army. Within thirty minutes, they had rearranged the new landscape of the ground floor of the house. Three other corpses had been unearthed, none of them Aubrey. The rooms became recontoured, new images of wreckage, as Zimmermann pursued Aubrey.

The stairs had collapsed. Zimmermann thought he recognized the shattered face of the corporal on guard outside their room when the shells struck. He could not be certain. Respectfully yet hurriedly he dragged the body clear.

'Somewhere here!'

He dragged one beam aside unaided, then the two privates joined him to move the shattered, gate-like sections of the balustrade. The dust rose around them until all three were coughing.

Arm, sleeve, civilian clothes . . .

Zimmermann uncovered Aubrey's face as gently as an Egyptologist uncovering the preserved form of a mummy, believing all the while that he would find a stranger staring lifelessly up at him. Dust-filled hair, a white skin, striped tie . . .

Aubrey.

'Thank God,' Zimmermann murmured, surprising himself with the warmth of his relief and gratitude. At least he had found the body . . .

He opened his cigarette-case and polished its silvered interior. Then he held it close to Aubrey's lips, snatching it away after a few moments. Clouded? Clouded.

'He's alive,' he breathed. 'Gently—move the rest of this stuff.'

The two soldiers lifted more shattered woodwork and a large, crazed piece of plaster away from Aubrey's legs. Then they brushed away smaller pieces of plaster and brick, splinters of wood. Aubrey lay exposed. His chest did not appear to move, his eyes did not open. Zimmermann, in a sudden doubt, used the inside of his cigarette-case again.

Clouded.

'Move him outside, into the sun—gently,' Zimmermann all but crooned. As they lifted Aubrey, his head fell loosely to one side and he groaned. 'Magnificent,' Zimmermann murmured.

They carried Aubrey over the new sand-dune formations of rubble, to the pavement. Here they laid him down very gently. One of the soldiers raised his head a little, and poured water over and into his dusty lips. Aubrey's eyelids flickered, he coughed, then groaned, and his eyes opened. The soldier eased more water into the now open mouth. Aubrey gagged on it, then swallowed.

'Can you hear me?'

Aubrey nodded, and groaned again. 'Yes,' he said faintly.

'Where are you hurt?'

'Everywhere,' Aubrey cackled, the strange laughter dissolving into a cough almost immediately.

A grey field ambulance drew up, as if on cue.

'You're alive—that's what counts,' Zimmermann said. 'You're alive.'

28 May 1940

'You see,' Zimmermann explained apologetically, yet with purpose, 'you were not in uniform when you were—captured. Therefore you cannot be a prisoner of war. You are . . .'—he looked down at his hands, clasped together in his lap as he sat perched on a hard chair—'a spy. You understand?'

Aubrey slowly nodded his head, absorbing the information. The room in the house in Courtrai, twenty miles east of Ypres, was shadowy. The house had been commandeered by an advance Abwehr unit. Aubrey fuzzily considered it was probably a unit to which Zimmermann had at one time been attached, since he seemed to know most of the officers by their first names. It was small and bare, with just sufficient space for the narrow cot and the upright chair.

'I see,' he said. He shifted on the bed, and his two broken ribs protested. His bandaged head ached. He was still aware of the weight on his chest and abdomen of the stairs and masonry slowly compressing his lungs, lowering down onto him until he would be extinguished. He shuddered. His broken ankle sent a stab of pain through his left leg. Nevertheless, it was difficult not to feel gratitude at his return to life, even in the face of Zimmermann's news. 'Thank you, anyway.'

Zimmermann shrugged. 'I am sorry.'

'What is the time?'

'One in the morning.'

'Oh.'

'Could you . . . ?' Zimmermann began. 'Could you move— travel?'

'Already?' Aubrey asked in sudden, alert alarm, his eyes roving the shadows of the small room.

Zimmermann laid a hand on his arm, patting it. 'No. To get out . . . ?'

'I—couldn't make it. Ribs, ankle. Feel so weak . . .' Aubrey replied. Self-pity welled up in his chest, pricked at his eyes.

'Not with my help?' Zimmermann was smiling in the light of the oil lantern. The electricity supply had not been restored.

'Your help . . . ?'

'Yes. My help. I don't want you on my conscience, you see,' he explained brusquely. 'I may have a great deal on it before we are finished. But not you, if I can avoid it.'

'How?'

Aubrey thought of the miles they had travelled in the back of a commandeered car, after the medical orderly had patched up his cuts and his ribs and ankle on the pavement in Ypres. Then the doctor Zimmermann had summoned to the Abwehr head-quarters; his painful gentleness. And the periods of fainting, of unconsciousness. He was helpless. Tears prickled at his eyes again. It was impossible.

'No?'

'Too far . . .'

'Listen to me, Kenneth Aubrey.' Zimmermann bent his face

268

over Aubrey, lowering his voice. 'I have a movement order, and a car. I'm trusted here, you see—known. Even admired by some, because I'm clever and don't care about danger. It was easy to persuade this unit that I wanted to get back to my own people. My unit's near Boulogne, still struggling to keep up with Guderian's Panzers. I have a movement order, to take the long way round, of course—and I shall be taking you with me.'

'Why?'

'Why? I've told you. I don't want you on my conscience. I don't want you shot as a British spy, even if that's what you are.'

'Why—why do you bother yourself?'

'Returning hospitality—call it that. You treated me well.'

'What about the danger?'

'There is none. I'm a German officer. This . . .'—he gestured around the room and beyond it—'this is all part of the Reich now. I'm a German in the greater Germany.' He laughed softly. 'Well?'

'Thank you . . .'

'Never mind. I must leave you for a few moments.' He stood up, pushing back his chair. 'Try to get into a sitting position by the time I return, please. We must hurry.'

Zimmermann closed the door behind him. He returned within five minutes, and seemed pleased that Aubrey was waiting for him, perched on the edge of the cot. Yet concern flickered in his eyes at the pasty, ill complexion the lantern revealed.

'I'm all right,' Aubrey announced with as much firmness as he could muster, before Zimmermann could speak.

'Good, good.' He addressed himself to someone Aubrey could not see, outside the open door. 'OK, get him to the car, you two. Don't be too rough on him. That comes later.' Zimmermann encouraged laughter in the two unteroffiziers who squeezed into the narrow room. They lifted Aubrey to his feet and assisted him out into the corridor. He groaned. One of the two men laughed, not unkindly, merely with indifference; as if he recollected some story or joke heard earlier.

They half-dragged, half-carried Aubrey down the stairs and out into the courtyard at the back of the house. An open Mercedes staff car stood on the cobbles, without a driver. An Abwehr officer lounged against the pale wall of the house. He grinned as Zimmermann emerged.

269

'I don't know why you don't stay with us, Wolf,' he said. 'A couple more days and you'll be able to shake hands in Dunkirk with all your pals!' The hauptmann exhaled smoke at the clear, soft stars overhead.

Zimmermann shrugged. 'I might get permanently assigned to this outfit,' he replied. 'My God, just think of having to put up with you all the time!'

'Take care, Wolf.'

'You know me, Hansie, only enough danger to get a medal—not to get killed.'

'See you in Dunkirk.'

Aubrey was placed not ungently into the rear of the car, and he subsided into a groaning heap of limp clothing, wanting only unconsciousness as an escape from the pain in his leg and ribs and head. He surrendered to Zimmermann's command of their situation. As the car pulled out through the archway from the courtyard to the street, Aubrey slumped further into the leather upholstery, and his sense of the cool night air rushing against his face diminished.

For him the night became a dream-filled sleep punctuated by the pain in his ribs and head, by scenes that flitted in and out of the darkness like moths, by the noise of the car's engine, by his own desultory, vague questions and Zimmermann's precise answers. These were occasional warnings, often associated with stops and murmuring voices in which Aubrey seemed to detect deference.

Questions popped into his reason and into his dreams. If he was conscious, he voiced them. Asleep, he asked them in his dreams and seemed to receive replies in Zimmermann's voice.

'How can you fool them . . . ?'

'The front's so fluid, we're advancing so fast, who's going to care which way round I go to get to my unit? . . . As Hansie Fischer said, in a couple . . .' The answer disappeared here. Aubrey did not hear any more.

Your papers? his dreaming persisted. *Who's going to care?* Then the dream-Zimmermann instructed him to go back to sleep. He felt hot, and sank into it.

Later, with a chill perspiration all over his body, he asked through chattering teeth: 'Which way are we going, anyway?' It seemed only a moment since he had asked about the transit papers and movement orders.

'North.'

'Where to?'

'Nieuport—we're attacking, but you're holding out. Unless things change . . .' Again the voice was lost, like intermittent reception of a distant radio station. Then, through the static of encroaching unconsciousness, he heard: 'It's on the coast. You'll be one of the first off . . .' Then the transmission was gone again.

A halt. Aubrey roused. *Where are we?* There was no reply. Had Zimmermann left the car . . .? Aubrey slept again.

'Where are we?'

'What's the matter with him, sir?' In German.

Aubrey protested something in German.

'Delirious,' he heard, and the laughter faded into static. Much later, he thought he heard Zimmermann reply: 'Dixmude—not far now.' Aubrey's mind grumbled at the slowness of their journey, then he slipped off the half-lit ledge in his mind into darkness again. Hot darkness, chilly darkness, hot darkness, chilly greyness, hot greyness, chilly light . . .

'What?' he asked plaintively.

'Wake up, Aubrey, wake up!' His face was gently slapped by a cold hand. Grey, early morning light.

'Where . . .? Your papers?' Aubrey asked confusedly, shivering violently, clutching his arms around his trunk.

'Listen to me, damn you! Up ahead, an SS patrol. You understand? *SS*? Stay awake and shut up!'

Then Zimmermann lowered himself back into the driving seat. Aubrey attended to concentrating on the German's face until he turned to look ahead once more, apparently satisfied. Lines of tension rayed out from his eyes like age's gullies. Aubrey shivered, felt himself retreat, tried to sit up, groaned. Zimmermann flinched at the noise as the car moved slowly forward into the single main street of a hamlet. Aubrey surrendered to his fever and the shivering of his body kept him conscious. He became aware of damp, salty sea air, and the smell of exposed mud and seaweed.

Zimmermann halted at the hastily erected barrier across the street. Beyond it, against the clammy grey morning sky, there were pillars of oily smoke. Buildings at the other end of the hamlet were alight, and distant fires hinted at burning farms or fields. A British tank had keeled almost onto its side just past the furthest house. A thin trickle of smoke came from its turret. Something charred lay near it.

The sea lay beyond the houses, and the straight road towards Nieuport and the German armour and the British lines. Smudges of smoke rose above the distant town. The sea seemed littered with a driftwood collection of small boats, beyond which the grey warships patrolled and lurked.

'Papers?'

'You got here quick,' Zimmermann replied, nodding at the SS collar tabs of the young, thin-faced lieutenant who commanded the barrier. Evidently the SS unit was acting in a police capacity, checking transport and men on the way to the eastern perimeter of the BEF's defences at Nieuport.

'Herr Hauptmann?' the lieutenant enquired, daring him to repeat the remark. Zimmermann shrugged. 'This is for Boulogne.'

'I'm taking the short cut—with him.' He indicated the slumped figure of Aubrey behind him.

'Who's he?'

'A British spy,' Zimmermann said calmly.

'We'll have him out, then.'

'Hands off, Herr Leutnant!' Zimmermann snapped. 'He's my property—Abwehr property.'

'So sorry,' the SS officer replied sarcastically. 'Does it speak? You—name, rank, number!'

Aubrey opened his mouth, and all that emerged was the sound of his teeth chattering. Most of the men in the guard unit guffawed.

'My God!' the officer said in disgust. 'Is this the best they have? He's half-dead already. No wonder they're losing . . .' He returned his attention to Zimmermann. 'You can't pass here, Herr Hauptmann. You'll have to go back—or lounge about here until the net closes. The Belgians have already surrendered, so maybe today, tomorrow . . . Then you can travel on to Boulogne.'

Zimmermann shrugged. 'I'll go back,' he said. 'And wait.'

The SS officer inspected Zimmermann's documents once more and then looked up, seemingly disappointed at their validity. He handed them brusquely back. 'Get moving,' he snapped.

Zimmermann turned the car in the street and drove out of the hamlet. A mile away, the ships at sea beckoned him. Behind him, Aubrey groaned with relief, or perhaps disappointment. He rounded a bend in the road and stopped the car.

Aubrey opened his eyes to witness Zimmermann standing on the bonnet of the Mercedes, field glasses to his eyes.

'What . . . ?'

'Good morning once again,' Zimmermann replied without looking at him. 'I can see our field HQ, our supply depot, our artillery and our reserves. The problem is, I can't see the British front line. Too far away. Mm . . .'

'Leave me here,' Aubrey volunteered.

'Not just yet. Yes, we'll take the officer's advice and go back, I think. Just hang on for a while. OK?'

'OK.' Aubrey replied faintly.

The car moved away, lulling him instantly. The artillery barrage was submerged beneath the regular engine noise. Zimmermann seemed to be talking, but Aubrey did not attend. Only scraps of it made sense, filtered through the haze of weary sleep.

'The Belgians have surrendered . . . gaps in the line . . . they'll bring up reinforcements—I would . . . head west, we might come across . . .' The rest of the transmission was lost as the static of exhaustion smeared across the words. From that moment, only the changes in temperature of his fever and the sharp movements of his head as he lolled against the upholstery distressed his even, deep unconsciousness.

Stop . . . ?

'Englishman, wake up!' It seemed like a different voice, and the first time of speaking, but something in Aubrey knew it had taken a long time to rouse him. 'Wake up!' Zimmermann commanded again, slapping his face. Aubrey blinked open his eyes.

'What . . . ?'

Light through heavily-leaved branches. Insect noises. He shivered and strained to keep his eyes open. Sunlight, splintered and dappled—warm. He felt a little warmer, but not hot and sweat-soaked.

'Now you have to walk. Understand? You have to walk!'

'Where . . . ? Don't want . . . can't!'

'You must, unless you want to be shot!'

'Where?' Aubrey asked more rationally, struggling into a sitting position, rubbing his head gingerly, then holding it.

'Down there.' Zimmermann pointed down a long, shallow slope, towards a dark hedge which lined a road. Moving along the road were olive-green vehicles; lorries and the occasional armoured car and tank. 'British,' Zimmermann announced. 'Heading north to plug the gap left by the Belgians.'

'Where are the Germans?' Aubrey blurted out, shivering once more, then clutching his broken ribs protectively.

'Behind us. Organizing for a push. Reviewing the situation or perhaps just tired out.'

'How did you . . . ?'

'You don't remember having rugs thrown over you, and a scarf in your mouth?'

Aubrey shook his head. His mouth felt dry, no more than that. 'No . . .'

'I'm on special patrol. Studying troop movements for Bock's GHQ. Who wouldn't respect that, except perhaps the SS? Now, out you get. Come on, come on . . . !'

Aubrey staggered out of the rear of the open car, his hands gripping the lip of the door for support. Zimmermann appraised him critically. It was evident he envisaged some cherished plan failing. Aubrey released the door with one hand.

'I—I'll try . . .'

'Come on, get moving. We won't be alone up here for much longer. Ready—a few paces first . . . Be careful of your ankle . . . One, two—let go of the door now—three . . . four—no, don't use the car . . . five, six, seven, eight—rest!' Aubrey had wobbled, limped in a stutter, a little way from the car, like a baby taking its first steps.

'My head's spinning . . . my ankle hurts . . .' he complained.

Zimmermann supported his weight. Then he said: 'Good luck, Kenneth Aubrey. Now—off you go!'

Aubrey staggered one step, then two, encountered the slope, stumbled, hopped, then began limping with exaggerated, listing, wide-legged steps, leaning his upper torso to one side and against the slope. Zimmermann watched him for a few moments, then turned his attention to the road only hundreds of yards below him. Lorries, armoured cars, a few tanks. Futile to prevent the victory of the German army, sufficient to rescue one English spy. He smiled, then shrugged, climbing back into the Mercedes. Aubrey, as if the child was growing older and healthier before his eyes, was now making a limping but steady progress. Zimmermann switched on the engine and put the car into reverse.

Aubrey, halting, so that he could retain his balance and rest his ankle while raising his arm to wave, summoned his energies to shout and heard the Mercedes' engine retreating into the distance.

PART THREE

WILD HUNT

He longed to be on the other side of the bars, as though he were actually a prisoner within the grounds of this centre of revolutionary plots, of this house of folly, of blindness, of villainy and crime.

—Joseph Conrad: *Under Western Eyes*

ELEVEN:

Penetration

Buckholz was dead. Aubrey, struggling through the vivid memory of his rescue by Zimmermann, was convinced that the CIA Deputy-Director had died instantly, and that his body had been taken away by the white-raincoated field officers who had failed to prevent his murder. He knew he was wounded himself. There was a single, distinct pain in his thigh. He considered attempting to move his toes and fingers, afraid of paralysis despite the location of the wound, but even as the image of a wheelchair came at him out of the dark, he drifted into unconsciousness again.

Hyde watched the doctor raise the hypodermic needle, squirt a thin stream of the sedative into the air, then pluck up some of the old, wrinkled flesh of Aubrey's arm and insert the needle. He was already unconscious when the sedative was administered.

'Well?' Alex Davenhill asked, voicing all their fears. The US army doctor looked up at them as they crowded like covetous relatives towards the bed.

'OK, I think. He can't stay here, but he's OK for the moment.' He stood up, surveying them. 'You guys play rough,' he said. 'It's got all the way down to shooting old men. You saving on pension payments?' He looked at each of them, then waved them back from the bed. 'Leave him alone now. I'll arrange for an ambulance to take him to the hospital—*our* hospital.'

'Thank you, doctor—Major.'

'Doctor will do, Mr Davenhill.' He grinned as he shut the door quietly and firmly behind them. Led by Davenhill, they trooped down to the house's principal lounge, overlooking the rear garden. During the day, the wooded slopes of the Taunus tumbled frozenly down towards the picture window. Now the curtains were drawn and there were guards in the garden.

'Drinks?' Davenhill asked, standing at the ornate cocktail cabinet and pouring himself a brandy.

'Scotch, please,' Shelley replied.

'Nothing for me.'

Davenhill studied Hyde for a moment, then merely shrugged. He handed Shelley his glass and sat down. Hyde remained standing, near the door, as if sudden escape from the room might be necessary.

'They think poor young Godwin will pull through,' Davenhill informed them. 'The hospital's pretty confident. Mind you, whether he'll walk again . . .' Davenhill rubbed a hand through his curling hair. 'My God, what a mess!'

'It's no bloody mess, Davenhill—it was a bloody massacre, and you know it. Petrunin broke the rules—*all* the bloody rules!'

'I understand your anger, my dear chap . . .'

'How can you? No one wants to shoot you.'

'Patrick——' Shelley warned, his glass halfway to his lips, his eyes attempting to calm Hyde.

'You know why it happened, Davenhill. What are you going to do about it? You're the ranking bloody officer here, now the old man's sedated. What do we do?'

'Nothing——'

'Bollocks to that! You heard what Aubrey said before they shut him up. The rules were broken because time's not on our side. If they kill all the principals—everyone in the know—then in a few days' time, when that bloody Treaty is signed, it won't matter. Whatever the consequences, whatever gang war there is between the CIA and the KGB, it will have been worth it. The poor old sod could see that with a bullet in him, for God's sake!'

'I'm not going to be responsible for starting the shooting war, Hyde,' Davenhill replied thinly over the top of his brandy balloon. 'I'm sorry Buckholz is dead. I realize the repercussions will be enormous. So, I imagine, does Moscow. But for the moment, we do nothing.'

'I understand, sir,' Shelley said softly, as if replying on Hyde's behalf.

Hyde walked to the middle of the room, and stood in front of the carved wooden fireplace and the heaped logs and pine cones in the grate.

'It's what *he* wants,' he said, his arm gesturing to the ceiling and the first-floor rooms above them. 'The only reason he isn't in hospital already is because he stayed to argue with you. Then, when he faints, you get the doctor to pump him full of quiet-juice! Give the poor bugger another shot of inertia, doctor, he looks like he wants to *do* something. Heavens!'

Shelley removed a smile from his face. Davenhill's narrow, saturnine, good-looking features were tinged with a blush of rage and insult.

'Nothing,' he said through closed teeth. 'Nothing will be done. You have your orders, Hyde.'

'We have to *know*!' Hyde stormed. 'We have to know. They tried to kill Aubrey, they killed Buckholz, they wanted Wei dead. Everyone who knows anything. Why? Is Zimmermann one of their people or isn't he? We must *know*, for God's sake!'

'The instructions I delivered from London remain unchanged. I have checked that with them . . .'

'Balls. Stuff London up a dead bear's bum, sport! You want the truth? I'll get you the fucking truth, mate. Where's that little yellow shit?'

'Hyde!'

Hyde stormed out of the door and up the stairs. Wei was being held under close arrest in one of the first-floor bedrooms, a small room with a narrow, barred window. Images of the two house-keepers, bound and gagged in the kitchen; of the empty room across the street that contained not even a spent cartridge case, and the family tied up in a downstairs room; the noise of cars departing at speed—all these pursued him up the stairs, hornets of ineptitude, his own furies of frustration and impotence.

Nothing. They were going to do *nothing* . . .

His mouth worked, his teeth ground together in uncontrollable rage. Godwin a basket case, Aubrey almost killed, Buckholz dead, Liu—Christ, Liu—nowhere at all, London sitting on its fat arse. His mind burned. Petrunin had taken the gloves off. It was eye-gouging, ball-booting time, and Davenhill wanted to sit back and applaud the boundaries . . .

There was a US marine in the corridor who let Hyde pass, even though his young eyes widened at the expression on the Australian's face, and a second guard inside the room who looked up from his magazine. Wei, his face suddenly alive and suspicious in the lamplight, was handcuffed to the bed.

'Outside,' Hyde snapped.

'Sir——'

'Outside! Let no one in—*no one*!'

'Sir!'

'Keys!'

The marine handed them to Hyde, and then closed the door

behind him. Wei could not prevent his eyes darting about the room, or the livid, unexpected fear from creeping like the accelerated symptoms of a disease across his face. He drew up his knees protectively, huddling on the bed. The room seemed small and shadowy, full of menace.

Hyde unlocked the handcuffs, then stepped away from the bed. Grinning as Wei scuttled into a corner like a frightened pet, he heaved the dressing-table across the stained, frayed carpet, placing it against the door.

'Sir . . . ?' he heard from the corridor.

'OK, sport—now it's my turn. You owe me your life. Now I'm going to collect on the debt . . .'

He advanced towards Wei, breathing heavily from anger and from his exertions with the dressing-table. Wei cowered, but his black eyes measured the Australian. Hyde dodged the first kick and hit Wei in the stomach, doubling him over. Wei groaned. Hyde lifted his head and banged it against the wall, splitting the plaster into a straggling spider's web of marks. He banged his head again, and again.

'It's all—your—fault—see?' he snarled, emphasizing his words with a bang of Wei's head against the plaster, now starred like a frosty window. Behind them, there was a knocking on the door. He heard Davenhill's voice calling his name, demanding he leave Wei unharmed.

Wei's dazed eyes seemed to gather hope and imprison it. Hyde shook him, shook his own head, let him drop to the floor. Then he knelt beside Wei.

'Hyde, leave him alone! Do you hear me, Hyde?'

The door heaved and thrust against the dressing-table, which squeaked in protest on the floorboards. The Heckler & Koch VP 70 was next to Wei's cheek, drawing his eyes like a magnet. The door eased open another few inches.

'Too late,' Hyde breathed. 'See, I've had it with you. I know you're a fake, and I'm pissed off with risking my neck for you. I'm going to blow your head off, mate.'

He pointed the barrel of the gun at Wei's head and squeezed the trigger. Wei's eyes had flickered towards the door, and to the marine's young face appearing round it, then had been drawn back to the hole in the gun barrel, the compressing finger behind the trigger guard.

'No——'

Hyde fired twice, raising the barrel of the gun a fraction so that the bullets thudded into the plaster an inch above Wei's head. The noise was deafening. The concussions of the bullets must have felt as real and vivid to Wei as impacts upon his skull. His eyes rolled, he screamed because he knew he was dying. He slumped on the floor as if trying to bury himself in the old carpet, screaming over and over again.

'Yes, yes, yes, yes, yes, yes . . . !'

The dressing-table was heaved aside, and Shelley and Davenhill spilled into the room behind the two marines.

'Hyde!'

'Listen, you Whitehall ponce! *Listen*!' He dragged Wei upright, the front of his shirt bunched in Hyde's hand. 'It's all a fake, isn't it? All a put-up job? Isn't it? Isn't it?' Wei's scream became a continuous sob. He could not speak, but he nodded his head, as violently as if Hyde were still banging it against the wall. Hyde let his body slump back against the skirting. Wei seemed no more than a dribbling, sobbing husk. Hyde stood up and grinned. 'Well?'

'Hyde—that was unforgivable!' Davenhill raged, his face white with anger. Shelley appeared confused, kneeling by Wei yet reluctant to touch him, as if the man were filthy or incontinent.

'Balls! You heard him—the whole bloody operation's one big fake . . .' Hyde paused, his eyes narrowing. 'You *knew* . . . ?' he breathed, then more loudly: 'You *knew*?'

'Outside!' Davenhill snapped at the two marines. The door was closed behind them a moment later. 'Keep your voice down!' Davenhill snapped at Hyde.

Hyde glanced at Shelley, who appeared similarly shocked.

'How long have you known?'

'I gather that matters were explained to the Foreign Secretary and Director-General of the intelligence service some time yesterday. A telephone call from Washington. The Director of the CIA, on behalf of—of the State Department . . .' Davenhill regretted having to inform Hyde, but he evidently assumed that only the truth would keep the man quiet.

'Just like that?'

Shelley stood up, and said: 'He's all right. Just scared stiff.'

'Never mind him. You mean the Foreign Office is just told to keep its hand off, and that's what happens—even if Aubrey and Buckholz get shot? That's it, is it? Do nothing.'

'What is there to do? You know, now . . .' Davenhill repressed a smirk of superiority, indicating with limp, dismissive fingers the crumpled, foetus-like Wei against the wall. 'We *all* know now. End of story.'

'You didn't know until yesterday?' Shelley asked, his tone carefully neutral. His eyes appeared distressed.

'Of course not!' Davenhill snapped.

Wei's blubbering sobs subsided. He was of no more account to the other three men in the room than a disregarded, hurt animal. Hyde slapped his arms at his sides, an expression of futility.

'And the Germans?' he asked. 'They're satisfied enough to stay away from this?'

'The BfV man I spoke to will want a fuller account—presently. For the moment, the German police and security service are satisfied that we cannot explain this . . . unfortunate action on the part of . . . persons unknown. It was as much a surprise to us.' The faintest smile of self-congratulation appeared on Davenhill's mouth for an instant.

'Shelley,' Hyde said, turning away from Davenhill. 'Give me my cover. Brief me.'

'You're not going in, Hyde.'

'Shelley, ignore him. You listened to Aubrey's ramblings, didn't you, even if *he* didn't. Zimmermann saved his life . . .'

'He was rambling . . .'

'Shelley, ignore him. Aubrey owes a debt. Get our man "Caspar" out of the DDR, if you can. Otherwise, get me in.'

'Why, Hyde? Tell me that. You know the score now. Why risk your life again?'

Hyde turned to Davenhill. Some communication of eyes had taken place between Shelley and Davenhill. It was as if Hyde suddenly felt the floorboards beneath him were treacherous, merely awaiting an opportunity to fling him into the room below. The moral and emotional atmosphere in the room seemed charged and murky.

'They call people like me—what is it, Emergency Response Facilities? Shit-shovellers,' Hyde explained limply. He anticipated he was being manoeuvred. Shelley and Davenhill stood on either side of him; childhood games of piggy-in-the-middle flashed on some mental screen. 'What is it?' he asked aggressively, hands bunching into fists at his side.

Davenhill rubbed his nose. 'Volunteers only,' he murmured

walking towards the bed. He sat down and studied Wei for a moment. Then he seemed to decide that the man was of no more significance, and said: 'I have, as you know, been in contact with London. With the Foreign Secretary and the Director-General. Naturally both of them are disturbed by the course of events, and by the—er, revelations that have come to light.' He indicated Wei with a tiny movement of his head. Hyde folded his arms across his chest and leaned against the wall. Davenhill continued to study the carpet near his feet. 'No one actually likes what is happening, you see,' he explained. 'It would seem that Presidential and State Department opposition, far from accepting defeat, has grown in direct ratio to the likelihood of the Berlin Treaty being ratified. Peking, of course, has always seen the darkest danger springing indirectly from a weakened or absent NATO presence on the western frontier of the Soviet Union . . .' Davenhill spread his hands. He seemed oblivious to their presence, merely rehearsing lines he had learned and would later perform. 'We, of course, have had to follow the American line. Which is why I arrived with cessationary instructions for dear Kenneth. However there is a powerful argument, which has been gaining ground in Cabinet of late, that the Treaty, by reducing considerably our NATO role, is something of a blessing in disguise . . .'

Davenhill looked up. Shelley nodded, almost fervently. Hyde had no idea how much Aubrey's assistant already knew or had heard previously from Davenhill. Some, perhaps, while Hyde had been across the street, in the dark bedroom which smelt of a smashed bottle of expensive perfume but which contained no other indications of an intruder . . . ? Probably. Davenhill had put himself in signals contact with London immediately he got into the house, and Shelley, though distraught on Aubrey's behalf, had operated the encoding console and the transmitter.

'So?' Hyde said surlily.

Davenhill looked up. Irritation, as with a lesser species, flitted swiftly across his handsome face, making it superior yet petulant.

'The PM is very conscious of the special relationship she has with the American President. She is also aware of the need to cut public expenditure effectively. Cabinet sees the withdrawal of the BAOR from Germany and a neutral Germany outside NATO, with no Soviet troops closer than Poland or Czechoslovakia, as a means of reducing at a stroke the defence budget for the next fiscal year, sufficiently to balance the total expenditure on the Trident II ballistic missile programme. You see, gentlemen, we would get Trident—retain our independent nuclear deterrent—for nothing.'

'So?'

'Therefore,' Davenhill continued, quelling his irritation, 'for the moment, the Foreign Secretary and "C" would both like to be kept up to date with the situation.'

'Meaning?'

'Meaning that *unofficially* they wish *Wild Hunt* to continue to run.'

'Christ . . .'

'I stress unofficially. Which is why I had to be certain that you would not give this matter up, let it rest. Your bloody-mindedness, Hyde, is our only weapon. You will see this agent in Wittenberg, "Caspar", find out what you can, and report back to Shelley. Whatever Aubrey intended will be carried out—for the moment.'

'And?'

'Cabinet meets to discuss this tomorrow. Foreign Affairs Committee only, naturally.'

'You're going to play games with the Americans?'

'That will depend. The Americans want the Treaty stopped. We may—*may*—want it to proceed. That is all I am prepared to say at present.' He stood up, briskly efficient, his pleasure at belonging to a covertness that transcended the intelligence service evident. 'I'll leave you to discuss details. I must arrange for poor Kenneth to be transferred to the British military hospital in Hanover. I'm sure you are going to need his sound advice in the immediate future.'

'Christ! You mean he doesn't even get time off to get better?'

'I'm afraid not. Time, as he observed himself, is of the essence, and not on our side.'

'Unless the Cabinet decides to go along with the Americans.'

'Exactly. Good luck, Hyde. Shelley——' Davenhill nodded, and crossed the room. He did not look back, and closed the door noiselessly behind him.

'Jesus . . .' Hyde breathed.

Shelley grinned nervously. 'I told him you'd still want to go in. He just had to be sure.'

Hyde rubbed his hands through his hair vigorously. 'Bloody

politicians!' he exhaled, lifting his face in despair to the ceiling.

'Election year next year,' Shelley murmured. 'Government borrowing, unemployment . . .'

'I know the song. Inflation, public spending cuts—they've had four bloody years to get it right. Now they can see a quick, smart, neon-lit way out.'

'Or see their way out going down the drain. If they have to keep BAOR in Germany . . . ?'

'No defence cuts, no election triumph.' Hyde tossed his head. 'Can't you get "Caspar" out?'

'Sorry, Patrick. He's on police probation for a drunken driving offence. Can't possibly get the necessary travel visas. Only saved from gaol, I gather, by his Party membership and his civil service status. You'll have to go in, I'm afraid.' He grinned unexpectedly. 'Like camping, do you?'

'No.'

'Pity. That's your cover—camping holiday, en route to Poland. You'll enjoy it.'

Hyde looked at Wei. The man was listening in a half-aware, withdrawn way. 'Never mind, you poor sod. We've both been used. But that's the job specification, isn't it?'

Wei's eyes remained closed, his face expressionless. He was a pawn removed from the game. Soon, Hyde realized, he would be grateful for that fact. His part in events was over.

'Good, but not very good—bad, but not very bad,' Petrunin observed to Petya Kominski, who had been made to feel, ever since the arrival of Comrade General Petrunin, a stranger in his own office. 'It means that we must continue stepping hard on their heels, hard on them.' He smiled, steepling his fingers so that they cast deep, almost impenetrable shadows on his face. Kominski, on the other side of the desk, nodded in what he hoped was a deferential manner. Once or twice already, he thought Petrunin might have spotted the sense of affront beneath his subservient façade. Petrunin was not someone whose displeasure he wished to earn.

'Of course, Comrade General,' he murmured.

'It has still been worthwhile, I think. Four days remaining. Confusion and loss of direction are the least we can expect from our . . . intervention. Whether it will give us enough time . . .' He shrugged. 'That we shall have to see. Meanwhile, I want Hyde,

Aubrey's assistant, and this man from the Foreign Office—all of them are to be watched and tailed. Organize that now.'

Kominski stood up, flushing at the insult of being so summarily dismissed from his own office, and left the room hurriedly lest his features betray him. Petrunin, however, directed his gaze at the open files on the lamplit desk. The files had arrived at the Bonn embassy by special courier that afternoon, before his own arrival in Germany. He had flown directly from Sydney to Frankfurt, once his operational scenario for the attack on Aubrey and Buckholz had been approved by Moscow Centre. The KGB Rezident in Bonn had put the operation into effect in Wiesbaden. Petrunin counted it a qualified success. Moscow Centre's reply to his signal indicated that approval would be withheld until a certain amount of tidying work had been done. Hence the Aladko files had become highly significant. Moscow Centre wanted any and all of Aladko's associates in Spain, during the period of Zimmermann's capture and interrogation, removed. Eliminated. Just for the sake of absolute safety. There was to be nothing to link Zimmermann with the KGB, with the Communist Party.

Petrunin had received one other order. He was to arrange a meeting with Zimmermann, to assess the man's capacity for surviving the pressures being placed upon him; the man's ability and will to succeed in the face of these new odds, too.

Petrunin was of the opinion—the long plane journey from Australia had made the idea more and more irrefutable—that Zimmermann should be persuaded, even forced, to resign. His departure, though risky, would at least create the possibility of cleaning up the Treaty, by removing from the public eye the focus of criticism. Either way, his own view or that of his masters, he had to arrange to meet Zimmermann.

Spain, then. And Zimmermann. The pressure was intensifying every moment. Petrunin was charged with the task of keeping the lid on events for four more days, until the Treaty was ratified, and in the euphoria generated by the bulldozing of the Berlin Wall and the rapid dismantling of the border wire, everything would be forgotten. Nothing would matter; no questions would be asked, no doubts raised.

He flicked through the files, turning over the past with rapid fingertips. Spain . . .

Who would still be alive? he wondered. Anyone? His fingers

ran down a list of names. The sheet was a photocopy of an old, stained, much-folded original. Lined paper. The embossed initials in Cyrillic of the NKVD. A Moscow copy of names that Aladko probably only carried in his head. The good, the bad, the ugly, the loyal, the useful, the crippled, the ambitious, the discontented.

How many of them would be left now, forty years and more later? One long index finger tapped his pursed lips as he squinted to make out the list of names. When they had been originally typed on the inappropriate, coarse lined paper, the typewriter had needed a new ribbon. Spanish Communists, one or two Americans, French—all of them in units of the International Brigade in which Aladko had enlisted; all of them known to Aladko.

Good God, most of them must have been dead for years . . .

He ran his finger down the list once more, the column for ages or, where known, dates of birth; the column next to the date of enlistment in the Party. No, some of them would be alive. Boys of eighteen or twenty here, men in their twenties and thirties . . .

Here is where the British would look for their answers. Spain was the plug in the bath. Then, he thought, let the water out. Drown London—drown Aubrey and Hyde. Pull out the bathplug. He picked up the telephone.

'Yes, Comrade General?' he heard immediately.

'Get me the Madrid Rezident in full signals contact at once,' he said, beginning to smile, action and the prospect of it heartening him.

Shelley looked at his watch. It had been light for a little over an hour. The traffic on the E4 autobahn between Frankfurt and Kassel was already heavy. The Volkswagen camper, with Hyde driving, was making reasonable time. Hyde had perhaps two hundred and fifty more miles to travel to Wittenberg, and "Caspar".

'Mr Aubrey will have taken off for Hanover by now,' Shelley observed as Hyde pulled out into the middle lane from behind a Total petroleum lorry. A Mercedes flashed its headlights at him, then overtook in the outside lane, its speed over ninety. Hyde tossed his head in envying disapproval.

'Davenhill certainly wants his pound of flesh out of the old bugger,' Hyde commented on Shelley's announcement.

'From all of us, apparently,' Peter Shelley replied drily.

'At least you're not lying on a stretcher being rushed across the tarmac at Wiesbaden Air Base, the nurses holding your drip-feed aloft and telling you not to worry.'

'The old man'll be all right, Patrick.'

'Maybe.'

'I'll see him in Hanover before I fly back to London. Give him your best wishes.'

'It's a shitty business, though—wouldn't you say?'

'I would. But don't worry. Aubrey's in no danger. He'll just be on hand . . .'

'And not in London, in case it's politic to deny everything and agree with the Yanks?'

'I suppose so.'

'It's a bloody shame this "Caspar" can't come out to play—at least, give us a call.'

'He's too important. Ever since that business two years back, when we lost no fewer than eight people because the East Germans had made advances in interception equipment, we can't allow our best people to use radios. Word-of-mouth only. Don't worry, you'll be in and out in no time flat.'

'We both hope.'

'All you have to do is collect whatever "Caspar" has discovered about Zimmermann's family and his trips to the DDR. And why they stopped. You're no more than a courier. And a very fetching one, too, if I may say so.' Shelley smirked. Hyde glowered from behind the clear-glass lenses of the old-fashioned spectacles they had supplied. His hair was untidy, unwashed. His cheeks were fattened with pads. He looked almost owlish. 'A fervent Communist with a love of the east European outdoor life,' Shelley added. 'Perfect.'

'It's my life, though,' Hyde replied, unamused. A Porsche 928, shark-jawed in the wing mirror, pulled out and glided past the camper. Hyde watched it as carefully as an enemy.

At first, David Liu assumed that Frederickson had come to exult in some way; gloat over him. Yet that did not appear to be the case. The cell became a cage which barely contained an ill-concealed, animal tension. Frederickson's mood pressed the walls in upon Liu, distressing him. He was strangely conscious of the atmosphere, and the setting of the confessional. Yet for some inexplicable reason, he was the priest, Frederickson the burdened penitent.

'What is the weather like outside?' Liu asked.

Frederickson turned on him angrily. 'What?'

'The weather?' Liu asked, indicating his cell.

'Fine. Warm day.'

'Thank you.'

Frederickson continued to move awkwardly around the strict confines of the cell. It was the distressed, repetitive movements of a tiger in a zoo. Eventually he said: 'It's all coming unglued.'

'What?'

'This!' he waved his arms to include the cell, the building around it; even China itself. 'All of it.'

'And I am not to blame?' Liu asked with a philosophic calm that surprised him. His detachment survived the intrusion of the American; grew from it.

'You?' Frederickson shook his head. The features now seemed coarsened by anger and disappointment. Sleepless stains, fine lines like the cracked glaze on a vase. 'No, not you. Buckholz is dead.'

'What? How?' Liu experienced surprise. There was curiosity in his reaction, but no anger and no satisfaction. 'Why are you telling me?'

Frederickson looked at him, his face puzzled. His hands moved as if to explain, and then hung at his sides. Liu guessed that the man had come to confide in the only other American in China who knew as much as he did himself. And the one harmless man in China. 'I——'

'How did it happen?'

'KGB bullet.'

'Where?'

'Germany for Chrissake. They were flying Colonel Wei home. The Brit, Aubrey—he's alive.'

'Why?'

'Maybe just to foul things up?' Frederickson shrugged. 'Who knows? Anyway, it's worked.'

'How?' Liu relaxed into the role of interrogator. It enhanced the unfeeling calm with which he had armoured himself, which had been induced by the silence, isolation and unvarying routine of his cell.

'Langley's trying to sit on its hands, that's how. Hoping they've done enough to pull the thing off.' Frederickson shook his head and rubbed his hands through his hair. 'Christ, I don't know. The Chinks are screaming for more action.' He squinted at Liu. 'Watch yourself, sonny. They're mad as hell.' He seemed to see caucasian features, anticipate an occidental mind, sense a camaraderie with his dupe.

'Did you come to warn me?'

Frederickson seemed surprised at the question, then merely shrugged. 'You're my responsibility,' was all he said.

'What about your position?'

'*My* position? I'm OK.'

'Is Zimmermann in real trouble?'

'Who knows? He hasn't resigned, I know that . . .'

'Will he?'

'Christ knows.'

'I'll get out when he either resigns or the Treaty is signed, yes?'

Liu realized, as he proceeded to what seemed an entirely natural question, that he had pricked the balloon of his own calm. When they locked him in that narrow room, his detachment had inflated to obscure the view of his own death. Now, as the balloon lost air, his extinction peeped out from behind the sagging sense of calm and indifference.

'Maybe. Look, Liu, I don't know what's going to happen now. These Charlie Chans are all screaming it's our fault.' He flapped his hands at his sides. 'I'll—try to watch out for you . . .' Again, he might have been talking to a Westerner. Liu's colour and bone-structure had ceased to be visible. He was an American.

'Thank you, Frederickson.' Despite the deliberation of his tone, Liu could not conjure back the detachment. The balloon had deflated. Self-delusion was no longer possible, and he began to be afraid.

'OK.'

Frederickson banged urgently on the cell door with the flat of his hand. If was as if he wished to flee the scene of an accident. Liu swallowed drily. The detachment gone, he was afraid once more.

Dust, the persistent smell of petrol. The blank-windowed hut, the lines of blue-and-white cones narrowing to a dead end. The line of cars and lorries. The periods of silence before each vehicle was released and drove off. The clicking of doors and boots. The rifles and machine pistols, the peaked caps. The formality.

292

Hyde had dropped Shelley in Braunschweig, where an SIS irregular, the son of a German recruited by the Control Commission in the '40s, was waiting to collect him and drive him to Hanover to see Aubrey. Thence to London. Hyde had then made good time on the E8 to the border at Helmstedt. Now he had been waiting twenty minutes in the queue of cars wishing to cross into the DDR. The wire stretched away on either side. It did not seem diminished by the immediacy of the Berlin Treaty's ratification.

Hyde's cover was standard fare. Shelley had coached him during the drive from Wiesbaden to Braunschweig. Communist Party membership, former university activist, trade union branch secretary, part-time teacher, demonstrator—twice arrested and fined—and an enthusiastic visitor to eastern Europe. It was one of hundreds of covers fed by double agents into the satellite country record computers every year; records which eventually found their way to Moscow Centre to be stored against future use. Until they were blown or discarded, they provided blanket coverage for SIS field agents. The camping Communist born in Australia was one of the covers available to Hyde personally.

He felt few nerves at the border crossing. Tiredness dulled his awareness, but his relative indifference sprang more from lack of purpose than from weariness. He was acting in the capacity of a courier because agent 'Caspar' faced a drunk-driving charge and couldn't cross the border into the Federal Republic. The elaborate, thorough cover seemed more than good enough. His fear and his growing anger were directed more at Davenhill and Whitehall than towards 'Caspar', the DDR or the CIA. The answer, after all, was available. Zimmermann was not a KGB agent, and never had been. It was a frame by the CIA and the Chinese. All he was now doing was obtaining background on Zimmermann which might or might not prove important, might or might not satisfy Aubrey's insatiable desire for the truth, his deep need to repay his outstanding debt to Zimmermann.

Then do it for Aubrey, he instructed himself. Not for Davenhill or Whitehall, but Aubrey.

The guard's face appeared at the window of the Volkswagen camper. Hyde blinked behind the clear glass of his spectacles, awakening himself into his cover. The peaked cap was piped with red. Border guard. His eyes studied Hyde. Already Hyde could see a promising contempt lurking in the man's eyes, twisting his mouth into a slight smile.

293

'Papers.' He held one hand up to the open window. Hyde yawned, then stifled it, releasing tension and exuding indifference. The guard officer's face thinned and his lips pursed. Hyde had begun to enjoy himself. He handed out his battered passport and the forged visas. 'Out!' the officer snapped while he studied the passport.

'What's wrong?' Hyde asked in a querulous and surprised tone.

'Out—search this vehicle!'

Two privates of the Border Troops moved forward as Hyde climbed down from the driving seat of the camper. His faded denim shorts occasioned amusement, likewise his rumpled check shirt which displayed its tail lapping down over the shorts. The officer examined him with contempt.

'Anything wrong?' Hyde asked, adding: 'Comrade . . .' in an ingenuous voice. The officer's face was a mask of suspicion.

'You travel a great deal, Mr Haynes. In Warsaw Pact countries particularly?'

'That's right, comrade.'

The two guards could be heard rummaging through the camping equipment in the rear of the Volkswagen, rattling pans and cutlery, unfolding bedding and clothes, opening the tight, neat bundle of the tent. It was unlikely they would find the gun or the alternative papers. It was simply not that kind of search. Nuisance value.

'Why do you keep using that form of address?'

'We're all comrades in the Party, aren't we?' Hyde replied, blinking owlishly. His voice was an uneasy amalgam of pride, respect and self-righteousness. He was rather pleased with it.

'Perhaps . . .' the officer admitted slowly. He appeared not to desire anything in common with the tourist whose papers he held.

'Sir?' One of the privates emerged from the back of the Volkswagen, a loose-leaf folder in his hand. 'This, sir,' he said. Good. They'd found the scrapbook.

The officer flicked through the pages of cuttings and photographs. The scrapbook of Haynes's fictitious political career, the pasted-in badges of his danger to the state, was a minor work of art.

'Why do you carry this with you?' the officer snapped, puzzled and intrigued.

'Makes for conversation,' Hyde explained cheerfully. He moved a step closer to the officer. 'May I, comrade?' he said ingratiatingly, and began turning the pages. A grainy picture of the American embassy, a police cordon being flung back by a surging crowd. 'A great day, comrade,' he announced proudly, his dirty-nailed finger tapping one of the display banners. It demanded an end to the Vietnam war. Another pleaded for the banning of napalm weapons, another displayed a crude cartoon of Nixon hanging from a gallows.

'I do not see you,' the officer smirked.

'Couldn't arrange that, could I?' He riffled through the pages of the scrapbook. 'Here's me,' he said.

Well-known union leaders in the picket line at Grunwick. Behind them in the crowd was Hyde-Haynes; the photograph was unfaked. Hyde had been there deliberately to establish part of the Haynes cover by having his picture taken in the vicinity of Shirley Williams and other prominent and more left-wing figures.

'So I see. You look younger there,' the officer said with vivid sarcasm. He handed the scrapbook back to Hyde with exaggerated indifference and returned his attention to Hyde's papers. 'This transit visa allows you only a single night's stay in the Democratic Republic. You must cross the border into Poland tomorrow.'

'Don't worry, I will, comrade.'

The officer handed back Hyde's rather grubby papers and rubbed the fingers of his right hand together, cleansing them by friction. Then he looked at the two privates, who now stood together beside the camper. One of them shook his head.

'You are free to go.'

'Thanks, comrade,' Hyde said, smiling confidentially.

The officer, scorn evident on his face, turned and walked back to the lorry behind Hyde in the queue. Hyde climbed into the Volkswagen and started the engine.

He grinned as he pulled out of the narrowing line of cones. The barrier swung up, and he entered the German Democratic Republic. Wittenberg and 'Caspar' lay eighty miles ahead of him. He would make the campsite by early evening.

'Good, Kominski. That is good news.'

'Why do you think he has entered the DDR?'

Petrunin sighed and removed his glasses. 'Zimmermann's background. I do not know, however, what he hopes to learn. We know what he *will* find, however . . .'

'Will it help them?'

'It depends on their motives.'

'I'll have him picked up——'

'No, not yet. Let's see who he meets. Then we'll have him. We might get an agent in place, perhaps more than one. We'll wait until tomorrow. Tomorrow will see the end for Mr Hyde and for our friend Zimmermann. We'll wait.'

TWELVE:

'Caspar'

The British military hospital on the outskirts of Hanover appeared almost deserted. Compensation had been agreed between the governments of the United Kingdom and the Federal Republic and, when the last British troops left Germany before the following spring, the hospital would become a German civilian establishment, serving the medical needs of the city of Hanover and its environs. Now it had a barrack-like order and quiet; its occupants might have been serving elsewhere in the world.

Peter Shelley got out of the car assigned to him by the consulate-general in Hanover—his driver from Braunschweig had gone back to his normal occupation as a taxi driver—and walked up the steps to the main hospital entrance. A soldier on guard, probably because of Aubrey, cursorily inspected his pass and held open the door for him. The foyer smelt aseptic, sickly-sweet, yet his imagination detected the must of disuse beneath the disinfectant. Again the lack of urgency, the unoccupied spaces, struck him. Sixty per cent of the British Army of the Rhine were already back in the UK. The Americans were withdrawing more slowly, but they, too, would have departed by the time the referendum on German reunification occurred in a year's time. Shelley felt oppressed by the ringing of his own footsteps along the empty, gleaming corridor.

Aubrey lay propped up in bed, a drip-feed attached to his forearm, the bedclothes tunnelled up over his damaged leg. He was freshly-shaved, and appeared very old. Shelley could not consider that his appearance was simply the effect of the drugs that must have been administered. Aubrey opened his eyes very slowly, suspicious of the intruder.

'Sir?' Shelley enquired, coming to the bedside.

'Wei?' Aubrey asked, his hand feebly patting the back of Shelley's hand as it lay on the coverlet.

'Safe,' Shelley replied. 'Under armed guard. I'm afraid he's finished, sir. Run out of steam.'

'Oh,' Aubrey remarked without interest.

'How are you, sir?' Shelley sat down on the hard upright chair.

'Not too bad. I—gather that my American doctor was—was proficient in removing the bullet and patching me up . . .' Aubrey seemed to gather strength in mid-sentence, and then his voice and attention faded again.

'That's good,' Shelley remarked in a soothing tone, and Aubrey's faded glance sharpened. He was angry.

'I'm not dying!' he snapped.

'Sorry, sir . . .'

'I—my attention span is short. I feel very tired,' Aubrey explained. 'Try to be patient, Peter.'

'Sir.' Shelley cleared his throat. 'Hyde is across the border . . .'

'How will you get him out again?'

'His papers are good enough—the second set. He could be back by tomorrow.'

Aubrey nodded, but the effort seemed to tire him. He was silent for some time, then he said: 'Why has he gone?' His eyes were very clear and bright. 'You and Davenhill . . . ?'

'We're to go ahead, sir. It may be that . . . HMG would wish to prove the innocence of Zimmermann.'

Aubrey was silent for a long time. The room was warm and quiet, except for the breathing of the old man and the occasional shuffle of Shelley's shoes on the linoleum floor. The hospital smells depressed the younger man. He tried to avoid looking at Aubrey and seeing his age and infirmity.

Eventually Aubrey said quietly: 'I understand. To put the clock back here would cost a great deal of money . . .' He sighed, as if the perception of events had exhausted his frail reserves. Then he added, more energetically: 'Very well. We will do as requested by our political masters. We will *prove* that Wolfgang Zimmermann has been severely wronged.' Aubrey smiled, and seemed immensely satisfied. Shelley was surprised. It was as if Aubrey was afflicted by a partial moral blindness. The shock and pain and sedation had reduced his perspective, his professional peripheral vision. All he now saw was the assistance he could render to a man who had once saved his life.

Shelley could not help but be disappointed in his superior. He had expected moral outrage, professional nausea. Perhaps it had been too much to ask.

'Yes, sir,' he said heavily.

'They use us as they must,' Aubrey explained, patting Shelley's hand with his own. Energy quivered in the old fingertips. 'At least we are not being asked to murder or invade, Peter.' He encouraged Shelley to smile. 'I always *knew* it was wrong!' he added with a brief and sudden anger. 'It was never right. I was not convinced . . .' His voice tailed off, and his eyes became moist. 'I'm sorry for poor Charles. He did not deserve to die. That was criminally stupid and dangerous on the part of Petrunin. He shouldn't be allowed to succeed, on those grounds alone.' He studied Shelley once more, his eyes bright and damp. 'And you, Peter? What's your next move?'

'London. Spain is the next area of interest . . . ?' Aubrey nodded.

'We want a survivor, someone who knows. Someone from Spain,' he said. 'When will we have a firm decision in Cabinet?'

'Tomorrow.'

Aubrey pondered, then said: 'I must know, Peter. Whatever decision our masters put into effect, I must know the truth, the whole truth, and nothing but the truth. There is a debt to Wolfgang Zimmermann. I must repay it. This thing must go on until I have done so.'

'Whatever?' Shelley asked.

'If necessary, *I* shall give Hyde his orders. If East Germany proves negative, then I shall send him to Spain. Tell me, what do things look like here?'

Shelley shook his head. 'Not good. They're hounding Zimmermann. Vogel's dropped another six points in the latest opinion poll. He's two points behind the Christian Democrats now. It doesn't look at all good.'

Aubrey shrugged. The plastic tube of his drip-feed joggled behind his head. He closed his eyes for a moment.

'Then it may well work. That is not properly our concern. The Treaty may well not be signed. We can do nothing about that. But——' He glowered at Shelley, and gripped his wrist with strong fingers. 'Zimmermann and Vogel should not be ruined by this—not utterly ruined, whatever happens. We must see to that, at least.'

'Yes, sir.'

'Get along now. Catch your flight to London. Try to be back by tomorrow.'

'I will, sir.'

Shelley stood up, his chair scraping back softly on the blue linoleum. Aubrey's eyes were closed again. As he opened the door and made to pass through it, Shelley heard Aubrey murmuring. He paused, and then went on, head down as if embarrassed or ashamed. Aubrey might as well have been delirious.

'Policy is not the province of intelligence services—intelligence is not the province of governments. These two arms of the executive, overt and covert, must not be confused. They must not mix or blend . . .'

To Shelley, it sounded old-fashioned, out of date, weary and anachronistic. It was everything Aubrey represented and believed. The old man was reciting it now like a passage from his memoirs or an introductory lecture to recruits. He seemed not to wish to inhabit the real world as fiercely as before. He was escaping, perhaps?

Shelley's footsteps echoed coldly in the empty corridors of the military hospital.

The campsite five miles south-west of Wittenberg was beside a small lake. It was clear, orderly to the point of being military, and possessed good facilities. It was crowded with late holiday-makers, but there was sufficient room for Hyde to be admitted. The sails of dinghies on the placid waters of the tree-fringed lake were orderly, too; set there to complete the pastoral scene.

Hyde drove the Volkswagen down to the lake. Insects buzzed in the warm, still air beneath the heavy, dark trees, despite the numerous barbecues and cooking fires; some splashed themselves like droppings or flecks of paint against the windscreen of the camper. The water of the lake was turning gold-red in the softer evening light as the sun dropped into a foretaste of autumn which dulled it to red. The thick air above the far trees was blue, almost misty.

Hyde got out of the Volkswagen, and removed the tent from the muddle of equipment, bedding and clothing that the Border Troops had left in the back of the camper. Swiftly, with an expertise born of urgency rather than experience, he pitched the small tent. Then he made a business of unloading his cooking utensils. A ring of charred stones indicated where he should make his fire. Two children banged enthusiastically at a rubber ball on a length of elastic across the clearing from him. Their mother sat plumply and indifferently in a deckchair while the father swatted away the first of the evening's mosquitoes and gnats as he erected the mast of a small dinghy at the edge of the water.

Hyde looked at his watch. Five-thirty. He wiped his hands on his shorts and climbed back into the Volkswagen. Two minutes later, he was turning the camper onto the main road to Wittenberg. He had had to divert to the campsite in order to establish his cover and have his transit visa stamped. Now he had a temporary home, a place of residence, if his papers were inspected.

The evening traffic was light, and he made good time through the small, straggling, untidy suburbs into the centre of the old town. Lutherstadt had failed to emerge from the chrysalis of the medieval town of Wittenberg. Its light industry and new shops and blocks of workers' flats seemed still-born. The town was only half-way to modern ugliness and seemed to have halted indefinitely in its journey.

In the still-cobbled main square the pavement tables and chairs of a café faced the griminess of a Gothic church that had become a museum. Hyde parked where the Volkswagen could be seen from the café and settled down to wait. Church clocks, rathaus clocks, struggled towards a unanimous assertion of the time. Six. 'Caspar' was due at six. If he was any good, he would have been there already, behind the anonymity of tablecloth, beer and newspaper, watching for him and any company he might have unwittingly acquired.

Hyde lazily wound down the window to its fullest extent. A round pink face stared into his own. An unlikely, pleasant, half-formed, unageing face.

'Open the passenger door, would you?'

Hyde leaned across and unlocked the door. 'Caspar' climbed into the seat, smoothing the trousers of his light suit when he had done so. He was well dressed, the beginnings of a paunch spoiling the waist-band of his trousers and causing his striped shirt to stretch open at his navel. His clothes were expensive. He regarded Hyde good-humouredly, but with something like amused contempt for the dishevelled condition of his appearance.

'Sorry,' Hyde said. 'Should have dressed for dinner.'

'Drive around, would you?'

Hyde switched on the engine and pulled out into the square's traffic. 'Caspar' patted his fair hair into place, winding up his window, despite the heavy warmth of the evening, so that the breeze of their passage would not distress the thick, waving hair.

'Have you got anything for me?' Hyde asked as they stopped at traffic lights. Bomb damage had been replaced by a wide, vacant-looking thoroughfare lined by the weatherstained sentries of workers' flats. 'Caspar's' nose and mouth wrinkled in disapproval at the perspective of the avenue, which led the eye only to some distant, bleak, dark monument. An upraised arm bearing a sword, some struggling heap frozen below the impending blow. The outline of the huge statue was clear against the crayon-vivid colours of the evening sky.

'I think so. Normal arrangements? I don't know when I shall be able to get out to collect—this damned driving charge. Sorry you had to come this far.' 'Caspar's' manner was almost caricature. His English was clipped, proficient, well-mannered; and old-fashioned. Hyde might have expected an older man from his voice, one trained by the generation preceding Aubrey.

'Normal arrangements,' Hyde confirmed. Then he added as they pulled away from the green light: 'Money'll be coming to an end next year, won't it?'

'Caspar' smiled. 'Don't you believe it. Anyone and everyone will want sources inside our civil service for years—just to know what's going on in the united Germany. They'll be keeping secrets from everyone then, and everyone will want to know.' He smiled, patting his hair again at the back where the breeze from Hyde's window disturbed it.

'Zimmermann?' Hyde asked, glancing into the wing mirror. Light traffic. No single car on their tail. If they were using a lot more than one, then it was too late to do anything anyway. For the moment, he would assume they were safe.

'Usual bonus?' 'Caspar' asked.

'Usual bonus,' Hyde confirmed.

'Excellent. I don't know why Britain has this reputation for being a bad payer. I have no complaints. And far less coarse and demanding than the Americans.' He inspected his nails.

The statue was a Soviet war memorial. Ugly, threatening; bellowing death rather than peace. Hyde skirted it, turning the Volkswagen into another avenue of grey concrete flats. He presumed the coloured panels in the balconies signified a better quality of apartment, or a differing social status among the occupants.

'What did you find out?'

'I won't say it was easy—oh, perhaps I will,' he added, smiling.

302

His teeth were very even and very white. His green eyes gleamed with self-satisfaction. 'Our civil service is very rigid and compartmentalized,' he explained, 'but moving around within it, if you're a member with a certain seniority, is not too difficult. Mr Aubrey would not want me if it were not so.' He coughed self-deprecatingly. 'I studied the family documents, back to the first war and beyond. Quite wealthy, once. Clever of him to live on the other side of the wire now. *His* sort would not be tolerated here. Not *real* capitalists—only pretend ones, like your humble servant——' He raised his hand to prevent Hyde's interruption. 'Their estate is now a collective, as you might have expected.'

'Family?'

'All dead—long dead.'

'Christ, "Caspar"!' Hyde blurted out, slowing the Volkswagen as a scruffy, thin mongrel crossed the road. It urinated against a lamp-post, and then sauntered unconcernedly on.

'I'm sorry,' 'Caspar' replied with genuine apology. 'I like English conversation. I do not have sufficient opportunity . . .'

Hyde accelerated bad temperedly. 'You're from the past, Christ!'

'Caspar's' hands indicated the broad, apartment-lined street. Lamp standards, concrete and bird-necked, leaned over the road. They seemed a stronger growth than the few stunted, almost leafless trees. It seemed to Hyde that the seasons were more advanced here. He suppressed a shiver.

'Would *you* wish to be of the present . . . here?' he asked lightly.

'OK. Go on.'

'As I was saying, all the family are dead. The brothers died during the struggle against the Fascists . . .' 'Caspar' grinned. 'Though the glorious Soviet liberators didn't kill either of them. One died in North Africa, the other on the Western front, in France in 1944.'

'Sister? Wasn't there a sister?'

'Caspar' pouted. 'Now you've spoilt my surprise.'

'What about the sister?'

'The reason for Zimmermann's visits to the DDR, for all of thirteen years during the 1950s and '60s, terminating in 1967. Regular visits, always sanctioned by the authorities . . .'

'Why?'

'To see his sister, of course.'

'Then they did have a lever they could use . . . ?' Hyde began. His voice tailed off as he entertained the implications of what had been discovered. If, after all, there was truth in . . . ?

'I suppose so. I wouldn't have thought so, however . . .'

'Then why didn't he get his sister out?'

'It was years before he found her.'

'So?'

A small, neat ordered park, children decorating the swings and roundabouts, a dog barking; opposite, across the cobbled street and the metal ruts of tramlines, a row of tiny, grubby private shops.

'Then he couldn't bring her out.'

'Like I said——'

'Forgive me, but no. He didn't *want* to—and it would have made little difference to her.'

'How come?'

'She'd hardly have noticed.'

'Look, I realize you like being mysterious, but is any of this fact?' Hyde glared at 'Caspar', who seemed unperturbed. Even in his irritation, Hyde realized what a gift had fallen into the hands of SIS when the man had enrolled. One day, if he kept his nose clean and to the grindstone, he could move to Leipzig or Dresden or even Berlin. The man really was good, and a real prospect.

Or Stuttgart, or Munich, or Bonn, Hyde reminded himself, in the new united Germany. The idea made him smile.

'The facts *are*,' 'Caspar' announced portentously, 'that Zimmermann's sister was a hopeless lunatic. Something as common and obvious as a gang rape by the Russians might have been the cause. I haven't seen the doctor's report, so I'm guessing a little . . . anyway, she was incarcerated in the asylum here for years, as good as dead. Then, by spreading money liberally about, your Herr Zimmermann located her. But . . .'

'But?'

'Successful businesman with political connections and ambitions? A lunatic for a sister. Great publicity, mm?'

A tram swayed ahead of them as they jolted over the cobbles. Blue sparks flashed as it passed beneath a dark railway bridge.

'You mean he left her *here*?'

'For thirteen years after he found her. Yes. Probably it was the kindest thing to do. She was a hopeless vegetable. Brain damage in the physical as well as the emotional sense. I think she was left for dead. The mother *did* die at the same time as the daughter's . . . accident?' 'Caspar' shrugged as they passed out into sunlight once more from beneath the cold, black arches of the railway bridge.

'Good God, man, it was his sister!'

'I would say that was debatable. Anyway, she died in 1967. Thus, end of visits by Zimmermann.'

'It could have been . . .' The street was clean of suspicious cars. There had been a fawn Wartburg, but that had turned off before it transformed itself from suspicion into a tail.

'Caspar' shook his head. 'I doubt it. Zimmermann, I'm certain, from the regularity of visits and other details, was spreading enough money about the district not to have been . . . compromised in any way. He was too good a source of revenue to be tampered with.'

'*You* think?'

'Yes, I think.'

Hyde digested the information. Zimmermann's behaviour had an ugliness about it, but it was difficult to see it as criminal or treacherous. No, it was Spain and 1938, if at all.

And it wasn't at all, was it? It was a frame, first to last.

'Mate, you're wasted in Wittenberg!'

'I know, my dear fellow. Perhaps next year . . . ?' He shrugged. 'Many of my superiors envy my taste in clothes, my taste in wine, my furniture and my lack of a wife. I have a great many enemies. However, I shall triumph, in the end.'

'You're sure the sister's dead?'

'Turn left here. I'll take you to see the grave. It's unvisited now, I'm afraid. He doesn't concern himself with her. That's it—straight ahead, my dear fellow.'

The second of the four cars being used to tail Hyde in a complex irregular, changing pattern turned into the shopping thoroughfare fifty yards behind the Volkswagen.

Somehow, even in his pain, David Liu understood the precise almost aseptic nature of the beating he had received. It had been a cold, impersonal expression of enraged frustration, exacted upon him merely as a representative of a different, and betraying service. Its ostensible object was to learn, precisely, the route and destination of his suspicions. They wanted to know how much Meng had told him, how he had guessed, what else he had learned.

And Liu would not tell them. Almost despite himself, despite his pain and fear, he clung to defiant silence. In a disloyal universe, he clung with an unsuspected passion to his newly-discovered loyalty to Meng's safety, Meng's life.

He lay, his head twisted, mouth dribbling saliva mingled with blood onto the thin, hard carpet of the third-floor office with the barred window. A wash of light from the illumination of Tiananmen Square was hazy and gauzelike at the corner of his wet, blurred vision. His own expressions of pain were dim, indigestive rumblings at the edge of hearing; more like the rumble of an an underground train transmitted through the floor of the room. His mouth kept filling with blood. He thought perhaps his nose was broken. His ribs and back were bruised. The pipelike leather coshes they had used were symbols of their disdain, their clinical exactitude and lack of personal animosity.

Quickly, and almost as if they disliked touching him, he was lifted to his feet and bundled into a hard chair, on which he slumped as if his spine had been damaged. His legs splayed out at awkward, rubbery angles from his body. His arms and hands hung down like those of a puppet whose strings had been loosened or discarded. He was no longer certain how many of them were were in the room. Two men with coshes? A man with a notebook and a small tape-recorder? Yes, he had seen him when he was first brought to the room from his cell. Interrogation regarding Meng, he had assumed. Then the man who had accompained them from the airport. He had been standing at the window, the lights of the square glowing behind him. The two men who had beaten him had entered swiftly—at some signal given by a buzzer beneath the desk?

He shook his head and groaned. Blood from his nose and mouth speckled his trousers and the carpet in front of the chair. The interrogation had been almost a formality, something to be gone through so that the beating could follow. They would probably kill Meng now, anyway. But not because *he* betrayed Meng. That certainly he had to retain. Not because of him. The beating was a coldly angry reaction to the CIA's handling of—what was it? What had he called it? Tiger something? *Jade Tiger*, yes. The operation's codename.

Liu spat into his hand. There were fragments of tooth in the pool of blood and saliva in his palm.

'Take him back,' he heard someone say in Mandarin. The voice sounded slowed down, tape recorded, a mere fuzzy boom, every word elongated. He shook his head, forgetting his pain, to clear his hearing.

Then he was dragged upright, pulled forward so that his legs buckled at the knees and his toes dragged across the room. He swung his head, but the face of the man who had come with them from the airport was obscure—a white blob. A shadow moved at the corner of the room—man with the notebook? The door opened, he was dragged through it, stumbling one or two steps until it became easier to let the two men holding his arms make all the effort and pull him along, toes turned in, hurting as they went down the first flight of stairs, almost twisting his feet from his ankles . . . He tried to catch up with them then, but he could not. His feet bounced down the stairs.

The bloodspecks were left behind almost before they formed on the polished wooden floor of the corridor. One of them speaking over his hanging head had said something . . . What was it? 'How many more times—how many times? More times?' No, those were not the real words, that was the sense of them coming through the tape-recorder of his woolly, slow hearing. *More* times? He said more times . . .

Corridor rushing past, yellow walls, uncovered faces staring at his, the blocks of the wooden floor rushing, melding into a race-track beneath his eyes.

Dead.

He formed the thought with great clarity and great effort. He was dead. Whatever he told or secreted regarding Meng, eventually they would kill him. He had become meaningless and unimportant. No longer valuable. He had become a devil doll, something to hurt so that the hurt would be transmitted to those in whose image he was made. He was an American. Devil doll. Pins, coshes, bullets, knives . . .

Cold air?

He retraced the last moments. Another flight of stairs, turn left, *left*, into a long corridor with green walls, a strip of highly-patterned carpet on the wooden blocks. Faces—ignore, not important—dark office doors, a twisting wooden staircase, then, down to some part of the ground floor—three floors up had they been, two floors?—his hands banged against the winding stair-case, then there were tiles rushing beneath his eyes, blue and white, black lines at either side of the corridor . . .

Take it in, *take it in* . . .

Or dead.

Where had the fresh cold air been? Not this chill down here, down the concrete stairs to the cells which he recognized lining this corridor. Up there somewhere. Yellow walls, stairs, green walls, carpet, carpet, carpet . . . ?

The cell door was opened, and he was thrust inside. He fell against the bed in an attitude that seemed to mock prayer; even hands together, holding his face, as if squeezing back through the pores and nostrils and mouth the impressions that threatened to evade him.

Carpet, carpet, *carpet, carpet* . . .

Small door, dark-almost-black wood, a white blob of a face above a dark suit, someone coming in, darkness behind him, the noise of a car . . . cold fresh air followed by the slightest whiff of petrol before he was too far along the corridor and the door was closed again anyway.

Outside—*outside* . . . escape . . . ?

British embassy telephone number. Peking in his mind like a map.

He turned. The light above him glowed, moved, enlarged, throbbed. He let himself be drawn up to it and it come down to him, the dark edges of his consciousness fold inwards, wrapping him in the dark. Escape . . . ? Had to . . .

Or dead.

Door.

Out—side . . .

He drifted in unconsciousness.

The rush-hour crowdedness of the café had subsided. Many of the tables were still occupied, but the crush of end-of-the-working-day drinkers and eaters had departed. Thus Zimmermann saw Petrunin weaving through the tables towards him soon after he entered the long, high-ceilinged room. He had never met the man before, but knew him. The formidable representative of a type. Petrunin, creating some fiction of his own, waved his evening newspaper in greeting while still ten or fifteen yards from Zimmermann's table.

Zimmermann glanced through the café windows, acting upon some old, buried instinct. Across the Marktplatz the town hall, the munster and the university lent solidity to the illusion that Bonn had become for him. What everyone called the federal village, no more than a staging post on the government's journey back to Berlin, had become more and more a neat, slow, rather boring provincial town which had happened to be Beethoven's birthplace. Cataclysmic events were happening in his own life, perhaps even in the life of Germany, and Bonn seemed inadequate to contain them.

Petrunin indicated the chair opposite him, smiling broadly, and Zimmermann nodded glumly. The Russian sat down. Zimmermann did not know the man's rank or seniority. He had not dared ask either the BND or the BfV, Germany's intelligence and security services, about the man who had telephoned to arrange a meeting. He could not make enquiries about KGB officers, not now . . .

From the corner of his eye, Zimmermann observed Petrunin unfolding the evening newspaper. He turned his gaze more directly to the window of the café, deliberately ignoring the black headline which contained his name. Women drifted past the window in summer frocks, men in shirtsleeves. Summer had come back for the day, as if mocking him. Just as tidy, dull, quiet, provincial Bonn mocked him, going unaltered about its business.

Petrunin ordered coffee and schnapps, and then addressed Zimmermann. 'Your position, Herr Zimmermann, is rapidly becoming untenable. You realize that, of course?'

Zimmermann's head snapped round, his eyes gleaming. Bonn glowed in evening sunlight at the corner of his eyesight. At the other periphery, the café retreated into a half-formed dark coolness, no more than the visual expression of the noise of customers. Petrunin occupied the centre of Zimmermann's vision; and his stage, he admitted to himself.

'What do you mean?'

Again Petrunin tapped the newspaper. Zimmermann flinched, but continued to gaze at the Russian and not where his tapping finger indicated. It was like resisting some enormous temptation.

Petrunin, dressed in a good lightweight suit, pale grey with a blue stripe, smiled: 'We both *know* it, Herr Zimmermann. My government is, of course, deeply indebted for your enthusiasm

and assistance towards the ratification of the Berlin Treaty . . .'
He paused, then continued: 'Yes, all that, of course. But now
Moscow feels that the time has come for you to—step down. To
depart.' He sighed theatrically, watching Zimmermann's jaw
emerge into sharper relief beneath his pale, stretched skin, and the
German's lips compress into a thin, colourless line. It was as if he
were adamantly refusing to swallow some food or drink being
offered, afraid that it was poisoned. 'Yes—all of us are deeply distressed, of course. But—to save what we have all worked for
during these past months, even years . . . You must do what is
best. The Treaty is dirty because of you. Your name is dirt, and
dirt sticks. Therefore, you must resign.' Again he tapped the
paper, but this time the gesture was emphatic rather than in-
dicative.

Zimmermann shook his head, 'No,' he said, and then his
mouth snapped shut again, as if foul air might enter it at any
minute, or some secret escape.

'No? Surely you don't mean that? A man as selflessly devoted
to German unity as yourself?' There was mockery, and anger, in
the Russian's voice. He did not look once at the waiter when his
coffee and schnapps were brought. 'Thank you,' he murmured.

Shadows stopped moving outside the window, probably to
read the menu. The sunlit evening was obscured.

'It is an entirely ludicrous situation when I am requested to
resign by an officer in the KGB,' Zimmermann observed. The
shadows moved on, and the golden, catlike evening spread itself
across the square once again.

'Perhaps. What do you intend doing?'

'I intend to sue for libel—each and every newspaper.'

'That will take too long.' Petrunin bent his head slightly,
sipped at his coffee. 'You can come back?'

'What?'

'When the Treaty is signed, it will no longer matter. You will be
back at Vogel's side before the year is over.'

'You're very kind.'

Petrunin tossed off the glass of schnapps as if it had been vodka.
He seemed disappointed with the liquor's bite and effect, then he
said: 'Let me make Moscow's position clear to you—just as the
ambassador would, were he here instead of myself.' He placed his
hands at either side of his coffee cup, as if to grab and choke it at
the right moment. Or perhaps only a man slipping his cupped

hands into water, sliding them beneath the fish's unsuspecting belly, ready to heave it out of the water . . .

Zimmermann dismissed the vivid, disturbing image. He had lost the skill, or perhaps it was the will, to deal with men like Petrunin.

'Very well,' he murmured. Petrunin bowed his head ironically.

'I am to make it clear to you that you must, and will, resign. Tomorrow. Before there are any more accusations, and before Chancellor Vogel's party loses any more ground in the opinion polls.' Petrunin's face was calm and unemotional, his words hard as flints. 'If the Treaty is to be ratified, and then to survive—you must go. You are now a carrier of disease. You must be—expelled.'

'What in heaven's name is happening here?' Zimmermann asked in a choked voice.

Petrunin shook his head. 'That doesn't matter. You must be concerned with results. *These* results . . .' He tapped the paper again. The golden evening seemed foggy at the corner of Zimmermann's eye. 'The campaign against you has been successful. You are finished. You must resign tomorrow. Do you understand me?' He waited, then: 'Do you understand?'

Zimmermann said only: 'Get out,' in a soft, weak voice. Nevertheless, Petrunin stood up, and threw some coins onto the tablecloth.

'Heed what I say,' he warned, and then left.

The evening had become fuzzy, barely coloured. Slowly but irresistibly, he turned his head to glance at the headline, and the picture beneath it. He could not, however, also avoid the results of yet another opinion poll in the adjacent columns. Vogel and the Social Democrats were now six points behind the Christian Democrats. Then his eyes were finally drawn to the obscene headline he had absorbed peripherally, almost through his skin and nostrils even before he had looked directly at it.

Obscene. Vile, untrue, obscene.

The picture was grainy, and of a complete and utter stranger who was described as his sister, Gretl. The unknown woman was posed against the white wall of a house with a husband and two children. Gretl. The headline read: WAITING FOR ZIMMERMANN'S TREATY?, and beneath it, a sub-heading asked: *Hostages to Fortune?*

Zimmermann read no more. His stomach revolted against such digestion. His eyes could not focus, except inwardly upon a simple grave, behind which hovered an empty, pale, youthful, idiot face, Gretl. All those years of empty visits, of talking to the empty head behind the empty face in disinfectant-smelling rooms. Empty tears—mostly his own—the unnoticed, casual wetting of under-clothes, the empty sucking of a thumb. All those years. Gretl.

He swept the newspaper from the table, knocking over Petru-nin's coffee cup as he did so. A dark stain appeared across the white tablecloth. Zimmermann's eyes streamed with tears he could not prevent or stem.

'What the state buries, the state also keeps tidy,' 'Caspar' ob-served, indicating the neat grave and its small marble headstone. There were no flowers, no pot or even a jamjar for them. Moss was a sheen of dark green on the gravel that covered the grave. It was one of a line of similar marble seed-boxes containing a level filling of gravel, bordering the hard dirt of the narrow path. There was no church. This was simply a municipal cemetery.

'Beloved sister,' Hyde read aloud, an acid irony in his voice.

'What did you expect?' 'Caspar' asked sharply, as if the tone had been directed towards himself. 'A hero?'

Hyde looked up. 'Maybe.' He glanced at the flanking graves. 'Why is she here? Where is the rest of the family buried?'

'Oh—village church near Pratau, where the family came from.' He shrugged. 'Perhaps he didn't think it mattered any longer. The mother's body was never located—or if it was it was never identified and interred in a fitting manner. One brother's buried in North Africa, I presume, and maybe the other's under the rubble of a house or a street in France. Who can say? At least he kept coming here until she died . . .'

'I suppose so.' Hyde's foot stirred the mossy gravel at one cor-ner of the grave beneath which Gretl Zimmermann had long since rotted. Then he looked up. 'OK, "Caspar". Thanks.' He turned to face back towards the haze that enveloped Wittenberg. It was almost dark. The sky was a dull red to the west. Witten-berg was a lumpy shadow pricked with tiny lights. Time to be going. He said, changing the subject: 'And you think the bribes would have been enough to keep them off his back?'

'You could answer that yourself. You disapprove of his be-haviour regarding—her.' He nodded at the headstone. 'She wouldn't have had the power. There was nothing they could do to her, after all. And Zimmermann was not a political figure, nor

312

were his business interests sensitive. No, I don't think you need worry . . .'

Hyde nodded. 'His public image,' he sneered. 'His social position.'

'Just so. I don't suppose he forgives himself any more than you forgive him. Shall we go——''

The first of the whistles cut across his words. It rang across the mound-like hill of the cemetery, and was answered by another from the far slope. Then a third. There had been other people, shadowy figures still and ornamental between the neat rows of headstones, but now, suddenly, there were more of them. The statue-like figures still did not move, but others were running, closing in.

'Caspar's' face crumbled into pain and loss rather than fear. It was as if he were some shallow poseur whose true origins and income had been revealed. He stared wildly at Hyde, whose eyes glanced between the chief components of the scene.

Agent-in-place, valuable . . . the headstone testifying to the man who was a lot less than heroic . . . the running, uniformed figures, directed by a man in a white raincoat which billowed behind him . . . headstone like a false affidavit . . . running policemen emerging into shape and colour and intention, moving to surround them . . . 'Caspar's' face, agent-in-place exposed, blown, ruined—so valuable . . . headstone, 'Caspar', the nearest policeman thrust off his feet as Hyde drove his shoulder into the man's running form, lifting him and sending him backwards onto Gretl's grave, winded and hurt.

Hyde ran.

Whistles more urgent now. Shots? No shots, take-him-alive, evidently. He had a chance. He ran headlong down the path, down the slope of the hill towards the small carpark. Police vehicles, a few cars, bicycles, the Volkswagen hemmed in by a Volkspolizei car and a barred-windowed, drab-green van. His escape was cut off, prevented. The gun and the papers were in the Volkswagen. Without them, he had no existence. No cover, no defence, no reality. Heavy feet pounded down the path behind him. He turned. A policeman, gun drawn, was careering after him. Hyde braced himself and waited. The policeman's face changed from triumph to anxiety, then Hyde moved to one side and heaved at the man who had to remind himself not to shoot. He was flung away by his own momentum and went rolling

313

between two graves, down the slope of the hill. White raincoats halted in a bunch fifty yards behind him. He turned and began running once more.

'Caspar' blown . . .

He cut off regret like the switching out of a lamp. *He* had to survive, get back. No one else counted. He vaulted the low metal gate from the carpark into the cemetery, and his body thudded into the hard body of the nearest policeman. Hyde was winded, fell, rolled, got up, kicked the uniform at the meeting point of jacket and trousers, hard. The policeman rolled away from him.

He tugged the keys from his pocket and unlocked the door of the Volkswagen. A second policeman reached the Volkswagen. Hyde fended off his reaching hand, and then slammed the door. There was a high, rabbit-like scream of pain. Hyde released the man's trapped fingers, slammed the door again. He started the engine—moment of coolness now, easy on the accelerator, *yes*— and it fired. He screeched the gearbox into reverse, and jammed his foot on the accelerator. The Volkswagen leapt backwards. Through the dirty windscreen he could see the white raincoats of the pursuit, the dark uniformed shadows just ahead of them. 'Caspar's' light suit was a glimmer farther up the slope, surrounded.

The Volkswagen crashed into the police car. He pressed the clutch, then released it slowly, accelerating. Metal ground in his head, jarring his teeth, hurting his ears. The police car moved protestingly. He ran forward, then crashed the Volkswagen back once more, scraping its side against the police van as he shoved at the car directly behind.

Through the gate now. Now they might shoot . . .

He ran forward once more, then crashed back. The car was suddenly alongside him, scraping its restraint and protest down the side of the Volkswagen. He swung the wheel.

Two shots. He felt one enter the wheel arch, the other perhaps hit the tyre. He accelerated towards the exit from the carpark, two policemen running far too slowly to cut him off. More shots, thudding into the rear doors. He turned the Volkswagen onto the minor road. Ahead were the headlights of the main road into Wittenberg. Behind him, lights flashed on, moved off, as the pursuit began. Without 'Caspar', he did not know the town or the countryside around it.

His wing mirror was filled with light, and when they bounced

314

out of view for a moment in some dip in the road, there was another pair of headlights close behind the first.

He swung onto the main road, still displaying no lights, and rushed into a gathering darkness occasionally flooded with lights. The two sets of headlights turned out less than half a minute behind. They would have lost him, but there was no thicket of traffic in which to hide. They would find him as soon as they overtook him—within minutes. The lights of Wittenberg had become a glow directly ahead.

Headlights—three, four pairs. Three sets oncoming. Ignore. Four pairs behind. First one moving too slowly, second and third pairs overtaking in turn. Fourth pair a heavy lorry. Coming up quickly, perhaps half a minute behind, no more. Closing that gap.

Darkness. They were rushing through trees. Wittenberg ahead. Ahead of him, the border would have been alerted, would be alerted at any moment. Even to get hold of the gun he would need to stop for more than a minute, another half-minute for the second set of papers. Far too long. Keep going.

There was no more response to the engine's increased revs. His foot was flat against the floor of the Volkswagen. The van was useless. Clapped-out. Knackered. He rehearsed the stream of abuse.

Seventy-five miles to the border at Helmstedt. He could cross nowhere else. No nearer place. Seventy-five . . .

Violently, he turned the wheel of the Volkswagen so that it bucked across the central reservation and across the northbound carriage-way. He heard the tyres protest, pulled onto the hard shoulder and stopped. Sweating profusely, he shuddered as a lorry passed him. Then he watched the two pairs of now-oncoming headlights move closer, draw level, pass . . .

Sweat broke out afresh as the lights receded in the wing mirror, growing smaller, diffusing into a dull, merged glow. He switched on the headlights and pulled out into the inside lane, heading northwards.

Berlin was less than forty miles away. Just over thirty minutes at top speed on the E6. West Berlin. The needle reached slowly towards sixty-five. Less than thirty minutes, once he picked up the motorway.

*

Peter Shelley hardly attended to the million diamond lights around Century House. His conversation with 'C' had been uncomfortable, unwelcome, unsatisfactory. The old man had been regretful, blustering, and defeated. He disliked the Foreign Secretary's orders, but he would put them into effect. He expected a Cabinet decision the following day, which would be conveyed to Shelley and thus to Aubrey. Confidentially, he expected the decision to be in favour—since both the Foreign Secretary and the PM were prepared to press for it—of pursuing the enquiries into Zimmermann's background and, if practicable, exposing the whole sordid operation to discredit him and the Berlin Treaty.

'C' evidently possessed the same kind of old-fashioned pride in the neutrality of SIS with regard to policy and the realms of legitimate government. Despite phone-tapping, mail-opening, Ulster, the employment of SAS and other army units in various parts of the world, 'C' like Aubrey seemed surprised at the CIA's behaviour with regard to Zimmermann and the British government's subsequent imitation of Washington's use of its intelligence service. Both old men behaved as if the intelligence service had never functioned otherwise than in an hermetically sealed world of its own, detached from Parliament, elections, budgets, armies, policies, foreign relations, business interests.

Shelley envied them both. He understood himself to be closer to people like Davenhill than to either Aubrey whom he admired or 'C' whom he respected. Yet he, too, wished for a moral vision, however impotent.

At least, he thought, tossing his head and staring blindly out of the window at night-town London, it might help one guard against excesses. Shelley regarded the American and Chinese operation against Zimmermann as an excess; wrongheaded, too, and creating an ill-considered, unstable future—but mainly excessive. Intelligence services ought not to go *quite* that far . . .

Aubrey very rarely came to the new headquarters at Century House, he thought. He preferred Queen Anne's Gate, even if half of the street had been demolished already and the rest was to follow shortly. Aubrey clung to the past. Even 'C' had moved in here.

The telephone rang. Startled, even though he had been waiting for more than an hour for the call, he picked up the receiver.

'Shelley.'

'Peter—John Lodge.' Computer Room senior officer. 'You owe me a pint. I've got three names, one of them really good, if you want them.'

'I'll be right down. Good lad.'

He put down the receiver, stood up and moved briskly to the door of his office. Next door, another and larger office waited for Aubrey to occupy it. He probably never would. Shelley shook his head. Hopelessly out-of-date. Clever as the Devil himself, but just as old-fashioned. More myth than reality . . .

He grinned as he made for the lift down to the basement. Spain. Three names for Hyde to check out. Only wise, he added to himself. Only sensible to get as much on Zimmermann as possible. It could prove very useful. No one wanted BAOR back on the Rhine, or the expense of keeping them there. Only sensible . . .

Shelley felt relief that the Cabinet decision had been to go ahead. Had they called a halt, Aubrey would have defied the order and sent Hyde or even himself into Spain in order to find, and produce, someone living who could clear Zimmermann's name. And that, Shelley realized, would have been uncomfortable, possibly dangerous to his own career. Aubrey would never have consented to drop the matter. It might have proved awkward— very awkward . . .

The lift doors sighed open. As they closed again behind him, Shelley was nodding in agreement with himself.

For once, the parameters of the investigation had acted in his favour. Berlin burned with light ahead of him, a huge, half-molten lump of fire, as he sat patiently in the Volkswagen, part of a long queue of traffic from West Germany, and from the DDR, entering the city to witness the historic event of the bulldozing of the Wall. There were Italians, Americans, British, too, and a dozen other nationalities. When he joined the queue of traffic waiting at the Dreilinden checkpoint on the E6, he became no more than another speck of curiosity drifting towards the city that would be no longer divided.

It took him an hour to pass through the checkpoint. On the DDR side, his papers were inspected, and he shrugged out an excuse that he had disliked the campsite at Wittenberg and decided to make a detour to Berlin. The van was not searched. He was informed that he had to cross into Poland the next day—an easy journey—by a pimply, bespectacled youth of no more than nineteen in a too-large uniform. He looked bored and harassed and tired. He had no interest even in the regulations he was attempting to enforce. He waved the Volkswagen through, blinking at the line of traffic still extending into the distance.

Hyde stopped at the first telephone kiosk on the Potsdamer highway and called the Consulate-General. Berlin Station appeared almost resentful of his arrival. He was an addition to a very busy schedule, a tired, drawling voice informed him.

'Stuff it,' Hyde told the voice. 'Inform Hanover. Get the message to Aubrey, then get me out of this place. Or get Shelley here to brief me. I don't care which.'

'Very well.' There was a tight, pinched sense of affront in the voice, but the names he had mentioned worked like a powerful nostrum. 'Which campsite will you be staying at overnight?'

'I won't, sport. Get me a hotel room.'

'You're joking, of course. Everywhere's full.'

'You'll fix it. It can be one of your last jobs in Berlin, mate. Send someone out here to collect me—OK?'

'I'll see what I can do.'

'Just do it.'

Hyde put down the receiver and stepped out of the kiosk into the cool night air. He felt grubby and tired and sorry for the engaging, efficient 'Caspar'. Somehow, the owner of the voice on the telephone represented a different kind of agent—the survivor. The ever-renewable old guard. The sort of intelligence agent who made Hyde heartily sick . . .

He stopped the accelerating train of thought. It was simply a transfer of guilt. *He* was responsible for 'Caspar' becoming defunct. No one else, just him. He should have known he was being tailed, however much they mixed up the cars and shuffled and reshuffled them. He should have known.

The slight, autumnal breeze cooled his face. His feet shuffled in fallen leaves as he walked moodily up and down near the telephone kiosk. A newspaper blew across his stout boots. He kicked it away, and it opened like a kite or the wing of some night-hunting bird. He saw the headline, and ran after it.

He folded the paper hurriedly. It was still damp from an early evening shower. The picture stared at him, the cosy little family group squinting into the sun behind the camera. A neat forgery, just a family snapshot we happen to have got hold of . . .

318

'Christ,' he breathed. He looked up as if he heard the on-coming rush of a vehicle or locomotive. In his head, he knew he heard the rushing inertia of the American and Chinese operation against Zimmermann, and he was enraged at his own impotence in the face of it. It was unstoppable.

He threw the newspaper away angrily. It fluttered to the ground like something wounded.

'Then they are even bigger idiots than I took them for,' Petrunin remarked icily. 'But, they do at least have this agent they pre-viously knew nothing about?' Kominski nodded. 'Even that declares their idiocy. Do they really think things are going to change in Germany? Are they that naive in the DDR?'

'I do not know, Comrade General,' Kominski replied in a studiedly neutral tone. Petrunin's anger arose from frustration and a growing sense of unease. The younger, ambitious man had decided it would not be wise to further enrage what might be a wounded, and therefore more dangerous, animal.

'Never mind.' Petrunin looked down at the papers that lay beneath his steepled fingers. He felt tired, and wanted to rub his eyes. Yet he was too much aware of the young man on the other side of the desk, too aware of how closely he was being studied, to permit himself such a solacing gesture. His neck ached with tension. 'Hyde must wait,' he added, though he did not mean it.

He knew the whole matter was refining itself, narrowing its horizon. Failure was becoming his personal liability. Moscow Centre had placed him at the dyke, thrust his finger into the leak; made it his responsibility, the whole thing . . .

And within himself, clearer and clearer, was growing the illusion that Hyde was to blame—entirely and solely. Hyde, with Aubrey behind him like a shadow. But, *Hyde*——

He wanted to clench his hand into a fist and bang the desk in enraged frustration. But, for Kominski, such a gesture would suggest loss of nerve rather than strength. He looked up and slowly, with fingertips that were still white from being pressed against each other, he picked up the list of names he had re-ceived. Days of work for a whole team simply to check and collate the material. Yet they had it now. Aladko's group, his intimates, his lieutenants. He could not be sure they had them all—but these names at least would be eliminated. No one would ever be able to ask them questions, investigate Zimmermann's past through them. They would cease to exist, this handful of old men who had survived the war, Franco and old age.

'These names——' he began. Kominski's eyes focused, and he reached out for the sheet of paper as it was offered to him. 'You will authorize immediate action through our terrorist contacts. The group will have to cross into Spain tonight or tomorrow. Every name on that list . . .'

'Sir?'

'I want them all eliminated—immediately.' Petrunin's tone sounded challenged. He stared at Kominski, who glanced slightly to one side, as if expecting some officer senior to both of them to enter the room. 'Yes?' Petrunin added with subtle threat.

'Moscow Centre?'

'I'm still in command of this operation—whatever it is. It's my decision . . .' He had manoeuvred the young man into one of the standard, and most unnerving of situations for a junior, but climbing, KGB officer. He could tell Kominski was weighing his loyalties and his career.

'I know that, Comrade General—sir, I'm just confused as to why——'

'Why such a drastic step?' Petrunin asked with false generosity in his voice. Kominksi nodded, settling himself to the recognition that Petrunin was as yet too dangerous, too powerful to be crossed or ignored. He would wait for his opportunity. Petrunin smiled blandly, hating Kominski. Timing, that's what it came down to. Report on your about-to-be-disgraced senior officer just a few minutes before his arrest, to purge yourself of unfortunate associations. Petrunin remembered his own identical techniques during the '60s, his decade of ascendency in the KGB. The similarity between himself and Kominski did not reconcile him to the younger man.

'Mm,' he murmured, then: 'The British—or it may only be Aubrey himself—wish to demonstrate that Zimmermann is not an agent of ours . . .'

'But why, sir?'

'Who knows. Economics, perhaps? They don't want their army back in Germany. Whatever, they don't appear to want the status quo. Of course, as I said, it could be only Aubrey's damned righteousness.' He smiled. Aubrey was an enemy he could normally accept, even admire. Not at that moment, of course.

Kominski was the sort of enemy he could only mistrust and fear. Now, of course, all his enemies—in Moscow Centre, in the Politburo, in the satellite countries and their security services, in the West—were indistinguishable one from another. All of them were part of the conspiracy to ruin him, to end his career.

'Yes, sir,' Kominski replied, plainly unconvinced.

'Good. This list may or may not be complete. Everyone on it will be eliminated within the space of three—four days at the outside. Every known, still-living asociate of Aladko during his period of service in Spain. Each name has an address. See to it, Kominski.'

'Is there an order of priorities, Comrade General?'

'The group can move south—in their work. The list is geographical, you will notice. In the case of the first name, Velasquez, it is also the correct priority. Velasquez was one of Aladko's closest confidants among the Spanish with whom he worked. Fanatical, trustworthy, brave. Ideal material . . .' Petrunin's eyes hardened, studying Kominski. 'The British will send someone to Spain, because in Spain lies the key to Zimmermann's innocence or guilt. Aubrey, especially, will be determined that no stone be left unturned. *He* will send someone to Spain. And if he has a list, then Velasquez will feature near the top of it.' He moved his hands apart. 'Now, no more timewasting. Get on with it. Give the orders.'

'Yes, Comrade General.'

Even before Kominski left the room, Petrunin's thoughts were rehearsing a growing chant, one that pounded like a fierce headache.

Send Hyde, send Hyde, send Hyde . . .

It was as if he were attempting some kind of remote hypnotic suggestion upon Aubrey. His hands clenched into fists, his neck and the back of his head were tense and stiff. His rage grew.

At least Hyde, he thought. These old men in Spain—*and* Hyde . . .

He might have prayed at that moment, had he a God.

THIRTEEN:

Final Decisions

Sir Richard Cunningham, Director-General of SIS, sat opposite Alex Davenhill in his study. Lady Cunningham had brought coffee before leaving for one of her charity committee meetings, and both men had, by a tacit agreement, drunk their coffee in silence before the subject of Davenhill's visit was broached. On the younger man's part there seemed a sense of the dramatic pause, while Cunningham merely felt a reluctance to begin the conversation which would inform him of the Cabinet's decision. When he put down his cup and saucer, he looked over Davenhill's head at the Childe Hassam Connecticut landscape in the style of Monet he had recently acquired. He felt almost that he wished to retreat into its pastoral calm. He roused himself when Davenhill spoke.

'I'm glad to hear dear Kenneth's making good progress,' he said. There was a hint of embarrassment and relief about his eyes. It had been his decision to transfer Aubrey to hospital in Hanover rather than London.

'Yes, quite. Now, of course, he mustn't be allowed to tire himself unduly,' Cunningham replied heavily, his eyes steady and hard beneath his bushy grey eyebrows.

'Of course not,' Davenhill snapped, as if refuting an accusation.

'Why did Cabinet meet last night rather than today?' 'C' enquired, erasing his reluctance.

'There was a great deal to discuss, of course—and a deal of urgency inherent in the situation. It was thought necessary to bring the Foreign Affairs Committee meeting forward to last night.'

'Urgency? I'm afraid I don't quite see . . .'

'Not urgent?' Alex Davenhill asked deprecatingly and with more than a touch of mockery. 'Surely that's a superficial view?'

'Enlighten me,' Cunningham replied with restrained anger. There was in the Director-General an instinctive dislike, even fear, of the Foreign Office Special Adviser to SISA.

'Cabinet wants the Berlin Treaty signed—if not in two days' time, then as soon as possible afterwards.'

'To save money.'

'It's not simply a matter of money, Sir Richard.'

'Oh? Then I must be mistaken. I thought we were talking about defence spending.'

'Only in part. If Vogel fails to win the next election, then we will be back to square one with regard to Germany, the EEC, NATO, and detente.'

'Where will you be if you reveal the Americans' part in this?'

'That—the man responsible is dead.'

'Buckholz wasn't responsible.'

'Do you think Washington will say otherwise, when the news is made public?' There was an arch, knowing smile on Davenhill's full lips.

'And the Chinese?'

'Ripe for the blame, perhaps? It could all be shifted their way. That isn't as dangerous—for us, that is—as the business Washington and Pekin have been up to.'

'Mm. Tell me what will be achieved by all this—*really* achieved, I mean. Before I begin making demands on time, effort and lives.'

'Oh, Sir Richard,' Davenhill smirked, shaking his head. 'All we want is proof. Not bodies.'

'Bodies you may get anyway. There have been some already.'

Davenhill spread his hands, inspected them, then steepled them as he leaned back in his chair. Above his head, the Hassam countryside beckoned, light through leaves leading to a peaceful, unpopulated distance.

'There are two weeks between the ratification of the Treaty and the West German elections. In that time, we must save Vogel from the consequences of having signed the Treaty. Clear this man Zimmermann, completely exonerate him. With him rehabilitated, and the Treaty purified . . .' Davenhill smiled. 'Vogel will carry the election, and German reunification will forge ahead, unblemished.'

'And that is our our advantage?'

'Cabinet has decided that it is.'

'In their wisdom.'

'As you say, in their wisdom. It enormously increases the reality of detente, opens up huge avenues of trade, drastically reduces our defence requirements, and keeps in power a good friend of ours in

Europe. There,' he added, 'I think that is a just summary. Don't you, Sir Richard?'

'Very well. What do you require of my service?'

'Evidence. The harder the better. A *living* witness. All the others are dead. We—Cabinet, that is—want to be able to prove conclusively that Zimmermann is not, and never has been, a Soviet agent. You already have a great deal of information that tends in that direction. It needs to be strengthened. Greatly strengthened.'

'The Russians do not seem to be similarly conscientious.'

'That's panic. They desperately need this Treaty. They *must* cut their defence spending. They have to buy their way out of trouble, and possess the funds to do it.'

'Agreed. Meanwhile, they're in the business of burying the very evidence we require.'

'I realise that, Sir Richard. Which is another reason for moving quickly.'

'For maximizing the risk.'

'As you wish.'

'You'll sour relations with Washington. I hope the Foreign Affairs Committee realizes that?'

Davenhill nodded. 'They are aware of that. It cannot be helped, I'm afraid. There will be sackings in the CIA, something of a scandal—but it can be contained. And despite the President's determination, America would be glad to reduce arms spending over the next few years. If a second term in the White House is to be ensured . . .'

'In other words, everyone can be persuaded to take the sensible view of things. *Our* sensible view.'

'Quite so.'

Cunningham sighed, and shifted in his chair. 'Very well, what do you want?'

'The most promising area would seem to be Spain. That is the hinge, the fulcrum. Crucial. Send some of your people to root out these three survivors of the Civil War. Get their evidence. Get *them*—one of them at least. A *living* witness, as I say.'

'I'll put that in motion,' Cunningham agreed, rising from his chair. Davenhill, sensing himself successful, and dismissed, also rose.

'If only we could talk to this chap—Liu, was it? The one who went into China. That really would prove illuminating.'

'Little chance of that. Complete loss of contact, I gather.'

Davenhill held out his hand. Cunningham shook it in a perfunctory manner.

'Spain, then,' Davenhill said.

'Spain,' Cunningham agreed heavily.

The idea had been ridiculous. Already he had gone far beyond husbanding himself, driven by the pain and grogginess into a desperate effort to remember the distances, the colours of the walls, the proximity of the guards. David Liu, his cheek pressed against the thin, stained carpet of the office, surrendered the attempt. He groaned. Blood and saliva dribbled from the corner of his mouth. His swollen tongue touched his teeth awkwardly and almost without sensation. He could not tell . . . His jaw might have been broken, for all the sense of it he had.

His hands were clutched around his genitals, his back arched, his knees drawn up. There was fluff on the carpet near his face. Beyond it, there were out-of-focus boots or shoes, no more than hazy dark shadows. The voices and movements beyond that were almost impossible to decipher.

He was dragged to his feet once more. He uttered a groan of protest. The pain seemed to spread through him, then retreat like a wave and localize in his ribs and back. He shook his head. The man who had been in the car from the airport, who called himself a colonel but who seemed something more and whose hands never touched Liu but seemed itchingly to want to, moved closer and lifted Liu's hanging head so that their eyes met. Liu was unable to decipher the complex emotions expressed in the colonel's eyes, but he sensed in some way that he had failed; that the MPT officer had become disappointed with him, as a child might have done with an anticipated yet mundane present. His head was allowed to droop on his chest once more, and he heard an order issued by the colonel. He felt his feet left behind, then begin to drag across the thin carpet towards the door. Guards held him, one on each side, fiercely gripping his arms. The interrogation was over. Liu opened his mouth in relief and the blood dribbled on his chin. He had not talked. He'd told them nothing about Meng. He was still loyal. Even though he knew they really didn't care. They only wanted to punish him for his cleverness . . .

The door opened. The corridor was cooler than the office, and he was grateful. Relief, a sense almost of escape, seemed to envelop him.

Escape . . . ? The word formed very slowly in his mind, but it brought no associations with it. It remained there, hanging in the darkness like a meaningless slogan. Escape . . . ?

The polished wooden floor. He trotted, bent forward, to keep up with his two guards. The pain subsided, as if relief were an anaesthetic. He had escaped from worse beating. They had tired of the sport. Escape . . . ? Yes, he had escaped.

Yellow walls. Wooden floor.

He spat towards the floor. The blob of saliva and blood coated one of his shoes. One of the guards laughed. They paused at the head of the stairs as if they intended flinging him ahead of them. His hands gripped their arms as they held his. He teetered on the edge of the cliff of stairs down to the next floor, to the strip of patterned carpet down the middle of that corridor. Green walls.

His toes bounced painfully on each step. The guards had dragged him off balance deliberately so that it happened. His ankles protested. His head cleared, each jolt awakening him further. Then his toes were dragging along the strip of carpet. The holster of one of the guards pressed into his hip and waist, thrusting against him like a solicitation of the crudest kind. A barred window showed him the inner courtyard of the building through a golden haze of evening sunshine. The sight of it brought useless tears to his eyes.

Escape . . . ?

The door triggered the slogan, the slogan now appeared with a rush of associations. Green walls, carpet, fresh air, smell of petrol, planning in his cell, the holster digging into his hip, the guards taken by surprise. Fantasy and memory were puréed by a surge of violent adrenalin.

Escape.

Door, almost past it already, strength husbanded? He couldn't answer that, didn't want to enquire. He had to try anyway. Door—other factor? *Other factor?* Don't resist, let yourself be dragged along . . .

Holster . . .

He twisted his arm in the slightly-slackened grip of the guard on his right, and swung his body against the left-hand guard, whose grip on his arm tightened for long enough to allow Liu's hand to reach the holster first. He flipped the tag and his hand closed

326

around the butt of the pistol. He heaved it free of the holster, and turned the guard off-balance, clutching him against his body.

Only now was the sensory information arriving that there was no one else in the corridor, that they were ten yards beyond the outside door, that the second guard's pistol was in his hand and coming level. The guard he embraced was beginning to struggle, to take him in a bearlike embrace and drive him backwards against the wall. His hand was coming up to claw at Liu's face. Liu fired twice. The second guard was flung against the opposite wall, his pistol discharging into the ceiling, his body becoming hard, soft, shapeless, still, all in a moment. Then Liu was slammed back against the wall by the guard he embraced. A clawed hand went over his eyes and mouth. He turned the pistol and squeezed the trigger. The body slid down his own, the hand raked lightly at his eyelids and lips, almost with a gentle touch. Then he, too, was still.

Reaction time, reaction time . . .

He made for the door. Other doors opened behind him, someone shouted, a woman screamed. The outside door was locked. He fired twice at the lock, then dragged the door open. Sunlight spilled into a narrow alleyway. He could not be certain whether or not the smell of petrol was only a memory. The air seemed cool. He slammed the door shut behind him.

The walls of the main building and one of its annexes rose on either side of him. Peeling yellow paint, barred windows, floor after floor. He went down a canyon of brick and stone, rounded a corner and found himself in a narrow space filled with parked cars, jammed as closely together as if they had been intended as a barricade to prevent his escape. With a single ninety-degree corner in the alleyway, he had lost all sense of direction; he had possessed no bearings when he first opened the door.

He looked up. The MPT buildings loomed over him. This was some overspill carpark from the courtyard. It lay like a pool of concrete between the two watersheds of the main building and one of its annexes. There seemed no way out of it.

He squeezed and slid between the tightly-jammed cars, feeling increasingly hampered and desperate. The evening sun glanced between the two buildings, illuminating the alley, lighting some of the blind windows. He listened, above the noise of his heart and lungs, for the noises of pursuit. An alarm sounded in the main building. He followed, like some blind, subterranean animal, the warmth of the sun between the two columns of windowed yellow stone. It could not be this easy, it could not . . .

He emerged into the vastness of Tiananmen Square. Instinctively his hand shielded his eyes; whether from the slanting sun, the crowds, or the size of the place he could not be certain. He thrust the gun into his waistband, seeing as he did so the blood on his shirt, its soiled and torn condition. He huddled his thin jacket around him.

He drifted into the crowd, becoming immediately imprisoned by them, captive and secure. He did not look back, or ahead. He moved with the homegoing crowd, and would only resist their pressure and their current when he was well away from the square and near a telephone kiosk. He felt his legs become rubbery. It had been so easy. He stumbled, someone lent him the support of his arm—he flinched as if that hand belonged to one of his guards, then nodded his thanks—and he moved on, shivering with reaction, his weariness and pain growing, his mind becoming increasingly numb as it attempted to accommodate the violent ease of his escape.

The city authorities had not attempted to prevent the erection of perhaps two dozen extra observation platforms—most of them rickety, entrepreneurial structures—near the one they officially sanctioned along the stretch of the Wall that hid the Potsdamerplatz on the other side. There was a brisk, resident-and-visitor trade in the use of the platforms. Ten or a dozen steps on the creaking wood, and the bulldozers could be seen on the eastern side, drawn up like a line of tanks.

The mined ribbon of ploughed earth had been freshly dug over. The wire had gone, though the high bright lights remained. The guards, too, remained. They seemed, however, unarmed. Occasionally one of them would wave at the heads that appeared above the Wall. Bulldozers and lorries and tractors were also drawn up at the Brandenburg Gate and the Friedrichstrasse's Checkpoint Charlie. At the moment of the ratification of the Berlin Treaty the day after next, the bulldozer blades would be lowered like visors, and the Wall would crumble. The potent images would be televised throughout the world. Already, the television gantries rose above the observation platforms on both sides of the Wall.

'Velasquez—same name as the painter,' Shelley was saying as

328

they crowded onto the platform and Hyde appeared to study the distant guards across the Potsdamerplatz. When one of them waved, Hyde made no reply. Cameras whirred and clicked around them. Shelley heard Japanese spoken, and American English.

'Oh, yes,' Hyde replied with apparent indifference. Already the autumnal coolness of the morning was disappearing and a hazy summerlike, humid, warmth surrounded them.

'Look, Patrick, I'm being pressured every which way with this matter. So is the Director-General. Your plane is booked, you'll be in Barcelona this evening. An interpreter will meet you. We— we're wasting time down here as it is. I could have briefed you quicker and safer at the consulate.'

Hyde turned to regard Shelley, and slowly shook his head. He indicated the expanse of the square beyond the Wall with a careless hand. 'This is it, though, isn't it? All fall down . . .'

'You? Sentimental?'

'No. Just wanted to see what I was doing it for. Everyone is shitting bricks in case it screws up.' He looked across into East Berlin. 'Like saying ta-ta to an old friend,' he said, grinning. Then he turned back to face Shelley. 'You don't want just questions asked, do you? You wouldn't be sending me if you did. You want Velasquez out—in Madrid or London?'

'What makes you think that?'

'You've got Wei in London spilling his guts, you've got my report from poor bloody "Caspar"—to make up the set you have to have Velasquez on film and tape, even in prison. A counter-hullabaloo in the press. You need Velasquez to prove the Yank and Chinese frame-up wasn't true by accident.'

'Yes,' Shelley admitted.

'Davenhill's a devious little funnel-web, isn't he?'

'Patrick, take my advice. Don't cross Davenhill.'

'And don't turn me back on 'im, eh, mate?' Hyde replied with a grin. 'What's Aubrey think?'

'Aubrey would order you in—whatever Cabinet said.'

'Why?'

'To discover the truth. To have a voice to pronounce Zimmermann innocent.'

'To repay Zimmermann for his life, forty years ago?'

'Exactly. And we both know you'll do it for Aubrey, don't we?'

'Fuck it—yes. In the end, yes, I'll do it for the old man. Sod it.'

329

Hyde grinned mirthlessly. 'OK. So give us me tickets and me papers, and I'll be off. Lunch first, mind. Your treat.'

'Of course,' Shelley replied, much relieved. They went down the steps once more, the bulldozers and the guards and the square passing out of their view. The graffiti of insult and protest on the Wall remained, and the lights on the other side reached into sight like the heads and necks of mantises.

Fuck communism . . . Stalin is alive and well and living in East Berlin . . . Rock against the Wall . . . the date and time of someone's death during a crossing, the stick-figure of a hanging man, swastikas. And the lights rearing above the breeze-block and capping stone. Once they reached the ground, there remained no change, and no apparent possibility of change in the situation symbolized by the Wall.

'How close was this Velasquez to Aladko?' Hyde asked as they walked towards Shelley's consulate car.

'Very close. During a period of months, perhaps as much as a year. Strong left-hand, as it were. Aragonese, knew the area well, staunch Communist. A bit dim. Who could ask for anything more?'

'And he was there?'

'He had to have been. He would have been there when Aladko talked to Zimmermann. He might even have been the muscle, the shit to Aladko's sugar in the interrogations. Anyway, he must have heard most of what passed between them . . .' Shelley was brightly, even artificially enthusiastic.

Hyde said cynically: 'You don't really care—as long as he can be got to say that Zimmermann wasn't a Communist.'

'What do you mean?'

'Aubrey wants the truth. HMG and "C" and Davenhill and you—all you want is a voice.'

'It was Spain, Patrick. It *had* to be Spain, if Zimmermann was ever turned.'

'Sure,' Hyde sneered.

Shelley turned back to the car and opened the door. 'Do you want a decent lunch before you leave?' he asked peevishly.

'Sure.' Hyde climbed into the car. 'Sure.'

'My old friend, I am desperately sorry that it has had to come to this . . . You know that.'

There was something insincere in Vogel's tone that jarred even on Zimmermann's misery. The characteristic bluffness and directness had disappeared to leave his residue of sanctimonious apology. Resignation. The letter of resignation, typed before Zimmermann had been summoned to the Chancellor's office in the Schaumberg Palace, lay on the large, ornate, eighteenth-century desk, a white stain on the otherwise empty, leather-bound blotter. Resignation. Abject, public, complete and final.

Zimmermann waved a feeble hand to silence Vogel.

'I understand,' he muttered thickly.

Through the latticework of his fingers, Zimmermann saw Vogel's moving bulk appear to come towards him, no more than a shadow haloed by a damp light from the window. Then he seemed to reconsider. He moved instead to keep the desk between them, and came to a pause in front of the net-curtained, tall windows leading onto the balcony. A bright late summer day lay outside, unregarded by either man.

'You do?' Vogel sighed. 'Thank God for that, Wolf. If there was any other way, you know I'd take that route first. This is really a *last* resort . . .'

Zimmermann swallowed, and looked up, blinking in the light from the window.

'Yes, of course,' he said with adopted firmness. 'But do you think it will be enough. Will it save the Treaty?'

'I hope so.' Vogel shrugged. 'It seems the only way left. The opposition to the Treaty, suspicion of it, has focused on you, Wolf. Look, I *know* it's scandal and no more—but it's working . . .'

'Are you sure you won't scrap the Treaty to save the election, Dietrich?' Zimmermann asked in a cold voice, a sudden and ghastly insight prompting the words.

'Of course not!' Vogel snapped almost too quickly and fervently. 'It's to save the Treaty—*our* Treaty—that I'm doing this at all!' Now he seemed to force himself around the desk towards Zimmermann. He added, standing over him: 'You can come back when all this has died down. When the Treaty's seen to be working, we can work together again.' His hand hesitated above Zimmermann's shoulder, and did not descend.

'Yes, of course,' Zimmermann said softly. He looked up into Vogel's strong, shadowed face. 'Of course,' he repeated. Vogel hastily drew back his hand as Zimmermann made to rise.

Zimmermann squared his shoulders, then crossed the room to the desk. He turned the letter of resignation towards him, and reached

331

into his breast pocket for his pen, ignoring the gold pen that Vogel had left resting beside the letter. Slowly, carefully Zimmermann appended his signature to the letter. He heard Vogel sigh with relief. Immediately there was a tension of urgency and hurry in the spacious, cool room.

'You wish me to broadcast?' Zimmermann asked maliciously.

Vogel's face signalled quick and surprised guilt, then he regained control of his expression and shook his head gravely. 'No, old friend. I wouldn't put you through that ordeal. It will be done—first news bulletins of the afternoon. You're not available for comment.' He studied Zimmermann, then added: 'You won't make yourself available, Wolf, will you?'

Zimmermann shook his head and replied stiffly: 'Of course not. I know the form, Dietrich.' Then he added, his eyes gleaming: 'I'm going to sue, of course.'

'Naturally. When?'

'Oh, next week.'

'Good. Next week, yes.' Vogel came towards Zimmermann, his hand held out, his face folding into lines of regret. To Zimmermann, his mouth seemed an exaggerated, painted expression of sorrow such as a whitefaced clown might wear. Similarly, the shadows under Vogel's eyes were no more than clever make-up to add to the sad gravity of the meeting. The dislike that Vogel's features evoked in him surprised, even shocked Zimmermann. His oldest friend . . .

Zimmermann cleared his throat, and said: 'Don't let it go, Dietrich. Not for anything. Don't let the Treaty go!' He realised his palms were damp, and he removed both his hands from the grasp they had placed on Vogel's hand.

'I won't, Wolf. I promise.'

'Very well. I'll leave you, then, to get on with the announcement of my resignation.'

'It's already——' Vogel began, then cut off the words.

Zimmermann nodded with a defeated, heavy irony. 'I understand,' he said. 'Goodbye, Dietrich.'

He crossed the room with what Vogel could only describe as a military step and bearing and, without turning back or pausing, opened the door and vanished. The door clicked shut behind him.

Immediately Vogel turned to the desk and picked up the letter. His sigh of relief was profound and genuine as he studied the strong, firm signature. Then he pressed the buzzer on the intercom to summon his principal secretary.

A bronze dragon clutching a flaming pearl in its claws stared balefully at David Liu as he mounted the steps. Stylized gold streamers of smoke issued unmovingly from his nostrils. It seemed a portent of the forces ranged against him. Even the giant pandas in Peking Zoo had seemed to stare at him from behind their bars with an infinite sadness, their great smudged black eyes doleful, hopeless. Now, as the daylight began to fail, he found himself in the Imperial Palace, preferring to think of it by its older name, the Forbidden City. That name seemed more in keeping with his situation.

He walked between the Tower of Enhanced Righteousness and the Tower of Manifest Benevolence, acutely aware of the irony of their names on his tourist map, towards the Hall of Supreme Harmony. The SIS officer to whom he had eventually spoken at the British embassy had arranged a meeting within the Imperial Palace, amid the crowds of shirtsleeved tourists. The huge courtyard in front of the Hall of Supreme Harmony dwarfed the throng of tourists. Liu halted and checked his bearings. Strangely, he felt little excitement. He experienced no more than the dull, microbe-like sensations of being part of an anonymous crowd. The telephone call, the identification he had supplied, the arrangement of the meeting place, all had left him numbed, weary, dispirited. He could not rouse himself from that warm, foetal anonymity he had felt drifting with the crowd, his body spent after the effort of his escape and the murder of the two guards.

Stone dragons glared; bronze lions mouthed their brazen roars in the dusk, seeming ready to spring. Upcurling eaves decorated with birds and small animals lowered in the failing light. Liu felt his temperature drop, as a reptile's might have done, with the loss of the sun. He shivered, and clutched his arms around his torso. His ribs and back and buttocks ached. In the toilets at the zoo, he had washed as much of the bruising and cuts away or into subsidence as he could. His face felt puffy and stiff and bloated. He leant against the stone balustrade of the stairs leading to the terrace upon which the hall was set. No one regarded him.

'I say, can you direct me to a restaurant serving English food?' a voice said at his side. Slowly, he turned his head.

'What?' He found the English difficult after the days of Mandarin. The accent, too, was strange, even unexpected.

'English food,' the young man said, smiling diffidently. 'Where can I get English food?' He seemed to prompt Liu, as if he might have been helping him guess the answers in a test. A camera hung from his neck, and he wore a shortsleeved shirt and light slacks and carried a large shoulder-bag. His face was pink with sunburn, his narrow nose showing signs of peeling. There were freckles, too.

'I—takeaway, you mean?' Liu replied with hesitation.

'Good chap. Hello. My name's Forbes. British embassy. You're David Liu, right?' Forbes's manner seemed casual, not unfriendly, patronizing. He seemed to supply Liu's name in case the man had forgotten it or lost his memory.

'Yes,' Liu said dully.

Forbes looked around him. 'Mm. Let's not stay here. Go through to the garden, shall we?' His hand indicated the sky beyond the red roof of the Hall of Supreme Harmony.

'Beyond Harmony?' Liu asked, shaking his head. 'Is there anything more?'

'Ha!' Forbes barked, patting Liu on the shoulder. 'That's the ticket. That's it!' He touched Liu's elbow, guiding him like a blind man down the steps into the vast courtyard, a sheen of summer grass on its cobblestones. The hall before them lost detail, gained bulk as the sun set. 'Have to get a bit of a move on, old man,' Forbes commented. 'These chaps are pretty keen on closing on time.'

Liu felt the comfort implicit in Forbes's hand on his elbow. He also sensed that the man's voice was belied by the keen glance with which he had been appraised while he fumbled for the reply to Forbes's indentification code. He had seen Liu's state quite clearly. His voice had become more jollying, more soothing. Also, there was in it an alarm-like quality that slowly but surely roused Liu.

Forbes merely contented himself with pointing out the features of the Imperial Palace as they passed northwards through it, eventually emerging into the Imperial Gardens. Liu was left with an ominous impression of the Forbidden City. Its stone and bronze and tile and gold weight seemed to press down on his head and limbs, oppressing both body and mind. It was an alien place, hostile to life. Stone elephants, gold lions, jade tigers, bronze

334

dragons. Curling, decorated eaves, flagged terraces, palms, shadows, failing light; the inner courtyards pressing in upon them until he wanted to run. The buildings looking like great, ornate ships frozen on collision courses with each other and with the helpless figures who slipped between them in the dusk. And always the animals; staring, basilisk, inhuman.

Liu sighed, paused, breathed deeply again and again when they had left the gallery surrounding the inner halls and court-yards behind the Hall of Supreme Harmony, then hurried down the stone steps into the deep shadows of pines and cypresses. Ancient China and the modern city beyond it, glimpsed occasionally as they walked, both disappeared.

'All right, old chap?' Forbes asked solicitously.

Liu nodded. 'Yes, I'm all right.'

There were benches beneath the trees, occupied by ancient Chinese who seemed to have ossified into the miniature land-scape of the gardens. Gnats and midges hovered like wisps of smoke. Liu brushed a cloud of them away. His breathing became easier. Forbes took a smaller bag from his large, bulky shoulder-bag.

'Shaving kit, change of clothes, papers,' he explained almost apologetically, handing the bag to Liu by its long strap. Liu nodded gratefully. 'You're from the south, Kwangsi Province. It fits your voice and intonation. On holiday in Peking. You should have a hotel reservation, but try any of the smaller, cheaper places. They aren't so fussy.' Again, Liu nodded. He relaxed into the embrace of Forbes's competence as he might have done into a warm bath. 'I think that's everything on your side—for the moment?'

Liu looked up at the interrogatory note with which Forbes ended his remarks. He wiped away at a reforming cloud of midges. The long, upturned roofs of the former imperial re-sidence were still distinguishable against the soft, darkening sky. Stars had begun to gleam within the dark blue. A tiny waterfall tinkled like small bells softly struck. Liu felt himself immersed in the sound.

'Is something the matter?' he asked with difficulty.

'You, I think,' Forbes observed. 'You're a long way away, old man.'

Liu rubbed his face. 'I—I'm sorry.'

'How many did you . . . ?' Forbes asked gently.

335

'Two of them.'

'I see. Sorry, but it isn't finished yet. Now—briefly, just the recorded highlights—what's your story?'

Forbes perched beside him on a low stone wall which imprisoned a rock garden and tiny shrubs and the musical water. Liu, speaking softly and with utter detachment, recounted his conversations in Wu Han, his subsequent arrest, the confession of Frederickson. He spoke without calculation, without reserve. The events no longer belonged to him. Forbes murmured from time to time, or swiped savagely at the gnats or simply rubbed his chin in silence.

When Liu had finished, Forbes said: 'I—think that's what is required. *That* truth.'

'What?'

'Don't worry. You're safe with us.'

Liu appeared startled. 'I never thought I wasn't.'

'Ah,' Forbes murmured. 'Your truth might have been embarrassing, even impolitic.'

'I—trusted Mr Aubrey.'

Forbes clicked his tongue. 'I see. Met him a few times. He does give that impression.'

'Will I see him?'

'I—er, he's indisposed at the moment. You'll be flown to London as soon as we can get you out. No doubt you'll see him there.'

'How will you get me out?'

'Ah. I'm trying to rig up something convenient and safe at the moment. There hasn't been much time . . .'

'And meanwhile?'

Forbes realised that suspicion had surfaced in Liu once more. He had shrugged off his drowsy, somnambulistic retreat from events, from murder and escape and the terrible, transient power of adrenalin. Now he was back in the real world.

'Meanwhile, your cover as a tourist is your best bet. You haven't work, or permits. In your bag you'll find a very small, very cheap camera. Use it. Tomorrow, take a trip out to the Great Wall. Everyone does. I can be there as another tourist. By then, I should have more news of your escape route.' He patted Liu's arm. 'Don't worry. People in London are *very* anxious to talk to you. You're quite safe.'

'And afterwards?'

336

'Don't worry. The usual bargain. New identity, pension, re-employment if you wish. Just drive a hard bargain.' Forbes laughed softly. 'Book a trip out to the Great Wall tomorrow. You should be there around midday, early afternoon. We'll talk again then.' The gardens were almost dark now. Shapes passed them. Someone was blowing a whistle. Liu flinched, but Forbes touched his arm reassuringly. 'Locking-up time,' he said. 'We must be off.' Forbes stood up. 'OK?'

'Yes. Thank you.'

'Don't mention it. See you tomorrow. Remember, you're a tourist.' He chuckled. 'And remember something else. You're almost home.' Forbes waved his hand, and turned away. Liu sat on for a while.

The whistle went on blowing, but he no longer shuddered at its sound. In his bag was a new identity, and he retreated to its safety. He was a few small steps, steps not of his own invention or volition, away from safe passage. He allowed himself to trust Forbes and the British because he was too tired and isolated not to do so. The midges hovered. The roofs of what had once been the imperial living quarters—a small grandness behind the public buildings—blended with the starlit night. The musical water continued to play. He closed his eyes. He could smell the pines.

Eventually he joined the last of the visitors to the Forbidden City and passed out of the Imperial Gardens through the Gate of Divine Pride. As he waited for a trolley-bus to take him to the crowded, cheap-hotel district near the main railway station, he watched the lights of the city and the colder stars above and beyond them.

The Madrid station interpreter's name was Fernando de Lorca. He was young, well-dressed, handsome and clever. He was waiting with evident eagerness, a sense of self-importance, and a willingness to please at Barcelona's Muntadas Airport, a Hertz car already rented. De Lorca had arrived at Muntadas only a matter of two hours before Hyde, on an Iberia shuttle from Madrid. The gun issued for Hyde by the embassy in Madrid was a new Belgian FN 7.65mm using redesigned bullets with a stopping power superior to most ammunition of the same calibre. Hyde had practised with that model only rarely, but made no complaint. The manner in which de Lorca informed him of the pistol he had drawn for him indicated that he considered it something of a coup over the Chancery armourer.

The Barcelona evening was dry, hot, redolent of petrol and dust. The lights of the city glowed to the north of the airport. De Lorca guided him to the rented Audi, and they drove out of the airport carpark, picking up the E4 only minutes later, and headed west.

'It will take us most of the night,' de Lorca explained apologetically. Hyde slid further down in his seat.

'That's OK, mate. You'll be doing all the driving.'

'I realize that.' De Lorca had replied without rancour or resentment.

'This bloke Velasquez. Where is it he lives?'

'Ah. He is a forester now. He lives right within the Ordesa National Park, up in the Pyrenees. He lives alone. He has no family.'

Hyde rubbed his arms. 'Not unusual,' he murmured. 'How far?'

'Maybe three hundred kilometres. A hundred and eighty of your miles.' De Lorca sighed, envisaging the road ahead as a species of melodrama.

'Where do we eat?'

'Lerida.' De Lorca smiled. 'I know a good restaurant in the town. We will be there in time for a late supper.'

'Good on you. You're sure Velasquez is there?'

'Certain.'

'And you know it's not just—conversation?'

'Yes. I, too, have drawn a gun, Mr Hyde. I realize we are going to kidnap a citizen of Spain.' Hyde looked up at the portentousness of the words. He saw de Lorca flash white teeth in the lights of an oncoming car. Hyde settled back in his seat once more. He'd do.

'They know what they have to do,' Kominski said with a trace of asperity in his voice. 'The first target, Velasquez, will be killed tomorrow morning. The others during the following three days.'

Petrunin understood the younger man's increased confidence. The order had come. The order for his return to Moscow, and it was not for him to be decorated or promoted. Moscow Centre had lost patience, lost nerve; sought only the scapegoat now. And Kominski knew it and revelled in it. Doubtless he had already submitted a record of his own doubts and increasing concern over the way in which General Petrunin had been running the operation. Some old college pal of his in the Centre could make certain it arrived on an influential desk, suitably backdated, before he himself arrived in Moscow.

'I hope we can trust to the complete efficiency of this group of yours?'

'If it were me, I would not keep an elite ETA unit on the French side of the Pyrenees just for their own safety,' Kominski replied with a touch of insolence. 'I don't suppose the Madrid Rezident does, either.'

Petrunin bridled at the younger man's tone. It was prophetic. His recall to Moscow was like adrenalin to Kominski, who was now pointedly studying his nails, as if waiting to be rid of a tiresome visitor. He had carefully omitted Petrunin's rank. The general clenched his hands into fists on his lap, out of sight behind the desk. Kominski's desk, he reminded himself. However, although the prospect of demotion, even punishment, seeped through his veneer of calm like a gas, he managed a thin, superior smile that threatened Kominski's future. The younger man appeared disconcerted by it.

'I don't suppose so,' Petrunin murmured in agreement. It was evident that something had struck Kominski, subdued his mood. Perhaps Petrunin's reputation for survival; he was notorious for surviving. It would not do to declare enmity towards him—not just yet. Petrunin placed his hands on the desk. In the pool of light from the anglepoise lamp, they were still and confident. 'Very well. Moscow Centre agrees with me that these eliminations are to go ahead. The smear attaching to Zimmermann must receive no further assistance. And, since Madrid confirms that the British have been interesting themselves in Spain and Aladko's old associates, it is felt safer that we leave nothing for them to find.'

'But, if Zimmermann is innocent——?'

'He *is*. But, people can be persuaded to say things, lay blame, suggest doubt. This way, there will be nothing that can be used against Zimmermann, nothing that can be twisted, distorted. Nothing that the Americans can use at a later date.'

'Sir, if we let Velasquez live, perhaps we could convince the British that——'

'No! Would you trust the British? Tomorrow, they may want

339

to believe, and say, that Zimmermann *is* a Soviet agent—the Americans may make them do it. Then Velasquez and the others will say what is required of them. *This* way, there can be no lies.'

'Yes, Comrade General.' Kominski evidently remained unconvinced. Had Moscow Centre not agreed with him, Petrunin realized that Kominski would have contacted headquarters direct, with the utmost urgency. As it was, he evidently despised the exaggerated caution the Centre seemed to be displaying. Weakness——

In my case, revenge, Petrunin reminded himself. Hyde must die, Aubrey must be cheated of proof . . .

'Comrade General,' Kominski began, carefully weighing Petrunin's rank, 'our reports do confirm that the British have been making enquiries regarding Velasquez and some of the others . . .'

'Unfortunately, Velasquez dies in the morning. It will have been a wasted journey for whoever they send . . .'

Send Hyde, send Hyde, send Hyde . . .

He could not control or still the chant in his mind. His desire for revenge had overridden his desire to escape from his situation. And his revenge had become precise and focused. He had failed to kill Aubrey, but he had to kill Hyde. Hyde *had* to die.

'You've given the necessary orders?' he snapped.

'Yes, Comrade General. The group is to prepare for a British presence—and to counter it to maximum effect.'

'Ah, the jargon,' Petrunin sighed. Then he added: 'Is my car ready? I will go directly to the airport.'

'Of course, Comrade General.' Kominski's former superiority of manner reasserted itself. With evident irony, he added: 'You will be in Moscow before dawn. I envy you your return.'

'We both know that is bullshit, Kominski.' The younger man seemed to think better of replying. Petrunin stood up. 'Very well, let us go. And, as soon as there is news of the progress of these eliminations—especially that of Velasquez—I wish to be informed. In Moscow.'

'Do you really think the British will send this man Hyde?' Kominski asked softly, startling Petrunin. The general turned on him.

'Yes, Aubrey will. *I* would, in his place.'

Kominski closed the door of his office behind them. The corridor was empty, but the noise of a vacuum cleaner sounded distantly in the building.

Send Hyde, send Hyde, send Hyde, Petrunin's thoughts repeated. Now, indeed, it did sound like a prayer.

'OK, that's good, Colonel. That's damn good,' Frederickson said as he stood at the window of the CIA Station Chief's office in the US Embassy on Guanghua Road, looking towards the twin strips of light along Changan Avenue and the ill-lit bulk of the railway station. The telephone receiver was slightly damp with the perspiration of excitement and relief. He had been waiting all night for this call from the MPT. 'Good,' he said once more. 'Very, very good.'

'Unfortunately,' the colonel continued, 'my men lost Liu somewhere near the railway station.'

'Shit!'

'I apologize. They will, of course, be disciplined. We have been and still are making a search of the area, checking all hotel and boarding-house registrations.'

'You'll find him?' The perspiration that Frederickson felt on his forehead was now chilly. He oozed anxiety, a sense of impending failure. 'He's made contact, dammit! He's close to getting out.'

'I understand the situation, Mr Frederickson. However, we know the man Forbes. We know *every* intelligence operative the British employ at their embassy. It is Forbes and the others we shall watch meanwhile. There will be another meeting, probably later today.'

'You sound pretty sure——'

'I am. Liu cannot enter the embassy without being stopped. The British will realize that. He will have to be got away unofficially. Such arrangements take time.'

'OK, I understand. Langley and Peking are in full signals contact. You know that?'

'Of course.'

'Your top brass and mine. I expect a decision as to what to do about Liu at any moment.'

'As do I.'

'What—result do you expect?'

'Elimination.'

'Same here. But—we don't have the guy.'

'We shall, Mr Frederickson. We shall. No one will lose Forbes, I assure you. And Forbes will lead us to Liu.'

'The guy has to go. I just hope Langley sees the necessity.'

'I am certain they will. Now, goodnight, Mr Frederickson. If there are developments, I will call you.'

'Sure. Goodnight, Colonel.'

Frederickson put down the telephone and rubbed his brow. His fingers were shiny with perspiration. Where the hell was Liu? To eliminate someone, you had to have a body so you could turn it into a corpse. They *had* to find Liu. Frederickson was sure Langley would want him buried. And expect an immediate compliance. Where the hell was he?

FOURTEEN:

Terminus

The field director who controlled the ETA group and who liaised with the Madrid Rezident was a French Basque. Over a crackling, distant telephone line, Petrunin had great difficulty in understanding the man's French. His own accent was smoothly Parisian, that of an educated and successful man, perhaps a lawyer or a doctor. A lawyer, he reminded himself; he had been taught his French by a lawyer with Communist loyalties.

'You understand?' Petrunin asked once more, raising his voice.

Outside the telephone booth, Kominski was laughing with the security men who formed his escort. One of them would be accompanying him to Moscow, ostensibly to protect him, in reality to ensure his arrival. Kominski was in profile to Petrunin, and evidently did not care that the older man noticed his lightened, satisfied mood. The terminal building was quiet, almost empty of people; light, high, glassy, aseptic, like some huge operating theatre awaiting patients and doctors.

'Yes.' The reply from the field director was faint, slurred by distance and regional accent. 'I understand, Comrade General.' The line was insecure, but it did not matter.

'You know what must happen?' Petrunin insisted.

'Yes.'

'That they must *wait* for a British presence?'

'Yes.' There appeared to be no hesitation by the Basque in accepting Petrunin's change of orders. The man would not seek confirmation from another source. He was prepared, in his undoubtedly unimaginative way, to accept the orders of the KGB general without hesitation.

'And there *must* be a termination.'

'I will give the order, Comrade General. There is just time before they cross into Spain.'

'Good. Good hunting.'

As he put down the receiver, which had become damp in his hand, his thoughts were at boiling point. He could hardly control

343

a tremor which possessed his body. Hated Kominski was still laughing beyond the glass of the booth. But Hyde——

Yes, he had him now. Oh, yes . . .

He stepped out of the telephone booth. Kominski turned a smiling, knowing, superior face to him. It beckoned like his cold, uncertain future. He shivered. He would warm himself on the flight to Moscow with drink and thoughts of Hyde's death and Aubrey's frustration.

To Hyde, it seemed that the night had been one long, unbroken climb into the mountains. Soon after their meal in Lerida, they had left the major road at Barbastro, entering Huesca Province and following the Rio Cinca north towards the Aragon Pyrenees. Frequently water flashed below them in the steady moonlight, or took up the gleam of their headlights as the car's nose dipped suddenly or rounded a bend. Hyde slept fitfully, never offering to relieve de Lorca at the wheel. In that tumbled, broken, wild country he had no confidence in his ability to drive safely at night. De Lorca, on the other hand, seemed untiringly alert and competent.

At Ainsa, they followed the winding C 136 along the bank of the Rio Ara as it retreated into the sierras and then the Pyrenees. Dawn slid like some exhausted creature into the river valley. Beyond Broto, they climbed more steeply towards Torla and the Ordesa National Park, the Ara rushing beside them, suggesting by its pace and hurry that they were going in the wrong direction. A tiny, dark café was already open in Torla. They ate warm bread hungrily and drank dark, gritty coffee. It was chilly outside in the tiny square, and the metal table and chairs were damp and cold from the night. The sun had not yet struggled above the peaks of the Sierra de las Cutas, but they were tinged with gold and the sky's small clouds were pinked.

'What do we know about Velasquez?' Hyde asked as de Lorca lit a strong-smelling cigarette. The smoke hung heavily, like that of gunfire, in the windless air. A rubber-tyred cart pulled by a headhanging donkey crossed the square slowly. An old man in a dark jacket and wearing a beret turned his head to study them.

'He has been a forester here for some years. It is a sort of retirement, I would think.'

'He's been in Spain all the time—the last forty years?' Hyde asked in surprise.

344

'No.' De Lorca shook his head. 'He was in France during the war, with the Maquis, of course.' De Lorca picked a shred of tobacco from his tongue and swallowed the last of his coffee. 'More?' he asked. Hyde nodded, and de Lorca carried the cups into the dark, aromatic interior of the café. When he returned, he pursued the conversation. 'After the war, of course, he could not come back here. Like many hundreds of others, he was branded a Communist and a Republican. He would have been arrested and imprisoned.'

'Where did he go?'

'Stayed in France. Just on the other side of the border, we think. Year after year. Think of it, my friend . . .' De Lorca leaned forward over his cup, his cigarette jabbing in emphasis between his fingers. 'Just by lifting his head, he could see mountains that were in Spain, *his* country. While Franco lived, of course, he could not come back. I think he probably crossed the border the day the Generalissimo died.' De Lorca smiled with a surprising bitterness. An old woman dressed in black seemed to pass like a slow wraith across the square. The sunlight had begun to spill over the raw edges of the sierra. The small clouds were deep pink, the sky beginning to become blue. 'He worked on farms, forested, poached —oh, I don't know. Anything the mountains could give him to do.'

'Any family?'

'No. None. You know, his way of life since the Civil War makes for megalomania, for a very difficult man. He will be tough and stubborn and entirely unwilling to become our prisoner.'

'I realize that.' Hyde drank his second cup of coffee. The tip of the church's spire had turned golden. 'How far now?'

'The Ordesa is very small. No more than seven or eight miles at most.'

'Can we make it in the car?'

'There will be some walking—perhaps the last mile. But it is quite easy.' He glanced at Hyde's suede boots. 'They will do. I have walking shoes in the boot of the car. We could hire them at the hotel, in any case. You are ready?'

Hyde stood up. 'Let's go.'

De Lorca left money on the table, and they climbed back into the Audi.

'How do you wish to get Velasquez out?' de Lorca asked as they followed the road alongside the Ara. The sun was above the peaks now. The river gleamed where it was not white with impatience. Buildings were whitewashed with light.

'You've got the papers?' De Lorca nodded. 'They want him in a hurry. Shelley's arranged to have us met, and Velasquez to be handed over, in Tarbes. They'll fly him out.'

'That sounds sensible. Yes, I can get him across the border with the papers Madrid prepared. He won't be cooperating . . .'

'I know that. He'll have to, won't he?'

'Yes.'

They passed the hotel and the campsite. Hyde entertained a fleeting image of the gnat-heavy evening air of the campsite near Wittenberg, but that swiftly brought to mind an image of 'Caspar', and he abandoned recollection before they crossed the turbulent Ara by the Puente de Los Navarros and entered the Ordesa National Park. The road twisted and climbed above the Rio Arazas. A vista of the main canyon of the park, running from west to east, opened up to Hyde. Sunlight drew out the steel and ochre colours of the cliffs on either side of the stream. Forests of dark pines, larches and beech trees climbed the lower slopes towards the bare rock of the escarpments.

'Beautiful,' Hyde remarked, since a comment seemed expected. 'Nice life for old Velasquez.'

'He has waited a long time for it,' de Lorca replied.

The sunlight slanted between the silver trunks of beeches on the stream's rocky bank. Hyde saw anglers dotted like bushes amid the briars and trees near the river. Something that might have been a deer or a chamois flicked away from a tiny clearing into deeper forest. His head turned to try to keep it in sight, but it had vanished.

'A goat,' de Lorca said.

The carpark was surrounded by beeches and poplars and ran down towards the stream. It was neat, orderly, unlittered. As much as was possible, it was apologized for and hidden by trees; a visitor who embarrassed and brought a slight sense of shame to the park. The air was already warmer, heavily scented. De Lorca parked the car, then changed his moccasins for walking boots. He pulled a map from beneath the dash and showed it to Hyde.

'Here he is,' he said, pointing to a cross he had marked neatly. He lifted his hand. 'Up there,' he explained, pointing north. 'About a mile or a mile and a half.' He shrugged and smiled nervously.

'Or four or five,' Hyde added. 'OK, let's go.'

'Yes.'

Automatically Hyde glanced at the other cars in the carpark. French, British registrations. They told him nothing. What, after all, did he expect? Anything? Nothing?

A door banged in the restaurant at the far end of the carpark. Its noise was like that of a gunshot. Hyde's hand jumped on the bonnet of the Audi as if he had burned himself. De Lorca studied him.

'Underneath you are tired, my friend,' he said.

Hyde nodded. 'Not a bloody great deal left, is there?' he admitted wryly. 'Still, enough for a bracing walk. Lead on, El Cid.'

De Lorca grinned. The expression might have been one of relief. 'This way—Ned Kelly?'

'. . . misjudged—seriously misjudged—the mood of Germany. It is with great regret, therefore, but in the knowledge that I am obeying the demonstrated will of the German people, that I announce that the so-called Berlin Treaty will not be ratified in Berlin tomorrow.'

Vogel leaned confidently forward, his hands clasped across the notes of his prepared statement. The television studio was small, with just two cameras directed at him. Behind him was a bare screen painted in a neutral colour. Yet at nine in the morning his speech was being broadcast to every television set in the Federal Republic, on every radio. It was being transmitted all over Europe, and by satellite to America. He knew, with a complete and utter certainty, that it was being monitored in the DDR and in the Kremlin. He was aware of himself as an actor holding captive a huge, surprised audience.

Dietrich Vogel and the SDP, his party, were trailing the Christian Democrats by twelve points in the opinion polls and in computer predictions he had himself commissioned. He would lose the election in two weeks' time. He was utterly certain of that fact. The Berlin Treaty had to be abandoned.

He wanted to clear his throat, even to sip from the glass of water on the desk. Yet he did not. He used the slight and growing huskiness of his voice to effect. It signified emotions he did not feel.

'You will conclude,' he continued, 'that this is a panic decision, dictated—forced upon me—by recent events and by the

347

opinion polls. Let me say that the libels and slanders directed at my close colleague, Wolfgang Zimmermann, and which have forced his resignation from my staff, constitute one of the blackest episodes in the history of the German media.' Vogel's mouth compressed into an angry, bloodless line. Then he said: 'When the truth emerges, as it will, you will see how deeply a fine man has been wronged.' He shook his head like a reproving parent, not utterly without compassion or kindness.

'As to the opinion polls,' he continued after a pause, 'they must be considered. Not as a guide to the result of the federal elections, but as an expression of the German people's lack of enthusiasm for the Berlin Treaty.' He opened his hands, moving them slightly towards the camera. 'I told you at the beginning that if your decision was not in favour of the Treaty, it would not be ratified. I am honouring that pledge now. There will be no Berlin Treaty. The time is not yet. When it is—when you tell me that you wish to see a reunited Germany, at peace with its neighbours—then I promise you it will happen.'

He converted the tickle at the back of his throat into a suppressed cough of deep and painful emotion. Then he added in conclusion: 'The greatness of Germany depends not upon treaties or trade agreements or fences or walls. It resides in, and depends upon, its citizens, and upon the political will of those citizens. The people of Germany cannot be misled or deceived. The Berlin Treaty will not be ratified because you do not wish it. For that reason, and that reason alone.'

He continued to look steadily at the camera, his face composed in as dignified and compassionate an expression as he could achieve. The red light on the camera winked out. Vogel relaxed. It was done. Without the albatross of the Treaty around his neck, he could still win the election. He was careful to let no new expression occupy his face, for the benefit of the television technicians. But yes—yes, he could still do it . . .

Poor Wolf . . .

He could still win. Poor Wolf . . .

The regret faded in his mind. Political necessity: survival. Everything was at stake. Germany would not be reunited in his lifetime. Dietrich Vogel would, however, serve another term as Chancellor. Poor Wolf . . . He dismissed the image of Zimmermann, and stood up, squaring his shoulders as he did so.

*

'There's one British car, and another with a Barcelona registration—nothing much else.'

The reply crackled from the R/T in the man's hand. He looked up towards the pine-clad mountains. Somewhere up there?

'OK, we'll look out. How long——?'

The man felt the bonnet of the Audi with the Hertz sticker and the Barcelona registration. It was slightly warm, warmer than the rest of the car. The engine had not been quiet for too long.

'Perhaps half an hour—no more than an hour,' he said.

'Good. Not too much of a start. We've still got three or four miles to go.'

'Shall I wait here—in case they come back this way?'

The handset crackled, the voice issuing from it was tinny and small and distant. 'No. Make your way to the next target— Pamplona. Set up the optimum time and place. I want that target dealt with by tonight.'

'OK. Signing off.'

He switched off the handset, and glanced around the carpark. Time for a coffee? Perhaps . . .

He patted the warm bonnet of the Audi, as if for luck, then walked towards the restaurant.

The chill of the underground marble palaces seemed somehow to have entered his bones like an ominous prophecy. As they left the bus, he rubbed his arms, the restored Badaling section of the Great Wall immediately before them. The small, cheap camera dangled from his wrist by a plastic strap. The tour party had been taken to the site of the Ming tombs, thirty miles north of Peking, before being brought to the Wall. What had been initially no more than a delay had become for David Liu a strange and powerful representation of his isolation. The huge, dead, echoing vaults, chilly, marble, subterranean, had oppressed him, accompanying him like an infection long after the bus had continued its journey to the tourist-favoured length of the Great Wall at Badaling.

The bus had travelled along the Avenue of the Animals towards the tombs. Elephants, lions, camels ranked with kneeling or standing human statues. The tortoise that marked the beginning of the avenue, even though he well knew its symbolism which expressed longevity, could only be regarded as an ironic comment. He was profoundly disturbed by the memorials of ancient deaths.

He had spent the night in a cheap, anonymous hotel squashed between shops and decaying, greystone houses near the railway station. He had slept fitfully, retracing the movements and tensions of identifying the tail, eluding it, fearing it would return. He knew they must have initiated a search for him, and in half-waking and dreams he had waited for the knock on the door that he expected would precede the dawn. Yet no one had come. However, his reserves of confidence and hope had been eroded.

He wandered the streets and inhabited dark, noisy, aromatic cafés for most of the morning, hardly able to eat, unable to relax. He had boarded the tour bus after lunch in gratitude and edgy weariness, but the optimism of driving north hardly lasted until they reached the suburbs and the first communes. The tombs had crushed him with their weight of dead authority and marble.

The newly restored section of the Great Wall lay like an endless snake across the retreating folds and peaks of the Jundu Mountains. There was no other way he could regard it. The thing lived, almost seemed to move, slithering away cross the landscape. He shivered, despising his heightened, runaway senses. Mile upon mile of it moved into the distance, coils dropping out of sight over one hill, then reappearing to slide along the backs of more distant ridges. Climbing, dipping, winding, it seemed to continue for ever, encircling the world.

Then the tour party moved briskly past the souvenir shops at the foot of the Wall, towards the nearest of the guard towers. Liu began to look anxiously for Forbes, for pursuit, for the gleam of recognition and identification on one of the faces surrounding him. An American accent, as they climbed the steps to the guard tower, pricked tears into his eyes, as if he heard the voice of a relative or friend from the other side of a prison wall. Germans, English, Americans, Japanese, Chinese. Fleas on the great snake's body. The Wall climbed and wound whitely in the sun against the green and brown of the mountains. The breeze was cold, a whisper of winter from the north. The guide went ahead of them, reciting all the facts she knew about the Wall and its building except the hundreds of thousands who had died during the centuries of its erection. Three thousand miles now; once it had been perhaps as much as thirty thousand miles long . . .

The statistics numbed him. The Wall was not a snake, it was one vast tomb. He looked about him almost frantically for Forbes, searching the white faces above the gaudy shirts and thin jackets

350

for one he recognized. There was no sign of the Englishman. The mountains stretched away around him. The guard tower beneath which they stood, gaping upwards, was small and futile. He was aware of himself in the middle of the vast territory of the People's Republic with no way of escape.

'OK, old chap?' Forbes's voice was soft beside him. The man's face was partly obscured by the camera into which he was squinting. Liu could see the smile beneath the Nikon.

'You——' he said foolishly.

'OK?'

Their guide was dismissing them, her arms indicating that they could walk in either direction at their pleasure. For thirty minutes, her voice cautioned.

'Yes . . .' Liu replied falteringly, looking around them. Now the rest of the tour party had become alien.

'Let's walk,' Forbes suggested. 'And don't look so worried. There's no one watching you.'

'Last night——' Liu began.

'You were followed?'

'I lost them——'

'Well done. They're not here, anyway.'

They walked out of the shadow of the guard tower's arch, into the sun. The breeze was chilly, plucking at their clothing as they climbed the hill towards the next tower.

'What—what has been decided?'

'A great deal, old chap. They want you in London very badly indeed.'

'Thank God——'

'More like political advantage, I'd say. Still—I have a way of getting you out. It does mean you'll have to spend some time in Peking, then in Tientsin. I've got new papers and that sort of thing.'

'Why Tientsin?' Liu shivered, rubbing his arms obsessively. 'How long?'

'Tientsin's on the coast. The Royal Navy has a frigate, HMS *Sabre*, one of the new Type-22s, about to pay a social call and drum up some armaments business from the Chinese. She'll be in Tientsin tomorrow. When she leaves for Hong Kong, you'll be on her!'

Forbes grinned with pleasure and satisfaction. He brushed at his fair hair as the wind distressed it.

351

'Thank you,' Liu said after a moment. Then, with more enthusiasm, he repeated: 'Thank you, thank you . . .' Forbes, even though he seemed to have expected praise, now appeared embarrassed by Liu's gratitude. He saw, for a moment, too deeply into the American's psyche, and retreated from it.

'Say no more, old chap. Simple, really . . .'

They had reached the summit of the hill. Both men were breathing hard after the long flight of steps. The wind whistled drily around them. Liu, however, no longer felt cold and frightened. Forbes was with him, and Forbes had a plan of escape. He was no longer a prisoner in this vast landscape.

When Frederickson put down the binoculars, the scene rushed away from him as if a camera had hastily retreated. Forbes had been brushing his hair like a signal, and Liu had been standing beside him. He'd picked up Forbes, having lost him after they arrived, as the two men had climbed away from the guard tower up the hill.

Two against two. The colonel from the MPT was with him, painstakingly assembling the rifle, fitting and finely adjusting the telescopic sight, then affixing the suppressor which would slow the exhaust gases to subsonic speed, preventing easy identification of their location. The rifle was, appropriately in Frederickson's mind, the M21, the US Army's standard sniper's rifle. The colonel's familiarity with the weapon and his expertise in using it had come as a surprise to Frederickson. He had expected them to have to rely on an MPT or army sniper drafted in. The rifle, to Frederickson's silent amusement, had probably been manufactured under licence in Taiwan, before being bought by the People's Republic. The 7.62mm bullets in the twenty-round box were a CIA adaptation of deer-hunting ammunition, partially-jacketed so that the soft, exposed point of each bullet would spread on impact. Insurance, the CIA considered them, since they increased the chances of an outright kill. Both Frederickson and the colonel had agreed they should be used in the elimination of Liu.

Eventually, as Liu and Forbes reached the summit of the hill and adopted their inviting, unknowing poses, the colonel pronounced himself satisfied with the rifle, its telescopic sight, the suppressor and the range of the target.

'I am now ready,' he announced with unemotional formality.

'We're at the edge of range. They have to come down the steps again towards us. Let's wait.'

352

The colonel shrugged. 'Very well.'

Frederickson and the colonel were concealed by short, stunted green bushes that surmounted a small knoll like tufts of hair, one of the hundreds of head-like domes of the landscape around the Wall. They were slightly above the Wall and six hundred yards from it.

Liu was, Frederickson concluded as he sat cross-legged beside the colonel, as good as dead.

'Well,' he said, 'all we have to do is wait. Langley and your people have agreed. We got the signal. So long, Liu.'

The colonel said nothing, but continued to inspect the target through the long telescopic sight, making endless tiny adjustments to the focusing wheel. Frederickson, despite his easy and convincing cynicism, felt no desire to use the binoculars. Instead, he shifted his position slightly until his back was to the Wall. The colonel would tell him, the colonel wouldn't miss. He didn't need to look.

The forester's hut which Velasquez inhabited was small and sparsely furnished. It was cool indoors after the long hot climb up through the pines. Velasquez offered them beer. His hospitality seemed grudging, no more than an extension of the suspicion with which he had regarded them as they entered the clearing in front of the hut where he had been sharpening a small axe on a creaking, heavy grindstone. His manner, as they sat around the scarred wooden table in the main room of the hut, also seemed charged with suspicion.

Outside the open windows, there was birdsong and the hum of insects. The sun spilled into the room, rejuvenating the faded colours of rugs and cushions. The place had a peacefulness that all three of them seemed to perceive vanishing as they talked.

At first, Velasquez was reluctant. He rubbed at his unshaven, lean cheeks or fiddled with the ends of his drooping grey moustache. He moved the beret on his head frequently as if it were a toupee with which he was unsatisfied. His throat was wrinkled at his open collar, but his body, though bent, was still firm and his eyes were clear and sharp like those of a young man.

The old Spaniard was taciturn and the conversatian only began to progress when de Lorca broached the subject of the Civil War, and especially the retreat of the Republican units into Aragon during the early spring of 1938. It was a story of hardship and defeat told with surprising bitterness after more than forty years. The old man's eyes gleamed. He was still angry, still proud. Cautiously. Hyde approached the subject of Aladko. The small tape-recorder lay like a gambling stake in the middle of the stained table.

Velasquez's suspicion suddenly intensified.

'Nothing to say,' de Lorca translated, shrugging.

'Ask him again.' De Lorca did so, but Velasquez shrugged in his turn. De Lorca turned to Hyde. 'Tell him Aladko's been dead for twenty years or more. He can't harm him now.' Hyde possessed no anger or irritation. Velasquez struck him as a bleak and lonely man, clinging still to an ideology that had blighted the greater part of his life. It was all he had had since Franco's victory and the beginning of his exile on the other side of the Pyrenees, and it would not be surrendered easily. Prising the past out of Velasquez was akin to the violent extraction of a betraying confession.

'He says he assumed that Aladko was dead. He wasn't young then.'

'OK. Ask him about the Germans they captured.' Hyde looked at his watch. They would have to attempt to persuade Velasquez to accompany them voluntarily before they had to settle, in all probability, for kidnap.

Velasquez spat with a rigid, expected contempt.

'He remembers.'

'Mention Zimmermann.' Then Hyde stared directly at Velasquez. '*Zimmermann*,' he repeated slowly and emphatically.

Velasquez found the name unfamiliar. Hyde drew from his pocket a small, twenty-year-old snapshot of Zimmermann, and placed it on the table in front of the Spaniard.

Velasquez nodded eventually.

'He remembers him.'

'Ask him, then.'

Hyde allowed de Lorca to conduct the argument, apply the pressure. Velasquez was sullen, uncommunicative.

'His contempt,' Hyde said. 'Use that. Exploit his contempt for the Germans.' De Lorca nodded. Within moments, Velasquez had launched into a bitter denunciation. His large-veined hands closed and unclosed on the table. He seemed to be staring sightlessly at the tape-recorder. Hyde let his gaze roam over the stone fireplace.

'He hated Zimmermann all right . . . arrogant bastard comes close to it . . . remembers the others, but especially this one . . . Aladko spent too much time with him . . . should have executed . . .' De Lorca translated in summary while engaging in a swift exchange of Spanish with Velasquez. '. . . all for killing the lot of them . . . always . . . Nazis . . . argued with Aladko, all of them were Nazis . . . Fascists every one of them . . .' Hyde stared at the beams above his head, dark with age and smoke. Hooks where meat had been hung to cure jutted from the beams. The past, filtered through de Lorca's hurried summary, invested the room, raising its temperature. The old man now appeared to be deeply engaged in a debate filled with anger and suspicion. His opponent was not de Lorca. It might have been Aladko. Velasquez was like a recording that had not been played for forty years, a voice from the past temporarily superseding the present. '. . . Aladko thought he had a convert . . . told him no Fascist changes colour . . . Aladko persevered . . . didn't even beat that one . . .' A dirty-nailed finger tapped at the table near the snapshot. '. . . just laughed all the time, strung Aladko along, never mind the wounded and dying . . . spent all his time with *that* one . . .' Again, the finger tapped the table. The hand curled into a fist behind the finger which pointed like the barrel of a gun. '. . . took some of them out and shot them . . . in the snow, just like that . . . left them for the birds . . . not him, though . . . he escaped . . . Aladko wasn't even surprised . . . though he was clever . . .'

Eventually the monologue petered out. In the silence, de Lorca turned to Hyde for instructions. Hyde said quietly: 'Ask him once more. Did Zimmermann become one of Aladko's converts?' De Lorca did so. Velasquez replied in vehement Spanish, shaking his head.

'He says no, and again no,' de Lorca translated.

'Then London wants him out.'

De Lorca glanced at Velasquez. His face was filled with reluctance. 'I don't know . . .' he began.

'He isn't going to come quietly, is he?' Hyde remarked. 'Not to help Zimmermann.' Velasquez' eyes watched the Australian with evident suspicion. 'Ask him what they talked about.'

De Lorca did so. Velasquex appeared to have lost interest.

'Politics, always politics, he said,' de Lorca commented. 'Intellectual crap about covers it, Mr Hyde. He didn't take much notice.'

355

'Ask him if Zimmermann was a Communist—go on, just ask him straight out.'

Velasquez laughed.

'No, he wasn't. He was a Fascist.'

'A real one?'

Velasquez became voluble.

'He says they are all real ones. This one was just smarter than the others.'

'Ask him again.'

'He says of course he was.'

'Did Aladko convert him—go on, ask.'

'He says not in a million years. There was no chance of it.'

'That's it, then. That's what we want him to say.' Hyde looked at the open window and the clearing and the dark, scented pines beyond. 'Ask him—politely—if he'll come to London to tell his story.'

'He won't come . . .'

'I know that. Ask him anyway. Give him the cover story.'

De Lorca couched the question with flattery and with an emphasis on the importance of Velasquez's evidence. Hyde guessed at his meaning, hearing in his mind the ploy they had agreed: Zimmermann's fictitious connections with neo-Fascist groups in Germany and England. It was poor bait, and Hyde suspected it would not be swallowed. He stared through the window, waiting for the end of the charade and the moment of abduction to arrive.

The man came cautiously out of the pines on the far side of the clearing. Hyde caught the vigorous shake of Velasquez's head from the corner of his eye, but his peripheral vision narrowed as he saw the gun carried across the man's chest. Then a second man emerged from the pines, his head swivelling cautiously and alertly from side to side. Velasquez was pronouncing his unwillingness to leave, beginning instead to demand their departure. A third man emerged from the shadow of the trees. For a moment, they formed a small tableau against the background of the pines and the bare mountain slopes beyond, then the foremost man began running towards the window of the hut, rifle still held across his chest in a military fashion.

Hyde stood up. Velasquez's eyes widened as he saw him draw the FN pistol from his waistband and slide a round into the breech.

'What is it . . .?' de Lorca began.

356

'Get down—get down!' Hyde bellowed. The man stopped, regained his balance, swung the rifle to his shoulder. 'Get down!'

Hyde fired twice through the open window.

Wolfgang Zimmermann was drawn to the television screen. They were withdrawing the bulldozers from the Berlin Wall. They no longer had the appearance of tanks drawn up, rather of ambulances being recalled. West German television was taking the DDR's pictures of the event. It was a deliberate, visual snub, an insult in reprisal for the abandonment of the Berlin Treaty. It was designed to hurt, to cause pain. It might, Zimmermann decided, have been intended entirely and specifically for himself.

The cameras roamed like caged animals along the Wall at the Potsdamerplatz. Long shots encompassed the whole scene, zoomed closeups revealed the faces of the army drivers and the re-armed guards and the Soviet officers supervising the withdrawal. In an hour, no more, everything would be as before, except for the units replanting the minefield and relaying the barbed wire. As before. Two Germanies, the obscene Wall . . .

Zimmermann studied the remaining liquor in the bottle of Asbach brandy, then refilled his glass. He could not, however, summon sufficient defiance to raise the glass ironically to the images on the screen. Instead, he swallowed the liquor with a deep, sobbing shudder.

Aubrey studied the youthful face of one of the military engineers relaying the anti-personnel mines in the ploughed strip of earth on the eastern side of the Wall. Behind him and out of focus, two men unrolled barbed wire from a slow-moving truck. Their huge bale of wire spun itself across the Potsdamerplatz like an irresistible spider.

A long shot, then, of the whole area of the Potsdamerplatz. The heads of West Berliners and tourists bobbed like dark patches along the bottom edge of the screen.

Aubrey, propped up against his pillows, thought of Wolfgang Zimmermann and felt the man's pain as his own, felt the unpaid debt of his life. He believed in Zimmermann's innocence, but that didn't repay the debt. He could only do that if Hyde found someone to tell the story of Spain in 1938. Hyde had to do that, had to . . .

*

357

General Tamas Petrunin sat in the cigarette-fugged atmosphere of the anteroom along the corridor from Chairman Andropov's offices, reminding himself of his KGB rank, reviewing his past career, and considering his future. His hands lay half-open on his thighs, fingers curled upwards, as if anticipating having to catch the trappings of authority and power as they fell from him. He was to be blamed. He knew that with a sick certainty. The Treaty had been abandoned. The Politburo, in its collective rage, needed a scapegoat. He had been selected. It was as simple as that, and as final.

Along one wall—the tall windows looked out over Dzerzhinsky Square, from which the muted noises of traffic ascended—a bank of coloured television sets were all switched on. Andropov's body-guards from the Ninth Directorate of the KGB lounged in easy chairs. Attached to each of the Japanese televisions was its own video cassette recorder. A quiet babble of conflicting soundtracks filled the room from the different films being watched by the guards; as palpable an irritant as the cigarette smoke. *Jaws* with its sinister bass and cello motif announced the imminence of destruction from one videotape; a cartoon mouse and cat chased and destroyed one another in endless variety and repetition. Gleaming bodies twisted in celluloid eroticism on yet another screen, to the accompaniment of impossibly sustained breaths and cries. James Bond expended technology at a terrifying, bank-rupting rate on the television nearest the windows.

On the set opposite Petrunin's chair, the Berlin Wall remained, weatherstained and immovable. There was no soundtrack. A guard had turned it down the moment Petrunin requested the programme, trying to hide his surprise at being kept waiting in that room. It did not augur well—no, it augured very badly. A species of insult and of warning. Andropov had been in his office for hours already. Petrunin expected to be kept waiting a great deal longer.

One of the guards laughed and whistled. Petrunin could not be certain whether it was at the antics of the cat and mouse or the copulators. It did not matter. In that anteroom, all activity could be made meaningless, humorous. The guards ignored him. Across the carpeted corridor beyond the door, a deep-seated, deep-piled waiting room probably contained individual officers still in favour, who still possessed power, who would be summoned to the Chairman's office with the minimum of delay and

358

be greeted with vodka or cognac. Petrunin choked back a sob not entirely caused by the thickness of the smoke.

He could be finished . . .

The upcurled hands flexed, then trembled. He thrust them into his pockets as if they were stolen apples that might betray his offence. He tried to ease his body into a relaxed slouch. It was difficult, but he felt a small pluck of satisfaction when he had achieved it.

On the television screen, the army engineers were relaying the minefield. An indrawn breath and a callous cheer made him look along the row of televisions. The huge shark's head and open jaws loomed behind a man flinging bloody bait into the water. Petrunin shuddered and looked back at his own screen. The guards were armed again in the Potsdamerplatz, the wire had been relaid, the red-and-white poles were back. West German television cameras watched the scene from scaffolds and spectator rostrums. The task was almost complete. No doubt the Soviet commentary he could not hear was becoming hysterical in its denunciations of NATO and the Germans.

He felt the trappings of power, privilege and rank retreat like a tide. He had failed. That is what he would be told. Demotion, a foreign posting, early retirement, disgrace, a trial . . .

The things that could happen to him: the list was endless . . .

Then there was a young man in a three-piece suit at the door, beckoning silently to him. He stood up, squaring his shoulders as he did so, buttoning his jacket.

Hyde, he thought. At least Hyde was going to go down with him. Hyde was a dead man.

The aide closed the door behind him, then preceded him along the carpeted corridor towards the door of Andropov's office.

'Well, Colonel?'

'Well, Mr Frederickson?' the MPT officer replied, turning onto his back and sitting up. The rifle lay across his lap. The breeze plucked at his jacket and lank dark hair, and billowed out the windcheater that Frederickson wore across his broad shoulders. Below them, Liu and Forbes had begun walking once more, slowly and methodically; as if they were two reincarnated guards posted on that section of the Great Wall.

'You satisfied with the turn of events?'

'I would have liked our scheme to have worked with a more

entire success. This'—he indicated the rifle by moving it a little—'is not the solution I would have chosen.'

Frederickson's face darkened. He had desired a small, shallow optimism from the Chinese officer, some mutual congratulatory sense of completion and success. It would have prevented him from considering that the target below them was someone he knew, someone who had obeyed his instructions and fulfilled them better than he should have done.

Frederickson did not enjoy the discomfort inflicted by his vestigial conscience. Perhaps he should have insisted on a CIA marksman. It would have made it easier. But the Chinaman next to him, the man who would kill Liu, was a stranger and a potential enemy. It was a situation that created an unbidden sympathy for Liu. He was a Chink, too, but he was American.

'Leave that, uh?' Frederickson warned him. 'Just tell me we won, OK?'

The colonel shrugged, admitting and signifying the gulf between their mentalities.

'Very well, Mr Frederickson. We have won. The Treaty will not be signed, and that is what *Jade Tiger* was created to achieve. Therefore, the operation has proven a complete success, for both our countries.'

Frederickson studied the colonel. His face was impassive, and his voice seemed incapable of irony. Yet Frederickson felt himself an object of amusement to a subtler mind than his own.

'Sure,' he said uncertainly.

'This'—again, the colonel indicated the rifle—'is no more than a detail. You must not think of it.'

The colonel sounded like a psychiatric nurse. Viciously, Frederickson swept the binoculars up to his eyes, focused them, and studied Liu and Forbes for a moment.

'You'd better hurry,' he snapped. 'Looks like they've almost finished. The guide's calling them together.'

The colonel rolled onto his stomach immediately. Frederickson dropped the binoculars into his lap, refusing to witness the events that were about to occur. Once more, he turned his back to the Great Wall.

Below Frederickson and the colonel, David Liu felt a rising desire to shake Forbes by the hand in gratitude. He ignored the political expediency that was the British government's only motive, concentrating instead on the fact of his escape, his future

360

safety. He had been betrayed and abandoned, arrested and beaten—he would have been killed—but now he was safe.

'Thank you, thank you,' he contented himself with saying.

'You'll lose yourself in London, or any of our large cities,' Forbes explained, and then flushed slightly despite the wind's chill. 'I—I'm sorry . . .'

'No, of course it doesn't matter. There are a lot of Chinks, yes?' Liu grinned. 'Perhaps I'll open a takeout—takeaway restaurant?'

Forbes was grateful for Liu's humour. He warmed to the man, understanding the acute and terrible loneliness he must have suffered from the moment of his arrest. Just for learning the truth, for being good at what he was trained to do.

'Come on, your guide's waving her arms and blowing her whistle, old chap. Don't keep her waiting. You've got the new papers?' Liu patted the breast pocket of his jacket, and smiled. 'They're better than the last set. Keep off the streets, of course. It'll be a couple of days, no more I promise . . . Come on. In a week's time you'll be off HMS *Sabre* and onto a plane for London. You deserve it, too!'

'I do,' Liu agreed. 'Yes, I think I really do!' He laughed. Like boys, they began to hurry down the steps and along the rampart of the Wall towards the little crowd of David Liu's tour party. Liu began jogging with unalloyed delight rather than haste. He heard Forbes laugh behind him. Liu felt pleasure bubble inside him, force its way into his chest and throat. Then he, too, laughed.

'Careful, old chap—you'll fall off!' Forbes called after him. Liu hardly heard the Englishman.

The tour party in the cold shadow of the guard tower joggled in his vision. His chest felt tight with emotion and effort. His head was light. He was safe, he was *safe* . . .

The sky and mountains seemed to open like gauzy curtains. He was no longer oppressed. The Wall lay no longer like a great snake on the hills; it was a pale-coloured streamer someone had left there after a carnival celebration.

There was a pain in his chest, then another which seemed to spread and expand within him like the joy he had earlier experienced. But this pain tore and burned after the first moment and knocked him sideways, tilted his angle of vision, showed him the parapet of the Wall, the brown earth and green bushes below, then closed his eyes tight with the deepest blackness he had ever known.

Forbes watched the body fall. Liu had tilted sideways, as if he had stumbled, almost like slipping on the music-hall banana skin, then his hands had clutched at his chest, then at the parapet, then at the air, clawing it for purchase as the body went over the Wall and tumbled to the ground below.

Forbes ducked involuntarily, crouching against the parapet. He did not expect any more shots, guessing that Liu had been dispatched simply to prevent any future embarrassment. Yet he shivered uncontrollably and, as he crouched there, he began sobbing while the closest tourists leaned horrified over the parapet to stare at the unmoving body below.

The running man stopped and skidded, as if in his dash he had collided with an invisible, solid object. His head snapped back at the second shot—the new FN pistol kicked more than Hyde remembered, and the barrel had lifted slightly—and a red stain spread immediately where his face had been. Then he fell back, writhed, and lay still. The two men behind him, recovering from shock, moved in different directions, out of Hyde's view.

Hyde dropped to the floor, pressing himself against the rough boards. The burst of fire a second later tore through the wooden wall of the hut, ricocheted from the stone fireplace and chimney breast, ploughed into the floor and the opposite wall. Before the silence there was a continuing noise like the tearing of something as flimsy as paper. A long freshly gouged splinter had appeared near Hyde's hand. He heard a single, low, exhaling groan, and sat up, alarmed.

Blood was spreading across the back of de Lorca's neat suit. The young man's empty, lifeless face was turned towards him. Beyond the body, Velasquez was rising slowly to his knees, his face uncertain, afraid, vindictive.

'Back door,' Hyde managed to say. Velasquez did not understand. 'Is—there—another *door*?' Hyde pleaded. The old Spaniard shrugged. '*Porte*!' Hyde shrieked, his nerves fraying. 'Une autre porte?'

'Oui.' Velasquez pointed. Hyde scrabbled across the floor on all fours, into the tiny kitchen behind the main room. The back door was open. He kicked at it, but it was like a stable door and only the bottom half of it swung shut. He slid upright against the wall of the kitchen, his gun pressed against his cheek. He listened above the noises of his own breathing and heartbeat.

Velasquez was moving about in the other room. A skinned rabbit lay on the dented wooden board of a table, hind legs dangling over the edge. Its skin lay alongside the pink and blue naked body. The sight of it revolted and unnerved Hyde. The skinning had somehow made its death utterly final, and his own more likely.

Cautiously, he peered round the open upper half of the door. A three-shot burst from a machine pistol chipped splinters from the frame of the door and the wall near his head. He knew too much about this operation. He knew the stakes, and the purposes, and and risk to his life enlarged until it was unacceptable. Velasquez continued moving. Hyde heard the snick of a rifle bolt, jumped in alarm, then realized that the old man must have a gun of his own. There was a bullet hole in the naked rabbit corpse.

Hyde listened. How many? He'd seen three. Who? ETA, some Basque unit. Petrunin . . .

He swallowed drily, fighting back the bile. It had to be Petrunin. The face of the running man had been dark and swarthy, not Russian. ETA, then, with simple orders. Tidy up. Get rid of the evidence. Kill Velasquez.

And, for the sake of completeness, kill Hyde. Yes, he'd have given that order, just for old times' sake.

He saw a shadow move within the pines, and fired twice, stiff-armed. Bushes rustled, but he did not think the man had been hit. He retreated, and a burst of fire caused the walls and windows to shudder. Splinters lifted in the table, and one of the small, dirty windows shattered. Hyde swiftly closed the upper half of the door and retreated to the main room once more.

Velasquez was crouching by the window, peering out, the long barrel of an old Lee Enfield bolt-action rifle nuzzling against his neck and face. He turned to look at Hyde. A stream of French issued from his lips. Hyde failed to understand most of it. The stain had stopped spreading across the shoulder-blades of de Lorca's suit. The body was very still, the young man's profile bland with death.

'Shut up,' Hyde murmured. 'Silence!' Velasquez stopped in mid-sentence, and spat quite expressively and expectedly. 'That's better.' Velasquez returned his attention to the window. Old and prized instincts were re-emerging. Hyde saw the process as a smoothing of the lines on his face, a narrowing of cheeks, a sharpening of jaw and eye. He felt relieved that Velasquez could be relied upon, that he wasn't a defenceless old pensioner needing his protection.

He had to think, anticipate the people out there . . .

What would they do? Quick, quick—in and out.

'The gunfire,' Velasquez said slowly in French, not turning his gaze from the window. 'It will bring help. The forest patrol will think they are hunters.' He spoke slowly and simply. Hyde understood with difficulty.

'Yes,' he said, then added in a murmur: 'I hope to God you're right, mate.'

Velasquez was right. They'd know that outside. They'd have to get it over with quick—a quick in-and-out. Blister and burn. SIS's scurrilous jargon would have called it a hand job. They'd already been on the scene for more than three minutes. Would they rush the hut?

'Other door,' he explained to Velasquez, aware of the hut as four walls and a roof now, a box that contained them. He crawled back into the kitchen, listening.

He looked up. The latch of the door was firmly shut. He breathed a sigh of relief. Yes, it had to be a rush. There was no time to wait . . .

He slid himself like a snake up to the level of the chipped, stained sink and leaned his head towards the shattered window. Insect noises, birdsong. Nothing. Time growing short, tea-leaves speckling the sink, the skinned rabbit as clear to him as if he were staring at it, the smell of grease coating the kitchen.

The noise was a tiny one. He turned slowly. The latch was moving upwards. He heard a sound like ragged breathing. The skinned rabbit watched him, front paws supplicatory. The upper half of the door moved very, very slowly. The breathing noise increased. He raised the pistol, remembering to aim just above the top of the bottom half of the door, and hesitated. The door had opened perhaps eight inches, then stopped.

Smell? Burning . . . petrol?

He felt choked with fear. The bottle with a flaming rag thrust into its neck appeared through the gap. Hyde fired. The hand withdrew, the bottle dropped to the floor and began to roll towards him, smelling of petrol. A wine bottle.

He tried to move. The rag flared. The bottle rolled. Outside, hardly apprehended, there was a groan and slow, dull footsteps away from the hut. He tried to move . . .

'Look out!' he yelled, staggering into the main room and throwing himself to one side of the door. 'Get down!'

The Molotov cocktail exploded, showering the room with streaks and gobbets of flame, blowing out the windows, splashing fire like a burst hydrant flinging water. Velasquez had risen half to his feet. His jacket was burning, but he had protected his head. Hyde moved to him, snatching up a rug. He wrapped it around the old man, beat at it with his hands, smothered the flames. Dark smears had appeared on Velasquez's face. He was wincing and dribbling with pain. The backs of his hands, too, were burned raw.

The kitchen blazed. The door frame into the main room and part of the wall were already burning. Then a sheet of flame roared at the window behind Velasquez as another bottle filled with petrol burst against the outside wall and exploded. Hyde backed away from the flames and heat, cradling Velasquez in his arms. The heat was intense, the smoke acrid and choking. Hyde began coughing. The flames raged, reaching into the room from the window and the kitchen, surrounding and isolating them.

Hyde saw the dribble of liquid from the fireplace sliding like a dark snake across the floor towards the fire. For one moment he thought it was water, then he knew. It inched towards the kitchen door and the flames. One of them was pouring petrol down the chimney.

He raised the gun above his head and fired four times into the ceiling. He could not tell whether he had hit the man. There was already enough petrol to mate with the fire. The snake had fattened as if it had swallowed a large rodent. Yet it moved quicker now, as if unrestrained.

Hyde dragged the whimpering Velasquez towards the door, cradling him still in the shawl-like rug, shuffling his reluctant feet alongside his own. The flames and smoke enveloped them, yet Hyde was still able to see the stream of petrol sliding to meet the fire. He rested against the door for an instant, coughing. His eyes were streaming, his lungs craved air, and the heat was beginning to scorch his eyebrows and hair. De Lorca's body was almost surrounded and consumed.

Outside, outside . . .

Into their gunfire.

He leaned Velasquez against the door, still whimpering between bouts of coughing. His eyes were wet with tears of pain and from the smoke. Hyde dashed to the centre of the room, where the table legs and the rugs had begun to burn. The trail of petrol was only inches from the fire spreading from the kitchen, soaking into a rug that was as yet only smouldering at one corner. His hands ached with pain as he dragged de Lorca's body across the floor, gripping the jacket which was already burning. Bending, he hoisted the body onto its feet, clutching it like a lover. He glared at Velasquez.

'Understand?' he yelled in French. 'You understand?' Velasquez nodded. 'Keep behind me!'

Hyde opened the door, screamed, and thrust himself, arms supporting de Lorca's body, through the door into the sudden air and sunlight. His legs moved fearfully and wearily, his lungs gasped at the air, he coughed. Bullets jerked de Lorca's corpse against his body.

Go, go, he told himself.

Velasquez——?

Go . . .

He flung de Lorca's body aside, clamped his awareness shut on the old man behind him, and ran. Wood crackled distantly, like radio static, and part of the roof of the hut collapsed. He held Velasquez's wrist, hardly noticing it, almost as if he had let go of the old man. The old Spaniard protested, yelped with pain, struggled to keep up. Hyde was out of the shadow of the hut now, on the sunlit grass. He stumbled on a tussock, fell, dragged the old man down with him. Bullets plucked at the grass around them, buzzed and whined in the air over their heads. The hut was engulfed in flames which roared into the sky. One wall subsided in a shower of sparks onto the dead de Lorca.

Hyde untangled the pistol from his windcheater, raised it, and aimed from a half-sitting position, squeezing off three shots towards a figure beneath the trees. The man staggered. Hyde got to his knees. There was a blue hole in the old man's left temple. There was no sign of the man on the roof, or the man at the kitchen door. He rose like a runner from starting blocks, and ran weaving and bobbing towards the trees. Gunfire pursued him, but in a desultory, hesitant, single-shot manner. He burst through bushes into the first deep shadows of the pines, flinging himself forward, winding himself, rolling, coming to a halt lying against the slim bole of a tree.

He sat up. The hut was already a dying bonfire, its flames pale

366

and innocuous in the midday sunlight. The clearing was redolent of burning. Velasquez's body lay, still half-wrapped in the dousing rug, on the grass fifteen yards from the hut. It was no more than a small, crumpled, dark interruption of the yellow-green expanse of the clearing. Grey smoke hung like a blanket in the almost windless air.

Swiftly Hyde removed the spent magazine and thrust another into the butt of the pistol, sliding a round into the breech immediately. The mountains had risen behind the trees to his left. How many of them alive? The last gunfire had been like a lone voice, querying support for its argument. One, then . . .

Unlikely. Impossible.

Footsteps crashed through undergrowth. Hyde rose to his feet, hesitated, and then began running, following the downward slope of the land, keeping to the shadows of the pines. There was safety only at the restaurant, with other people, with telephones. He careered on, guessing the direction of the twisting path which had brought them up from the road to the forester's hut. He blundered upon the path unexpectedly and paused, bent double with effort and lack of breath, feeling his legs immediately weak and clenching his hands upon his knees to prevent their quiver. He listened. Blood and heartbeat interfered, working on behalf of his pursuers. His hands were black with scorching. The whole of his body ached and protested at further effort.

Shouts behind him . . .

He turned slowly, reluctantly, lifting the FN pistol like a heavy weight. He could not understand the Spanish he heard. He waited, lips stretched in a snarl of rage and weakness. His eyes searched the gaps between the straight pines. A darker shadow emerged from shadow, halted in a splash of sunlight. The man moved the machine pistol awkwardly. One of his hands was bandaged with a white cloth or handkerchief. The Skorpion machine pistol still had its stock folded over the barrel. The man was trying to align it with one hand. The Skorpion wobbled. Hyde fired twice. The man staggered, then stumbled behind a pine.

Hyde ran on, down the path. He was a mile or more above the carpark and restaurant. The twists and doublings of the track appeared in vivid, jumbled recollection. Too far. He ran on, skipping, stumbling, half-jumping down the track, looking back from time to time, seeing no one. The trees were close about him, occasionally parting to show him, like a prize he could not expect, the vista of the Ordesa Park; the opposite wall of the canyon, the gleam of the stream below him, the dots of buildings, the neat square handkerchief of the carpark.

A steep cliff face rose opposite him as he turned to follow one twist of the track. He teetered on the edge of a dry waterfall. A hundred yards away, a swift shadow moved through the air. A young chamois posed on an outcrop as if demonstrating its superior adaptation to the terrain. Then the huge eagle took the kid, lifted it from the rock, began to plummet, employed its vast wings, and rose again, sweeping low over Hyde's head. The speed and finality of the execution made him shudder, drained him of remaining strength. Reluctantly, he put his body into painful motion again.

Trees again. He felt safer, enclosed in scented shadow. He staggered into a shaft of sunlight, stumbled against rock, and pressed his face to it, hands clawing at it as if to open some secret door through which he could pass into hiding, even oblivion. He crept along the surface of the rock, his cheek touching it where it was warmed by the sun, his eyes shut. His feet stumbled on roots and stones as if he had never learned to walk. He was finished.

Something constricted his throat. He did not open his eyes. For a moment, he simply tried to breathe more deeply, and to swallow. The grip tightened on his throat. It seemed like an attack of some kind brought on by over-exertion. He gurgled.

The face was partly obscured by the halo of sunlight around it. It was dark, intense, weary, determined. Hyde did not know the man, he was a stranger in a black jersey. Sweat glistened on his sallow forehead and on the hairs of his narrow moustache. He had both hands on Hyde's throat, choking him. That knowledge filtered into Hyde's awareness slowly; the noises of a warning bell deadened by fog.

Hyde raised his hands, gripping the man's wrists. The man rammed his knee into Hyde's crotch. Hyde's legs collapsed. He closed his eyes with the pain, seeming to fall forward into the grip of the man's hands, accelerating his own death. He wanted blackness now, the end of the pain shrieking through his frame.

He did not know the man . . .

Black . . . did not know him, they were . . . black . . . strangers, complete strangers . . . black . . . no grudges, no enmity . . . blackness . . . no air . . . blackness, blacker . . . stupid . . . for . . . black . . . what?

Black.

His hand floated behind him. His mind kept losing contact with it and its intention—the pistol in his waistband. His other hand was on his crotch, cuddling it, soothing. He could not remember why his right hand was reaching behind his back . . . why?

Floating behind him. Clutching something cold, drawing it free. Bringing the object—pistol?—to the other man's side— finger squeezing instinctively on the trigger . . .

Black.

Two noises, explosions in the blackness. He fell backwards, released. He wanted to fall forwards, bring the dark back, finish it, give up. Dive into it like a pool. He fell backwards, body arched, throat hurting as he coughed. He pressed his eyes shut when they attempted to flutter open, not wanting to wake up. He was finished.

One hand on his crotch. Pain going. Other hand on his stomach. Left hand soft, right hand heavy. Heavier . . .

He coughed in a spasm, then opened his eyes. His right hand was holding the pistol up for inspection. He let it flop back on his stomach. Christ, the bloody organism wouldn't give up, he thought, almost disappointed.

He lay there for some time. Small birds inspected him from the slim branches over his head. Ants crawled past his wet cheeks. The pines rendered him their scent. There were no noises other than innocent ones. Other directions, other tracks . . .

He did not know how long he lay there. Eventually he struggled upright, climbing up the face of the gnarled rock until he stood on his feet. He leant away from the rock gently like an invalid and took a few tottering steps. Slowly he continued his descent of the track, wary of his footing after he almost stumbled over the prone, black-jerseyed body of the stranger. Now he was beyond knowledge; beyond enmity, struggle, ideology, murder.

He reached the restaurant perhaps a half-hour later. He had encountered no one else. He had no idea why they had not continued the pursuit. Perhaps the others, if there were any, had given up simply because they had identified Velasquez's body. He neither knew nor cared.

He pushed open the door of of the restaurant bar. The barman and two customers looked up at him.

'Good heavens!' he heard the man exclaim, before looking in

369

polite enquiry at the barman, who shrugged suspiciously. Above the bar, a television set had been switched on. Hyde did not understand the commentary, but the images fascinated and appalled him. He dragged a chair away from one table, and slumped into it. The woman customer allowed her eyes to inspect him with growing distaste.

On the television, the wire was back, the bulldozers had gone. The mantis heads of the lights rose above the scene. The Wall. Potsdamerplatz. The Treaty had been reneged upon anyway.

'Oh, *shit*!' he moaned, letting his head slump forward onto his arms, which lay folded on the table awaiting their burden.

'Never mind, dear,' he heard in reply.

'Shit!' he repeated.

He had lost. It had all been for nothing. Everything had been for nothing. He allowed himself to plunge forward into the blackness of utter exhaustion, grateful for the absence of awareness.

He failed to hear the arrival of the Guardia Civil truck in the carpark outside.

BIBLIOGRAPHICAL NOTE

The People's Republic of China has in recent decades adopted a specific system of alphabetic script known as *pinyin*. This is gradually replacing systems such as that invented by Wade which is still widely used in the West. The author of a novel which uses Chinese proper and place names is therefore confronted with a minor problem, i.e. which system to adopt. There are two ways of highlighting the differences between the *pinyin* and Wade systems. The city of Peking, as Wade renders it, becomes Beijing in *pinyin*. Obviously, any Western novel set in Peking would lose by employing the new system. This is true also of places like Canton and perhaps especially Shanghai.

Therefore, the reader familiar with Chinese as rendered alphabetically must forgive me for employing a rather random selection of both systems. I have chosen convenience of recognition and familiarity above considerations of accuracy or exclusivity. Thus we have Peking, Shanghai, and Canton, while we have Deng rather than Teng in rendering the name of the most powerful man in post-Mao China. I only hope that he, and the reader, approve my eclecticism.

In researching this novel's background, I was indebted to the Nagel Guides to Spain, China, and the Federal Republic of Germany, and the Michelin Guides to Spain and Germany. Also, that valuable (and shorter!) volume, Keijzer & Kaplan's *China Guidebook*. In Australia, Roma Dulhunty's two books on Lake Eyre and Michael Page's *South Australia* kept me company.

Other principal sources of reference employed during the writing of the novel include *The Chinese War Machine*, edited by Ray Bonds; *British Intelligence in the Second World War* by F. H. Hinsley; Terence Prittie's *The Velvet Chancellors*; Purnell's *History of the Second World War*, vol. 2, and *The Encyclopaedia of World War II*, edited by Thomas Parrish.